STORY

Coming of Age in an Era of Change

Anderson Andrews

Inspired by a true story
Some characters and events have been fictionalized

Transformational Novels ™

www.TransformationalNovels.com

STORY OF A HIPPIE
Coming of Age in an Era of Change

ISBN - 978-1-944781-39-2 - Paperback

Copyright © April 2022 - 1st Edition

Author: Anderson Andrews
Editor: Debra DeLung

All rights of ownership belong to the publisher.
Transformational Books & Novels
For contact information, please go to:
www.TransformationalBooksAndNovels.com

The Literary Works of Anderson Andrews
www.TransformationalNovels.com

STORY OF A HIPPIE, Coming of Age in an Era of Change
www.StoryofaHippie.com

PEACE CORPS NEPAL, A Search for Enlightenment
www.PeaceCorpsNepal.com

THE DARK SIDE OF LIGHT, Amorous Memoirs of a Former Trial Lawyer
www.TheDarkSideofLight.com

A SENSUAL SEDUCTION, Transformation of the Shadow Self
www.ASensualSeduction.com

THE CRYSTAL TRILOGY, A Story of Conscious Transformation
www.TheCrystalTrilogy.com

> **THE CRYSTAL PRISON - Part One**
> www.TheCrystalPrison.com

> **THE CRYSTAL CHRYSALIS - Part Two**
> www.TheCrystalChrysalis.com

> **THE CRYSTAL CASTLE - Part Three**
> www.TheCrystalCastle.net

THE ACTIVATION, What if God Were One of Us?
www.TheActivation.net / www.WhatifGodwereOneofUs.com

'NEW' BOOK OF THE DEAD, Transformation for the Afterlife
www.NewBookOfTheDead.com

Transformational Novels

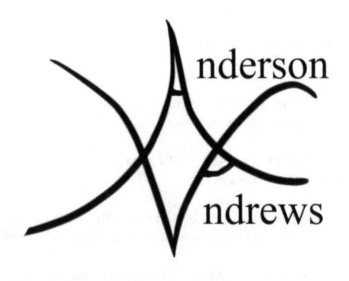

Anderson
Andrews

ABOUT THIS BOOK

People always say to me…*I wish I'd been born in the Sixties*…!
Or they'll say…*I wonder what it was like to be a hippie*…?

I was in college during that wonderful time…and was very much involved in the new *'peace & love movement'*…as well as the protests against the Vietnam War and the military draft. I often found myself having to choose between the peace in my heart and the anger I felt for what our country was doing overseas…as were millions of others.

I wrote this story so that others would know what it could have been like to have lived during the Sixties, and to show some of the dilemmas you would have faced…many of which, were not always so peaceful, much like what so many young people are facing in today's world.

This book is about historical events, but it's also a work of fiction. People's names, what they said, what they wrote, what they thought, or what they did…may not be totally true, factual, or accurate…and even some actual dates *may have been slightly altered* to fit the story.

In portions of this book, you will find quotations and even entire paragraphs that came from several different historical sources.

I've tried to give credit where credit is due…but I did not document from where the source of each of these passages originated.

♥ ♥ ♥

The hippies were 'heroes' during the turbulent 1960s because they were able to prevent an armed American revolution from taking place, but there were other heroes as well…like Martin Luther King Jr., and other leaders of the civil rights movement…plus, those who fought for the rights of women and gay rights. The Sixties was a time when so many Americans found the courage to stand up to our government, to speak up, and to be heard, no matter what the cost…but this book is dedicated to the hippies, whose goal…*was to bring an end to war*.

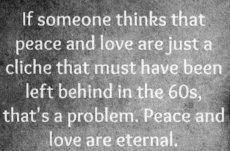

If someone thinks that peace and love are just a cliche that must have been left behind in the 60s, that's a problem. Peace and love are eternal.

"When the power of love overcomes the love of power, the world will know Peace."

~Jimi Hendrix

Peace Love & Happiness

PRELUDE TO THE SIXTIES

Where have all the soldiers gone…long time passing…
Where have all the soldiers gone…long time ago…
Where have all the soldiers gone…gone to graveyards, everyone…
When will they ever learn…when will they ever learn …?
(Artists: Peter, Paul & Mary)

Most people don't realize just how close we came to another armed American Revolution during the Sixties. History wants us to believe it was nothing but a time for wearing bell-bottom pants, bright beads, and rose-colored glasses…unless you were drafted and shipped overseas to fight in Vietnam or involved in one of those 'weird new movements.'

Others might tell you…*about the drugs, sex, and music*…however, from 1964 until 1970 a small counterculture of peace-loving American youth gave their lives to save the ravished soul of our nation from an armed uprising, right here at home, due to a war we had no business being a part of in southeast Asia. They were able to do so *by creating a revolution of consciousness of love and peace*, one our government dreadfully feared. But they were never recognized as '*the real heroes,*' during that important time of great transformation…until now.

They were called, *hippies*…and this is their story.

It's about those who heard the sound of a different drum beating in the winds during that turbulent and magical time in our nation's history.

Discover how the peace & love movement began, and how it ended.

It's what a lot of young people are going through again right now.

This is a transformational book that was written to wake people up to the lessons that our country '*should have learned*' way back then.

Now, it's as if we're having to learn many of them all over again.

Perhaps this time, hopefully…*we'll actually get it together.*

SEX, DRUGS, AND WAR

Coming into Los Angeles...
Bringing in a couple of keys...
Don't touch my bags if you please, mister customs man...
(Artist: Arlo Guthrie:)

Sex and drugs were always at the forefront of the Sixties.

It was during the Sixties when the recreational use of certain drugs became popular in the United States, Canada, and Great Britain.

Many of these drugs had actually been invented much earlier during the World War II era, by both the American and German military.

The drugs they experimented with most often targeted the brain for the purpose of trying to create some kind of *'truth serum.'*

By the time the mid-Sixties arrived, many of these drugs had found their way onto the streets and into the homes of America with no labels or instructions for their use...those who began to experiment with these drugs were changed...and became the *'seekers of truth.'*

For a long time, hallucinogenic drugs such as LSD, psilocybin, and mescaline were not illegal to use. Drugs like marijuana, cocaine, and heroin were...but when the Vietnam War started to become unpopular, the war against the recreational use of many more drugs began.

The U.S. government actually believed it was the drugs themselves that were turning the American youth against the war. To the existing establishment...*it was better to make war...than it was to make love.*

Keep in mind...that the prescription drugs we purchase for health are also controlled substances, but the government requires that they come with warning labels and instructions. When used properly, they are generally safe. Therefore, one could certainly make the argument that recreational drugs would also be safe...*if they were properly used.*

The truth is…almost all drugs are subject to abuse and addiction, but because recreational drugs do not come with any *warning labels* or instructions they are much more likely to be used wrongly. Therefore, abuse lies with both the user of the drug, as well as the failure of the government to educate the public as to how illicit drugs should be used.

Even illegal drugs should come with instructions and warnings.

So instead of education…the government went into fear by taking the position that anything that might make someone feel good inside or make them happy…*should be outlawed and declared illegal.*

This book does not condone the use of illegal drugs…nor does it approve the government's laws and actions regarding them, but before using any kind of drug…whether it's for medical or recreational use, legal, or illegal, you should educate yourself, and become familiar with potentially harmful effects of the drug upon both your mind and body, as well as the laws and punishments regarding its possession.

As to the issue of sexual activity in this book, please keep in mind that before the sexual revolution of the Sixties occurred, being open and vocal about sexuality had been severely repressed by the media.

In the Fifties, television shows always portrayed married couples sleeping in separate beds, and any idea of sexual activity was such a taboo subject it was rarely discussed publicly, or even privately.

But with the dawn of the Sixties, sexual expression began to take a new foothold in America as the use of psychedelic drugs and marijuana brought down the walls of previously pent-up frustration.

As a result, sexual freedom finally began to awaken.

This change in attitude soon became *a sexual revolution.*

Back then, the HIV virus and AIDS did not exist…and the other sexually transmitted diseases that did were often easily treatable with a single shot of anti-bacterial medication…such as penicillin.

Although condoms existed, the youth of America were more prone to use them to prevent pregnancy…rather than infectious diseases.

So with the advent of the pill and diaphragms as an alternative for birth control people began to engage in indiscriminate sexual activity without worrying much about catching a sexually transmitted disease.

Group sex, called *love-ins*…were just orgies…but in most cases, there wasn't a lot to worry about in the way of repercussions.

♥ ♥ ♥

Today, however…the world has become much different.

People should be more discerning about their sexual partners than their predecessors were…and the sexual activities they engage in.

But history has a way of repeating itself.

Now…a new sense of sexual liberation is taking place again among our nation's youth. Porn sites on the internet are free, for anyone to see, and dating sites encourage their users to engage in sexual affairs.

For some, oral sex is not considered to be sex at all.

In the Fifties, you were lucky if you got kissed on the first date, but these days…getting laid is almost expected…not to mention the fact that anal intercourse is now considered by many…normal.

Still, even though sexual consciousness is expanding and evolving, one should be discerning when engaging in sexual activity.

♥ ♥ ♥

I suppose the bottom line would be this. Yes…the over-indulgent use of mind-altering drugs and the indiscriminate pursuit of the sensual carnal pleasures may not always be the safest thing to do…but they're here to stay…and let's face it, there are a lot of things far worse.

War is much unhealthier…*for children and other living things.*

Perhaps someday, someone will invent 'a drug' that prevents war, and at the same time…makes sexual activity safe.

After all, it's better to make love…*than to make war.*

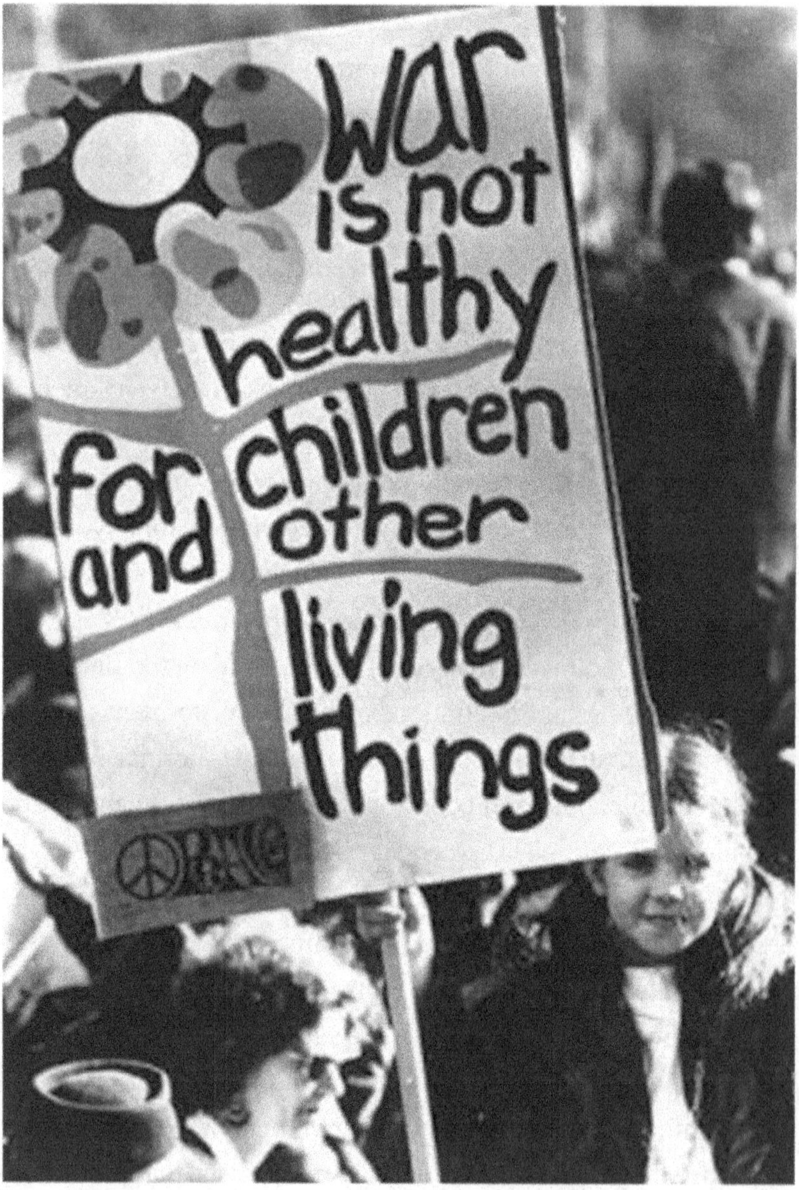
war
is not
healthy
for children
and other
living
things

Table of Contents

We Have Got to Get It Together.. 1

California Dreaming 11

Mr. Tambourine Man... 35

If You're Going to San Francisco... 59

White Rabbit.. 71

The Times…They Are a Changing.. 95

And the Beat Goes On 119

It Ain't Me Babe... 139

Parsley, Sage, Rosemary and Thyme 167

Sounds of Silence 179

Fire and Rain.. 195

A Whiter Shade of Pale 209

A Bridge Over Troubled Water 225

Purple Haze All in My Brain 247

By the Time We Got to Woodstock 261

Jumping Jack Flash... 271

You Say You Want a Revolution 303

The Eve of Destruction... 323

Commentary: When Will They Ever Learn?.............................. 341

We Have Got to Get It Together

Call out the instigator…
Because there's something in the air…
We have got to get it together…sooner or later…
Because the revolution's here…
And you know that it's right…
(Artist: Tom Petty)

It was time to wake up from the American dream.

Some people will tell you it happened on February 3, 1959…which was later to become known as '*the day the music died.*'

That's when the young lives of Buddy Holly, Ritchie Valens, and the Big Bopper were tragically taken in the same plane crash.

After that, the music would never be the same again.

Just as music reflects the mood of a country, the untimely death of these musical icons symbolizes the death of an older consciousness.

That's also when the lives of everyone *'coming of age'* during that time began to transform into something different.

Successful television shows like *Leave It to Beaver, Donna Reed,* and *My Three Sons* would never again be the preferred role models for American families. Instead, to grow up in a dysfunctional family, or to be a single parent, would become the norm of our society.

As a result, divorce became more and more widely accepted.

Never again…would war be so intensely glamorized and glorified.

Never again…would the young men of America be seen running off to the nearest Army enlistment center to fight the enemy *over there.*

Never again…would 'people of color' be required to drink from a public water fountain marked *For Colored People Only*…nor to be forced to sit in the back of a city bus full of so-called, *white people.*

Never again…would the young women of this country be seen in long petticoats. No longer…would Ms. Liberty stay at home with the kids, with open arms and open legs, just waiting for her man to arrive.

Never longer…did those who were gay be forced to hide in a closet.

No, the times were definitely changing.

'American Pie' is a term that has often been used to refer to the simple, innocent, and uncomplicated way that life *seemed to have been* in our country from the late Forties to the early Sixties.

It was before Civil Rights, before Women's Rights, before all of the protests began…and before the unjust…Vietnam War.

During the Fifties, the closest thing to hippies were *the Beats*…or what some later referred to as *Beatniks*. They were made up mostly of laid-back artists and blues musicians who haunted the back streets of New York City's Greenwich Village and smoked a lot of 'reefers.'

When the Sixties arrived, *everything was changing.*

It was a different world than our parents grew up in.

Weekly television shows that had nothing to do with family values were popular, such as *Dallas, I Dream of Jeanie, Mission Impossible, The Man From Uncle, Get Smart, Batman,* and *I Spy* with Bill Cosby.

Some believe…life was much simpler back then.

The world's population was only three-and-a-half billion people.

One-hundred-and-eighty million people lived in the United States.

Unemployment…was close to four million.

The national debt…was three hundred billion dollars.

The average income…was five thousand dollars per year.

The minimum wage…was one dollar.

The life expectancy for men…was sixty-seven years.

For women, it was… seventy-four years.

Small wisps of pubic hair began to show up in Playboy Magazine.

Miss America was no longer just a simple, innocent girl. Not only was she getting a face-lift, and showing off her boobs, but was dealing with lots of other issues as well. She was hot, bothered, and had some four-letter words she wanted to say to men, without feeling guilty.

We didn't really have much in the way of *freedom of speech* back then, but it wouldn't be long until you could say almost anything.

The warm nights at the high school gym 'sock hop' were also over, and America's youth were all seeking out new ways to have fun.

The lives of many so-called *baby boomers* had become filled with new ways to play. They were getting high on marijuana…and were in the midst of discovering a whole new sense of sexual freedom.

There was also a new kind of music…more guitars and drums.

It was defining a new consciousness for the young Americans.

Drugs, sex, and rock & roll…became a new way of life for many.

The young people who tuned in to this new energy were considered '*to be hip*'…and soon, a new generation of *hipsters* replaced the older and outdated Beatniks. Eventually, *they became known as the Hippies.*

The Vietnam War became *totally un-hip*…when the government began drafting every young man who wasn't in college.

The hippies reacted, protesting both the war and the military draft.

However, the use of psychedelic drugs was also taking a foothold within the culture thanks to people like Timothy Leary and his friend, Richard Alpert, two former university professors who had conducted experiments in mind research for the U.S. Government.

After being under the influence of these experimental 'truth serum' drugs like LSD, hundreds of thousands of young Americans (many of whom were in college) began to see a whole new truth, one that altered their reaction to the military draft…and to the idea of war itself.

Instead of launching a revolt against the war and the draft, it was decided to create the *anti-war* and the *anti-draft* movements…which would not be carried out with violence, but with peace and love.

As a result, the new *peace and love movement* was given birth…and it drove the established government crazy, not only at the federal level, but at the state, county, and local government levels as well.

Thus…the *war on drugs* came into being all across our country.

Not only were concepts about our role as a nation-changing, but so were traditional concepts about religion. With the plane crash in 1959, it really did become '*bye, bye, Miss American Pie*'…and the three men we admired most…*the Father, the Son, and the Holy Ghost*…they caught the last train for the coast…only to re-surface five years later in San Francisco. But this time they were wearing bell-bottom pants, had flowers in their hair…and were tripping their asses off on LSD.

It's no wonder these times…*seemed to be so spiritual.*

But it could no longer be said that God was a man…but was instead perhaps a woman…a goddess, who was all about peace and love.

Yes, something touched us deep inside…*the day the music died.*

Wars and revolutions were going on all over the world.

The long and drawn-out *Cold War* in Europe appeared to be ending, but the fear of nuclear attack by Russia was always in the backdrop.

Students in all of the schools were told to prepare for such a war.

Once a month, they'd practice by crawling underneath their flimsy desks just in case an atomic bomb should actually be dropped on them, pretending that in some way their lives might somehow be spared.

The Middle East was in turmoil, and Israel's fate was uncertain. The Shah of Iran's *American-supported government* was always on the brink of being overthrown by radical Islamic groups.

More and more third-world countries were turning to communism.

There were violent revolutions in Central and South America.

The life of Cuban revolutionary, Che Guevara, became a legend and was considered to be a hero for young radical Americans.

Mao Tse-tung's communist Red Army now ruled in China.

His 'Little Red Book' (*a communist manifesto*) was banned in the United States, a country that was supposed to have freedom of speech.

Insurgents in other third-world countries all over the planet were preparing similar assaults on democracy and sovereignty. During this time, the so-called 'free-world' was facing its biggest challenges.

In an effort to help ease world tension, President John F. Kennedy decided to try an experiment. He hoped to stop the growing flood of revolt and communism by making Americans more popular.

His idea was to send thousands of recent college graduates to live in remote villages. If they could do something…anything…to benefit the people living there…then that would be great…but the main goal, was for local tribesmen to make friends with these young Americans.

For if they did…they would never turn against the United States.

To do this…he created the *United States Peace Corps*…in 1961.

On November 22, 1963…Kennedy was assassinated.

After Lyndon Johnson became president, the war effort in Vietnam began to escalate. In 1965, thirty-five hundred combat-ready Marines landed there…to defend the American air base in Da Nang.

Then, Johnson authorized the use of explosive napalm firebombs on the Viet Cong, made by Dow Chemical Company…which would shower explosive pellets upon impact…and scorch entire villages.

The use of napalm would burn to death every man, woman, or child who lived there…and if that didn't work, helicopters sprayed tons of *agent orange* over the treetops, which would defoliate the jungle.

That way…*the enemy*…wouldn't be able to hide.

It didn't seem to matter what the consequences might be.

After all, it was only about winning.

If any country was going to bully another country, the United States was determined to prove…that it could be the biggest bully of all.

It's no wonder…so many servicemen suffered from nightmares.

It's no wonder…the god-damn war was so unpopular at home.

♥ ♥ ♥

Within our country, we had our own internal wars to fight.

Racism against blacks was still rampant.

Women were demanding equal rights.

The gay community was fed up with being put down…

And the war on drugs was just beginning.

We were a country founded upon principles of freedom, justice, and human rights, but those terms were still in the process of being defined.

Amidst the chaos, there was another and even greater movement going on…*the search for higher consciousness*. Somewhere within this turmoil of war and social upheaval, you could also find truly intelligent discussions about how to change our current reality.

There was hope…that the new *Age of Aquarius* was on the horizon, but no one knew when that would be. We believed…it would be a time when peace would rule the planet…but even if you weren't a hippie, or into the New Age, people still talked about freedom, what it meant to have human rights, and how to achieve world peace.

Environmental awareness, and the protection of endangered wild animals, became prominent issues that hadn't existed before.

One could sense the beginnings…of a new consciousness.

For many, it was about growth, transformation, and enlightenment, because the survival of both our country and the planet was at stake.

Fortunately, '*We the People*' finally stood up to the establishment and said, "*Fuck you. No more war! We're not going to take it anymore.*"

For some, it meant going to jail or running off to Canada to become a fugitive, but thousands were willing to take this risk.

It was a time for just about everyone...*to come out of the closet.*

Whether you were black, a woman, or gay...it was time to stand up and be counted...and be recognized as a voice of American society.

With Lyndon B. Johnson as president, there was no hanky-panky going on in the White House. After all, President Kennedy had been having more sex parties than *The Rolling Stones*, but the news media would cover up anything that might threaten the American Dream.

With more than nine-hundred-thousand *war-baby* freshmen about to enter college, L.B.J.'s *Great Society*...turned out to be a *great flop.*

Everything was changing, and the establishment could do nothing about it. Real freedom of speech was taking place within the various countercultures, and new movements were sprouting up everywhere.

Besides the anti-war and the anti-draft movements, there was the Civil Rights movement, the Black Power movement, Gay Liberation, Sexual Revolution, Environmental Awareness, Women's Liberation, and just about anything else you could imagine.

At the same time, Be-Ins, Love-Ins, communal living, weed, hash, LSD, and even cocaine, were taking a foothold throughout the country. It wouldn't be long before college campus protests, rallies, and rioting would be seen as common occurrences throughout the nation, as the youth of America openly burned their draft cards.

Even though people were demanding respect...the Vietnam War continued to escalate. Any young man in good health who wasn't in college and was under the age of twenty-three...would be drafted.

Initially, the anti-war and anti-draft protests were peaceful, but with the sometimes violent Civil Rights movement growing in the south, and moving northward, it wasn't long before the government began to view any kind of rally as potentially explosive and dangerous.

It didn't matter if you had flowers in your hair or not.

If you spoke up or joined a protest of almost any nature, it would be likely that a National Guard trooper might point a gun at you.

Over time, both the civil rights protests and the peace and love movement quickly spread to every city in the country. Each started out following the principles of non-violence, based upon the teachings of India's great soul, *Mohandas Mahatma Gandhi*, which he used in his people's struggle against England some twenty-five years earlier.

Within only a short time, open combat and riots became the norm. During one civil rights protest, the City of Detroit was literally burned to the ground and looted, and thousands of people were shot, injured, and arrested by the police who then became known as '*pigs.*'

It was against the law to burn a draft card or to wear anything on your body that looked like an American flag, and draft dodgers were running off to Canada in droves, where they could still get asylum.

The first talks about an armed revolution against the government were beginning to stir…even if no one knew really knew what it meant, but it was certainly a topic of debate in colleges all over the country.

Was Chairman Mao right when he said…*power only comes from the barrel of a gun*? Many…were beginning to think so.

But real hippies…were not violent people.

They rebelled against the old ways…smoking pot, dropping acid, and experiencing a new kind of sexual liberation through communal living based on principles of happiness, peace, and love.

It was revolutionary and represented a huge leap in consciousness.

They were responsible for preventing an armed assault against the established government…from the radical factions of our own society.

However, the peace & love movement only lasted a few short years.

But…what was accomplished during that time was incredible.

It left its mark upon the face of our nation…in the form of a peace symbol…that looked like a B-52 bomber with a circle around it.

There are lots of theories about why it ended.

It might have been the switch from psychedelic drugs to the more hardcore drugs…like cocaine and heroin. Or maybe…it was because '*hippiedom*' became an accepted part of our American culture.

Or maybe it was just the Seventies…and time for another change.

In May of 1970, gunshots were fired by National Guard troops at Kent State University that killed several unarmed students.

It brought a tragic end to the peace and love movement, as innocent blood spilled on college soil. The shots were heard around the world, just as the Redcoats had shot the Minutemen on Lexington Green.

That caused the Colonists to take up arms in defense of their liberty and touched off the American Revolution. And now…the very same thing was about to happen again…two hundred years later.

Civil rights and anti-war protesters were now targets for the police, but what were the actual events that led up to all of this?

Why had students all across the country become the new enemy?

Why were peaceful people beginning to arm themselves with guns, and seriously considering another American Revolution?

Was it because…*they heard the sound of a different drum?*

Was it because…*the magic of the music had changed them?*

Was it because…*of the mind-expanding drugs?*

Was it because…*of the new sexuality and their search for freedom?*

Was it because…*of the impact the protest marches had?*

Was it because…*the soul of our nation was actually bleeding?*

Perhaps it was all of those…but it's the story millions of young men and women all experienced together…*during the turbulent Sixties.*

California Dreaming

All the leaves are brown, and the sky is gray,
I've been for a walk, on a winter's day,
I'd be safe and warm if I were in L.A.,
California dreaming, on such a winter's day...
(Artist: The Mamas and Papas)

♥ ♥ ♥

The First Day of Spring (1965)
Lower Bucks County, Pennsylvania

It wasn't about winning or losing. That's what I realized on that cool and crisp equinox night as I ran through the fresh-cut dew-covered grass of Lower Bucks County Veteran's Memorial Park Soccer Field.

It wasn't about power either. It was just about playing the game, doing the best you can, and having fun while doing it.

Barely able to see the small shadow of the football in the backdrop of the large halogen lamps, I ran as fast as I could and held out my arms. If I could catch it, fine...but if not, then who would care?

After all, it was a friendly and innocent game of touch football, but then...just as the ball landed in my arms, I noticed something strange.

It wasn't a smell or a noise...but a feeling I was sensing.

Little did I know that my life was about to change forever.

Tonight, my eyes would open to a new era in American history that was just beginning to unfold. I could barely feel its vibration, but I was certain...that there were millions of others just like me...who were hearing the *sound of a different drum* beating in the winds.

At eighteen years old, I was coming of age during the mid-Sixties and was about to enter a whole new world.

This evening, I was with my two best friends, Ronald and Byron, and another friend, Stanley. Yes, I'd caught the football and scored the touchdown, but it didn't matter. Nobody cared, and nobody cheered.

I threw the ball back down the field to the others and then tried to find my lukewarm can of Samuel Adams Beer, hidden next to a fence, just in case the cops came by to check us out.

"Let's take a quick break!" I shouted to my three sweaty comrades. "It's almost ten o'clock, and I have to be home by eleven."

"You're such a good boy," Ron sarcastically pointed out.

Suddenly, we all stopped in our tracks and looked in awe at an event that was taking place not too far away. It was something I'd read about but had never actually seen before…until this night.

Just across the street from where we were playing was the county administration building, and we could see a small group of young men wearing war paint, like American Indians…shouting something.

Some of them even had scarfs tied around their heads.

They stood on the front steps, waving several banners.

One sign read, *Peace*. A bigger one read…*Make Love, Not War*.

"What do you think they're doing?" I asked.

"Oh, it's just a bunch of hippies," replied Byron.

"Yeah, they're protesting the Vietnam War," Stanley explained.

Whatever they were doing, it seemed to be a lot more important than the game of football we were playing and a lot more fun, too.

Only a few bystanders were watching as the wild group of youthful hippies proceeded to pull a large metal trash barrel off the sidewalk and set its contents on fire. Then, they raised their arms and began to chant protests against our current President…Lyndon B. Johnson.

"Hey, hey…L.B.J., how many kids have you burned today?"

They also protested *using Napalm on Vietnam villages* by lighting pieces of white paper on fire…which Byron said, were 'draft cards.'

Then, they proceeded to burn an American flag as well.

They waved it around several times…and dropped it into the barrel of burning paper. I could tell that Stanley was getting pretty pissed off about the whole thing, but we were outnumbered, so he just watched.

Not only were they triumphant in their endeavor, but seemed to be very proud of it, as they shouted out loudly…*Fuck the war!*

Then, they made peace symbols with two fingers of their hands.

Moments later, the small group of renegades fled into the darkness of the night as quickly as they had appeared, leaving the barrel on fire, apparently wanting to disappear before the police could arrive.

Although I'd seen news reports of such protests on television, I had never actually witnessed a live incidence of civil disobedience over the Vietnam War until now…and quite frankly, I was impressed.

"Hey, guys," I called out to my friends. "We better get the hell out of here. The cops might think we're the ones who burned that flag, and I don't think any of us want to spend the night at the police station."

We were just seniors in high school who lived in a small town in eastern Pennsylvania across the river from Trenton, New Jersey.

Just a few miles downstream, was a well-known tourist attraction, a town called *Washington's Crossing*…located at the historic site.

Lower Bucks County was an interesting place to live, being rich with the history of our country's beginnings and safe from the chaotic hustle of cities like Trenton, Philadelphia, or New York.

I had always been amazed by the fact that the Colonial Army came very close to losing the Revolutionary War, and in fact, they had not won a single battle until the night General George Washington crossed the Delaware River over to Trenton one fateful Christmas Eve.

As the story goes, our beaten-down soldiers were only able to win that night because the Hussein troops were drunk. They had already declared a '*time-out*' truce to celebrate the holiday.

Because we violated that Christmas Eve ceasefire, it seemed to me that our country had been founded on some very underhanded dealings right from the very beginning…and perhaps we hadn't really changed all that much over the last two hundred years.

I also found it strange that the Declaration of Independence had been written on paper made from hemp, which comes from the stalk of marijuana plants. Perhaps it was a symbolic secret message that the founders of this country were nothing more than a bunch of potheads.

Not only that, but all over this area there were signs that read, '*George Washington slept here.*' It was pretty obvious that gorgeous George had been doing a lot of sleeping around back then, much like Thomas Jefferson had. So it seemed our forefathers may have actually been the inventors of the 'free-love movement.' Therefore, it was no surprise that the 'Father of our Country' died of venereal disease.

Regardless of the disloyal ideas, I had back then, I was still pretty much an all-American teenager…a good one, too, having become an Eagle Scout just a year before my family moved to Pennsylvania.

I was born into a white, middle-class, Anglo-American Christian home, and when I was younger, I had even thought about becoming an army officer, commanding a fleet of tanks like General George Patton had done in World War II. I also played basketball throughout my four years of high school and had never been in trouble with the police.

Why hell…I even belonged to the local church youth group, but it was because of all the sexy girls who attended, not because of Jesus.

I was eighteen years old, so I was old enough to be drafted into the army but not old enough to vote for a president who would end the war.

Back then, the voting age was still twenty-one.

Even though I was old enough to kill on the battlefield, I was also too young to drink a six-pack of beer…at least in Pennsylvania.

The drinking age was eighteen in New Jersey. All we had to do was drive over the Delaware River Bridge into Trenton, and we could get a six-pack of beer whenever we wanted. The Jersey shore wasn't too far away either (only about an hour with no traffic) and the three of us would often drive to the small, quiet ocean town of Surf City in the light blue, 1956 Chevrolet I'd bought for less than a hundred dollars.

Along the way, we would always pick up a case of Schmitz beer.

I remember the time Byron drank half of the case before we arrived which caused him to become car sick. To make matters even worse, he thought the window was down, which it wasn't, and he got sick all over.

I stopped the car, opened the passenger door, and pushed him out into someone's front lawn. It was an old car, and because the smell was terrible, we found a nearby garden hose and sprayed the entire inside of the car until it was completely clean again.

However, I could never drink that brand of beer again.

In only a few more months we would all be graduating from high school. I was planning to go to college, but I didn't know where yet. Maybe the University of Pennsylvania, or Penn State, or maybe go back to Houston, where I was from. I didn't really care which one…and it really didn't seem to matter. All I knew was that my parents had said, *"When you graduate, you have to go to college somewhere."*

We called Ron the *Pollock* because his family was Polish, and we referred to Byron as the *Dago* because his family was Italian. Our other friend, Stanley, was simply known as *Stan*, who by today's standards would be considered something of a studious geek.

My name was Andy, but the three of them called me Tex.

That's because I'd lived in Texas until I was in the eleventh grade.

Being the new kid in school, I found myself playing second-string on the high school basketball team. Byron had played football in the past, but neither of us were serious jocks. Ron was a bit of a poet and musician, while Stan did nothing but study. In my opinion, the four of us looked and acted like your basic normal American teenagers.

We were required to have short hair in order to play sports, and the high school rules didn't allow for any hair to be grown on your face. Blue jeans were not permitted, but we were allowed to smoke cigarettes at school during lunch, so long as we had our parent's permission slip with us, which would usually be forged anyway.

The music of the Beatles ruled the airways, but everyone could see that the music and their images were transforming. They were no longer just an English rock band saying, "I want to hold your hand."

Instead, they were creating a whole new music that represented the growing psychedelic freedom movement among the youth culture.

We could feel the shift of consciousness growing within ourselves, but we didn't dare try to express our own individual transformation, especially with only a few months to go before graduating.

Besides, none of us understood what was getting ready to happen to the world. When we were in high school, we didn't know anything about what would soon become known as the '*love generation*,' or about hippies, yippies, or yuppies. Instead, people who had long hair, smoked pot, and dressed in funny clothes were just known as weirdos to many people, or as freaks, especially to those my parents' age.

On one of our trips to the Jersey shore, I had what some people might call *a near-death experience*. Between the four of us, I was the only one who owned a surfboard. On one spring day, we put the board on the roof of my car and drove to Surf City, and as usual, we drank a few too many beers. However, the waves were too small to surf on.

Instead, we decided to swim in the ocean, as far out as we could, using the surfboard as a float. We were all wearing wetsuits, and I'm sure we looked like a bunch of seals bobbing up and down in the water.

As it turned out, this almost became a tragic mistake.

We swam for about thirty minutes until we were far beyond the point of safety. As the shoreline became harder to see, we all became aware of something coming toward us from the opposite direction.

Three dark fins were approaching at a rather rapid rate.

In my scuba class, they had taught me that one of the ways to avoid a shark attack is to go underwater and blow bubbles, scream, shout, and generally make a lot of noise, so that's what we all proceeded to do.

When it didn't seem to work, the four of us tried to climb onto the surfboard all at the same time. Not only did the combined weight of our bodies push the surfboard underwater, but it flipped us over as well, spilling all of us back into the ocean of doom. At that point, our failed attempts to scare the sharks away by blowing bubbles and screaming under the water transformed into hysterical laughter.

So there we were…laughing at the face of death just knowing we were going to die. The fact was, we were panic-stricken, but there was nothing we could do about it except to go into uncontrollable laughter.

A philosopher once said, "How simple it is to see that we can only be happy in the present moment, and there will never be another time, other than now." We certainly weren't trying to be philosophers back then, but we were certainly laughing our asses off about the thought of being eaten alive…wondering who would fall off the surfboard first.

Finally, just as it appeared that all was lost, and we'd be eaten alive, one of the three dark fins swam right up to us. Then, the menacing beast poked its head right out of the water. It was a bottlenose dolphin, and it looked at us…like we were just a bunch of crazy humans.

After that, all three of them slowly swam off.

I don't know about my three friends, but I never viewed death quite the same again. For someone else, it might have been only some foolish incident, but ever since that day I've never had any fear of dying…and without the *fear of death*, most of your other fears disappear as well.

In May of 1965, students at New York City University created the Committee to End the War in Vietnam (CEWV) and organized one of the earliest American anti-war teach-ins on the NYU campus.

A week later, a demonstration in Washington, D.C. took place that involved more than fifteen thousand students who opposed the war.

After watching the protest on television, I found myself drawn to apply to NYU, even though I had just been accepted at Penn State.

Something inside of me was calling out to go to New York City, but I had no idea why other than being so intrigued by all the drama and the fact that it actually *meant* something.

It was too late for me to get accepted for the fall term, but if I did get accepted, then I could transfer my credits from Penn State to NYU and go there in January of the following year.

I hadn't dated too many girls at that point in my life but had come fairly close to losing my virginity the previous year in Texas during a drunken *going away party* I attended just before I left.

However, I couldn't actually remember if I did or not.

Now that I was living here, and was a high school senior, not only did I want to get properly laid, but to have a steady girlfriend as well.

Ron worked in a bakery that was owned by Ed, a strong muscular man in his mid-forties. Jackie was a slender and sexy high school junior who worked in the bakery as well. Jackie had long dark hair that hung down to her waist and worked there after school. She went to a different high school than I did because she lived across the river in Trenton.

Because Ron and I were best friends, we'd often have food fights in the back of the bakery on Sunday with the leftover pies, cakes, and donuts. Sunday was Ed's day off, so he didn't ever know about it.

That's how I met Jackie.

Jackie and I went out several times, and I even took her to my senior prom. One night, we finally wound up making love in the front seat of my Chevrolet at a drive-in movie theater. It was more of a memorable experience than a pleasurable one…but there were footprints on the windshield the next morning, and I was certain I was in love.

Two weeks later, I discovered through Ron that Jackie was banging the boss in the back of the bakery after work. And so, like a young, angry, jealous idiot…I confronted her, to see if the story was true.

She didn't deny her affair with Ed and said she never wanted to see me again because of my jealous attitude. Of course, that pissed me off even more. On the way home, a song by the Beatles came on that said, *"It's a fool who plays it cool, by making his world a little colder."*

I learned a lot about anger and jealousy from that experience.

It doesn't get you anywhere…but alone.

After losing Jackie to Ed due to my own stupidity, my attitude about women became like a popular song by the artist, Stephen Stills.

If you can't be with the one you love…love the one you're with.

That's when I met Diane, a girl at school I had never really noticed until I saw her in a bathing suit at a Red Cross Water Safety Instructor class I was taking. Not only did she have an extremely firm six-pack for a stomach, but this chick had more curves than the Indy 500.

Standing by the pool in a white two-piece bikini, she reminded me of the actress Ursula Andress…from the James Bond movie, *Dr. No*.

Diane was different than a lot of girls…in a lot of ways.

She was stunning, smart, loved to sing…and was an artist.

But she was a little too trusting, always believing what anyone said.

On the surface, she seemed to be a happy person, but I could sense that she had been hurt deeply by someone, almost as though she was carrying some kind of dark secret within her heart.

She also appeared to be shy at times, but she wasn't at all.

It was just that she didn't like to share all of her feelings with people for fear that the secret might accidentally be revealed.

A week after our high school graduation ceremony, Diane and I met with Stan, the Dago, and the Pollock, along with their dates, under the bleachers of the football stadium and proceeded to drink beer and dance until midnight. Afterward, we all split up and I took her home.

Surprisingly, Diane's parents had gone away for a long weekend, so she invited me into her bed. Unfortunately, I'd promised my parents that I'd be home by two o'clock in the morning.

I found the whole situation to be somewhat awkward, as we were both pretty drunk and totally inexperienced at this. So before we started getting too passionate, she played a song on her guitar by Juice Newton that went…*just call me angel, in the morning.*

The next day, I was certain that this would be my chance to finally fall in love with someone….and I thought for sure we would hook up again in just a few days. However, without any explanation, or even calling me, Diane left town before her parents returned.

Her mother told me she had gone 'out west' to see her older sister for the summer. Since I was planning on going off to college around the middle of August, I doubted that I would ever see Diane again.

At this point, you might ask, *why am I telling you all these stories?*

It's to show…those were my biggest concerns back in high school.

It was about drinking beer, playing sports, thinking about college, feeling sexual urges…and discovering what women were like.

Things like the Vietnam War, or Civil Rights, were not exactly on my list of priorities…but that was all about to change.

I believe we are constantly being given clues in our lives that show up as signs and signals from the universe about what's going on, and if we are aware and awake, those communications become rather evident.

That summer, a second near-death experience happened to me.

I was driving my mother's 1960 Volkswagen Bug one afternoon and took a sharp curve at about fifty miles per hour. Back then, that model didn't have independent suspension. Instead, it had something closer to a straight axel, and when I rounded the curve, the right rear tire buckled under…and the car flipped over…at least ten times.

Stan was behind me in his car…watching in awe.

Afterward, he told me…it was the worst accident he had ever seen in his life. I wasn't wearing a seat belt, but I was able to ride out the crash by falling over into the passenger's seat beside me.

The roof of the car was crushed, *almost flat*, and had I been buckled in and sitting up, there's no doubt my neck would have been broken.

As I was rolling over, I asked for help. It was kind of like praying, but not to God. Rather, it was like calling out to some kind of guardian angel, although I didn't know about such things at that time.

In the middle of all the chaos, after I asked for help or some kind of assistance, there was the sound of a small voice that actually replied, *"We are with you. Everything is going to be all right."*

After finally coming to a stop upside down, I was still able to move and nothing seemed to be broken. The doors of the car were sealed shut, so I kicked out what was left of the front windshield and climbed out.

After having yet another close brush with death, and again coming out unharmed, I began to think that my life might have some meaning, or that maybe I was protected. What if there was some destiny I was here to fulfill? What it might be, however, was totally unknown to me.

♥ ♥ ♥

It was the summer of 1965. New York City wasn't far away at all, and I had already been there several times before both by car and train.

My friends and I would simply catch the commuter train in Trenton, and for just a couple of dollars, we would be in Grand Central Station about an hour later. The very first time I saw it, I instantly loved the majesty of New York City. I found the energy of Times Square to be absolutely fascinating, and the gentle tranquility of Greenwich Village touched my soul with the sounds of rock music in the air, along with the aromas of incense coming from the numerous head shops.

I clearly remember the day of my first protest march against the war when the three of us walked out into the streets of Manhattan from the train station and were once again instantly surrounded by the dazzling magnificence of the city that never sleeps.

"Look at that!" Ron shouted while pointing at a big red neon sign that read "*Blarney Rose*" over the top of an old Irish bakery.

"What about it?" Stan asked.

"Blarney Rose sat on a tack. Then, Blarney rose," recited Ron.

"That's really dumb, you stupid Pollock," Byron replied.

"Oh, yeah? Then tell me, can you speak Polish or write in Polish?"

"No," replied Byron.

"Then that makes you dumber than a Pollock," Ron told him.

"Hey, guys," I intervened, "I heard there's supposed to be a rather large anti-war protest march this morning somewhere in Central Park this afternoon. What do you say we go and check it out?"

"Aren't you afraid of getting arrested, or maybe getting your head smashed in with a nightstick?" asked Byron. "Last week, more than thirty people were injured and a whole bunch of hippies and other marchers got carted off to jail for smoking pot."

"I'm not afraid," I replied. "What about you, Ron?"

"In case you didn't already know it, I'm a revolutionary Marxist, so let's go and kick some capitalist pig ass."

"It's supposed to be peaceful," I replied.

"All right, I'll go," recanted Byron, "but just so long as the Pollock doesn't start spouting off to the cops and calling them pigs. My father would kill me if he had to bail me out of jail for protesting the war."

"Do either of you know how to get to Central Park?" I inquired.

"No," replied Ron, "but that taxi driver can sure take us there."

We were let off a few blocks from the park because the road had been barricaded and was being patrolled by policemen on horseback carrying large wooden batons. You could hear some drumming in the background and the sound of someone speaking into a microphone.

It was turning out to be a windy, cool, and cloudy springtime day and looked as though it could possibly rain. Still, folks had started to gather in large numbers. Within an hour, a rather large crowd gathered together to be a part of something that seemed to concern all of them.

Within a large open area of the park, they got organized. There were the young, the old, men, women, and children, not to mention a large number of dogs. Some people were throwing frisbees, and others were huddled in small groups to talk…or just to smoke and share a joint of marijuana. Although I had never gotten high on weed before, I found the smell coming from the nearby smokers to be quite appealing, and of course…felt the temptation to join them. I just couldn't bring myself to do it in front of my friends, but I suspected that Ron had tried it.

All I knew about marijuana, was the fact that it was illegal.

People were holding large signs and banners with slogans that read, *Get Out of Vietnam Now…No More War…Hell No! We Won't Go!*

The energy of the crowd was high, but it was obvious there wasn't going to be a huge turnout today, perhaps maybe a thousand people.

That was fine with me. After all, it was my first protest march.

We were there to observe, bear witness, and see what it was about.

However, a part of me was hoping to participate…just a little.

Beautiful people with long flowing hair were everywhere wearing tattered, colorful clothes. I'd never witnessed so many gorgeous young women with flowing flowery skirts, or so skimpily clad…and watching braless breasts gently bounce under tie-dyed shirts…blew me away.

It felt like the circus had come to town, or that someone had thrown a costume party in the park. I found it to be so awesome, I unbuttoned my shirt, took off my shoes and socks…and tried to fit in.

The mounted police were on the outskirts of the crowd and seemed to be ready to move in at a moment's notice if violent behavior erupted. However, some of the people jeered at the police and held up their fists as a sign of defiance. There was another small group gathered nearby, those who supported the war and were waving American flags.

Some held signs that said…*America, Love it or Leave it.*

As the time neared for the rally to begin, the number of protesters had gathered in strength, and several of the organizers began speaking. Standing on a newly constructed wooden platform, they talked about the atrocities and evils of war itself and explained why the Vietnam War was wrong. They said it was important that the public be made aware of why protests against the war were necessary.

Then the crowd cheered when a funny-looking man came onto the stage wearing a red and white top hat that reminded me of the book by Dr. Seuss, *The Cat in the Hat*. Later, I discovered this person was known as, Wavy Gravy, and was a former New York City comedian, who had now become a hippie…and anti-war activist.

"Hey, people!" he shouted. "Please listen! President Johnson has just announced…*that the military draft quota is going to be doubled.*

"Can you believe it? He's going to increase the troop levels that are already in South Vietnam…and turn this into a major fucking war."

The crowd booed and hissed loudly.

"This afternoon's march to protest the war will begin in just a few minutes. Please remember…this is a *non-violent* protest. Do *not* throw rocks, bottles, or *anything* at police or bystanders. We want to show the world we can do this peacefully and *without* any violence."

Some of the people in the crowd cheered.

"We are beautiful people who believe in loving all other beautiful human beings, and we don't believe in killing those who are innocent. We don't believe in the war, and we are here to give the rest of the world a message…*to wake up and to stop the madness*…and to stop the senseless slaughter of innocent people in Vietnam."

This time the entire crowd roared with approval and shouted out, "*Peace now…no more war! Peace now…no more war!*"

Wavy continued and said, "We will be leaving out from the east side of the meadow and down Fifth Avenue. The march will end when we get to Washington Square in the Village. If for any reason the march is broken up or disrupted by the police before we get there, then we'll all meet back here again next weekend. We'll regroup and do it again and again and again…until our voice has been heard!"

As the crowd egged him on, he then yelled at the top of his lungs, "Power to the people…power to the people!"

Then, he made a fist with his right hand and thrust it into the air.

The crowd responded in the same manner and shouted back loudly, "Power to the people…power to the people!"

The tone had been set as the large number of assorted freaks and non-freaks began to move out of the park and into the streets.

You could tell the police were nervous.

Even though this was to be a peaceful protest, it was new back then.

No one had any idea what really might happen.

Everyone knew…things could get out of control quickly.

It recently happened in Birmingham when the civil rights activists protested segregation in Alabama and Mississippi.

As the crowd marched out of the park and into the street, the three of us remained off to the side in case we wanted to leave but chanted along with the group and even held up our fists in defiance of the war in order to fit in. However, we still didn't feel as though we were really part of it. After all, we were still living in the other world…the one that believed '*America would never do anything wrong.*'

It was my very first protest march but would be the first of many. This time, however, I didn't feel quite right about it, having not yet made that leap in consciousness. Of course, I didn't know it at the time.

The protesters continued to chant and make a lot of noise as we marched down Fifth Avenue. Even though it was to be a peaceful event, many of the onlookers were obviously angry and upset.

The people on the sidewalks looked at us with bewilderment as if wishing to say…*why on earth are all of you against the Vietnam War? It's just another one of those situations where America must keep those evil communists from taking over the world! I mean, really, I just don't see what all of these young people are so upset about.*

It was about an hour into the march when I first met Drake.

He was about my age with long blonde hair that hung down to his shoulders. He sported a scraggly mustache, bright purple sunglasses, and a red-striped shirt tucked into his blue denim bell-bottom pants.

He also had two big round buttons on his shirt. One of them read, '*My button is trying to communicate with your button*'…and the other one read, '*I am a human being. Please do not fold, spindle, or mutilate.*'

"Hey, guys, what part of the world are you from?" Drake asked.

"We're from a small town in Lower Bucks County, Pennsylvania. It's not too far from Washington's Crossing," I replied.

"I know where that is. I'm from Long Island myself, but I'm going to college at Cornell in Ithaca this year. Is this your first protest march?"

"Yeah, how can you tell?" I asked him...as if it was too obvious.

"By the way you're dressed...how you look. I can see you're a little up-tight and apprehensive, but that's cool," he replied with a smile.

"Nice to meet you," I said.

"My name's Drake. Are you guys in college?"

"Well, yes and no. Actually, we just graduated from high school last month but I'm planning to be in college in September. I'm Andy, but these people call me Tex. This is Byron and Ron, also known as the Dago and the Pollock. And this is Stan. We just call him...Stan."

"That's far out. Where are you planning to go to college, Tex?"

"Well, I've already been accepted at Penn State, but I'm seriously thinking about NYU for next January."

"Good choice," Drake responded, "so am I...Cornell is just a little too stuffy for me and by next year there should be a lot of protests going on if this war thing doesn't come to a stop. We've got to get it together."

"We have to get organized. Did you know that people are actually talking about having another American revolution?"

"No, I didn't."

"Well, it's almost here, man, and it's written in the Declaration of Independence that we have the *right*, and the *authority* to do it."

"It is?" I asked somewhat confused.

Drake thought for a minute as if to get the words right in his mind.

"This is pure Thomas Jefferson," he explained, "*Whenever any form of government becomes destructive of these ends, it is the right of the people to alter or abolish it, and to institute a new government.*"

He paused for a moment before continuing.

"We have the absolute right to end this illegal war…one way or another…even if it means overthrowing the government to do it."

"Pretty cool," I replied. "It almost sounds like fun."

"Yeah, man. There was a fucking big teach-in about the war that was held on the NYU campus in March. In April, a bunch of us took a bus and went down to Washington D.C."

"Really? How did that go?" I asked.

"Well, we got chased around by the cops, but it was a fucking hoot. We slept outside next to Washington Monument, smoked a lot of pot, and spent a lot of time playing Frisbee and freaking out all the tourists. So yeah, man, you got to come to NYU. You'll have a ball."

"I know. I'm really thinking about it."

"As far as I know, this is the last protest march scheduled for the summer, but there will be another one in September, right after school starts. It'll be kind of like a fraternity rush party for the hippies."

"Cool, I'll try to be there," I replied.

"And if you get the chance, dude, you should check out California. I mean, that's where it's all *really* happening."

Before I could ask about that, Drake became distracted and said, "Hey, I'll have to catch you guys later. There was this really hot chick who I was talking to earlier. I need to find her to see if we can hook up after this is over. You know my brother…love is where it's at, not war. So make damn sure that you come back again."

"We'll try to," I replied. "Maybe we'll see you later."

Drake patted me on the back, said goodbye to my friends, and then moved toward the front of the crowd until he was out of sight.

We continued to march with the crowd for another hour and were getting pretty close to Greenwich Village. Before we arrived, however, the three of us decided to pull out for a moment to grab a hot dog with sauerkraut and mustard from a nearby *Nathan's* street vendor.

Eventually, we caught up with the marchers again just as everyone was about to enter Washington Square Park. It had been an uneventful but very fun day for all of us. There had been no violence at all, and as far as I knew, the police didn't arrest anyone, but still, I just didn't feel that we'd changed the world all that much…one way or the other.

It would soon be time to head home…to do so, we would have to take another taxi to the train station, but two things were on my mind. One was the fact that I had a date lined up with a girl named Rosie, and had planned to see a new controversial movie called *Rosemary's Baby*.

I think she was mostly interested in seeing it because she had the same name but probably knew nothing at all about the subject matter.

I had sat next to Rosie for most of the semester in my English class, but I knew nothing at all about her politics or religion. All I knew about her was that she was five-foot-two, had a nice figure, was a little shy, very friendly, and definitely…had a great set of boobs.

Before leaving the city, I wanted to stop by the park to see if Drake was there. For some reason, I already felt a certain connection to him and thought that perhaps I should get his telephone number so he could help me understand more about the political atmosphere before going off to college. With his red shirt, it didn't take me long to find him.

After finally reaching the arch at Washington Square, I briefly left my friends so they could walk around while I went to look for Drake.

"Hey! It's me, Tex!" I shouted as I saw him throwing a Frisbee to an attractive young lady wearing a long flowing, blue velvet dress, and a circular crown on her head…made of yellow daisies.

"Tex! Yeah, man. Far fucking out. What's your bag man?"

"I wanted to get your telephone number, so I could call, and maybe talk some politics, or about California…and maybe hang out."

"Hey, that would be so far off the wall…right on man.

"This is my new friend, Annie, that bad-ass chick I told you about."

What I would give to have a new friend like that…I thought.

"Yeah…hi, nice to meet you," I said.

Annie just smiled.

"Man, we just smoked some killer weed, and man, we're like a little fucked up right now. Would you like a toke?"

"No thanks," I politely refused. "Heading home, some other time."

I was still feeling infatuated with this young, skinny blonde wearing bright silver bangles that dangled from her wrist.

She just stood there…with a shit-eating grin.

She was obviously very stoned…and I really wanted to hug her.

I noticed she was wearing a couple of buttons on her dress as well, so I leaned forward to see what they said.

One of them read…*My button loves your button.*

The other one read…*Ban the bra.*

It was obvious, she was practicing what she preached.

"I like your buttons," I said to her.

"Thank you…" she replied.

In my mind, I thought…*I think you should ban the panties, too.*

"Tell you what, Tex," Drake said. "I don't have a telephone right now, but I'm taking a Buddhist Sutra course every Wednesday night here in the Village this summer with an old Tibetan Lama. Right now, we're studying the Buddhist Mahayana teachings. It's for training the mind and he teaches us how to meditate. It's a small group and it's open to anyone. You just donate whatever you can afford, you know, maybe a couple of bucks. Why not meet me some evening, and we can talk more after the class. It begins at 7:00 p.m. and is usually over by 8:30.

"That's the best I can do for now, man. Are we cool?"

"Yeah, we're cool. That's a great idea. I'd love to do it."

Drake wrote down the address where the class was being held and said, "Perhaps, I'll see you in a couple of weeks."

"So hey, Brother Drake…keep the faith," I replied clumsily, trying to sound as hip as I could…and said goodbye.

After a few minutes, I found my three amigos watching a troupe of Hari Krishna devotees singing and dancing in front of a small crowd.

We left the park, hailed down a taxi, got out at Central Station, and boarded the next train back to Trenton. Within just over an hour we were back in my car again and on the way home.

I still had plenty of time to keep my movie date with Rosie, but by now I was worn out, exhausted, and tired, and the bottoms of my feet really hurt. However, I was still looking forward to seeing her.

As soon as I dropped everyone off, I returned to my parents' house, jumped into the shower, and then immediately sped off again.

Rosie was very interested in my story about the protest march and said that if the war didn't stop pretty soon…she was going to protest the war as well, in the fall, when she went to Notre Dame University.

She had read something about the movie we were about to see and pointed out that she didn't like scary movies all that much.

That's also when she told me…she was Catholic.

Rosemary's Baby was based on a novel about a coven of witches who assist in bringing about the birth of the son of Satan, who would eventually take over the world. Rosie wasn't sure she should watch it, plus, there would be…brief frontal nudity.

I tried to explain to her…that the movie wasn't supposed to be all that scary and had a lot of famous actors. I also said…that Satan, or the Devil, represented change, and change is what people fear the most.

Reluctantly, she agreed to go.

Rosie didn't get the least bit turned on by the nudity, and I didn't get laid that night. She told me, on the way home, that the movie had only strengthened her desire to become a nun someday.

Taking her to see that movie was an obvious mistake.

I was jealous, that she'd give her body to Jesus…but not to me.

When I dropped her off, I gave her a peck on the cheek and left.

Even if I'd tried, I probably wouldn't get to second base with her.

Rosie was a pretty girl, but I didn't plan on seeing her again.

That night as I lay in bed, I said to myself…*I thought you were over those stupid jealousy issues*, but then I realized…it wasn't jealousy.

It was envy that I was feeling.

Drake was probably shacked up right now with that skinny blonde hippie-chick, Annie, smoking a joint together, naked in a bathtub.

Here I was…with a girl who could care less about sex.

Maybe Drake was right about California.

Then, I began to remember the events of the day.

The protest march against the war had been a lot like the movie we saw, because both had been about giving birth to something new, that could actually change the world, and would perhaps ultimately destroy the established order. I was beginning to see why the older generation viewed hippies as if they were the children of the devil, especially with their new sexual freedom, their drugs, and their music.

The naive Rosemary, from the movie, represented the intellect and innocence of the 1950s and had been the vessel through which the child of Satan was successfully and secretly born into the world.

Although the protest march wasn't what I expected it to be, meeting Drake had opened a huge door for me, and it was one I wanted to enter.

I couldn't just go off to college…when I still had so much to learn.

There was an inner knowingness inside me that said...*a whole new consciousness was about to be given birth to*, and I wanted to be a part of it, although I had no idea if it would ever change the world or not.

What I did know, was that I wasn't afraid of the devil, and I wasn't afraid of change. Hell, I wasn't even afraid of death, but I wanted to know what Drake meant...*that California was the place to be.*

It had to be more than Hollywood, 'Beach Boys' and surfer girls.

Maybe I should go to California...I said as I fell asleep.

That night, I dreamed about California and was about to catch a really big wave on my surfboard. It turned out to be the coolest trip of a lifetime. What a ride it had been, although sharks were everywhere.

There were other surfers nearby and some were holding up signs.

I saw Rosie on a surfboard holding one that read, '*A war to achieve peace is like fucking for virginity,*' and next to her on another surfboard was Jesus who was holding a sign that said, '*Who would I bomb?*'

There was also a beautiful girl looking just like Annie who paddled over and said she was going to ride next to me. Then she handed me a marijuana cigarette, and I gladly accepted it. As I took the first puff, the next thing I knew...we were on standing on my surfboard together just as a huge wave lifted us high into the air. Then we began to make love right on top of the surfboard...as we swiftly glided across the water, washed up on the beach, and rolled into the sand, naked and laughing.

Then, amid all the crashing and pounding of the surf, I could also hear the voice of Drake shouting at me in the distance.

"*Hey Tex, now that's what I call...California dreaming.*"

Then I woke up in a hot sweat, feeling warm rushing sensations throughout my entire body. It had been an amazing experience.

It must be a sign from God...I thought. The next morning, I felt the decision was made...but I didn't know for sure when I could leave.

Mr. Tambourine Man

Hey, Mr. Tambourine Man, play a song for me…
I'm not sleepy and there is no place I'm going to…
Hey, Mr. Tambourine Man, play a song for me…
In the jingle jangle morning, I'll come following you…
(Artist: Bob Dylan)

♥ ♥ ♥

The next time I went to New York City it was a hot summer evening during the first week of August. The Pollock was on vacation with his family, and the Dago had found a night-time job…so I decided to go by myself this time. College wasn't scheduled to start until a week after Labor Day, but I wanted to see Drake before he left for Cornell.

When I got off the train, I found myself right in the middle of the five o'clock rush-hour madness of Grand Central Station, and still had two hours to kill before I had to be in Greenwich Village.

Drake had given me an address for a headshop on Waverley called The Hungry Eye, which I thought was an odd place to have a class on Buddhism. He said the meeting would be held on the third floor.

I could either take a taxi or walk down Fifth Avenue. Rather than spend five dollars for cab fare, I decided to go on foot. I loved being in the energy of this city and was now more determined than ever to come here and go to school if I could get accepted at NYU.

Before proceeding towards my destination, I decided to take a quick detour and see all the lights in Times Square. There was just something about all the hustle and bustle of the city that totally fascinated me.

Someday, I'd just love to live here…for maybe a year.

Almost immediately I was approached by a couple of good-looking whores on Seventh Avenue. I do declare, if I'd been just a little more lonesome, then I might have taken some comfort there...but I did not.

The sultry babes were wearing tight-fitting blouses and miniskirts that were looking pretty damn good. After all, I was grown up now and had to start learning to go with the flow. Perhaps the time had come to learn the ways of the street. To have a good education was one thing, but if you don't know your way around the shadows of life, then you may not survive the tough times when they happen to come up.

"Hey, sailor. Looking for a date?" a young Puerto Rican gal asked.

"I'm not a sailor, but you sure do look like a nice port to sail into," I replied noticing her black leather hotpants and red vinyl go-go boots.

"What's your name, honey?" she asked as she dropped her blouse a little lower than the law permitted, briefly exposing a great set of tits.

"My friends just call me Tex."

"Hey baby, my name's Kitty. Where are you off to, anyway?"

"Well, Kitty, at the moment I'm on my way to the Village to meet a friend, and then to sit down to study with an old Tibetan Lama."

"Now, Tex...what's some old toothless Lama going to do for you that a young lady like me can't do a hell-of-a-lot better?" she laughed.

"You know, that's exactly what I'm hoping to find out! Maybe I'll catch you on the way back and then I'll let you know. I think it's about learning how to train your mind, and not get distracted by the cravings of the world. If that's the case, I might not be interested anymore."

"Well look at you," she shouted. "The man from Texas is going downtown to get himself all holy. Yawl be sure and come back now, you hear, even if you're not into sex anymore. We can just talk about philosophy and other shit, right? I do that with customers all the time. You know...sex and politics...it's all the damn same thing."

"You're probably right!" I noted.

Just then, a young girl who I seriously doubted was eighteen, butted in and said, "What she means to say…is that sex and politics are both about power, manipulation, and control. So if you're one of the few not already corrupted, stay away from them. That's my advice."

Those were some strong words, and right from the dark side itself, but I didn't think I was here to learn about pain and suffering. I had to meet Drake, and then hopefully learn something a little more uplifting from a Tibetan Lama, so it was time to get the hell out of here.

"Well…, I need to think about that one," I replied. Then I waved to the girls and continued on my journey towards Greenwich Village.

Yeah, baby, this was one hell of a far-out-city…and I was feeling *kind of groovy* just by being a small part of its microcosm.

It was getting near six when I reached the Village, so with almost an hour left, I decided to check the place out a little closer. I was able to cover a lot of territory in the small amount of time that I had.

I explored what was happening on Bleecker Street and around the traditionally Bohemian area of the Village. There were a number of performers who were listed to be playing that night in the numerous coffee houses and clubs, such as Tom Paxton, Phil Ochs, Tim Hardin, Leonard Cohen, Tom Rush, Eric Anderson, and many others. But most impressive was the fact that Bob Dylan would also be playing.

Bob Dylan had recently appeared at a folk-rock festival at Newport, Rhode Island and performed with an electric guitar for the first time. Purists in the audience were so angry, they booed him off the stage.

Artists like him often found themselves caught in such a time warp, being somewhere halfway between the past and the present.

At 6:45, I made my way down to Waverley Street and easily found *The Hungry Eye*, a small headshop located four feet below street level.

It sold things like incense, t-shirts, sunglasses, and had a lot of those buttons that I liked…so I bought three buttons for fifty cents each.

One button read, '*Hop, skip and go naked,*' and another one asked the question, '*What if they threw a war and nobody came?*' The third one I liked the best because it read, '*Student Power.*' I didn't know how it would have gone over in high school, but I was finished with that and was now moving on…*with the power to do whatever I wanted.*

Next door to the Hungry Eye were some steps leading up to a door that led to a stairway going up five flights. On the third floor, there was a large room that had once been a dance studio but was now being rented out to anyone who needed space for thirty or forty people.

There were a handful of people sitting on the floor on top of soft cushions with their legs crossed in a meditation-like posture. Several of them smiled at me when I walked in, but no one said anything to me.

Instead of asking a question, I quietly walked toward the back of the room and sat on an empty cushion next to a young, attractive girl.

I crossed my legs in the same way as many of the students were doing…and sat there looking around, but I didn't see Drake anywhere.

As more people arrived, the room started to feel overcrowded.

Candles were lit, which added to the strong smell of sandalwood incense in the air, giving the former dance studio a mystical feeling.

I sat there quietly for another five minutes, finding it uncomfortable to be still for so long without shifting my position.

It was obvious I wasn't very experienced in meditation.

Then Drake arrived and I signaled to him. With a big smile on his face, he came over and sat next to me. In doing so, he lightly elbowed me in the ribs and whispered, "I'm glad you could make it."

A few minutes later an old Lama arrived with several other students in front of him and behind him, apparently acting as escorts.

As soon as he entered, everyone stood up and some of the regular students began to prostrate themselves three times by placing their palms together and then bending down and touching their foreheads to the floor in the traditional Tibetan manner. Drake did the same thing, but most of us remained standing with our hands together next to our chest in a prayer-like position. The escorts lighted even more incense and candles and prepared a special place for the old Lama to sit down.

When everyone was seated, the elderly Rinpoche looked around the room and smiled at the gathering of people. Then, three times, he began to chant the words to the mantra, "*Om Mani Padme Hum.*"

"That means, *praise to the jewel in the lotus,*" Drake whispered.

Wearing only a crimson robe and sandals, he rang a small brass bell several times with his left hand while throwing bits of uncooked rice into the air with his right hand, making sure that at least a few pieces of rice fell on everyone who was sitting in the room.

"This is for purification and blessings," Drake explained.

Then, in a very hard-to-understand broken English the Lama began by saying, "Homage to all of you, all who have come here this night. *You are Maitreya…*future Buddhas and Bodhisattvas of this Age.

"The sound of the bell is to purify the energy in the room and to remove any negativity that might be present. The rice is made as an offering to the many deities that have come here to be with you this evening. Yes, they are here, and they welcome you."

The crowd laughed and looked around as if trying to see one.

"If one has gained a human form, possessing both the eight freedom and the ten endowments, then one should therefore be able to reap the benefits afforded by this auspicious situation.

"The final attainment of a completely enlightened mind, or what is known as 'Bodhicitta,' depends upon having a suitable physical life form, as well as a suitable environment and harmonious friends.

"The first of these is produced by the practice of ethical discipline, the second by the practice of generosity, and the third by cultivating patience. Each of these practices is best performed by a man or a woman having the freedoms and endowments we discussed last week.

"The best ethical discipline is the path of individual liberation, and this can only be taken by one who is a human being.

"Other forms of life are unable to generate such awareness and knowledge. In other words, animals are aware of what is outside of them, but humans have the ability to be aware of what is within them.

"A dog cannot become enlightened, nor a bird attain Buddhahood. This is the immediate benefit of being human. That is to say, you have the opportunity to expand your awareness far beyond that of the animal kingdom, but looking at today's world, you might doubt that."

The crowd laughed.

"Dharma means *truth* or *the law*, and it is what the Buddha taught during his lifetime. Why must I practice the Dharma, you may ask?

"Were it not so difficult to regain a human life after death, perhaps it would not be necessary to practice Dharma. However, because there are so many other souls already in line, it can be very difficult to attain a human rebirth. So sometimes…you must wait hundreds of years.

"Merely to gain rebirth into one of the higher realms of existence requires some discipline, but in order to gain a physical form with the eight freedoms and the ten endowments, one must have a very strong discipline, and this is extremely rare in the present age.

"Take advantage of this valuable life you have found and extract its essence by striving for the attainment of enlightenment.

"Granted, your death will become certain one day, but there is no guarantee that your death will be followed by another state of freedom. Beings do not disappear into a state of nothingness when they die, but rather they take rebirth in accordance with the karmic forces and the psychic propensities they have sown within themselves during their life on Earth. So now, let us begin where we left off last week."

After this brief introduction, the regular students began to take turns reading from the *Prajnaparamita Sutra*. As Drake explained to me, this text expounds on the doctrine of the non-reality of the world as it is conventionally experienced. He said that most of the things humans normally ascribe to their daily experiences are a product of intellectual analyzing and thinking, or else they are simply a perception that comes from the senses. He said that according to Buddhist philosophy, instead of making any references to God...or to any form of Supreme Being, they go beyond the mind and instead refer to a state of *emptiness* that's often referred to as, *the void*, which in Tibetan is called *Shunyata*.

Carl Jung described it as...*the Empty Center*.

After reading from the text for thirty minutes, the old Lama began to explain the meaning of what it all meant.

"What this is saying...is that objects are merely attached to words. For instance, the term 'chair' is associated with a collection of four legs, one back, and one seat. However, 'chair' is neither one of the parts taken on its own, nor is it detached from those parts. If 'chair' were the composition of the parts, this would mean that each part would be a chair, or that the composition would not have any parts. For that reason, 'chair' does not really exist other than as a designation, but you still believe that 'chair' exists, *even though it does not.* This illustrates the way of thinking and reasoning that we use in Buddhist philosophy."

I was confused and didn't understand.

"As a consequence of this insight, we find there are two types of reality. One is the *relative reality*, which is the world of appearances. This reality is necessary to be able to act, move and relate to others.

"On the other hand, there is also the *absolute reality*, which may be characterized by the absence of any inherent existence at all.

"That is what is meant by *Shunyata*. Recognize *emptiness* in all things by following the path laid out by Buddha twenty-five hundred years ago. It will eventually lead to the attainment of enlightenment.

"Again, I urge you to abandon all negativity in this life, for it will only cause a lower rebirth. Instead, learn to harvest the causation of joy. The method for gaining freedom from the six lower realms of rebirth and attaining the state of ever-lasting joy is two-fold.

The first is to take refuge in the *Three Jewels*, and the second is to live in accordance with the karmic laws of *cause and effect*.

"Next week, we'll discuss more about what the Three Jewels mean, which I'll remind you now are the Buddha, the Dharma, and the Sanga.

"*Buddha* means…the example set by the teacher. *Dharma* means… the teachings of Buddha, and *Sanga* means…the harmonious friends you surround yourself with…like those who are here tonight."

The crowd looked around at each other and quietly laughed again.

The Lama continued, "We will also begin discussing what Buddha discovered to be the cause of pain and suffering in the world."

I poked Drake in the side and quietly remarked, "I already know the answer to that … sex and politics."

He just gave me a weird look in response.

"Now, please go into the rest of your evening with peace in your heart and a smile upon your face. Be kind to everyone you meet, and help the world to live sanely and saintly. Goodnight my dear friends, or as we say in India, *Namaste*. It means…*I honor the Soul you are*."

Then, the old Lama bowed his shaved head and placed the palms of his hands together as he touched his wrinkled fingers to his smiling lips.

Everyone sat quietly until he had gotten up with the assistance of his escorts, and then left the room in the same way he had come in.

Drake jabbed me with his elbow and said, "That was some heavy shit, dude! You shouldn't be making fun of it. Let's have a cigarette."

♥ ♥ ♥

As soon as we hit the sidewalk, Drake lit up and offered me one.

"I've got some of my own, thanks."

"Let's take a walk down Bleecker Street and find us some dive bar where we can just hang out," he suggested.

There were a lot of people out on the street that night and I was feeling good, especially after that session with the old Lama.

"I enjoyed the meeting a lot. Thanks for inviting me. You know, Drake, I'm interested in hearing more about how to get involved with what's going on in the world. Today I met two whores and one Lama for the very first time. I feel as though I've lived a sheltered existence, and don't even know what's happening to people my age.

'I want to be part of the solution, not part of the problem. You dig?"

"There's a whole lot of cool stuff going on right here in the Village, but as I told you before, California is where it's happening. New York is still stuck somewhere halfway between here and there. We have a lot of hippies living here, but we also still have the Beats."

"The Beats? Who are they?"

"The Beat generation…Beatniks, poets, singers, and artists such as William Burroughs, Gary Snyder, Michael McClure, Allen Ginsberg, and a whole lot more. Ever since Allen came back from India he seems to have traded in his poetry, and now sings a lot of *Hare Krishna* songs.

"He's also become very active in the anti-war movement."

"I've heard of him, but I still don't understand what the difference is between Beatniks and Hippies," I confessed.

"Beatniks have been hanging around New York City since the late Fifties," he clarified. They're the '*old school*' radicals, who years ago, began to reject the boredom of a post-World War II consumer-society."

"I still don't quite get what you mean," I asked.

"I mean, what exactly was it that they rejected?"

"People like your own parents…who live in white suburbs, watch television sitcoms, drive identical cars, and pretend they're Ozzie and Harriet. However, Beatniks reached a peak, in terms of consciousness, and are now stuck in their own patterns of worn-out thinking, meaning that when it comes to Beats and politics, there's nothing new anymore. In my opinion, the Beats were not able to expand their minds far enough to become completely free, but for those of us who are now becoming much hipper, we've become the new generation. We've got a stronger awareness of where we're going…instead of where we've been."

"Now I get what you're saying."

"What also makes us different is that we're going to be successful, by changing the world from the inside out, and it's already happening in California. It's like the pioneer days because a lot of people are trying to discover a whole new identity for America. We have this ingenious sense of a new consciousness that's being given birth to right now and many people are beginning to wake up and see the bright light of the sun, but the sun is shining inside of them, not out there…somewhere. It's a new day and a new dawning, and I'm telling you that California is the place to be if you really want to get an education in life."

"So why aren't you out there yourself?"

"I was out there for a while last year…but it's like this man, some of us have to remain here…in order to help bring the east coast and the west coast together. That's what I'm doing. I'm like one of those early colonists, you know, like Benjamin Franklin."

"These are exciting times we're living in," I commented.

"You have no idea just how important these times are. You see, there are certain points in the history of every nation that are like huge portals, or thresholds. It's like a time warp, an opening that leads to other dimensions, or a doorway that allows the consciousness of people to expand in ways that will advance the civilization forward."

"Is that what Chairman Mao Tse-tung is doing in China?"

Drake paused for a moment to think…and then continued.

"What he's doing…*is a cultural revolution*, but what I'm talking about for America…*is a consciousness revolution*…one that will be a total assault on this country, and the rest of the world. Just listen to the music and how it's changed. *Our music…is what's changing people.*

"That's how powerful it is because it has a new vibration.

"*A different drummer is drumming*, and it will continue so long as we make use of every tool and every kind of media that's out there."

"Far fucking out," I noted.

"Can you imagine a world without war because of music? No one knows how long these times will last, but the frequency that's coming in right now is affecting everything from art to books, to posters, to our clothing, and the way we grow our hair, the way we smoke dope, and even the way we fuck, eat, sleep, and piss. But ultimately, it's just all one message man, and the message is about freedom, the mind-blowing fucking freedom to just be you…*just because you are here, and just because you exist,* and for no other reason in the entire fucking world."

"Wow!" I replied in astonishment.

"*Fucking wow*," Drake mimicked. "You were born on this planet. It's your absolute birthright to use it and enjoy it however you want. It's not right for someone else to fuck it up just because they're a rich, greedy scum bag, capitalistic pig. That kind of shit has to stop."

"Right on," I said. "Power to the people."

"Yeah, Tex, there's a whole new way to view the world.

"*We've got to get it together*…not only as a nation but as a planet. However, they're going to try to stop us, stomp us down, beat the crap out of us, and cut our balls off…but it's not going to happen that way."

As he was talking, I felt a chill run down my spine.

I hadn't heard any of this in high school.

"What we're about is freedom of speech, freedom of art, freedom of sex, and freedom of love. We're about expressing ourselves, doing what we want...and becoming *real human beings*."

"It seems so simple, doesn't it? But we make it so hard," I said.

"It's just as the old Lama said...it's about being in the energy of those whom you choose to surround yourself with. Do you want to wear a stuffy starched shirt with a suit and tie, and work your whole life, maybe fifty hours a week, just to be like everyone else on your street who no one gives a shit about? Or do you want to become a free and enlightened human who lives in a world without borders or boundaries? That's what this is all about, man...can you dig it?

"I mean, what do you think? Am I right, *or am I right*?"

After that speech, I didn't know what to think. All I knew was that yes, I wanted to be free, whatever that meant. Perhaps it was just what he said, 'that I exist,' and have every right to be here on my own terms, not on what someone else, or some government is telling me to do.

"I thought it was interesting what the old Lama had said about how we need to let go of all the negativity in this life," I replied to Drake. "I'd like to find out a whole lot more about enlightenment."

"I think I'd try to explain it this way...that somewhere within us is pure consciousness, but the mind we use on a day-to-day basis has its limitations because we live in this limited realm we call 'Earth.'

"We all hold within us the original *Source consciousness* of that thing we call, *God*, which is pure, unlimited and perfect...but because we're born into this imperfect world we take on a body with limitations, and we forget 'what it is' we really are...and go through life believing we're separated from God, feeling that the world we live in is for some reasons unfriendly and are always in danger...being in survival mode keeps our enlightenment elusive because we've chosen fear over love, so we continue to feel limited...rather than be *the gods* that we are.

"That is unless we somehow free our minds from this global prison we've all been born into. To me, that would truly be enlightenment."

"And how would we free our minds from this prison…meditating naked for twenty years in a frozen cave in Tibet?" I jokingly asked.

"Well, yeah, that's one way. What I'm saying is that now there's a new drug on the street called LSD, and man, that shit will open up your mind big time! It allows you to tap into that original consciousness we once had before we were born and to see beyond the illusions of what we call reality. It's what the old Lama was talking about, you know, that there are two types of reality. Well, LSD allows you to see that other reality, which is a separate and absolute reality. Personally, I think it's a shortcut to attaining enlightenment."

"I've heard of LSD, but what is it really?"

"It's a mind-expanding drug that increases awareness and removes the limitations of our ability to think. When you've seen beyond your limited self, you find an inner peace of mind that's always been there just waiting for you. It's the empty space we call God, and the Shunyata the Lama talked about. I'm telling you…this stuff is going to allow lots of people to become enlightened really fast…without go to India.

"It's going to change the way we see everything."

"Have you ever tried LSD?" I asked.

"Yeah, once, about a month ago, and it was fantastic. It's still a little hard to find here in New York, at least for right now, but there's tons of it in California, so it won't be long before we have it going on around here too. There's this guy out there named Timothy Leary, and he and these two other dudes named Ken Kesey and Neal Cassady have this bus, and all they've been doing for the last few months is going around California getting thousands of people turned on to LSD. And you know what's really cool? It's not illegal either. At least...not yet."

"Wasn't Timothy Leary a college professor?"

"Yeah, he has a Ph.D. in psychology, and man, this cat is smart too.

"He says…reality is just a crutch for people who can't handle drugs, and that LSD is better than chocolate…because it melts in your mind, not in your hands. Isn't that absolutely brilliant?"

"Yeah…incredible."

"Hey, Tex, what do you say we go inside this place here and have a drink…we can even light up a joint if you want to."

We ducked into a darkly lit hovel of a club called, *The Cellar Door* and paid $2.00 each to a man sitting on a stool at the entrance.

The dimly lit hallway that led to the inside had several 'black-light posters pinned to the walls. At first, I had trouble seeing where I was.

About thirty people were sitting in a single large room.

Some were seated on old worn-out couches, dirty sofa chairs, or on the shag-rug floor that was littered with large colored pillows.

Drake and I found some empty cushions in front of a small black wooden stage that had a couple of chairs for performers to sit in.

As my eyes adjusted to the light, I could see we were sitting next to a group of people who were smoking cigarettes and drinking beer.

I could also smell the familiar scent of marijuana, and upon closer inspection, I saw a small cannabis roach being passed around.

"Come on, let's light up and smoke some weed, too. I've even got a joint right here in my pocket. You've smoked before, haven't you?"

"Actually, no," I said, a little embarrassed. "I haven't, but I'd really like to try it. Do you have any pointers?"

"Wow, I guess you're a virgin midnight-toker, eh! Okay, well…just breathe it in slowly, hold it in for a few seconds, and then breathe out.

"Then, pass it back to me or someone else.

"And…be sure not to *Bogart that joint.*"

"What does that mean?" I replied with a nervous laugh.

"I don't know. I think it comes from the movie, *Casablanca*, where Humphrey Bogart was always sucking on a cigarette. You see, the gods created pot for people to share with each other and throughout history, there's always been a certain sacredness about smoking the herb with other people because it brings you all together into one mind. You know, the freedom to get high with all of your friends is part of what this whole new consciousness is all about."

Drake pulled out a rolled joint and handed it to me while he lit it. Then I took a few puffs, held it in, and then passed it back to Drake.

Within only a few seconds I could feel the change come over me, and minutes later I was feeling very lightheaded.

I started laughing at the absurdity of everything.

"So," I began, "you think the whole world is stuck in the mud with a stick up their ass, and that LSD and the hippies are going to change all of that by just getting high and playing music…is that right?"

"Yeah," Drake replied, blowing out a large puff of smoke, "if we can't change the world, then who else is going to do it? It sure as hell won't be *Che Guevara* or *Barbarella*. You see, there are three kinds of revolutionaries. There are political revolutionaries, there are cultural revolutionaries, and there are consciousness revolutionaries."

"Okay, I dig you so far."

"A political revolution is about politics, and a cultural revolution is about culture, but they may not affect consciousness.

"A consciousness revolution affects both politics and culture…

"I want to be a conscientious revolutionary. *Viva la revolution!*

"Here's to consciousness…and the evolution of humanity."

"That's all well said," came the voice of someone sitting beside us as Drake passed the joint back to me. "Now let's see if you can go out there into the world…and really do it."

I turned my head and tried to see was talking.

It was a young man with a boyish grin and dark hair that hung down over his ears. He looked familiar but I couldn't place his face.

"Hey, dude," replied Drake, "good to see you again. I didn't know you were going to be here tonight."

"Yeah, man, but just for a few more minutes. Then I have to do a gig that's going on down the street."

"Bob, this is my friend, Tex. I think his name is Andy but for some stupid shit reason he just goes by Tex."

I glanced at Drake and replied, "That's what my friends named me when I moved here from Texas, not for some stupid shit reason."

"Hey, man, it's cool," Bob responded.

I shook Bob's hand and passed him the joint after another toke.

"Groovy," Bob said, taking the joint and small puff. Then he handed it to a girl with long blonde hair sitting next to him.

"So…how do you like New York?" Bob asked me.

"I like it here a lot and I hope to go to NYU…but at the moment, I'm thinking about heading to California, just to check it out, the only problem is…I don't know anyone living there," I replied.

"You should go to San Francisco," he recommended, "if you do, you're going to meet a lot of gentle people, I promise."

"Just be sure to wear some flowers in your hair," the girl sitting next to him noted. "Summertime is like a love-in there."

Feeling really high, I blurted out something that was totally random and made no sense at all by saying, "Well, I probably wouldn't feel so all alone…if everybody would just get stoned."

Bob laughed out loud and retrieved the joint from his lady friend. As he passed it back to Drake, he echoed…*everybody must get stoned.*

"Hey, that might be a good line for my next song."

For a brief moment, Bob started to slowly hum out a new tune, then picked up a tambourine that was lying next to him and began to sing.

Well…they'll stone you when you're riding in your car.

They'll stone you when you're playing your guitar, and I would not feel so all alone…everybody must get stoned.

"Far out, Bob," Drake replied.

At that moment, we were interrupted by someone tapping on the microphone. It was open mic night where anyone could get up and say what they wanted, sing a song, or read one of their poems.

A young man stood up and said he was going to recite a poem he had written just the night before and called it…*Ode to Vietnam.*

Slowly, he began to read his poem to the audience…

He walked alone in the jungle heat,
    the jungle grove looked quiet and calm,
    It was time to stop, and get off his feet,
    in this torturous hell called Vietnam.
Behind every bush awaited death,
    but here he had stopped to take his rest,
    And as he sat just to catch his breath,
    a machine gun echoed into his chest.
Blood gushed out on his khaki shirt.
    The Cong jumped out and grabbed his gun.
    He lay there motionless in the dirt.
    His eyes just focused on the setting sun.
Death had not taken his body yet,
    for life still remained inside this man.
    In the game of survival, he lost the bet.
    The Viet Cong had won the hand.
In pain, he sought to remember the past,
    to times when he had been but a youth.
    His life was now over much too fast,
    and now too late he was facing the truth.

He had been in a hurry to conquer his fears,
    quit school, and enlisted at seventeen.
    But was so scared in battle he held his ears,
    being too young to hear men scream.
Only a month until his enlistment ran out,
    into the jungle, he had started to roam.
    Now as he lay there, he tried to shout,
    wishing to be next to his girl back home.
His regrets were many, his joys few.
    He died, but the grove was quiet and calm.
    Here lay a young man dead, all covered in dew,
    in this tortuous hell called Vietnam.

When he was done, the crowd clapped with approval.

"Right on!" someone shouted.

I felt as if the effects of the weed were changing the chemistry of my brain when another young man quickly took the stage and started to talk. He spoke of things I had never heard before that touched my soul. What he said, and what I felt inside, may have changed my life.

"The government's view is: *if it feels too good, it should be illegal.* My philosophy is: *if it feels that good, then why aren't you doing it?*"

The crowd laughed.

"Let me tell it like it is brothers and sisters. A hand on your cock is more moral, and more fun, than a finger is on the trigger of a gun."

Everybody clapped and cheered.

"I'm here tonight to talk about freedom. Now I've got a few things to say to all you folks, but first…let's have a little quiz."

"Who said this? *'Those who desire to give up freedom in order to gain security will not have, nor do they deserve, either one.'*

"That was from Thomas Jefferson," someone answered.

"Hey, you're smart...so how about this one, '*How many years can a people exist before they're allowed to be free?*'"

"That comes from our dear friend, Bob Dylan, sitting right there," someone else answered while pointing out Bob.

Bob stood up and took a bow.

I couldn't believe it. Bob Dylan had been sitting right next to me all along and we had even smoked from the same joint.

Then the man on the stage continued his freedom monologue.

"So if you want to be free...*be free* because there are a million things to be. And one thing I can tell you is you've got to be free!

"Nobody can stop me as I go walking down my freedom highway.

"Nobody living can make me turn back. This land is your land.

"This land is my land, and this land was made for you and me.

"I mean, listen, people, I do my thing and you do yours.

"The only rose without a thorn is friendship and a true friend is someone who lets you have that total freedom to be yourself.

"You are you. I am me. And I am you and you are me. We are one.

"I am not in this world to live up to your expectations, and you are not in this world to live up to mine, but if by chance we should find each other, and if the energy's right, then it's going to be beautiful.

"Just think of all the hate there is in Red China, and then take a look around to places like Selma, Alabama.

"Whenever you find yourself on the side of the majority, then it's time to pause and reflect. For you see, my friends, true freedom is in your mind. Sure, they can throw your ass in jail, but they can never put your spirit anywhere it doesn't want to be. Listen closely to what I say.

"You must become the change you want to see in the world, and that change is freedom. You see, battle lines are being drawn right now, but nobody's right if everybody's wrong. Young people are speaking their minds, getting so much resistance from those who are still behind.

"So come on board brothers and sisters…because the ship is getting ready to sail and it doesn't matter at all if you're getting on late because we're all going to reach the opposite shore at the same time.

"Henry Thoreau once said, '*Live the life you've always imagined.*' Mark Twain said, '*Go confidently in the direction of your dreams.*' Robert Frost said, '*I took the road less traveled by, and that has made all the difference.*' Of course, if I went through life just quoting other people then I would be nobody. So I just have one last thing to say, and that is…*always question authority, enjoy life, and let freedom ring!*

"Peace to all of you, my brothers and sisters, goodnight!"

Everyone applauded.

We had a bit of a break before the next performer, so I turned to Bob and asked him, "How did you get started in this business?"

"I'll tell you, Tex, there was already some band that was playing in my head the day I was born and the next thing I knew, I just felt like getting high and so I did. Then one day, I got on a stage and started telling people what was on my mind, and it hasn't stopped since."

"Far out," I replied.

"Hey everyone, I've got to go now and do my gig down the street. I'll see you guys again sometime. Tex, be sure to look me up when you come back here for college and if you want, you can come backstage.

"Thanks again for the song."

"See you later, Mr. Tambourine man," I replied.

I was still in shock that it was him!

After Bob left, Drake and I continued to talk a little more about Timothy Leary and about what was happening in California. After that, and after getting high one more time, I got it in my head that I wanted to live in a Buddhist culture someday, maybe in Tibet, but first I wanted to live in California for a while, and also go to college.

However, I wanted to go to California soon, before I missed out on something really special. Besides that, I also wanted to try some LSD, so we talked for about an hour before I had to catch the midnight train.

I was pretty stoned, but I figured I could still manage my way back home safely…knowing my parents were probably going to be just a bit pissed off about me getting back so late.

As I was getting ready to flag a taxicab, Drake tapped me on the shoulder and said, "Hey, Tex, before you go, I just made up this little rhyme: *Southern change is going to come at last! Now your crosses are burning fast. Hey, Southern Man, you're going to be all right.*

"By the way, Tex, if you do go to San Francisco, bring me back a couple of bags of acid, will you? Whatever we don't take ourselves, we can easily sell and make some good money. I'll catch you later, dude."

On the train coming back, I realized more than ever that I wasn't ready to jump into the box my parents had set out for me, which meant I wasn't ready to go to college yet. I just couldn't bring myself to go to Penn State, at least for now, and I was going to have to face my parents with this fact and tell them I was seriously thinking about moving to California for a while. After all, I had a little money saved, and I could sell my car. Maybe once I got there, I could get a job…or something.

It was actually a question about either being true to me and seeking my dreams, or following the dreams of society, and I didn't want to be just another brick in the wall. No…walls were built to prevent freedom, and I wasn't someone's military son, so I didn't have to play the same game my parents had played. It was a new dawn, and a new age was upon the land. It was a seasonal shift, and the winds of change were here. It was time to expand my consciousness and be a part of the change going on in the world. Drake's words were having a profound effect on me, and I knew there was no turning back.

Maybe it was just the time of year, or maybe it was the time of man, and I didn't know who I was, but I did know...life was for learning.

Besides... it was just time to go out and do my own thing.

♥ ♥ ♥

The next morning, I slept in late, not wanting to get out of bed and face a new reality. What I wanted...was what the old Lama had said, *to seek freedom and become free*, even though I still had no idea what true freedom actually meant. I was also sure that pain and suffering had more to do with that unfound freedom than with sex and politics.

I don't know why I thought that whore was so smart.

Enlightenment and freedom must be connected...I said to myself.

Then, I realized the similarity. They both had to do with the absence of limitation. No walls, no barriers, no borders...just the emptiness of Shunyata, total freedom of consciousness. Nothing within your mind holds you back from anything. No fear, no cravings, no nada....

I wondered if LSD could accelerate that process...I certainly didn't need to use reality as a crutch...*because I didn't even like reality.*

♥ ♥ ♥

My parents weren't happy that I wasn't going to school in the fall. I told them I was torn between NYU and Berkeley in San Francisco, and I wanted to check out the campus at Berkeley before making my final decision. I had to promise that I would start school in January.

When my parents saw my determination to take the semester off, they finally agreed to let me go even though I was over eighteen and couldn't be legally stopped anyway...so my mother bought me a new suitcase, and even gave me an extra hundred dollars.

♥ ♥ ♥

That summer, President Lyndon Johnson sent even more Marines into Vietnam and deployed another 50,000 troops. No doubt, the U.S. had now become the aggressor and was on the offensive.

Now, I was facing the real possibility of being drafted into the army, because I wasn't enrolled in college and without a military deferment.

The U.S. military draft had gone into effect in 1948, shortly after World War II, but even though the war in Vietnam was heating up fast, I didn't think I would get called up immediately. So I sold my car and my surfboard…and then took a Greyhound Bus across the country all the way to San Francisco, having no idea what I would find there.

I traveled across the wheat fields of Kentucky, to the California sun, and along the way, I heard Bob Dylan's songs ringing in my head.

How does it feel, to be on your own…?

With no direction home, like a complete unknown…

Like a rolling stone…

For me, the adventure of a lifetime was just beginning.

I said to myself…*to be a rolling stone, feels pretty good.*

If You're Going to San Francisco

If you're going to San Francisco…
Be sure to wear some flowers in your hair…
If you're going to San Francisco…
You're going to meet some gentle people there…
(Artist: Scott McKenzie)

The bus arrived at noon in the City of Berkeley. I left my suitcase in a locker and decided to check out the student life on campus.

The fall semester at the University of California had just begun.

I was immediately impressed by the beautiful and lush landscaping on the campus. Besides the massive number of green lawns, there were lots of trees and streams with squirrels running everywhere.

It was very pleasant to be surrounded by all this nature.

Between classes, you could lay down on the lawn to be in the sun.

All of the buildings were impressive, as was the whole campus.

I found the Student Union Building where I picked up some papers about admission procedures for next January from the Bursar's Office. By then, it was close to one o'clock, so I decided to have some lunch and quickly found the student cafeteria located in the basement.

Not knowing anyone, I sat at a table near some other students and quietly began to devour my Monterey taco salad, the special of the day. Sitting next to me was a small group of long-haired students, mostly dressed in tie-dyed t-shirts, bell-bottom pants, and leather sandals.

"You see, man," I heard one of them say to the others, "I met this guy yesterday who had just come from a trip around the world.

"Really, this cat was far out. He'd been to Kathmandu in Nepal and also traveled around India. He's been with gurus...he even went to one of those Hare Krishna ashrams for a while, but now he's just a roofer here in Oakland. Can you dig it, man? Doing all that cool shit, learning all about eastern religions, and then becoming a roofer! I'll bet he hits every nail on the head just perfectly...*with total awareness*."

As I listened to the conversation, I became even more interested in what was being said. After having spent only an hour with the old Lama in the Village, I had become intrigued with the idea of actually going to Tibet someday. I had read about the Chinese invasion of Tibet in 1951, and that the Tibetan borders had been closed to people from the Western cultures. The closest anyone could get to Tibet was to go to countries like India or Nepal, and the capital of Nepal was Kathmandu, which is where this fellow had apparently been to visit.

I didn't know if I would ever be able to visit Tibet or Nepal, but if the opportunity ever arose, I was definitely going to do it. But for now, it was nothing more than a simple pipe dream. What I did know was that I needed to find a place to spend the night, and I didn't want to pay for some rundown, star-cooled hotel room if I didn't have to.

I decided to check out Telegraph Avenue in the Haight-Ashbury district. That's where Drake had said a lot of students and hippies were living, so perhaps I might find a room where I could permanently live, or at least find a really cheap place for a few days. Not only that but staying there would give me the opportunity to get more 'tuned into' what this new California consciousness was all about.

It was only a short walk before the scenery began to change.

The first thing I noticed when I reached Haight Street was all of the funny-looking shops, and...the just-as-funny-looking individuals.

Talk about people strutting their stuff...!

It was like being at a circus where everyone was dressed in bright colors with long hair and flowing clothing, coming in and out of the various stores and headshops that had colorfully painted entrances.

I had never seen so many people going about the daily business of *hippie-mania*…not even in Greenwich Village.

I was feeling kind of lost and needed to stop to regroup. Then I saw an old brick building with a sign that read "Sexual Freedom League."

Inside, they were having a meeting sponsored by a student group called the C.S.R.F. (Campus Sexual Rights Forum).

It looked pretty interesting, so I decided to check it out.

When I walked in there was a large room just to my right where the meeting was going on with about twenty people sitting in chairs.

A guy named Mike had just introduced himself as being the vice president of the student group and had a number of topics to discuss, including whether or not the C.S.R.F. should continue to organize nude parties. He said the *Sexual Freedom League* was already performing that function, and to do so might damage the reputation of the C.S.R.F., or worse, imperil official campus recognition of the student group.

The C.S.R.F. was to be concerned only with matters that affected the campus community, while broader issues (like legalizing abortion) would be left up to the *League* to pursue.

However, there were two other issues that needed to be voted on. They concerned the distribution of birth control pamphlets to students living in the dorms and allowing nude movies to be shown on campus.

I found it interesting that students were so involved in such matters, so when the meeting was over, I hung out for a while to meet some of the people. One of them was an older man in his thirties named Henry.

He said…he owned a building across the street and had a furnished room for rent that was well within my budget, so I took it.

I liked it here…and it seemed the energies were flowing with me.

It was only a small room, with just a mattress on the floor, an old chair, and a beat-up dresser. The bathroom was down the hallway and had to be shared with several other people who I had not met yet.

Henry was a likable character with a broad mustache and long hair with a receding hairline, and we seemed to hit it off pretty quickly.

After paying him the first month's rent, he said, "My friend Mike and I are having a little party tonight in my apartment downstairs and you're welcome to come. As you can tell from the topic of discussion today there may be some nudity and drugs...so don't be shy."

"It sounds pretty cool," I replied, not believing my luck so far.

After retrieving my suitcase from the bus station, I got a bite to eat at the Flying Biscuit Café across the street, unpacked, took a shower, and then rested before the party began. It had been a perfect day.

There were only a few people present when I made it downstairs to the party that was supposed to start at eight o'clock. I began by going into the kitchen to thank Henry again for the room. He was setting out party goods and introduced me to Mike, the speaker from the afternoon. I also met the other people who were helping out in the kitchen.

I helped them prepare several cookie sheets of brownies that had been mixed with marijuana, called *Alice B. Toklas Brownies,* and also helped to prepare some kind of party punch by pouring several cans of pineapple juice and orange juice into a large bowl.

When it was done, Henry said he was going to place several tabs of acid into the punch. Of course, I had never done acid before, but I didn't tell him that. I simply said, "This should be a great party."

Then he proceeded to open a small baggie of orange pills and mixed them in. Several minutes later he handed me a cup and said to drink it.

I nodded my head and took a small sip, being a little apprehensive about getting too fucked up on my first acid experience.

"Don't worry," Henry stated, "I only put a couple of tabs in there, so you're not going to trip out or even hallucinate, but if you mix it with a brownie or two...*you'll be feeling really groovy.*"

Shortly thereafter other guests began to arrive, and the aroma of weed filled the front room as they quietly sat on couches and on the floor passing joints. Then a cup of punch with a brownie was handed out to everyone in the room. Mike placed a Tahitian Calypso fire dance on the Garrard turntable in order to pump things up a bit. Then the two of us sat down on the floor alongside everyone else.

As soon as the titillating melody began, someone else began beating bongo drums that were on the couch. As the sound of the music played, the energy in the room changed, and people began to get involved.

A tall girl with long dark hair stood up and swayed to the sounds. Then, she began to slowly remove her purple dashiki dress, until she was down to a black-laced bra and a pair of silky black skimpy briefs.

She continued to move her body until the rhythm hit a heightened peak...and then it suddenly ended. She collapsed onto the floor and folded herself up into a little ball. Everyone clapped, and moments later she got up and walked out of the room, and into one of the bedrooms.

By now the room was tense and hot, especially after some of the people began to remove their own clothing as well. At about the same time, I began to feel the first tingling sensations of the acid kick in, often feeling as if my stomach was in a tight knot. I didn't know if that was supposed to happen, or if I was just getting nervous.

A guy sitting next to me apparently felt my minor distress and tried to calm me down by saying, "It's all cool man. It'll go away soon."

I got up and went into the kitchen to find a beer and relax. Everyone else seemed to know each other, so I felt just a little odd being the only new guy in town. A few minutes later I returned to the living room and sat down on the floor again, only this time next to a hot-looking slender blonde named Andrea, and a dark-haired Latin man named Ernie.

After a brief conversation I learned that she was a graduate student at U.C., and Ernie was a research assistant at the Radiation Laboratory. On the weekends, they performed a sensual salsa routine together at the *Coffee Gallery*, a famous nightclub in San Francisco. They'd decided to perform their dance routine this evening, right here in the room.

Andrea stood up and placed '*Black Magic Woman*,' by Santana, on the turntable, and then began to dance by moving her body in a slow and seductive fashion. Ernie got up off the floor and elusively moved around her in a stalking manner. From behind, he quickly removed the black bow tied to her hair…and allowed it to fall over her shoulders.

Reaching around her waist, he then tried to unbutton her blouse, but she resisted his advances, until it gently slid off, revealing a bursting zebra skin bra. Moving gracefully to the music, they faced each other.

She pretended to protest when he tried to kiss her, so he captured her in his arms, twirled her around…and quickly unfastened the bra. When it fell to the floor…her large white breasts were unleashed.

After that, Ernie slowly stepped back…as if to examine his prize.

The dance culminated when he reached forward and grabbed the front of her loose-fitting dress and flung it into the corner of the room, revealing her last vestige of clothing, a pair of crimson panties.

When the music came to an end, everyone applauded, and they both disappeared into one of the bedrooms just as Rita had done before.

I really needed to check out what was going on in that bedroom.

As the evening wore on, the effects of both the spiked punch and brownies were causing me to feel as if the walls were moving. I decided to sit down beside a big heavy-set guy named Roy, whom I had met earlier in the kitchen, and tried to start up a conversation.

He wanted to introduce me to his date who was sitting by herself on the floor a few feet away staring into space. She reminded me of Cher Bono because her jet-black hair hung down to her hips.

When Roy introduced me, I knelt down and simply shook her hand without speaking. He said her name was Leanna and told her my name was Tex. Strangely, Roy walked off leaving the two of us together.

It was awkward at first because she didn't seem at all interested in having a conversation, so I asked her if she wanted to dance.

She just shook her head to decline my offer since the glassy-eyed girl didn't seem to be capable of speaking, so I cautiously got up from the floor and carefully made my way back into the kitchen where Roy was pouring himself another glass of the magic punch.

"Isn't she the most fantastic girl you've ever met?" he asked.

"She seems to be awfully quiet," I noted.

"That's because of all the acid she took. She dropped a couple of tabs about an hour before we got here, and it's really kicking her ass."

I nodded in acknowledgment of her condition because I had only had one glass of punch and was pretty much feeling the same way.

Then I followed him out of the kitchen and returned to the living room, feeling alternating waves of chills throughout my entire body.

I was having a lot of things going on in my head at the same time, most of which were just random thoughts that didn't make any sense.

Music was playing from the *Jesus Christ Superstar* soundtrack, and it occurred to me that it would be an absolute tragedy to have lived your life for such a glorious and serious cause, and then after you die for some Hollywood asshole to turn it into a musical.

When that song ended, several of the couples began to dance to *Good Day Sunshine* by the Beatles. Roy was sitting on the couch again, but I sat down on the floor next to Leanna instead. I suppose she was happy I came back because she apologized for not wanting to dance.

She said…if I would help her get up, she'd like to move around and get into the beat of the music. So I gently pulled her up and then guided her to the middle of the room to join the other couples.

At first, I simply watched her very sexy lean body sway back and forth in front of me, then I attempted to do the same thing by closing my eyes, allowing the vibrations to guide my movement.

As we came closer together, we moved our arms around each other without actually touching at first, but then she turned and moved her back firmly against me. I placed my hands onto her slender torso and felt nothing but soft skin underneath her skimpy dress. Then she turned to face me, and we began a rather long and passionate kiss.

Leanna worked her tongue inside my mouth until I was filled with emotions that were unbearable. I wanted desperately to ask her to come upstairs to my room, but I hesitated, knowing that Roy was nearby.

She must have known I wanted to make love to her right there in the middle of the dance floor, in front of everyone, so she took me by the hand and led me into one of the dimly lighted bedrooms where other couples were sprawled out across the floor. Instead of beds, the room was filled with large pillows and futon mattresses.

Just inside the door was some empty space where we could sit, and then she pulled me to her and lay back, spreading her legs just far enough apart so I could sit comfortably between them.

The sensations coming from the acid were like nothing I had ever felt before. I was definitely feeling horny, and somehow, all I wanted to do was to merge completely with her sensual body.

I could tell that she wanted to make love as well, so even though Roy was in the other room I didn't care. However, as my eyes became accustomed to the light, I became aware of things going on around us.

The room was almost filled with naked bodies…gently caressing, making love, smoking from a large hashish pipe, or just talking.

Henry was right next to me and asked, "Do you mind if I join you?"

By now I had to take a really wicked piss, so the way I figured it, since he had rented me the room, and was the one who invited me to the party, then he could stay with her while I went to relieve myself.

"Of course, I need to take a break and go to the bathroom anyway," I replied. "Why don't you keep Leanna here company for me?"

Leanna didn't seem to mind but did say, "Don't be gone long."

"It's the door beside the kitchen," Henry said.

I got up and went back into the living room only to find two other people waiting to go in. I got in line and watched what was going on.

A guy named Rodney was with a short slender black chick named Greta who was upsetting several people, claiming to be with the F.B.I., and saying that everybody in the room was now under arrest.

Meanwhile, Rodney was declaring himself to be God and claimed this party was simply a manifestation of his almighty works.

Greta and Rodney both seemed to be quite annoying.

Another person named Joseph had set up a strobe light in the corner of the room, and its flicker caught the dancing couples in a series of motionless frames. Standing there waiting, I watched the shadows as they danced along the walls and across the ceiling.

When it was finally my turn to go in I pissed for what seemed like hours but when I came out I immediately noticed someone sitting in the corner of the living room on the floor who I recognized.

Thinking I must be hallucinating, my eyes tried to focus on her face. Through the flicker of the strobe lights, I saw the girl from high school who I'd made love to shortly after my graduation. It was Diane!

♥ ♥ ♥

A young guy with shoulder-length hair was sitting next to her, and then her face disappeared as they began to kiss. I watched them until her face reappeared again. *Yes, it was her…and I was ecstatic.*

I went back into the kitchen to think for a moment about how to handle this new revelation. When I returned, they had disappeared into the back bedroom where all of the orgies were going on.

She hadn't noticed me, but she looked a little spaced out and was probably tripping pretty hard as well, so I walked into the bedroom to find her. Upon entering, I noticed that many of the couples were now with new partners, and there seemed to be no fuss or hassle. There was no jealousy, just people sharing each other. It seemed as if everyone there was just doing their own thing…yet all together, free and easy.

So this is what they call, a 'Love-In'…I said to myself.

In the darkness of the candle-lit and incense-filled room, I finally saw Diane, who I never expected to see again. *Yet here she was*, sitting on the floor, totally in outer space next to some long-haired dude, right in the middle of a bunch of naked people who were all on drugs.

I sat down beside her without saying a word.

Then, I slowly slipped one of her hands into mine.

She turned her face and looked at me.

"Andy…holy shit, you found me. I can't believe you're here."

Without saying another word, we embraced each other, as a rush of energy emanated between us that was overwhelming.

Then, she introduced me to her friend who had been sitting there watching the whole thing without comment. His name was Tom.

"You know," Tom said, without showing any emotion about my unexpected interruption, "this is one cool party, and I don't believe it's ever going to stop. It's just going to keep going and going and going…"

"Hey, Tom," I replied. "Good to meet you."

Tom leaned over and hugged me.

"Why don't we go back to the living room," I proposed to Diane, not wanting Tom, or anyone else, to start humping her here on the floor.

Now that I'd found Diane, I wanted her all for myself.

She agreed, so the three of us went back into the living room where several couples were still dancing. Alex was still proclaiming himself to be God and was now rapping with Greta about how girls being on top during sexual union went against the laws of nature…as far as God was concerned…men should never have allowed this to happen.

"That's why the women are now beginning to take over the world," God proclaimed, "because men allow women to get on top during sex. Once they are there, they like it way too much and then desire more. Everyone calls it *'free love'*…but nothing is free, if she's on top during the sexual exchange, a woman can steal a man's energy and his power."

Greta, the alleged FBI agent, then told God…*he was full of shit*.

We sat down on one of the couches and Tom went somewhere else. It seemed as though the party was beginning to break up because other couples were also making their way out of the bedroom. Those without clothes were looking around trying to find their garments to get dressed. Apparently, Henry was right, the acid-punch hadn't been that strong.

After feeling a gentle buzz…they were now back to normal.

"Where are you living?" I asked Diane.

"The guy you met earlier, that's Tom, he's just a friend…I've been staying with him at a house with six other people…he plays in a band, and the house is like a little commune. I'm not seeing anyone right now, so I'd like to stay with you if I could," she replied. "How about you?"

"I'm staying in a room very close to here. I just got into town this afternoon, and then I met Henry, and he set me up with a place to stay. The next thing I knew…there was this party, then I dropped some acid, I got introduced to a lot of strange people…and then I found you."

"Wow, that's some real far-out synchronicity shit!" she declared, "but like…what are you even doing here? I thought you were going to Penn State, or something like that…this is just so fucking freaky."

White Rabbit

One pill makes you larger,
One pill makes you small,
And the ones that mother gives you,
Don't do anything at all…
(Artist: Jefferson Airplane)

I told Diane…the reason I was here was because of this guy I'd met in New York…who told me I should come to California and see what's really going on in America. I was honest…and admitted that I wanted to go to NYU in January but hadn't been accepted yet. For now, this was all a new adventure for me, and we'd just have to see where it led.

But now, Diane was back in my life and was a genuine hippie chick. For the first week, all we did was make love and get high.

We'd spend an entire day walking all over the City of San Francisco barefoot. She wore braided flowers in her hair, and I took off my shirt to soak in the beautiful sunshine and feel the earth beneath my feet.

We had the most fantastic time tripping on acid one day, trying to cross streets, dodging cars…and finally making it back to my apartment by taking the trolley. Then, we stayed up for the remainder of the night just feeling all of the loving energy that surrounded us.

One day while sitting in the park, she asked me, "Did you do know, the world is on the verge of the dawning of the New Age of Aquarius?"

"I've heard a little about it…but what does it *really* mean?"

She just stared at me with a loving smile.

"What it means, my dearest one…is that when the moon is in the second house, and Jupiter aligns with Mars, then peace will guide the planets…and love will fill the stars with harmony and understanding."

"You're such a poet," I replied.

"Actually, I have a friend who's writing a musical, it's called *Hair*, and those were some of his lyrics. What it means is that a New Age is about to begin, we are the children of that New Dawn, and we are here to give birth to a New World…and to let the sunshine in."

"And…what does that mean to you?"

"It means we're here to put an end to war, to anger, to hatred, and to all that's negative in the world. We're here to bring peace and love, and to teach the rest of the world to share it, openly and freely."

Diane was normally shy and reserved, but whenever she was on the topic of higher consciousness, she became the goddess of gab.

"And just how are we going to do that?" I asked her.

"Just by being here and now, at this moment, and learning to walk our talk. Everyone will have to be educated about the fact that peace and war are nothing more than choices, and when you think about it, there really is no choice. Why would someone choose to break their own arm? Not only do people have to understand the truth, but they have to live that truth every day. What I'm saying is that we have to *become* peace, and we have to *become* love. By *living love*, the rest of the world will follow our example. I'm really excited about being alive during this time in the history of the planet because we are going to be the founding fathers and mothers of a whole New World."

"That sounds really cool."

"Do you know what would be sort of a shame?" she asked me.

"No, what?" I replied.

"Someday, the human race will come to an end, and it would be the ultimate tragedy if the Akashic Records of galactic history showed that the human race had destroyed itself during times of war, rather than to be absorbed back into the Universe during times of peace."

"Wow, that's pretty far-out heavy shit. Who said that?"

"I did…just now."

There were lots of love-ins going on around the Haight-Ashbury area, but for now, I wasn't interested in being with anyone but Diane. She was all right with that, but she asked me not to get jealous just in case something ever happened while we were in an altered state.

I told her I wasn't really the jealous type, having already learned that lesson, but I felt a deep love for her in ways I had never felt before. It was my preference not to be sharing her with total strangers.

Her reply was, "Always remember that we are embarking upon a New Age. We have to own that, which means not only letting go of anger and fear but that of jealousy and envy as well. Love gives not, but of itself…and love taketh not, but from itself. Love possesses not, nor will it be possessed, for love in itself is enough. Understand?"

"Didn't the prophet, Khalil Gibran, say something like that?"

"Think of it this way," she said. "We've got this gift of love inside of us, but love is like a precious plant. You can't just accept it and then leave it in the cupboard, or just think that it's going to get on by itself. You've got to keep on watering it and giving it sunlight. You've got to really look after that love and nurture it. We have to love everyone, not just people we happen to like, and if along the way they make a mistake, then we have to find it within ourselves to forgive one another."

Sometimes Diane sounded like a saint…essentially spouting out the same rhetoric as the old Lama in Greenwich Village had done.

Despite my concerns, and because of the free-love lifestyle and communalism that existed there, Diane and I did occasionally wind up swapping partners when we attended love-ins. I just became *all right* with it over time, and actually enjoyed making love to different people.

Because of her acquaintance with Tom's band, Diane was able to get us into some incredible concerts with some of the up-and-coming rock groups. Sometimes, we even got to go backstage and hang out.

Tom still had a bit of a crush on Diane, so over the next month, he invited us to some very wild and private parties. In fact, we had the opportunity to meet 'The Rolling Stones' the first time they came to America, and we got to know a lot of other people who were starting to become famous, like Sonny & Cher, Janis Joplin, and Grace Slick, who was creating her own successful band, *Jefferson Airplane.*

♥ ♥ ♥

One sunny afternoon, we were day-tripping in San Francisco at Golden Gate Park sitting down on the lawn and having lunch when we met another rising star named Jim Morrison. He lived in Los Angeles but was here visiting for the weekend. Jim had studied filmmaking at UCLA and had just started a band called The Doors, which was based upon Aldous Huxley's book, *Doors of Perception.*

We were getting to know some pretty interesting people, and they were getting to know us, so it was all very exciting.

Jim invited us to see him play in Santa Monica where he was doing a gig at a new club called The London Fog located on the Sunset Strip. He would be playing alongside another rising rock artist, Frank Zappa, and his psychedelic band, *The Mothers of Invention.*

The three of us sat in the park for several hours talking about what was meant by "love and freedom," and if they could be the same thing. To me, love meant *expansion,* and so did the word *freedom.*

Jim considered himself to be very unique…liberated, radical, and a free thinker. His ideas actually got me thinking even more about what Drake had said, about becoming a consciousness revolutionary.

"Whoever controls the media," Jim explained, "controls the mind as well. The media's job is to create fear. So you have to learn to expose yourself to your deepest fears, then after that, the fear that the media puts out has no more power over you, and then the fear that you once had of freedom shrinks and vanishes. After that, you are totally free."

I told Jim the story about the fear I had the time I swam far out into the ocean and thought I was going to be eaten by sharks, and he thought the story was funny. Then he told me one about the time he was being held at knifepoint in Los Angeles by a Mexican gang and thinking he was going to lose his testicles, however, all they wanted was his guitar.

"The most important kind of freedom," Jim continued, "is to be who and what you really are. Most people trade in their true nature for a role that society places on them, and then they call it reality. However, there are two realities...*societal reality* and *your personal reality*.

"If you're following societal reality, then you're putting on a mask and giving up your ability to truly feel the life you were given."

"You mean, like someone who doesn't believe in war but still gets drafted anyway and is put on the front lines?" I asked.

"I mean, *everybody*. Everyone who's a part of mass consciousness, especially if they have ideas about overthrowing the established order. You see, I'm interested in anything about revolt, disorder, or chaos, and activities that seem to have no meaning. That's freedom, man.

"You see, Tex, it seems to me that along the road toward freedom if we can truly express our external freedom...then that's also a way to bring about internal freedom. You know, it's all connected."

"Well, I have my doubts that overthrowing governments will create enlightenment, but I think what you're saying is that if you become a famous rock-musician, then you'll have even less freedom."

"I've thought about that, and you know what? If I ever become too famous, I may just fake my own death and then I'll be totally free."

Diane was quick with a comeback as we passed around a newly rolled joint of weed and said, "Let me tell you what's really subversive, it's love. Yeah, man, love is everything that it's cracked up to be and even more. That's why people become cynical about love because it really is worth fighting for, being brave for, risking everything for, and even dying for. If you don't risk anything, then you risk everything."

Taking a deep drag of smoke, and looking at her with awe he said, "You know that it would be untrue, and you know that I would be a liar if I were to say to you, babe we just can't get much higher…because when you talk like that, you know…you really light my fire."

Shortly after that, '*Light My Fire*' became Jim's first big hit.

There were all kinds of counterculture and spiritual groups that were springing up all around the Haight-Ashbury District, and some of the communes were becoming almost self-sufficient by providing things or services that other people in the hip community wanted.

Notice boards and leaflets were everywhere…in communes, in the shops, and on telephone poles…advertising things like yoga classes, meditation classes, and talks by self-proclaimed gurus.

Just about anything you wanted was available here; acupuncture, sex therapy, bioenergetics, mind control clinics, Kabala, Scientology, massage, Zen Buddhism, Tibetan Buddhism, Hinduism, swamis, and even Hare' Krishna's. There were psychics, shamans, witches, pagan and Wiccan groups, along with all kinds of crazy wizardry. There was even a UFO group for flying saucer watchers. All you had to do was to step outside to see that the circus had come to town.

There was such an incredible smorgasbord of new and interesting things to learn. Diane and I wound up joining several of the groups. Almost every night we went to a different meeting and met some very incredible people…however, the LSD parties still continued.

I had fallen in love with Diane, while at the same time my mind was being expanded by using so much LSD. Everyone was right about this being the New Age. It really was about freedom, peace, and love, and my awareness of the world was growing exponentially every day.

I felt that I had learned more about the universe, and about people, during these last two months, than I had during the first eighteen years of my life. I could feel my consciousness evolving, almost as if I were becoming a completely different re-invented person.

October turned out to be interesting…because Jefferson Airplane made their debut at San Francisco's Matrix Club. Since we had already met the band, we were allowed to come backstage after the show.

After getting pretty fucked up, we ended up watching a new release of a soft-porn movie based on *Alice in Wonderland*. Shortly thereafter, the words to the song '*White Rabbit*' were born.

Speaking of airplanes, America's Gemini-5 space capsule made one hundred and twenty orbits around the Earth while at the same time the Beatles flew to America to meet with Elvis Presley.

I can't remember which of those two events was more exciting.

One weekend, we decided to go to Los Angeles to see Jim Morrison in concert. We drove with Tom and two of his friends in a brand-new Volkswagen minibus on Friday night smoking lots of pot on the way.

Tom was supposed to meet with a song producer in the city the very next morning, so he dropped us off in another part of town several miles from there. It was at Diane's older sister's place…where Diane stayed when she first moved to California. Kathleen was extremely happy to see Diane again, having been worried about how she was.

Their parents had been calling from Pennsylvania every week to just see if Kathleen had any news of where Diane was.

The only reason she hadn't been labeled *as a runaway* was that she was over eighteen years of age…and Diane had threatened to tell the police the truth about what her father did if she was ever caught.

"We were sure you'd been kidnapped!" her sister shouted at her. "Why haven't you called anyone?"

"I don't know, just too busy, but I'm all right. Andy and I have been together for a while now and everything's just fine."

Diane confided to me that she didn't care for her family very much. Her father had molested her and her sister when they were younger, but her mom didn't believe it, and Kathleen wouldn't admit to it. Then, after Kathleen moved out, Diane vowed to leave home right after she graduated from high school and never look back. Which she did.

The next day, we decided to hitchhike into Santa Monica where Jim was scheduled to play that night. Tom had agreed to meet us after the concert and drive us back to Oakland. Kathleen warned us to be very careful because there had been a lot of rioting and looting going on nearby in the Watts area of Los Angeles for the last five days.

♥ ♥ ♥

Watts was an area with a lot of poor housing, was overcrowded, had high unemployment, and a pretty high crime rate as well.

A white police officer had stopped a twenty-year-old black man and accused him of drunk driving. A large crowd started to gather as the questioning continued, and soon began taunting the officer. A second police officer showed up and one of them said something derogatory to the observers, and then hit one of the bystanders with his police baton. That led to the first major race riot in our country's history, in which more than thirty-five thousand Afro-Americans took part.

Interestingly, as we hitchhiked to the concert, we were picked up by a black driver, Tony, and he began the conversation by asking us how we felt about the racial dilemma and the civil rights movement.

"Do you know what the hardest thing in the world is?" he asked us.

"I guess not, what?" I replied cautiously.

"Being black…in a white America," was his reply.

"We've heard about the riots. What's up with that?" Diane asked.

Tony replied, "Until the philosophy that holds one race superior and another race inferior, is permanently discredited and abandoned, then there is going to be war everywhere. Do you dig?"

"Yes, I do," she replied.

"Poor brother, Malcolm X, was murdered six months ago by a black man who was paid off by the CIA. You know it won't be long before they come gunning for Martin Luther King…too."

Diane and I did not reply but just listened.

"I mean, look here, man," Tony went on, "black is beautiful, and one way or another, we shall overcome. Just so you know…it's off with the heads of any of those donut-eating pigs who stand in our way!"

Diane rolled down the window and began to sing one of her songs, *"Come on people, smile on your brother…everybody let's get together and try to love one another…right now."*

A police officer standing on a nearby street corner pulled out his pad and wrote down Tony's license plate number.

Tony said, in his opinion, we were *'all right white folks'*…and then drove us safely to Santa Monica for the concert.

The next day the National Guard was called in to restore order, but thirty-four black Americans died protesting. Altogether, more than a thousand people were hurt, over four thousand people were arrested, and property damage was estimated to be at over forty million dollars.

It was now November, and I remember waking up one morning to hear on the radio that Pope Paul VI had just made a very radical decree. He said, "Not all Jews should be blamed for the death of Jesus."

I wondered why it had taken two thousand years to figure that out, but what I needed to figure out...was how to get some more money coming in, because right now...I was close to being dead broke.

We began to sell lids of weed and tabs of LSD at Golden Gate Park. I was surprised at how many different names there were for marijuana. You could call it cannabis, bud, dank, dope, ganja, hashish, Mary Jane, herb, moss, pot, rope, swag, skunk, skank, smoke, grass, or weed, and some even called it whacko tobacco. There were almost as many names for LSD as well, but the most popular one was called, *Orange Sunshine*, and we were certainly doing our part by letting 'the sun' shine in.

One day while we were out near the Berkley campus just doing our thing, we saw a large group of protesters that had gathered on the lawn. I had heard there was going to be a protest rally and march against the war that had been organized by the Vietnam Day Committee, but I had no idea that there would be this many people attending.

The leaders of the committee were joined by the former beat-poet Allen Ginsberg, and acid-guru Ken Kesey, who had also brought along some of his friends...the so-called...*Merry Pranksters*.

Up until now, I had only heard stories about Ken Kesey.

He was a former songwriter...and had used his money to purchase a large bus. Then he, along with the *Pranksters* and Timothy Leary all teamed up in 1964 to distribute tabs of LSD all over the southwestern part of the country. They were known as the *Merry Pranksters* because the group would throw a party and spike the drinks with LSD, which up to now, had not been declared illegal. Within months, because of the efforts of Ken, Timothy, and the Pranksters, thousands of people on the west coast had been turned on to the hallucinogenic world of '*acid.*'

They believed...this new drug would change consciousness.

Even to this day, some would argue...*it did just that.*

♥ ♥ ♥

When we arrived at the park, I could hear Allen Ginsberg finishing up a speech he was giving before the protest march began. He reminded everyone, "This procession should be led by grandmothers carrying flowers, young women with babies in their arms, and girls dressed up in pretty costumes. We expect the Oakland Police to try and stop us, so when they do, please just sit down, stay calm, and remain peaceful."

Up to now, Diane and I had avoided participating in marches that had the potential for violence. Diane was against the war, but it seemed that more and more people were beginning to fight with the police.

This time, Diane and I just instinctively decided to join in with the marchers as they were beginning to leave the Berkeley campus. It was scheduled to end at the Oakland Army Terminal.

Right at the city line, the police intervened as Allen had predicted, greeting us with full riot gear, including tear gas, shields, gas masks, and guns. As Allen had instructed, we did not react, but just sat down in the middle of the street. After a while, someone would occasionally take a moment to stand up to give instructions or to make a speech.

"Are you scared?" I asked Diane.

"Hell no," she replied, "I'm loving this shit."

As long as we continued to sit peacefully, the police did not try to attack us. In fact, it was an incredibly successful display of non-violent disobedient protest. There were no arrests made, or any casualties that day, but at one point there was a confrontation between Allen and Sonny Barger, who was president of the Hell's Angels.

Sonny swore he'd beat up anyone who marched against the war.

The Hell's Angels' official position was that anti-war and anti-draft marches supported communism. Allen was tripping on acid, and when the argument between the two became heated, he began to chant from the Prajnaparamita Sutra, which came from old Buddhist teachings.

To our surprise, one of the Angels began doing the same thing.

Within moments, the entire crowd was chanting mantras consisting of Om's, Ah's, and Hum's, which completely alleviated any paranoia that had been there before. Astonishingly, everything ended peacefully, all due to the power of those sacred vibrations.

Afterward, I told Diane I was excited to be a part of this new peace and love movement, but there was a part of me that wasn't completely into it, almost as if one of the key elements seemed to be lacking.

"What do you mean?" she asked.

"You know, the only reason we're even here is that we accidentally stumbled upon it as it was happening. We didn't seek it out, that's the part of it that still seems to be missing. It came to us and called to us, but perhaps we should have been the ones calling to it."

"I don't know, baby, but the fact is that you and I are here right now and who knows, maybe we didn't discover it, maybe it discovered us. There are no accidents in this world and no coincidences. Perhaps we were both looking for each other. Who's to say who found who first? Either way, it's meant to be. Your Higher Self wanted you to be here today, and now you're here. So just accept that as being the way things are supposed to be. Don't feel like you have to have so much control."

Diane was right, but I also believe that one of the reasons I was led to be there, was so I could meet Ken Kesey, and during the sit-down portion of the march, we actually got to talk for several hours.

He told me about his adventures during the last several months, and how the police were starting to make raids on many of the people who were dropping acid in order to find other drugs that were not legal, such as marijuana. Ken said that he, Timothy, and his friend, Neal Cassidy, were pretty high on the police hit list and he was feeling a little paranoid about the number of police who had now surrounded the marchers.

He thought that maybe…they were looking for him.

"You know, Tex," Ken said, quoting his own famous words, "you're either on the bus, or you're off the bus."

"And what does that mean?" I asked.

"It means that if society wants me to be an outlaw, I'll be an outlaw and a damned good one, too. That's something people need these days. All societies need to have more outlaws. It's the outlaws that prevent the government from having total control, from trying to strip us of our freedoms, and turning us into remote-controlled robotic zombies."

I nodded my head in agreement and tried to visualize what it would be like to actually have the police or the FBI watching your every move. It didn't sound very pleasant…but knew it could actually happen.

"What we want to do next," Ken continued, "is to start conducting 'acid tests' involving large groups of people. We're planning a really big concert, and everything there will be spiked with acid."

He said that the first of many big acid tests would be next month on November 27th at a chicken ranch near Santa Cruz, called *The Spread*, and he invited us to attend. At first, I didn't think too much of the idea since we had already been doing acid for some time, but when he told me Timothy Leary would be there, I knew that I had to go.

As the day wore on and the sun began to set, we weren't moving, and neither were the police. Eventually, the march was canceled, and everyone was allowed to go home peacefully.

After that, Diane and I began attending as many protest marches as possible, regardless of whether they might become violent or not.

Just before we arrived at *The Spread*, there had been a week-long battle in Vietnam that left two-hundred-and-fifty U.S. soldiers dead and five hundred more wounded…so in response to that battle, more than twenty-five thousand anti-war and anti-draft protesters marched upon

Washington, D.C., which was the largest protest turnout anyone had seen thus far. I wasn't there, but I was sure Drake had been part of it.

On the day of the first-ever *acid test,* more than two hundred people showed up to participate, drinking from a large batch of red Kool-Aid that had been spiked with hallucinogenic drugs.

Ken was apprehensive that the party might get raided by local law enforcement…but the ranch was very secluded, and he'd been cautious about passing out flyers. He even had two people posted at the front entrance with a big bell that would ring if the cops did show up.

Timothy Leary supplied the LSD, called '*clear Sandoz,*' packaged in small red capsules. This was the maiden voyage of an experiment to try and raise mass consciousness to a whole new level. It later became known as…the *Electric Kool-Aid Acid Test.*

For those who participated, everyone said…*it was a beautiful thing*.

Allen Ginsberg started off the event and set the tone by chanting Hindu and Buddhist mantras from the small outdoor stage. After that, Neal Cassady and Timothy Leary rapped into an open microphone for almost an hour. They explained how psychedelic chemicals had helped mankind to explore the far and infinite regions of human consciousness by the expansion of universal awareness.

Timothy had been both a brilliant and well-respected psychologist at Harvard University. He believed…that to alleviate mental suffering, something more than behavioral analysis was needed.

As a result, he began experimenting with hallucinogenic drugs and had received funding to conduct his experiments from the U.S. Army.

This evening he talked more about his first acid trip.

"You're never the same after you've had that first flash glimpse down the cellular time tunnel," he told us. "You're never the same after you've had the veil lifted. When I took my first acid trip, I could look back and see my body on the bed. I relived my life, and re-experienced events that I had forgotten. More than that, I went back in time, in an evolutionary sense, where I was aware of being a one-celled organism. All of these things were way beyond what my mind could understand.

"Just knowing that the human brain possesses an infinite number of potentials that can operate in other space and time dimensions left me feeling exhilarated, awed, and quite convinced that I'd awakened from a long ontological sleep. This profound transcendent experience left me a changed man who is now living a totally changed life."

So after all of the big pep talks about what everyone could expect to experience that night, the music began, most of which was supplied by Jerry Garcia and *The Warlocks*, an acid-rock band that soon became known as *The Grateful Dead*. They played long into the night and the event lasted until the early hours of dawn. Everyone seemed to have had a good time until someone suggested that we should sacrifice a chicken in honor of the event. After that, some of the people got just a little bummed out, and the party slowly broke up without any further incident…and without any harm to the chickens.

The party ended…without getting raided by the police.

Diane and I threw a blanket on the grass and watched the sun come up, grooving on each other's bodies while we were coming down from this delightful hallucinogenic mixture. However, I was still definitely tripping and was beginning to have some new revelations about my life.

I realized that much like Timothy Leary; my life had also changed.

Like the song said…I had become '*a rolling stone*'…a turned-on, tuned-in, dropout…and was going nowhere fast. I hadn't spoken to my parents in quite some time, and I was wondering if I had been accepted at NYU. I decided I needed to call them.

I was learning a lot about freedom, and about love, but some of the things the old Lama had said came back into my memory.

He'd also mentioned compassion for all the suffering in the world and said that people who truly aspire to become Buddhist monks must first take the *Bodhisattva vow*. They promise…that they'll take refuge in the Buddha (*the teacher/guru*), in the Dharma *(the teachings)*, and in the Sanga (*their spiritual friends*), and will devote their life to the elimination of human suffering through compassion.

"Where is my compassion?" I asked Diane, as she lay next to me. "What am I doing to alleviate suffering in the world? Is this it, just getting high all the time, feeling the love, and grooving on the music?"

When I looked over, I saw that she was softly crying, obviously caught up in her own internal drama.

"What are you talking about?" she asked.

"Nothing," I replied.

Later that morning, Ken invited a group of us to the main farmhouse for breakfast with some of the organizers of the acid test.

That's when I finally got to meet Timothy Leary.

The people who were sitting at the large table were talking about the good old days, but as I sat there listening, I could tell that Timothy viewed the use of LSD from a much different perspective than they did. He believed that taking acid should always be a spiritual experience and taken in a peaceful setting instead of in a party type of atmosphere. He said…that loud noise and partying would distract a person from the whole process of raising one's consciousness.

"*You have to be out of your mind…to use your head.*

"LSD allows a person to bypass their brain…and go directly to their consciousness, which in turn…changes the brain. So really, that's what we're trying to do here. We want to create *brain-change*…which is a profound, spiritual, and transcendent experience that leaves in its wake a transformed person with a changed life," he tried to explain.

Because of his unique beliefs, Tim had recently created a group of acidheads that called themselves The League of Spiritual Discovery. The group's co-founder was Dr. Richard Alpert, another psychology professor, and also a colleague of Dr. Leary. After traveling to India and staying in an Ashram, Richard changed his name to Ram Dass.

Timothy went on to explain that the term '*hippie*' was nothing more than an establishment label for a profound, invisible, underground, and evolutionary process. He said, "For every visible barefoot, flowered, and beaded hippie, there are thousands of other invisible members of the same turned-on underground. They are tuned in to their inner vision through the use of LSD and have dropped out of the television comedy of American Life. They are living everywhere in this country."

Afterward, I sat outside with Timothy on the porch and shared a joint of freshly cut weed. I told him that I could relate to what he said, but I was in a bit of a dilemma about what to do with my life.

"Should I keep doing what I was doing, or should I go to college so that someday I could help those who were suffering?" I asked him.

"Tex, my advice to people like you, is that if you are willing to take the game of life seriously enough, and if you take your nervous system seriously enough, and if you take your sense organs seriously enough, and if you take the energy process seriously enough, then you have no other choice but to turn on, tune in, and drop out."

"That's my dilemma. I don't want to drop out. I mean, look at you. You've already got your Ph.D., so it's easy for you to say to drop out."

"But you see, Tex," Tim further explained," the term 'drop out' doesn't mean to become a jellyfish. It means simply to drop out of the old patterns of thinking that have been handed down from generation to generation. Did you know that ninety-five percent of what people believe is what someone else told them, and they just accept it as true?

"That's what religion is all about. What if everything people have said for the last two thousand years is not correct information?

"Then, what does that say about everything you believe to be true?"

"Are you saying that if everything I believe in was created by my mind, then there's nothing in my reality that's real, not even God?"

"Oh wow," he replied. "I haven't considered that possibility."

We talked for another hour after that and became close friends, but I could see that he was right. Dropping out really meant for us to stop being so serious about what was going on 'out there' in the world, and to get serious about what was going on inside of us, personally.

When Diane and I returned to our apartment in Oakland I went to a payphone and called my parents. Naturally, they were concerned about not hearing from me for so long…but were fine once I told them that everything was all right. My parents said I had been accepted at NYU and had been offered an academic scholarship. It would not only pay tuition but room and board as well. That was really great news for me, but the bad news was…that I'd also just received a draft notice and was supposed to report for a physical exam in two weeks.

My father had already called the draft board…they said I could take the physical in California instead of Pennsylvania. They said that even if I accepted the scholarship, and planned to return to school in January, I still had to take the military physical exam. Then, after I was actually enrolled at NYU, I would come off the draft list as a student deferment.

It didn't take long for me to make my decision.

I certainly didn't want to get drafted or move to Canada, so I'd take the physical exam here in Oakland, accept the scholarship, and then go home for Christmas, with the intent of going back to school in January.

The problem was…what to do with Diane?

I just had a feeling she wouldn't be willing to leave and go with me.

A week later, I arrived at the 'Oakland U.S. Army Testing Center' for my physical examination. It took more than three hours because of the large number of young men who were there. Outside the facility were hundreds of protesters, some of whom were trying to convince the new inductees to burn their draft cards and not go in.

The medical exam was a routine procedure, checking our eyes, ears, and reflexes, but at one point they made all of us get naked, and then face each other while standing in a large circle, which was very strange.

Then the medical officer walked around the circle to see if anyone was sporting an erection. I suppose this must have been their only way of trying to figure out if any of us were homosexuals.

At the end of three hours, I stood in line waiting for my results, and as I got close to the end I could hear the medical officer saying to the first guy, "You're 4-F,"…and then to the second guy, "You're 4-F too."

(The term, 4-F, meant you were medically unfit.)

When he got to me, the medical officer yelled out loud, "All right, we've got us a new warrior! You're '1-A'…congratulations."

At that point, the prophetical words of Ken Kesey really hit home, *"Either you are on the bus, or off the bus."*

I said to myself…*I suppose it's time to get on the bus.*

♥ ♥ ♥

When I returned home, I had a whole new perspective.

Protest marches against the war and against the draft suddenly held a whole new meaning for me. I had just been listed with a 1-A rating, which meant "medically fit for fighting." If I wasn't in school, then Uncle Sam would immediately draft me and send me to Vietnam where I would probably die. It was almost like a death sentence, and now this whole war thing became a whole new reality. That's what happens when you're the one who's about to be placed on the firing line.

Ken invited Diane and me to attend the second acid test, which was to be held at a house near San Jose State University. Because we had such a great time at the first one, we decided to go.

The Rolling Stones were scheduled to play in a nearby auditorium that evening, so the Pranksters decided to hand out crayon-lettered handbills at the concert that had the address of their get-together, and a simple sentence that read...*Can you pass the acid test?*

Over four hundred people showed up after the concert was over, around midnight. Jerry Garcia had become known as...*Captain Trip.* He and his band, the *Warlocks,* played for several hours until the cops arrived...who proceeded to send everybody home without any arrest, but since Diane and I were staying at the house with thirty other people, we were allowed to remain. That's when I got the opportunity to meet Timothy Leary's partner in the League of Spiritual Discovery.

Dr. Richard Alpert (*Ram Dass*) was the son of a wealthy lawyer, the president of the New York, New Haven, and Hartford Railroad, and founder of Brandeis University. Alpert studied psychology and earned his Ph.D. from Stanford University. He had also conducted research at Harvard where his explorations of human consciousness led him to conduct intensive research with LSD and other psychedelic drugs.

That's where he met Dr. Timothy Leary.

Because of his student involvement in this controversial research, both he and Dr. Leary were dismissed from Harvard in 1963.

After that, the two of them proceeded to 'turn on' literally millions of American youth to the wonder of their own acid trips.

Richard's message to everyone that night was just to '*be here, now*' at this moment, because this moment is all that anyone truly has.

"How easy it is to see that this moment is the only time we will ever have when we can truly love each other," Richard stated.

Richard was planning to go to India to live in the ashram of some famous holy man he had heard about. The Beatles also planned to do something similar, so this was becoming a trendy idea. Richard said that once the war in Vietnam was over, people would turn their focus to Eastern spirituality. That would mark the beginning of the New Age of spiritual discovery and enlightenment. He also believed the war in Vietnam would be the last war our country would ever fight.

Paul Kantner, from Jefferson Airplane, was also there staying at the house and tried to explain to everyone that 'rock and roll music' was the new form of communication for our generation.

"When the truth is stoned," he said, "we are floating on time, and the music we play is like time travel. It gets you there on time, so we have to learn to ride on time, through the music."

As it got into the early hours of the morning and after I had finally come down from a fairly nice trip, I told Diane about going back to school in January at NYU, and that my parents had wanted me to come home for Christmas. I told her she could come with me if she wanted, but she immediately shook her head back and forth.

"I can't go back there. I won't go back to my parents' house ever again, and I don't like New York City. San Francisco is my home now, and that's where my friends are living. Why are you doing this to me?"

"Because I don't want to wind up being nobody, on my own, like a complete unknown, with no direction home, like some rolling stone. The truth is, I want to be like Timothy Leary and Richard Alpert. I want to get my college degree and then go out and do something to help the world to be a better place. That's what I have to do."

"So in order to save the world…you must leave me?" she asked.

"I'll be back," I promised.

"In fact…if you want, I'll even stay for Christmas."

"Fuck Christmas," she replied.

"I'm not going to hold my breath waiting for you."

"Well, then...I'll hold it for both of us," I replied.

Then she began to quietly sing a song she had recently heard at one of the parties we had been to. It was from a play called 'Hair' that was soon to be released on Broadway in New York City.

How...can people be so heartless?

How...can people be so cruel?

Easy...to be hard.

Easy...to be cold.

For the next few hours, we lay there next to each other not speaking about anything. I don't remember if we slept or not. I was in love with Diane, but I had to decide, and the decision had to be made now.

I would never get another scholarship to NYU, or anywhere else.

If I stayed with her, who knows what direction my life would take. Being here now might be good for Richard, and to tune in, turn on, and drop out might be good for Timothy, but neither one was good for me.

The next morning, Diane just hugged me and then said goodbye. She was going to be staying at the house for a few more days and then Paul would take her back to Oakland, She was hoping that I'd be gone before she got back so she wouldn't have to say goodbye a second time.

She looked sad and depressed, knowing I wasn't going to change my mind, so rather than mix words, I agreed to do as she requested.

I realized that more than likely she would go back to live with Tom, and if not with him, she'd easily find someone else to hook up with. Any way you looked at it she was going to be all right.

So I left San Jose without her and drove back to San Francisco with Ken and his group of Pranksters. Along the way, we tripped again, and I became even more aware that I was making the right decision.

Diane's words, however, kept ringing in my ears for days.

Easy to be hard...easy to be cold.

♥ ♥ ♥

It had been a wild and crazy six months. I'd experienced more of life than my entire previous nineteen years. I was now a completely different person than I had been when I graduated from high school.

I had longer hair…dirtier clothes…and even a small beard.

I thought back to how different life would be right now if I hadn't met Drake or ended up in the Village that day. What if the Pollock, the Dago, and I hadn't gone to New York City and joined that first protest march in Sheep's Meadow? It was almost like the whole thing was a setup from the very beginning. If that hadn't happened, I'd be a student at Penn State and would have joined a fraternity. Maybe I would have smoked a little pot, or attended a rally or two, but that would be it.

Because of a simple twist of fate, I'd met some incredible people who were all in the process of changing the world.

Plus, I had the privilege of expanding my mind along with them.

I realized…just how close I'd come to dropping out and spending the rest of my life with Diane in some whacked-out hippie commune, stoned every day, 24-7. Yes, I'd made the right decision. I was making a conscious choice to go to NYU to get my degree. I wasn't doing what my parents or Diane wanted, but what I wanted, which was to become like Drake, a revolutionary thinker and activist in the peace and love movement, raising consciousness. Not only was I ready to get started, but I believed…our efforts to stop the war were paying off.

In December of 1965, the *Gemini 7* space capsule orbited the Earth over two hundred times, convincing the U.S. that it was now possible to reach the Moon. At the same time, the media was reporting a huge recent loss of over four hundred American lives in Vietnam.

American losses in the war, since it began in 1961, now exceeded thirteen hundred dead, and over six thousand wounded, and as a result, the U.S. temporarily suspended its bombing runs in the North.

The Times...They Are a Changing

Come gather round people wherever you roam...
And admit that the waters around you have grown...
And accept it that soon you'll be drenched to the bone...
For the times...they are a changing...
(Artist: Bob Dylan)

♥ ♥ ♥

The year 1966 proved to be full of paradoxes and contradictions. The first draft card burner was convicted while Pope Paul VI appealed for peace in Vietnam. We were the most progressive nation in the world, but *One Million Years, B.C.* was the number one movie at the box office. We were also the most charitable nation in the world, but *How the Grinch Stole Christmas* was the number one television show. The establishment's *moral majority* were against the use of any drugs, but *Valley of the Dolls*, a book about drugs, became the number one bestselling book and was written by a woman who didn't do drugs.

*Women's Liberation...*became a new term on the street, coined by the "National Organization for Women," who frowned upon female stereotypes. At the same time, Lesley Hornsby, an anorexic young model who went by the name Twiggy, was the top model of the year.

The Civil Rights movement was split between two major factions, the advocates of *nonviolence* and those supporting *black power.*

Both groups were met with strong angry resistance by believers of white supremacy. Racial demonstrations and riots began erupting all over the country as National Guard troops used real bayonets against the very people they had been sworn to protect.

Bombing resumed in North Vietnam. By now there were more than four-hundred-thousand servicemen in Southeast Asia, and more than five thousand dead U.S. soldiers, being a far greater number of deaths than that of South Vietnamese soldiers, who we were there to help.

Both the CIA and the FBI were convinced that antagonistic forces within the anti-war movement were being organized and financed by foreign powers such as Russia when everyone else knew it was mostly made up of nothing more than a bunch of kids throwing empty beer cans at the police. The true organizers were only a handful of creative free-thinking radicals who believed that war was morally wrong.

The government was also convinced that the widespread use of LSD was the primary reason for the war having become increasingly unpopular. Based upon this theory alone, the government decided to declare LSD illegal, not because it was a dangerous drug, but because it was a subversive drug. The effects of LSD were making too many people love each other *and that just had to stop.*

Psychologists say that those who make rules (i.e., the government and the church) fear sexually liberated groups and individuals the most because one who is sexually free can no longer be controlled.

I spent the holidays with my family and also got to see Stan, the Dago, and the Pollock. They didn't think much of the lifestyle I had been living in California, and the fact was that it scared them.

Ron and Byron were still teetering back and forth between the two worlds of consciousness, to follow society's reality, or follow their own personal reality. Ron was in school at the local community college for a degree in sociology and therefore had a draft deferment. Byron was working full-time at a steel mill in Allentown, but because of flat feet, he was exempt from military duty. Stanley, however, had enlisted in the Marines and was scheduled for boot camp in February.

In mid-January, I went to New York City to start my first semester of school at NYU. I heard that Ken Kesey and the Pranksters recently held a third acid test, but Ken and his girlfriend, 'mountain girl,' were busted by the police for possessing a large quantity of marijuana.

The word on the street was that Ken and several of his friends had fled the country and were now living in Mexico.

I was on an academic scholarship, but it would only pay for housing if I agreed to live in one of the old brick university dormitories.

My roommate, John, turned out to be a total nerd, and the whole situation soon became unacceptable. I needed my own place, because having my freedom was important, so I was determined that by the next semester I would find a small loft somewhere in the Village.

I decided to sell marijuana on campus in order to raise the money necessary to finance an apartment, but at the same time, I wanted to get serious about going to school. Therefore, I promised myself not to do any more LSD trips during the school year when I was trying to study.

♥ ♥ ♥

About two weeks into the semester I met Donna. It happened one day while reading a book in the library. Sitting across from me was a petite girl with short brown hair, blue eyes, and a nice-looking body.

Instead of reading, I couldn't keep myself from looking at her.

Noticing that she was noticing me noticing her, I finally wrote out a note from my spiral notebook. Then I passed it to her across the table and continued to read my book, pretending to ignore her. It read…

"Hello, my name's Andy. I'm sitting here trying to study, but I keep getting distracted by an incredibly attractive girl sitting across from me.

"I also noticed…that you were checking me out as well.

"So I'm getting a little uncomfortable because we're not allowed to talk inside the library…I could just get up and leave, but then I'd never know for sure if there was a chance you might go out with me.

"I mean…we're both stuck here for the next few years, trying to get a college degree and it's going to be really hard to study if we're always looking for someone else to be with…so wouldn't it be nice to know you've always got a special person to hang out with after a hard day of classes…someone to talk to, to have a beer with, or share a late-night cup of coffee with? So do you think you'd be interested in meeting me later to discuss the possibility of long-term coexistence? If it works out, then we can sit back, relax, and enjoy the rest of the time we have here. If you say no, then at least I can get the rest of my homework finished."

A few minutes later…we went to the coffee shop to talk.

Donna told me this was her second semester in accounting and had gone to high school in Boston. The two of us hit it off right away.

Not only was she very smart but was into politics as well.

Diane had been the ultimate hippie chick, with flowers in her hair, who loved to get high, believed almost anything anyone said, was like a saint with no religion, and would probably fuck anyone who asked her nicely. Donna questioned everything, believed Jesus was still the hope of the world, didn't buy into the hippie-communal-lifestyle shit, and didn't do drugs. However, she was against the war in Vietnam.

It was obvious that she viewed herself as a liberated woman.

Donna was also an avid supporter of the new woman's liberation movement, and a supporter of other political revolutions going on in the world, especially those which would enhance the rights of women. She also admitted that she had once been in a relationship with another woman but believed that monogamous heterosexual relationships were important. She was turned off by the free-love movement, claiming that men got more out of it than women, who were treated like fuck-toys.

I told Donna about my anti-war involvement over the last couple of months in California, but not the story about Diane, or using LSD.

She hadn't undergone the same kind of mind-liberating experiences that I'd gone through, so I was cautious about the things I told her.

One of the problems with orgies is that sometimes, there's just too many arms and legs, and if it's too dark, that presents a whole other set of issues...so I really wasn't going to miss the love-ins, all that much. Even though California had spoiled me sexually, I was willing to give the monogamy thing a try for the long haul...although I'd never done it before...I agreed to make our relationship 'a one-woman show.'

The first new friend I met was Tomás...from Peru, who was also a freshman. He had wavy-black combed-back hair, a clean-shaven, and olive-skinned face, as well as a good sense of humor. Tomás enjoyed smoking pot and had tried cocaine but said...he would never do acid.

As with Donna, and most of my friends, I kept my background to myself and didn't let him know about all the LSD I had already done. What had seemed so natural in California, now had to remain secret.

Tomás was also a psychology major like me. His parents wanted him to become an architect, but he said it was just too hard and wanted to enjoy his time in the United States. His girlfriend was Debbie, a cute long-haired brunette with dark-rimmed glasses and large seductive lips.

The three of us spent a lot of time together in the Student Union coffee shop after classes, often comparing notes about revolutions in South America...to what was happening here in the United States.

Gary was Tomás' roommate, a journalism major who also had a job working part-time for a printing company. Gary appeared to be a rather clean-cut individual, with blonde hair that was combed-back like Elvis.

He had a tall lanky build and was usually conservatively dressed, but deep down, Gary was totally anti-establishment and a true radical.

He also had the 'gift of gab' to go along with his extremist views.

Gary had trouble finding women who could actually relate to where he was intellectually. Although he'd dropped acid on several occasions, he dressed in a way that was much too straight for most hippie chicks, and the more fundamentalist babes found his demeanor to be just a little too far off the edge for them. Gary was definitely not…a chick magnet.

He and Larry…were the only ones I could be totally honest with.

Larry was Gary's first cousin, who stood six-foot-three, and was a very handsome twenty-five-year-old man. I met him one day while he was in Gary's dorm room selling lids of weed to the undergraduates.

He lived in Greenwich Village by himself and didn't go to college, having recently returned from combat in Vietnam, where he had been shot at quite a bit. The stories he told us often sounded unbelievable.

Larry said…he had been medically discharged from the Army for traumatized insanity but claimed to have faked the whole thing.

He told the doctors of nightmares, crying at night, wetting his bed, and banging on lockers in the early morning hours…pretending to have flashbacks of combat, and screaming at the top of his lungs.

It wasn't that I didn't believe Larry's story…but I could tell by the way he acted at times that he'd probably been severely shell-shocked (*later to become known as post-traumatic stress disorder*) and didn't have all of his marbles in a row. He may not have faked anything at all, and perhaps the Army's diagnosis of his condition was correct.

When I first met Larry, he was a lot like Gary, but with brown hair. He was straight-looking and had blue eyes. Larry supported himself financially by selling pot on campus. After we became friends, he put me in touch with his supplier so that I could do the same thing.

Within a few months, Larry was dropping acid regularly, growing a beard, letting his hair grow long, and was becoming active in the new underground anti-war movement. Soon…*Larry looked a lot like Jesus.*

Scott and Bill were brothers but were only a year apart. Scott was a freshman and Bill was a sophomore. They had a friend named, Arnold, and the four of us would often hang out together at the local bars and drink a lot. None of them did drugs, and for the most part, we would just have drinks together while exploring the city nightlife.

Since I had sworn off LSD…*at least for the time being*…I decided that they were the kind of guys I should be hanging out with instead of those who would appeal to my Scorpio moon tendencies, such as Larry.

Another person I met was a guy named Eddie, who was a friend of Arnold and was kind of a creepy weirdo. He had dropped out of college during his first year in order to start his own band. At first, he tried to play the guitar and sing, but having no voice, he moved to drums.

The name of Eddie's band was called *The Hairy Dogs* and often played at different clubs around the Village. Eddie didn't believe I had actually met people like John Lennon, Grace Slick, and Paul Kantner, and he refused to believe that I knew Jim Morrison and Timothy Leary.

Kathy was Donna's roommate…a delightful, bleached blonde with obvious dark roots, big boobs, a slender waist, and a great ass that could have been on a pin-up photograph. Kathy began dating Arnold, and at times, the four of us would go out together on a double date.

♥ ♥ ♥

Out of all the friends I had Drake was probably the one with whom I had the closest karmic ties and was the only one I could be completely honest with about the life I'd lived in California. Having been like a brother since the day we met, I could often feel his joy…and his pain.

"Right on!" he shouted. "You've experienced more during the last six months than most people do in their entire fucking lifetime."

Drake had transferred from Cornell and was now living at NYU.

I said to him one day, "You know, during one of my acid trips I had an incredible vision of the future. I was feeling totally overwhelmed with the spiritual connection of what we were all about, and I could feel the intense love that existed between the people I had met.

"Our souls were acting together in concert…trying to give birth to the New Age…as if we were born with the same blueprint inside of us. When this time in history arrived, a quickening-of-consciousness took place, and with the use of drugs, all our brains changed very quickly.

"Then, I saw a gathering of people who had come together in the name of peace and love to teach the world how to do it. America is supposed to be the cradle of freedom, but we would teach them what freedom actually means. We would teach them to give up their ideas of nationality, and instead, teach them how to become world citizens.

"We would be instrumental in helping to create a brotherhood and sisterhood of one unified world, instead of this individuated, one nation under God bullshit. That would be both the goal and the prize, and after that, once the whole frigging world got on the same page, then drugs would no longer be necessary because society as a whole would have made the great leap in consciousness. We would all 'live in peace' and still have our freedom, too. I mean really, can you dig it?"

"Wow, man, you have done a lot of fucking acid," Drake replied.

I explained that instead of tuning in, turning on, and dropping out, I was going to try and get serious about school. That meant I was going to be disciplined and stay off drugs until it was all over.

"Why?" Drake replied. "Are you planning to run for President of the United States or something? I study on acid all the time."

"I don't know what the hell I want to do with my life at the moment.

"Maybe I'll climb Mount Everest…and when I get to the very top, I'll smoke a joint and plant a flag with a peace symbol on it.

"But I do know this. I don't agree with everything the leaders of the movement are saying. All I know…is that I'm a part of the change."

"Change is good," Drake remarked, "that's what humans fear most. The only thing that stands in the way of changing people…is people. However, we could sure use the expertise you've gained from being in California to get our political movements going on campus. One of the groups is getting together next week to schedule protest rallies and marches for the next couple of months, so please…come and join us."

I promised Drake I would show up for the meeting and be looking forward to becoming more politically active. Not only did I want to be a campus advocate for change…but also within the city, thinking that this year, 1966, might be the start of something really big.

The Cellar Door was a good place to meet the new, up-and-coming celebrities in the world of music. Scott, Bill, Arnold, and I would often go there on the weekends to watch Eddie on the drums. During one of those nights, we had a brief encounter with Jimi Hendrix.

Jimi was tripping his ass off and couldn't talk much. In fact, he kept saying something about how all he could see was a purple haze inside his brain and wanted to know if anyone in the room had experienced more LSD than he had. A few months later, his band became known as *The Jimi Hendrix Experience,* which was exciting, sexy, and unique.

He didn't really have that good of a singing voice, but he made up for it with his guitar because the music was insane, often being a bizarre mixture of blues and rock. Personality-wise, Jimi was a very sweet guy, although he did seem to be just a bit confused at times.

His ramblings didn't make sense until about a year later when he burned his guitar on stage in front of a thousand screaming fans and said, "It's going to be purple haze every night, you know, because I've got this song in my head, inside my brain, and I'm going to play that song '*Purple Haze*'…until I get sick of it. And man, I sure as hell don't want to have to keep burning a new fucking guitar every night."

Another time, at the same club, we also met a recently famous group called *The Monkees*. They were there to do a film segment for their television show. Davy Jones, Peter Tork, Mickey Dolenz, and Mike Nesmith were actually on stage with Eddie's band to play their newest releases, '*Last Train to Clarksville*' and '*I'm a Believer.*'

It was at the Cellar Door that I also met the man who was Larry's contact for purchasing marijuana. His name was Marcus and he only sold weed by the kilogram. The cost of a kilo back then was only about fifty dollars, and Marcus had a new truckload shipped to New York every two weeks from Los Angeles. His contact there would bring in a *couple of keys* from Mexico at a cost of about ten dollars each.

By selling one pound of pot every week I made enough money to support myself for the entire month and still have money left over.

Back then, a lid of grass that weighed one ounce sold for ten dollars, so by spending one hundred dollars a month for two kilos, I could make a five-hundred-dollar profit, even after giving out free samples.

Most of my customers were just other students who I knew from my classes. I never sold to anyone I didn't know and was very careful not to get busted. There was a lot of paranoia about "narcs" on campus. Fortunately, most of the students who smoked pot were pretty close and shared any information they had about any funny business that might be going on. If anyone was suspected of being a narcotics agent or working undercover for the police, word spread quickly about who that person might be. Then, everyone would run home and vacuum up all the scattered pot seeds from their shag carpets.

One snowy day, Larry and I shared a joint as we hoofed around the Village. For some reason, he felt compelled to tell me his life story.

Being quite stoned, Larry just began to ramble as we walked.

"You know, Tex, I grew up with *Buffalo Bob* and *Howdy Doody, Buster Brown, Davy Crockett, Roy Rogers, Sky King, Queen for a Day, Froggy the Gremlin, The Lone Ranger, The Cisco Kid,* and *Sea Hunt.*

"As a child, we had twenty-five cent Saturday matinee movies and nickel cherry Cokes. Life was fun in the fifties. I was a kid, and I didn't have to worry about anything except where my next candy bar was coming from, where my bags of marbles were, or if my parents would let me watch *Frankenstein* and *The Wolf Man* on late-night television.

"The worries of life were there for my dad and mom, but for me, my life was structured, ordered, consistent, nice, and neat."

I was really impressed by the fact that Larry was being so candid about growing up, so he continued his ramblings almost as if I were a priest, and he was making his last confession.

"Watching *Leave It to Beaver, Ozzie and Harriet, My Three Sons,* and *Groucho Marx* on the television made for both a wholesome and humorous home life. When I was growing up, it seemed that all the black people lived in their own part of town, kept to themselves, and never caused any trouble. The grocery store had two water fountains.

"One said, '*Whites Only*' and the other said, '*Colored People.*'

"One day, when no one was looking, I sneaked over and tasted the water from both, and you know what? They didn't taste any different.

"Then, my body began to mature. Hormones blossomed, my dick had constant erections, girls looked prettier, school got tougher, and the metamorphosis from a child to a teenager began to unfold.

"High school in the Sixties brought about some of the greatest times I can remember. There were no drugs, no gangs, and no suicides, and on Friday nights we drove our cars to the Tasty Freeze for all the gossip on who was going out with whom, who won the game, and the teachers we disliked the most. Occasionally, someone would get in a fight over something stupid, but no one got killed over it. We didn't even discuss the Vietnam War in the early Sixties. It was just some news story we might hear over my dad's shoulder after dinner while he was watching television with Walter Cronkite at six o'clock…every night.

"When I started out in high school, all the boys had crew-cut hair styles and all the girls wore skirts about one inch past the knees.

"Then, one day, I heard a song on the radio with a new sound, and with it came the words, 'I want to hold your hand.' The D.J. said it was from a pop group in England called *The Beatles*. My cousin even said, 'How strange for a band to be named after an insect.' But I liked their beat and just knew their song would go to number one overnight.

"That was the first thing I remember about the winds of change. The winds of life force energy on the planet were definitely changing directions. Within the next six months, hysteria, long hair, girls wearing slacks, and some really bizarre anti-establishment buzzwords began to appear everywhere. I'm sure that must have had a subtle and unsettling effect on everyone, especially our parents, who had been mired in the old traditional ways a lot longer than we had.

"Within the next two years the Vietnam War finally grew to a boil, and I started to listen to the news a little more. I mean, hey, that could be me over there getting killed. So I began to question a lot of things and wondered if I should get a college deferment, a medical deferment, or just run off to Canada? What would I do? Where did all this new catastrophic emotional stress and trauma I was feeling suddenly come from? I surely didn't create it, nor did I want any part of it.

"I had been very happy up until then, just playing football, dating my favorite girl, and looking forward to living a peaceful life, but like so many other adventuresome boys, I was lured by the curiosity of war.

"As a way to ease my stress, I surrendered to any fears I had and went ahead and joined the Army. Of course, I got sent to Vietnam.

Then, people started shooting at me, and friends I had started dying. That's when I wound up with this post-traumatic stress syndrome."

"Yeah. What is that exactly?" I asked.

"It's the delayed release of fear, anger, and stress…as well as a lot of other abnormalities that are buried in the dark recesses of our minds. Most people can't deal with witnessing horrific acts, or participating in the savage murder of innocent villagers," he explained.

"Once I went to Vietnam, it was as if somebody changed the mold in the middle of the pour. I saw whole villages swallowed up and burned as people ran from their huts still on fire only moments after being struck by napalm bombs. I witnessed screaming women holding babies who had become nothing more than charred carbon.

"I hated my job. I was manning a machine gun in a helicopter, and we would go in after the fighter planes dropped the napalm and shoot at anyone who might still be alive. I'd already done it before, a couple of times, but now, it just felt different…I just couldn't do it again."

Listening to him, I was pretty certain I wouldn't ever do that either, but I just kept quiet as his dark confession continued.

"There were five of us in the chopper that day. The pilot, a young lieutenant, another gunner, the ammunition assistant, and myself.

"When the lieutenant told us we were flying into the same zone where several choppers had been shot down the day before, all of us voiced our protest. He replied, calling us a bunch of sissies and ordering us to shoot anything that moved…be it was a man, a woman, a child, or even a dog. When he said that, my body became frozen. I couldn't pull the trigger on my machine gun…even if I had to defend myself.

"All of us looked at each other not knowing what to do, and out of pure rage I absolutely freaked out. Grabbing him by his shirt collar with one hand and drawing my revolver with the other, I shot the lieutenant in the back of the head…and threw him out of the chopper.

"In slow motion, I watched his body fall into a rice paddy below."

There was a long moment of silence after he told me that.

"The other three guys weren't all that upset about what I'd done, and one of them even admitted that I'd probably saved their lives.

"The other two said they didn't see what happened.

"As far as they were concerned the lieutenant was hit by enemy fire, then lost his balance and fell out accidentally.

"At that point, we turned around and went back to the base.

"The sad part of the story is that it wasn't just an isolated incident. While I was in the hospital, I heard all kinds of similar stories about commanding officers being killed the same way."

"Really?" I asked in disbelief.

"That day was to be my last run. I just couldn't take it anymore.

"I couldn't bring myself to go on any more airstrikes that would kill anyone else. I just had to get out of Vietnam...that's when I started to pretend that I'd gone crazy...to receive a medical discharge.

"To this day, I still have nightmares about what I saw over there.

"Occasionally, when rushing to a meeting, or trying to keep up with some schedule, I'll get stressed out and just stop. Then I'll look around at small children who are laughing and playing with smiles on their faces and remember the times I had when I was a child...a child who had no worries, except where his next sandlot ball game would be.

"Then I think about the children in Vietnam that I shot and killed or watched as they burned to death. I realize, how they must have felt and how terribly scared they must have been.

"That's when I start to cry."

Larry and I eventually made it back to his apartment and then I left. His experience in Vietnam was never mentioned again between us, but deep inside I knew that for him to tell his story to someone who would not judge him for what he did had been extremely therapeutic.

In February I attended the meeting about the rally and protest march Drake had told me about. I gave them some ideas and was asked to help with publicity. It was set to be held at the same place where the other march had taken place the previous summer in Central Park.

By now I was much more tuned in and turned on about the anti-war effort which had now become very personal for me. The week before the event, Gary and I snuck into the print shop where he worked and ran off several hundred fliers which were later distributed to the public. It felt good to know that my efforts would make the march a success.

When the day arrived, Donna was with me as well as my friends Tomás, Debbie, Arnold, Kathy, Larry, and Gary. Drake, of course, was there too but was busy getting the marchers prepared to leave.

This time, it was extremely cold outside, and instead of people wearing long flowing cotton dresses and multi-colored tie-dyed t-shirts, everyone was all bundled up, walking proudly in their winter coats, wearing smells from laboratories, and talking about our dying nation.

My friends and I shared a couple of joints just before the crowd of about a thousand protesters began to march. Donna took a few puffs herself, even though she normally abstained from getting high.

The problem was that one of our organizers had failed to get the proper parade permit to the right people. As a result, the march was broken up by the mounted police on horseback who blocked our path. Those who tried to break through the barricade were hit with batons, but due to the cold weather, most of the people were happy to abort the mission in order to get back to where it was warm. There was another one planned for the spring, so we weren't all that disappointed about it.

♥ ♥ ♥

Our little band eventually wound up at Larry's apartment, and after about an hour of smoking joints…we all became quite stoned.

The conversation turned to politics, and we began to talk about the difference between communism and socialism…how they were both just a huge conspiracy but the communist party would never admit it.

"To me, communism is nothing more than the rebirth of Russian Imperialism," Tomás tried to explain since he was from Peru and had some first-hand experience with the socialist movement. "And it is very much a part of your American Democracy. Communism is actually an international conspiratorial drive for power on the part of men in high places who are willing to use any means necessary to bring about their desired aim, which is nothing less than global conquest. In reality, it is a conspiracy to seize power, which is as old as history and Julius Caesar himself. Its most effective weapon has always been the big lie because most people believe anything you tell them."

"Are you saying communism is not really a movement for all of the down-trodden masses to rise up against their exploiting bosses, or for the poor to finally stand up to the rich?" Donna interjected.

"Totally," said Tomás. "All of them…Mao Tse-tung, Ho Chi Minh, Fidel Castro, and Tito…they're all the same. You see, they learned this trick from the great Chinese warlord, Sun Tsu, who said…*you create psychological warfare through the creation of diversions*. That's what socialism is…a diversion that opens a doorway into world domination. It was invented by people like Marx, Engels, Lenin, and Trotsky. They are the ones who created all that linguistic bullshit about the bourgeois, proletariat, dialectical materialism, and pseudo-economics."

"What they said," replied Larry, "was that before you could have true communism the proletariat must first undergo a cultural revolution that would establish a socialist dictatorship to represent all the people.

"Then through that dictatorship, they would first begin to establish the elimination of private property, the dissolution of the family unit, and the destruction of the great opiate of the people, which is religion.

"That means, to have communism, you need a dictatorship first."

"That's correct," Tomás explained, "but there's a catch to all of this. According to the Communist Manifesto, they just assume that the new dictator-led and all-powerful socialist state would then miraculously somehow wither away and lend itself to some kind of purified version of communism. Eventually, you wouldn't need to have any government at all, which is what real communism is supposed to be in its true form. In theory, everything would become peaceful, and everyone would live happily ever after for the rest of their days. The question is: do you really believe that an omnipotent state led by a dictator who is hell-bent on world domination would just voluntarily dismantle himself for the good of the people? No, he wouldn't. That's the big flaw in the theory.

"Once a leader has power, they become obsessed with it and refuse to let go of it. That's why true communism has never existed."

"What you're saying, is that communism has existed, but it hasn't ever been practiced in its purist form," Donna noted.

"Correct again," Tomás added. "The principles of the Communist Manifesto, written by Karl Marx, were set down over seventy years earlier by a guy named Adam Weishaupt who was the founder of the *Order of Illuminaté* in Bavaria. They had to go underground, and later became known as the *League of Just Men*. Eventually, it evolved into the *Masons*, who are made up of families with famous names such as Rockefeller, Ford, Kennedy, Rothschild, and Warburg, all of whom were Masons, and as you know these guys have ruled the world's banks since their inception. What people don't realize is that the Illuminaté was a radical branch of the Jesuits, from the 'Society of Jesus,' and was the right arm of the Catholic Church in Rome. When America was first colonized, Catholics were looked upon with disdain because most of our founding fathers were Protestant. That was the last thing Rome wanted to have, which was an enemy in the new world."

"What you're saying," answered Larry, "is that the Masons were a secret society of Protestants who supported the Jesuits because it was the only way for Catholics to get a foothold in the new world."

"Well, yes, but what I'm really saying is that the Catholic Church in Rome is the organization that financed the American Revolution as part of its goal of achieving world domination. You see, the Pope didn't want the American colonies to become hostile toward Rome the same way England did, so they planted the Masons into the various colonial groups, like spies with double identities…and gave them great fortunes in land and money…to people like George Washington…and even to Benjamin Franklin…almost all of your original founding fathers."

"Are you saying the Catholic Church put these guys into power?"

"Yes," said Tomás, "the Church in Rome orchestrated the entire American Revolution from its inception…they created it, paid for it, and finally won it by sending in French war ships to prevent the British from leaving. Everyone knows the French are primarily Catholic.

"Ever since you won the American Revolution, the United States has been run by either Catholics or Masons…all of whom are directly connected to the Illuminaté…socialists who have pledged allegiance to the Roman Catholic Church, all in the name of world conquest."

"Why would the Catholic Church want socialism?" Larry asked.

"Just read your New Testament Bible," replied Tomás. "What Jesus taught to his disciples…was communism in its purest form.

Jesus said…*love your neighbor as yourself…if you have two coats and your neighbor has none, then give one of the coats to him.*

He also said…*damned, are the money lenders.*

Jesus taught…that you shouldn't lend money, but to give it to those who have none. So like I said before, to have communism, you must have a dictator, and that's what Jesus was…*a very loving dictator.*"

"You're saying, Jesus believed in a communist society?" I asked.

"Yes," he replied, "but Jesus didn't teach world domination through violence, only through compassion...which is the way a loving dictator should be. Jesus expected his followers to do whatever he said and was willing to forgive them when they didn't listen. Today, the Church still believes that it's their mission on Earth to spread the teachings of Jesus in order to create world domination, but the problem is, that the Church has become corrupt with power. However, it is still their goal to control politics, the military, and the money of the entire planet...and not only are they doing it, but we're also letting them get away with it."

"That's some pretty heavy shit," I replied.

"What you still don't get is that your country's leaders are Masons who have connections to Rome with the same goal, *world domination*, but instead of using love as Jesus did, they use violence. Your country is like a brutal dictator to many third world countries...which is the same goal as socialism...here you may practice democracy...but to the rest of the world you are seen as nothing but hypocritical tyrants."

Then Donna interjected her two bits by saying, "You think that's some heavy shit, man? Let me tell you how most wars are paid for. Those banker guys you were talking about earlier, well, their families have been financing world wars for centuries. What's worse is that they loan money to both sides...because they still get repaid either way.

"For example, the same financial institutions loaned money to both the North and the South in the Civil War. Now in Vietnam, American banks are loaning money to Russia, and Russia is loaning that same money to North Vietnam, and they're the enemy who we're supposed to be fighting against. Now that's some real shit, isn't it?"

"And what's all this crap about Columbus discovering America?" asked Tomás. "You can't discover a land that's already inhabited."

"Yeah...that's a fucking far-out concept, man!" shouted Larry.

And the conversations went on...well into the night.

♥ ♥ ♥

By now, it was the middle of March, and I hadn't heard anything from Diane. I was becoming worried about her, so I tried to write her a letter by sending it to the old address, not knowing if she would even get it. To my surprise, it was forwarded to her new address, and she even wrote me back. In her usual style, the letter was more like a poem.

She was living in a more upscale commune than she was before, this time with several famous Hollywood celebrities. They were living just outside San Francisco in a big house that was overlooking the bay near the Golden Gate Bridge…wanting me to come back.

What she wrote was based on a song written by a very good friend of hers, David Loggins…but wasn't released until many years later.

Dear Andy, it read…

'Please come to Oakland for the springtime. I'm staying here with some friends, and we've got lots of room. I'm living in a house that looks out over the ocean, and some stars fell from the sky and are living with me up on the hill. I'll be selling my paintings out on the sidewalk, by a café where I'll be working soon. So please come back to me and live forever…we'll move up into the mountains so far that we can't be found. This drifter's world goes around and around and I doubt if it's ever going to stop…but of all the dreams I've lost and found you're the only one I still don't have. It's you I want to cling to, it's you I want to sing to. Each morning I throw '*I love you*' echoes down the canyon, and I lie awake at night until they come back around. Life without you is just too hard to bear, so would you please come home to me.

'I know you've heard me calling, so hey…rambling boy, why don't you settle down and come back to me? After all, this place is your kind of town. There may not be any gold, but there's no one else like me.

'I'm your number one fan, why can't you see?

'Loving you still…Diane.'

I tried writing back but didn't hear from her a second time. At least I had the location of her address just in case she was serious about still being in love with me. Maybe she was tripping on acid or something when she wrote it. However, I decided to go back to see her once the semester was over. Maybe we could make love again just like before. As the time got closer, I started to look forward to it.

♥ ♥ ♥

Back in those days, the dormitories of men and women were always in separate buildings. Members of the opposite sex were not allowed in without special permission. The only way Donna and I could have sex was to use the apartment of one of our friends. Up to now, we had been mostly going to Larry's place...but it was inconvenient and dirty.

Arnold was also disenchanted with the dormitory situation but had recently rented a small flat with the aid of his parents...so now, he and Kathy, who was nineteen years old, could get easily together and ball.

One afternoon I showed up unannounced and knocked on the door.

"Who is it?" I heard Arnold shout from inside.

"It's me, Tex."

"The door is unlocked, just come on in."

As I entered the room it was dark, but I smelled the familiar aroma of freshly smoked weed, and a faint melody of a hit band, *The Animals*.

At first, I couldn't see anyone, so I shouted, "Where are you?"

"Back here in the bedroom, come and join us."

The bedroom door was open, the music stopped, but I heard rustling sounds from the bed. As I entered, I could see that Kathy was snuggled under a white sheet next to Arnold...and both were naked.

"Hello, Kat, hey Arnold...now look, I don't want to be interrupting something that might be going on here," I proclaimed.

"Hell, you can get in with us if you want," Arnold noted, laughing.

"No you can't," said Kathy, "but you can have a hit of this roach."

"The sex I can do without," I replied, "but I can't pass that up."

"Sit down and talk to us for a while," Arnold suggested.

She handed me the joint as I sat on the bed and stretched my legs but couldn't help but notice that I was sporting a rather large hard-on.

After taking a few puffs I replied, "This is a great place you have. Maybe Donna and I can start coming here instead of going to Larry's."

Being quite stoned and without thinking, she noted, "Sure you can, but I think you'd prefer your own place. Arnold and I are much happier, and from what I hear, your sex life sucks…but don't worry, I go down on her almost every night, so she gets a pretty good workout."

"*Every night?*"

"Well…she is my roommate, so at least a couple of times a week.

"I had no idea, but that would sure explain her lack of interest."

"Yeah, it would, but please don't tell her I told you."

After receiving that information, I didn't think twice about going back to California and hanging out with Diane for a while.

That little two-faced dyke…I quietly said to myself…*good for her.*

I hadn't cheated on her all semester…but it was time to catch up.

After all, sometimes 'payback' can be a real bitch.

By now it was mid-April, and we were preparing for another rally just as Drake had predicted. This time the police wouldn't try to stand in the way because the organizers had correctly followed all the rules and obtained the proper permits…which pissed the authorities off.

Just a few days before the march I received a telephone call from my father. Byron had called him and asked my parents to tell me that our friend Stanley had been recently killed in Vietnam. Byron said his platoon was trying to defend some useless hill and was hit by our own bombers after calling in for help. Stan was a victim of '*friendly fire.*'

That night I went out with my two friends Scott and Bill. We went to a bar for the sole purpose of getting drunk, and even though they had never met Stan…they could feel my pain. Together, we made several toasts to his death, and people we didn't even know joined in with us.

After that…I became even more committed to getting serious about doing whatever I could to put an end to this damned war.

When the march was announced for April, Gary and I printed even more fliers than before. At the bottom, it read, "This march is dedicated to the memory of Corporal Stanley Levitt…he was just one of the many who was exactly like us, and senselessly lost his life in Vietnam."

No one but me knew who Stan really was, or how he died, but there were times when the entire crowd of marchers would begin to chant, "Ban the War for Stan! Ban the War for Stan!"

By the time the march ended, rumors had started, and the word was out that Stanley Levitt had been a former hippie who had somehow made it over to Vietnam and single-handedly tried to keep the soldiers from going out to fight by handing them flowers. They said…his death occurred when he accidentally stepped on a land mine, and his body was blown apart. Some people were saying that flowers had begun to bloom immediately right at the spot where Stanley died.

To many, he was not only a hero but now qualified for sainthood.

It was a fitting tribute…to a very good friend.

Before I knew it May arrived…final exams were over, and although it had been *a hazy shade of winter*, my first semester at NYU had been for the most part a successful one (both academically and financially).

Donna was going back to Boston for the summer and had obtained an intern position with a social advocacy group for women's rights.

For me…it was time to go back to California…and to find Diane.

I'd made enough money selling pot that I could easily afford a small flat in the Village next fall, but for now, I was going to take a break.

I planned to take the next flight out…looking forward to being back in the Golden State…physically, mentally, emotionally, and spiritually.

The U.S. finally admitted to firing on military targets in Cambodia for the first time. In response, twelve thousand anti-war demonstrators picketed the White House, involving minor skirmishes by the police.

A new heavyweight boxer name Cassius Clay was becoming quite a spokesman for civil rights. He wound up beating Henry Cooper in the sixth round in London, thereby retaining the world championship belt.

He told the world…*I am the greatest.*

Shortly thereafter, he officially became…Muhammad Ali.

And the Beat Goes On

The miniskirt's the current thing, uh-huh.
Little girls are still breaking hearts, uh-huh.
And men still keep on marching off to war…
And the beat goes on…and the beat goes on…
(Artists: Sonny and Cher)

♥ ♥ ♥

It was the summer of 1966. The moment I stepped off the airplane I could tell the next three months were going to be long, hot, and angry throughout the Haight-Ashbury district. Underground newspapers all across America were asking for people to rise up and demonstrate even more aggressively against the Vietnam War than ever before.

In early June, James Meredith, who had been the first black student to attend the University of Mississippi four years earlier…was shot in the back during a civil rights protest march. He was immediately taken to a hospital in Memphis and somehow survived.

Martin Luther King continued to lead civil rights marchers through Mississippi, starting from the point where Meredith had been gunned down the day before. To everyone's surprise, Meredith rejoined them near Jackson where a major civil rights rally was held that night.

That same month, an American pilot admitted to shooting down two South Vietnamese planes…while he was high on marijuana.

♥ ♥ ♥

When I arrived in Oakland, the first thing I wanted was to locate the return address posted on the letter Diane had sent me. I took a taxi directly from the airport…with no idea at all what I would find or who she might be shacking up with…but according to those who were there, she hadn't been seen since May and was nowhere to be found. It seems that Diane had become depressed, had taken too much of something, and ended up in the hospital. The rules at the commune where she'd been staying said…*if you overdosed, you were out*…so she left.

The rumor was…she'd gone back to live somewhere near the same place that she and I had met the previous fall.

There was a new head shop on the corner of Haight and Ashbury called "The Psychedelic Shop." Almost immediately, it had become the favorite place for people to hang out, and where runaways could find a home. Everybody who was anybody knew somebody living there.

Before that, it had just been the local laundromat.

The Psychedelic Shop stocked many things like books about drugs, books about oriental philosophy, rolling papers, roach clips, candles, bells, beads, flutes, posters…and a full range of *hippie paraphernalia*.

They'd even sold tickets to Ken Kesey's acid tests.

Some of the people working there knew me from when I lived in the neighborhood and told me Diane had recently come in. I continued to ask around until someone finally clued me as to where she was.

I finally tracked her down at a commune called *The Family Dog*, which was only a few blocks from the Psychedelic Shop. The head honcho of the Family Dog was Chet Helms, who was also managing Janis Joplin's new band…*Big Brother and the Holding Company*.

At this point…Janis was just becoming a well-known artist.

Helms had lived in San Francisco since 1962 and had tried to make a living as a poet, but after hearing Janis sing he convinced her to leave Texas and hitchhike to California where he promised he could make her into a huge rock star. Chet had been impressed with the fact that Diane knew so many famous people, so he welcomed her into the pack.

Chet also had some business dealings going on with Jerry Garcia's new band, which was now being called *The Grateful Dead*.

The Family Dog commune was an integral part of the Haight Street community. They believed in both drugs and free love, so Diane's most recent overdose was apparently not a problem.

The commune would often promote free concerts in the middle of the street with bands that never received any payment. Another thing they had become famous for was psychedelic poster art and t-shirts, as well as painting murals on buildings. That's how I finally found her.

A girl outside the commune said she was working on a project only a couple of blocks away. She had been asked to paint a freaky-looking picture of Frank Zappa on the outside of a café overlooking the ocean, just as she had said in her letter. However, she usually made a living by creating custom-designed, tie-dyed psychedelic t-shirts for five dollars, and of course, all of her money went into the communal kitty.

♥ ♥ ♥

Excitedly, I yelled loudly, "Diane!"

She turned around slowly and smiled.

"Andy, you found me. I knew you would."

"I've been looking everywhere for you."

"Well, I've been coming here and you've been going there, but now we've stopped...so now we're here and there together. Pretty cool!"

Diane was obviously high on something, but it didn't matter to me because I was elated to have found her. As we talked, however, I came to find out that she was not only doing acid and weed regularly but had also moved on to some of the harder drugs like cocaine and speed.

She had even tried heroin, which was on the night she accidentally overdosed, and said she had not used it again.

"I'm not doing those drugs anymore," she swore. "From now on, it's just orange sunshine, mushrooms, and mescaline for me."

"How do you like living at the Family Dog?" I asked her, changing the subject to see if she could leave with me.

"It's just a place to crash for a while until I was ready to leave."

I was totally honest with her and said that I wanted to be with her, but when the summer was over, I planned to return to school.

She shook her head back and forth and said, "It's all about living in the now moment. You never know, things might change. New York may not even exist anymore by then. Fuck, who knows…we could be living in outer space. We'll just deal with it when we get there."

Diane wouldn't be able to live at the Family Dog any longer if she hooked up with anyone outside of the communal group. So she put her paints and brushes away by placing them in the store where they were kept and found us a place to stay near the Psychedelic Shop.

The free-love movement in the Haight-Ashbury district was more intense now than it had been the previous summer, to the point that people were almost fucking in the streets. It's no wonder the latest hit song by The Beatles was called, *Why Don't We Do It in the Road?*

Because I was living so close to the Psychedelic Shop, I got to know the owner, Don. The local underground newspaper in the area was called the 'Berkeley Barb,' and it covered most of the social events around Haight-Ashbury. However, the people living on Haight Street wanted a newspaper of their own. I convinced Ron to print a weekly local paper for them and said I would help him get it started.

I had gained enough knowledge from my experiences in New York to get a similar paper going on here. Besides, I needed something like this to keep me busy for the rest of the summer.

Don wanted to call the newspaper, *The Psychedelic Oracle.*

The first weekly issue turned out to be just a little on the amateurish side, mostly because I didn't know exactly what he wanted.

Some of the things we were headlining…were often articles like… *Concentration Camps have been prepared for Subversive Activists*, and *Here's a New Recipe for Chocolate Chip Hash Cookies.*"

Over the summer the paper became much more respectable, but it was still being written for all the stoned hippies who lived in the nearby psychedelic community. It was the first official underground paper that represented the growing "turned on" national underground movement. It made me feel like the reincarnation of a young Benjamin Franklin, stirring up a new American Revolution with my little printing press.

There was no doubt that the lines of demarcation were being split because of the Vietnam War. However, there was confusion about how this new underground movement would actually be any different than the established order we were rebelling against.

The police were beginning to crack down heavily in the area, and the people on Haight Street demanded that everyone calm down, rather than have the neighborhood turn into an anti-police war zone.

This dilemma of how to deal with this situation was also taken on by a person named Emmett Grogan. That wasn't his real name, because he'd changed it after being kicked out of the Army after a self-induced psychotic attack…much like Larry had done. Grogan had recently founded a new communal group in the district known as *The Diggers*, who were very much against having a capitalistic society.

Emmett and The Diggers would encourage people to give their things away for free and recycle. They asked people to barter and trade, rather than bow down to the 'God of Money.'

The Diggers were not into drugs as an expression of freedom but believed that freedom could be attained by letting go of our American beliefs and ideals. So they tried to live outside the box of profit, private property, or the hunger for power that was driving our Western culture.

They were certainly freethinkers…but perhaps ahead of their time.

The Diggers offered free food to those who had no money if they were homeless or runaways, and there were many of those. Their small commune had lots of women whose jobs were to prepare the food, while Emmett, Slim, Peter...and the others, would solicit handouts from the food markets and butcher shops.

The Diggers had no official leader and didn't want one. When they couldn't get food for free, they would steal it from local shops and their suppliers, then gave it to those who didn't have anything.

One day, Emmett was arrested for stealing a side of beef from the Armour Meat Company. When he came to trial, the judge accepted his modern-day Robin Hood defense and only gave him a suspended jail sentence, plus payment for meat he had stolen.

Although they were known for stealing a lot of food, they remained popular with the locals because their offerings of free food and other essentials gave hope and a promise of a new way of thinking and living.

As far as The Diggers were concerned, their heroic effort was a big contribution to the rise of the hippie counterculture.

One week, Emmett wanted to run an ad in the Psychedelic Oracle that read, *"Free Food at the Ashbury Panhandle at 4:00 p.m. every day. Bring a bowl and spoon. It's free because it's yours. The Diggers."*

Don agreed to run the ad even though he knew the food was stolen.

Many of the boutiques and shop owners of Haight Street were doing very well, financially, much like the Psychedelic Shop. Don and several other merchants got together and asked everyone to invite a policeman to share a meal with them. By doing this, they hoped the police would see the hippies as being good, quiet, and peaceful citizens.

The Diggers saw this move by the shop owners as a bribe, or as some kind of payoff to the cops. In response, they distributed a leaflet that read...*if you take a policeman to dinner, it feeds his power to judge, prosecute, and brutalize the people...and the streets of our city.*

♥ ♥ ♥

Another interesting person I met that summer was Wavy Gravy, the guy who had spoken at my first protest march in New York City.

He was a former comedian and poet named Hugh Romney and had studied acting. He was known throughout Haight-Ashbury under his new name and had met Diane at the commune she was in.

Wavy had lived in several communes and had also been a friend of Ken Kesey, but with Ken being in Mexico as a fugitive, Wavy teamed up with what was left of the Merry Pranksters and went off with the Grateful Dead to put on a number of free concerts, as well as to conduct even more of the notorious Kool-Aid acid tests.

That summer, Wavy settled down in the Hollywood Hills outside of Los Angeles after he had bought an old pig farm on a mountaintop in the San Fernando Valley. Many of his friends from Oakland arrived and colonized some of the nearby shacks, or just put up some tents.

The farm mascot was a very large pig known as 'Pigasus.'

When Diane asked me if I would like to experience life in a rustic, country-style commune, I said emphatically, "Most definitely."

One day, she saw Wavy in town and asked him if we could visit his farm, called *The Hog Farm Commune*. When he said, "Yes," we went there together to visit what would eventually become renowned as one of the most famous California communes of the late Sixties.

The land was located on a large ridge covered with pine and oak trees that descended on three sides into the canyons. It had one passable access road, which was later temporarily closed by a Sonoma County judge after there were reports that someone had been smuggling in drugs from Mexico, thereby causing people to walk down, up, and out to the roadway to get to the neighboring ridge. It turned out to be quite the hike, which everyone called 'woodsy aerobics.'

Hitchhiking was not only quite popular but was a necessary form of transportation. The walk via the access road from a drop-off on the main road consisted of a two-mile walk up to the front gate.

During this walk, people who lived there were usually laden down with packs or groceries and would sometimes have to stop in the shade for a rest and take a hit from a refreshing joint.

There was running water near the garden in the center of the land, and people would haul their water up from there, usually in gallon jugs, or from a tiny spring on the east canyon side where you could sit and contemplate nature the entire time it took to fill a gallon jug.

Being that the land was located not far from the ocean, it was often visited by fog and morning mist. The weather, as the climate goes, was mild, though the roughshod buildings always intensified the impact of any season. Regardless of the weather, it was a good place to be.

Most of the abandoned or dilapidated houses came in many shapes and sizes. Each had its own unique personality and earthy appeal.

Everything from a comfy mattress under a shady tree, to a two-story and many-windowed mansion, could be found on the property.

Scrap lumber, canvas, aluminum, and plastic were among the most common materials used in the creation of each new masterpiece, and structures were added to, or subtracted from, as different people moved in and out. The main thing was that everyone seemed to be happy.

There was no electricity when the land was purchased. For months, people used kerosene lamps, gas lanterns, or even a twelve-volt hookup to someone's car battery. Heat radiated from crackling fires in glowing woodstoves and bathrooms were only a shovel and a roll of toilet paper. Showers were often taken with wash pots down at the creek or you'd make a trip to the hose in the garden. People who visited would share space with others, or if the weather permitted, just slept in the woods.

Many would try and perfect just the basic skills for living…such as cooking on wood stoves, learning how to split wood, or doing home improvements…just *making do* with what was available.

One unique invention the community took part in at the commune was known as *canyon calls*. People evolved their own unique call while walking to a friend's house by announcing themselves a few hundred feet up the hill. If the person called back, it meant they were home and receiving guests. If not, it meant they were away or having a private moment. This saved the visitor from having to walk all the way to the house and finding no one there, or from intruding. So it wasn't unusual to hear a lot of weird-sounding calls echoing in the background.

Those who were drawn to live at 'The Hog Farm' didn't necessarily have all that much in common other than the simple desire to be there and to get back to the land *and set their soul free*.

They wanted to live and feel a simpler way of life in a more natural environment…away from the rigidity of mainstream society.

There were all kinds of people helping to set it up, sages and seers, gardeners and builders, lovers and musicians, poets and orators, parents and painters, geniuses and scholars, old soldiers and survivors, hippies and trolls, mystics and dropouts, as well as a cowboy or two. Most of the residents sported full tans because wearing clothing was an option while you were living on the land. It wasn't unusual to see a couple, or for that matter, three or four, strolling together naked in a nearby field.

People gravitated into their own groups of friends, which became like neighborhoods, each with unique personalities.

There were many families either of a few or of multiples, and there were couples and singles, but all these could change in a heartbeat.

Special occasions were celebrated with a bountiful feast and were always accompanied by music. The steam baths and sweat lodges were also considered to be great celebrations of cleansing and community.

Even peyote was sometimes consumed for added delight, although just being in the steam was often a consciousness-raising experience.

A large fire lined with rocks burned for hours on end, until the rocks were red-hot and ready to go into the sauna hut. Bay leaves would be gathered and used by dipping into a bowl and sprinkling the water onto the hot rocks, creating great clouds of steam.

The sauna itself was a dome of branches covered in canvas, inside of which was a fire pit with lots of room for the people to sit.

They would crouch in the glowing heat and humidity, sweating and glistening, with their minds filled full of intensity and wonder…each person in their separate space, yet they all remained as one.

For anyone who felt too overcome, all they needed to do was to speak the word 'uncle'…and the flap would be opened to let them out. Afterward, there was cold water from the hose to diminish one's body heat and lots of water to drink…to invigorate the soul.

Music was always in the air, and a stroll around the land was sure to bring you within earshot of someone who was jamming. People were known to break into song at any given moment, or just to whistle.

Many times someone would grab a guitar, or other types of musical object, and begin to play. In no time at all, a rhythm section would magically appear and would tap, bang, or thud on anything handy.

Inverted pots and pans worked well, or an upturned oatmeal box was excellent, and harmonicas were in the pockets of many.

The music on the land was stilled when the people would leave, but the beat of freedom never died from the hills. It just continued to beat and echo on and on, so if you listened quietly, you could still hear the rhythm of all the drums and music that was there.

The main point was…that fun was usually had by all.

Sometimes there were so many people at the Hog Farm Commune on a Sunday afternoon that it was hard to walk through the crowd.

Many times, I found myself having to weave my way around to avoid running into people. Some were pushing strollers, some were walking their dogs, and some were not paying any attention at all and bumping into each other among the throngs. Although pleasant, it was chaotic and at times, almost overwhelming.

One Sunday afternoon while the bands were playing, we decided to drop a couple of tabs of Orange Sunshine LSD, and in no time at all, we were tripping really hard, so I had to stop to get my perspective for just that moment. All of a sudden, it looked as though the crowd parted right before me…just like the Red Sea had done for Moses.

Then I saw him! There, right behind a small group of guys passing a joint was someone who resembled a holy man. He was dressed in a long orange gown and had black curly hair almost like an afro.

By some telepathic means, he identified himself as, *the Master*.

He was standing there right in front of me with his arms wide open as if to be welcoming me. He looked radiant as he was bathed in golden light. He was a handsome man, and although his skin was dark, he had an incredibly clear complexion that almost glowed.

He was ethereal, and yet *very real* at the same time. It began to feel as though time had stopped…but I noticed a familiar stillness in the air, one that I will remember for the rest of my life.

He looked right at me and smiled which caused a feeling of pure divine bliss to envelope my entire being. It felt as if it came from inside of me, and from all around me, all at the same time.

I'd been reawakened…just by his presence.

The Master told me…*what he does is to awaken the light already there within*. I was almost too overwhelmed to move. It was like he'd cleansed me of my entire twenty years of residue from living on the Earth. I wanted to rush over to him, but as soon as that thought entered my mind, the crowd closed again, as the Red Sea did to the Pharaoh.

I looked all around but he was gone.

I knew I wouldn't find him again that day.

Once again, the crowd became a sea of moving people just going about their business. I could feel the warm sunlight against my skin and the sounds of talking and laughter returned to my ears, yet the blissful feeling of *the Master's* emanations still remained.

Then I walked over to a bench and sat down while still in a state of utter amazement. Yet, I felt sad because I couldn't see him anymore.

I put my head down in despair only to find that sitting right in front of my feet was a card someone had dropped on the ground. It was only 4 x 6 inches in size. In large print, the card read, *"The time is now."*

"Andy, there you are," Diane said, who had also dropped some of the same acid that I had. "I've been looking all over for you."

"Wow. This stuff is some pretty heavy shit…you know?"

"I know. I've been hallucinating like crazy!"

"What have you been doing?" I asked.

"I had to get away from all the people, so I was talking to the trees, and then I had a long conversation with Dan, one of the horses."

"He wanted me to find him an apple, so I did."

"That's cool," I noted. "How about you…I'm feeling really tired. Why don't we go back to the cottage and lay down for a while?"

"Great idea," she replied.

On the way back to the cottage, I held Diane's hand. I was going to miss being with her, and she was so beautiful and innocent.

I asked myself…*why did I leave her? Why did she wait for me?*

As we passed by some more horses, Diane let down her long blonde hair and shook it out. Then, she petted a beautiful palomino mare that shook out its own blonde mane as well. I realized, that in some other lifetime, Diane must have been a horse, and judging by my hair, which was a very dark brown, I must have been a bear, or maybe a wolf.

Once we reached the cottage, Diane found a blanket. It was such a beautiful day, so she spread it out on the grass instead of going inside. Then we sat down, and I took off my shoes while Diane lit up a joint. Soon, we were joined by two other friends Paul and Elle, who were also tripping and just happened to see us sitting there.

Paul decided to greet us with a familiar song. He began to sing, "*One pill makes you larger, and one pill makes you small.*"

Then, Elle joined in and sang, "*But the ones that mother gives you don't do anything at all. Go ask Alice…when she's ten feet tall.*"

Then, they sat down and joined us in smoking the joint.

I took a toke of the joint and kissed Diane while blowing some of the smoke into her mouth before passing it over to Paul. After taking a hit, he passed to Elle and loosened his neckerchief. He held her hand, put it on his heart, and said, "I would do anything for you."

After taking a lungful of smoke, she replied with a sheepish grin and a laugh, "Then let's make love right here."

Diane was not in the mood to watch this, so she quietly said to me, "Let's take a walk before we go inside," then pointed upward at a sky full of storm clouds that seemed to be filled with thunder and rain.

Paul and Elle didn't seem to mind us leaving. Diane took my hand and together we ran up a small hill behind the house.

"Did you ever read *Lady Chatterley's Lover*?"

"Line by line," I replied.

"Do you remember that one part where Oliver takes Constance from behind and mounts her like they were a pair of wild horses?"

"Yeah, I think so. What about it?"

"I don't know. It just popped into my mind."

In the distance, three horses were grazing in a meadow…and she began to run towards them…like long-lost friends.

I followed, right behind her…which then became a chase.

At first, I had to pursue her around a tree but then chased her down the other side of the hill where I finally caught her. We both fell over into a large patch of clover and we rolled several feet.

"Crimson and clover over and over!" she shouted out loud.

The same thought popped into my mind as I considered taking her from behind. It might have actually happened, but it began to rain.

We were laying there together in this empty green field...totally connected to each other. The rain was drenching us both, but it actually felt really good as we continued to lay there and feel the raindrops.

After a time, we returned to the cabin. Paul and Elle were nowhere in sight, so we went inside to get out of our wet clothes and to lay down.

I must have slept for over an hour. I dreamt that I was sitting on the white sandy banks of a desert river. It was warm and dry, and I could see desert shrubs in the distance of the river, but then, I saw *the Master* standing next to Dan, the horse. He looked at me with eyes that pierced deep into my soul, and proclaimed, *"The time is now."*

I felt completely content just sitting there in the blissfulness of his presence. With a look of great compassion, he said, *"I want you to tell the world what is happening because it will happen again."*

He reached out and gently touched my third eye in the middle of my forehead. At the point where he touched me, a white light entered my body and filled me with a gentle feeling of infinite divine love.

In a flash, I awoke feeling happy, but still tripping very heavily.

I didn't see Diane anywhere, but I wasn't worried. I decided to lay back down. I began to think about her and about the world.

For me, this had been a 'summer of love.' I also knew it wasn't just about this summer. It was about an entire saga that was being played out during this time in history. I felt as if *the Master* wanted me to write the story of what this whole thing was about. However, I didn't really understand what he meant or when I was supposed to do it.

Then, I felt myself rising up and away from my body. It was gentle at first, with the subtle presence of a brightness that seemed to be with me. Then, without any effort, I began climbing higher and higher.

The speed of my ascent accelerated. The light became ever brighter, and I flew at an astounding rate, faster than any plane could fly, while at the same time the light kept increasing in intensity.

I had never before seen or experienced anything that bright, yet it didn't hurt me in any way. I was fully conscious and awake as I moved without effort toward the light which had no center or outer boundary but seemed to be everywhere. It was within me and without me.

In an instant, a thought emerged into my awareness like a bubble rising from a pool of still water. It wasn't even a thought…it was an impulse, *almost a feeling*. I was afraid. It was that deep sort of fear like when something jumps out at you from the dark when there's no time to think, just a primal fear, and a fear of the unknown.

I had been conscious throughout the whole ordeal, but instantly it was over. I looked around and I saw that I was still on my bed. I could hear the creek across the road through the bedroom window. It felt good to be in the reassuring warmth of the house.

I sat up slightly…carefully resting upon one elbow, trying not to make any noise. I desperately wanted to tell Diane what had happened, but I didn't know where she was, so I went to find her.

She was in the front room asleep on the couch. I was careful not to wake her. She looked so beautiful in her restful slumber. Even when she is awake, she was the one who always turned heads whenever we walked into a room. I realized I was still very much in love with her.

A cool, spring breeze blew through the open window pushing one of the shutters closed. She stirred, drew a deep breath, and slowly opened her deep blue eyes. She looked a bit disoriented as if she didn't know where she was and said, "Where am I?"

"You're with me, babe!"

She shook her head back and forth and said, "Wow…that was so weird. I was dreaming when something woke me up."

She turned on her side so that she was facing me. She pushed her hair back over her shoulder and said, "I dreamed you moved away, and I tried to find you, but it was too late. Then, I went somewhere else."

"I had a really weird dream, too. At least…I think it was a dream."

I described to her what had happened in as much detail as I could remember but she seemed distracted. When I finished, she just looked away and said, "It sounds like the guy who's always got a joint on him."

"Are you talking about Ernie?"

"Yeah, that's him. He's got dark skin and a black afro hairdo."

"No, it wasn't Ernie. He was like a holy man from India, or maybe somewhere like that. I felt like I was his disciple."

"Fine, whatever," she said, sounding annoyed.

We had pretty much started to come down from the acid by now and Diane said she had to rush off to do something that she felt was more important than being right here with me. She left quickly, so then I was left alone to think about what had happened.

I didn't have a clue if it had been just a dream or something more. Over the next few years, my life was going to change in ways I could have never imagined. The experience I had that afternoon was only a mere foreshadowing of the magic that was to eventually come. In fact, it was several years later that I recognized the man I saw in that vision. He was one of the holiest avatars who has ever lived, *Sathya Sai Baba*.

By now, we had been there for almost a month, and it was time for us to leave and head back to Oakland. It had been a fucking incredible visit, and one of the best acid trips I had ever experienced. I was sure that my friends back in New York would never believe any of this.

I thanked Wavy Gravy for allowing the two of us to be a part of the Hog Farm…and told him I knew we were bound to meet again.

Before I left California that summer, the Beatles were scheduled to play their final live concert at Candlestick Park in San Francisco.

The four of them were being attacked by the press due to John's earlier statement about being more popular than Jesus Christ.

In every city they went, the press had a field day, and the headlines reflected a tired and somewhat bewildered group. It's no wonder they flew in and out so quickly and rode around in armored cars.

Their only official meeting with the press in San Francisco was a brief stop at the airport, but unofficially, there were rumors that some of the press people would be allowed backstage at the concert itself.

Since I was working with Don and his paper, "The Oracle," I was given a *press pass* and was allowed to hang out with the other reporters.

The stage was being erected on second base, and a chain-link fence surrounded the plywood stage, which would be taken down once the concert began. Fans had also gathered early in the afternoon to put up posters all around the infield to express their joy.

The Beatles' bus arrived at the ballpark early and caused a lot of commotion. I wasn't far away and ran to that end of the stadium where I could look down on the small crowd.

As the bus rolled in directly under me, I could see George Harrison raising his own camera to shoot a picture of the crowd. John was seated immediately behind George and the other two were still out of sight.

Once the bus came to a stop, the group was quickly hustled out and taken downstairs to The Giants' locker room. That was supposed to be their dressing room, and where they had agreed to meet with several reporters who had been following them for quite some time.

Fortunately, I was one of them.

Much to my surprise, John Lennon actually remembered me from the party that Diane and I had been to with Tom, and he graciously gave me a front-row seat ticket. Needless to say, it was a fantastic concert.

After all of the warm-up performances were done, the Beatles emerged from the Giants' dugout to take the stage. They walked out right in front of me, and from where I was sitting, I was probably one of the closest people taking photographs of the event.

In less than a half-hour…it was all over.

Without doing an encore, they ran back into the dugout, and this time got into an armored car. They were gone almost as quickly as they had arrived. That night was the last time that I, as well as many others, ever got to see the Beatles perform in person again.

Based upon the vision I had at the Hog Farm, I returned to Oakland and wrote a story in the Oracle calling this "The Summer of Love."

Much to everyone's surprise, the term caught on really fast.

From what I saw taking place in California, the flower children of our country were indeed creating a very "dropped out and tuned in" loving, sexual community, but I was very dismayed by what I saw, and it prompted me, even more, to go back to school and to finish fulfilling my vision for a creating a New World.

I was in search of finding some kind of happy medium between the conservative mind of mass consciousness, and the irresponsible bullshit found in the psychedelic community of transcendentalism, promoted by the self-proclaimed, media-fabricated shamans who were espousing the *be here now…tune-in, turn-on, drop-out and jerk-off* ideologies of the legendary Timothy Leary and Richard Alpert.

If all I have to do to find enlightenment… I said to myself…*is to go to India, find a guru, and sit next to his smelly feet, then I should go.*

Then perhaps…he might throw me a few crumbs of wisdom.

It was now the end of August, so I had to say goodbye to both my old and new friends…but I made a promise that I would try to return again over Christmas break. Diane understood that I had to go back and finish school…and she was all right with that.

"I never expected you to stay," she said. "I'm just glad that you were able to come back and see me. I've already found a place to live."

Just before I left, the U.S. Government announced a draft call for more than forty-six thousand more troops, just for October.

It was the highest one ever done so far.

I felt certain…that the next semester would be even more active than before…with anti-war and anti-draft protests and marches.

I was excited…and looked forward to it.

It Ain't Me Babe

You say you're looking for someone…
To pick you up each time you fall…
A lover for your life, and nothing more…
It ain't me babe, it ain't me you're looking for, babe…
(Artist: Bob Dylan)

It was late September in 1966 and time to be getting back to school. Newspapers reported forty percent of the U.S. population was under twenty-five years of age. Seventy million children from the post-war baby boom were now either teenagers or young adults, and the general feeling among them was not to trust anyone over thirty.

The new generation had moved away from the conservative fifties, but unlike the Beats, we'd become more empowered with the aid of the anti-war movement, the civil rights movement, LSD, and marijuana.

We were also developing revolutionary and evolutionary ways of thinking. In some areas, real change in the cultural fabric of American life was taking place. Many of us were no longer content to be images of the generation ahead of us. Instead, many young people who lived in America wanted radical change. It seemed as if the first stirring of another American Revolution was close at hand.

♥ ♥ ♥

I'd truly enjoyed being in the energy of that new, wild, and crazy California consciousness. The East Coast was beginning to catch on, but it just didn't have the same sense of freedom…or perhaps, it was the suicidal recklessness of the West Coast I found so appealing.

After all, people seemed to have no qualms about building houses on the sides of mountains that they knew would someday wash away or to live right on top of the San Andreas Fault line.

I looked forward to coming back for Christmas if I could, but my primary focus right now was to find an apartment in New York City.

Without much effort, I found a one-bedroom flat in the East Village on the third floor. It was already furnished with a double bed, a dresser, a desk, a couch, an end table, and a lamp. That was all I needed anyway. Donna was happy with it as well because we could now come here to make love...and not have to rely on going to Larry's or Arnold's.

I could tell that something had changed in our relationship. I didn't bother to ask if she had been sexually involved with anyone over the summer, and likewise, she didn't ask me. Donna was still my beautiful, brown-eyed girl, but I would not get jealous if she strayed off the path. However, she was still curious as to how I could afford an apartment, instead of staying in the dormitory for free with my scholarship.

I couldn't tell her the money had come from selling marijuana on campus, so I said that my family was supporting me in the same way Arnold's parents had. Donna was from Boston and her parents were supporting her, so it made sense, but I wasn't sure she believed me.

Interestingly, LSD became outlawed in the U.S. about the same time Walt Disney died, which was sad because everyone I knew had tripped out more than once while watching *Fantasia*. His studios in California had created the ultimate entertainment for hippie freaks long before the advent of psychedelic art. He truly had been a visionary.

In mid-September, U.S. planes accidentally bombed a friendly South Vietnamese village, killing twenty-eight women and children. Then, twenty U.S. soldiers died a week later while they were on patrol when an American fighter plane dropped napalm on them by mistake.

Two weeks later, the largest demonstration in the country so far took place. Fifteen thousand protesters marched down Fifth Avenue in New York City. Allen Ginsberg was there wearing a 'stars and stripes' hat like Uncle Sam...while objectors to the demonstration jeered and booed. Newspapers reported that the protest was a peaceful one, but for my friends and me, it was our first close encounter with the police.

There was only a small group of us, but we were separated from the others when we slipped into a side ally to light up a joint. A couple of mounted policemen saw us and decided to get tough. They wanted to get their rocks off that day by bashing our heads in.

After running behind buildings and hiding behind cars we were able to escape. When the coast was clear I mentioned to Drake that even though we were just smoking weed this encounter somehow reminded me of the Boston Tea Party, which had not only been a significant part of the American Revolution but an act of patriotism as well.

"Oh, hell yeah," he agreed. "Those tea-party people were really a bunch of potheads, you know...hell, I'll bet it wasn't even the price of tea they were protesting about. It was probably the price of marijuana. There's a lot about the history of our country that people don't realize."

Not only were the New York City police starting to kick everyone's ass, but cops all over the country were not taking any more shit from anyone because of all the rioting and violence that had previously sprung up in Watts and was now taking place throughout the South. Police and sheriffs all across the nation were extremely nervous about the civil rights movement. Over the next few months, it got especially rough, not only in New York City but also in California.

The young people of our promised land, both black and white, were becoming very angry and were just as fed up with the police as the police were with them. Many were starting to fight back.

The militant Black Panther Party had been formed by Huey Newton and Bobby Seale in Oakland, and branches were springing up on other college campuses. Students were prepared to take over the government. They were meeting and talking, trying to figure out ways to seize the administration buildings on campus as a symbol of student power.

Rioting was increasing in almost every city, both on the streets and on college campuses. At times, it seemed as though we were living in a country at war right here at home with regiments of National Guard troops standing on the corners of our major cities…holding rifles with bayonets. It may have been winter…but as each day was becoming shorter, the light was becoming dimmer. We were all getting worried because the melting pot of America was about to boil over.

FBI Chief, Edgar Hoover, said all the evidence had suggested that Lee Harvey Oswald acted alone in killing President Kennedy and wounding Texas Governor John Connelly, but Connelly swore he had been hit by a second bullet, not by the same bullet that had killed the President. Taped evidence showed Connelly was hit 1.3 seconds after Kennedy, but Oswald's rifle could only fire once every 2.3 seconds. Therefore, Connelly's bullet must have come from a second assassin.

"Life Magazine" demanded the case be reopened, and rumors were being spread that Kennedy had been murdered by the CIA because of his White House connections with the New York Mafia.

Shortly thereafter, Kennedy's secret lover, Marilyn Monroe, also died in what appeared to be an accidental drug overdose. However, we believed that Marilyn had been murdered because she knew too much. She was an actress who was very outspoken with the press and may have been considered to be too much of a risk.

Perhaps the CIA and the FBI thought she would spill the beans about Kennedy's Mafia connections, or about all of the wild sex parties going on at the White House that Kennedy shared with his close friend, Frank Sinatra, who was also believed to be involved with the Mafia.

Overseas, casualty reports showed that five thousand U.S. troops had been killed in Vietnam since the beginning of the year, and over thirty thousand U.S. troops had been wounded. The U.S. now had more than four-hundred-thousand military people fighting in Southeast Asia.

About halfway through the semester, Donna and I began seeing less and less of each other. Since she was an accounting major, she said she had to study longer hours than I did. However, I also knew that Kathy was there to take care of her…should she really need a friend.

My own sexual hunger was sporadically being fed because I'd often meet good-looking and rather uninhibited women while spending time hanging out with my beer-drinking friends, Scott, Bill, and Arnold, or with my pot-smoking buds, Gary, Larry, and Tomás.

For example, one afternoon Scott and I had just finished off a round of beer at a local Washington Square tavern. We were coming up the stairs to my apartment, but as we passed the second floor and turned to go up one more flight, a girl with long strawberry hair stuck her scantily clad body out from her door wearing nothing but a short black teddy.

She was older than us…close to thirty, and said her name was Jill.

After a short conversation, she then invited both of us to come back and see her *anytime we wanted*. When we got to my apartment, Scott immediately said that he wanted to go back down there right away.

"No," I reasoned, "she spoke to me first, so I should go first."

"I tell you what," he suggested. "We're friends, so why don't we stop arguing…and both just do her together?"

Jill seemed to enjoy taking us both on, one after the other, giving each of us a short rest in between trying to please her. As for me, it was my first experience with someone who was a true nymphomaniac.

Gary was considered to be '*a square*' (which by today's standards meant a '*geeky-looking*' kind of dude). His cousin, Larry, however, had most certainly become an official hippie, with his medium-length beard and long brown hair. He was a very handsome man, and never had any problem meeting hippie chicks...or getting laid.

One time, I went to Larry's apartment and found him in the bathtub with three naked girls, and they were all sharing a joint. Immediately, the four of them invited me to climb in with them...so I did.

I can't explain...how five grown naked people were able to fit into that bathtub. Then again, how do ten people fit into a telephone booth, or...how do twenty people fit into a Volkswagen Beetle?

Somehow, we just did it...with the help of a bottle of baby oil.

There was also a girl I met that semester named Patty.

She was a tall, blonde-haired freshman who always sat next to me in American History class. Patty was married to a medical student who was working some very long thirty-six-hour shifts.

We had some verbal foreplay in class, and then a discussion in the coffee shop afterward. She told me...she'd only had sex with one man in her entire twenty years of life, and that was with her husband.

She said...she wanted to see '*what it was like*' with someone else.

I was happy to oblige her...right after class, every week.

It was a lustful relationship that went on...the entire semester.

Sexual incidents seemed to be a naturally occurring organic event.

I didn't try to make them happen, but when the prospect came up, I allowed myself to experience them. It was as though '*free love*' had taken a hold on the consciousness of our nation. It wasn't just for those who were involved in the '*peace and love movement*,' but for everyone.

It seemed…sex had become 'a new realization' within itself.

I suppose I did feel a little guilt about hiding all of this from Donna and knew I wouldn't be able to keep up the deceit much longer.

Soon, I would have to make a decision…either become a faithful lover…or let her go. I'm pretty sure…I already knew the answer.

LSD was now illegal, so the subculture that made up the drug-using community began to branch out and try different things. Among those were drugs like speed, cocaine, and heroin. For the hippies, those drugs were not the drug of choice because hippies were more into drugs that expanded consciousness, not the ones that stole a part of your soul.

Therefore, hallucinogenic drugs like mescaline and psilocybin started to become very popular with us. For those who don't know a lot about the various drugs that were being used back in those days, I'll tell you what I experienced, but please understand that this is simply from my personal point of view. It is not to be taken as gospel, for I'm sure that many people would not agree with all of my revelations.

First, let's briefly talk about drugs in general.

I believe that everything was put upon our planet for a purpose and for our benefit, and anything or any experience can be viewed as being positive or negative. These are simply judgments and are nothing more than one's individual experience. They're personal and subjective and dependent upon the individuated consciousness of that experience.

Positive experiences result from one's *intended* use, while negative experiences result from one's *unintended* use.

Unintended use might cause you to feel out of balance, or if you are already depressed, it can make you feel even more depressed.

If you look at history, hallucinogenic drugs should not be outlawed (*in my opinion*). Over the centuries, men and women of great wisdom, including medicine men, shamans, priests, warriors, and holy men, have used mind-expanding drugs to enter altered states…to heal the members of their tribe, to gain wisdom, knowledge, or personal power, and to defeat their enemies. So really, the use of these drugs is not new, and when used with the proper intent, honor, and respect, they can be beneficial to your mental, emotional, and spiritual growth. However, in our country, there are a lot of unwritten laws about using drugs…like, *"If it's fun, or feels too good…then, it should be illegal."*

Granted, there will always be those who abuse drugs, and yes, there have been those who have overdosed or tried to commit suicide while taking some drugs, but these kinds of incidents are more likely to be seen with prescription-type drugs, like tranquilizers and sleeping pills.

The number of people who have experienced a so-called, 'bad trip' on LSD, mescaline, psilocybin, or other hallucinogenic drugs, are few and far between, especially when compared to the amount of drug use that's involved in our country either back then, or even today.

The police, and other anti-drug factions of the establishment, will often take one or two isolated incidents of abuse and try to place that guilt upon everyone else. If the establishment wants to control the more dangerous substances, like cocaine and heroin, that's fine…since those drugs create chemical addictions, which are medical conditions, which then begs the question…why should someone have to go to prison for five years or more…simply because they have a medical problem?

LSD was a hallucinogenic drug that was created around the end of World War II in chemical laboratories by military scientists who were trying to create new formulas for a 'truth serum.'

It's taken orally, and the duration of the 'trip' is about eight to twelve hours. It takes about thirty minutes for the effects to begin.

However, different formulas cause different effects to occur.

Some forms of LSD are more visual than others. Some will actually cause muscle cramps, body rushes, or create hot and cold flashes.

The hallucinogenic experience is usually a combination of strong body rushes, visual stimulation, and mild hallucinations, accompanied by heightened awareness and a lot of mental gymnastics.

At first, everything seems to be funny...you can laugh your ass off at almost any little thing. Then, as the trip continues, your mind seems to expand so you 'see and understand' things in a whole new light.

If you hear a song, for example, you think that you understand the original meaning of the song from the mind of its artist. Everything you think about is suddenly seen in a new perspective.

As the trip wears down, some people feel a mild sense of fear and paranoia, but that usually occurs only if you've never tripped before.

It happens because the user doesn't understand what's happening.

The user may feel out of control, or that the trip will never end.

If you plan to take an acid trip, make sure you don't drive any sort of vehicle, don't walk around in scary neighborhoods, avoid the police, and allow for a full day to rest (that being, the next day).

Some of my most memorable trips were during the daylight hours in an outdoor park with my girlfriend, walking barefoot in the grass, rolling down hills, being close to nature, feeling the warmth of the sun while lying on a blanket...and then, to go back home and make love.

For me...they were 'the days of wine and roses.'

My worst trip was the time I was driving at night and the brakes on my car went out. Instead of leaving my car and walking, I tried to drive home, crossing intersections with what felt like...no brakes at all.

I had to drive very slowly...and use my emergency brake.

Somehow, I made it back, all in one piece.

Most of the fear involved from doing any kind of drug comes from the fear of not being in control, and this can scare people a lot.

That is…until they learn how to relax and just enjoy the ride.

What LSD tends to do is to amplify whatever mental state or mood you're in at the time. So if you are already in a loving and happy mood, then that is what's going to be magnified to a greater height.

A so-called "bad trip" would only occur if someone were already very depressed, then that would be amplified as well. So before you do any acid, make sure that you are in the proper frame of mind to do it.

Acid is literally a 'mind expanding' drug…so taking LSD with a spiritual intent is the most rewarding way to do it. If you are lucky, you might get to meet Jesus, God, Goddess, or who knows what.

Actual suicides from taking LSD are extremely rare, but once again, be forewarned, and only consider taking LSD if you are in a good mood and have a stable disposition at the time.

Being able to have orgasmic sex on any drug pretty much depends upon your personal physiological makeup. Some can and some can't. Just because you are feeling horny doesn't mean you can get off.

All drugs, even aspirin, can cause physical changes in your libido and physical metabolism. Some people are able to screw like rabbits on drugs, while others either just can't or just don't want to.

Some drugs make you feel extremely sexually stimulated, but you can become so over-stimulated that achieving an actual orgasm may become nearly impossible. All of our bodies are wired differently.

So for guys especially, don't get upset if you're feeling super horny but can't get an erection. For girls, have compassion for the guys….

For me personally, I found that most drugs affected my libido in a very positive way, and that's why some of my most memorable sexual adventures took place while I was on a drug-induced high.

By now, you're probably sick of hearing me talk about having great sex on drugs, but *understanding* sexual energy is important stuff.

There are many different types of energy in the world, but humans can only experience a limited number of those energies.

The highest vibratory energy available to humans is sexual energy, and the most famous of all has been called...*Kundalini energy*.

However, as the Kundalini energy travels up the spine from the root chakra, it then passes through the second chakra which is the center where sexual energy tends to be released during an orgasm.

If it is not released through an orgasm, and if it consciously moves upwards with proper intent into the higher chakras along the spine, then Kundalini energy can be used for great transformational power.

Some ancient traditions believe the Kundalini energy can even be used in ways that some would call *sexual magic*.

This is one of the reasons why the energies of 'power and sex' will often work together, hand-in-hand. Sometimes, sex becomes power.

Hallucinogenic drugs can amplify sexual energy so intensely that even if one doesn't know how to consciously move that energy up the spine and into the higher chakras, it doesn't matter. Just being able to *feel the intensity* of the energy as it emanates from the sexual center is often enough to experience the *power* of the energy itself.

A second drug that was very popular in the Sixties was mescaline. This is the chemical derivative of peyote, a plant native to Mexico and certain parts of the southwestern United States and can be natural or synthetic. Mescaline is a hallucinogenic, somewhat similar to LSD, and it does cause stomach cramping. Some people report having contact with beings from the spirit world when they are on mescaline.

Carlos Castaneda was a popular author back then who wrote about the Yaqui Indian tribes of Mexico. He reported that by ingesting peyote buttons, he would contact a spirit-being called *Mescalito*, who could be called upon to create both power and magic.

Psilocybin is a chemical derivative of psychedelic mushrooms and can be taken orally, made into a tea, or smoked in a pipe.

Drinking them in a tea…was always my favorite.

The mushrooms themselves can easily be grown in your own dark basement if you have the correct spores. The psychedelic effects of psilocybin are also similar to LSD, but I've found it to be a much smoother trip with fewer stomach cramps and gentler body sensations.

It's a more relaxed high but still allows you to hallucinate. Also known as "shrooms," they sometimes cause one to have an out-of-body experience. If you want to travel around the universe and visit other planets, mushrooms are the best way to go.

Marijuana is mind-altering but is not hallucinogenic. The buds and leaves of the plant are smoked like tobacco in cigarette papers or pipes, but you can also use it to make tea, mix with brownies, or add it to any kind of food. There are also varying degrees of potency for marijuana.

Depending upon the variety, some of the plants are mild, and others can be powerful. The effects of smoking pot are almost instantaneous, whereas ingestion through the stomach may take up to an hour or more. The more often you get high, however, the more you learn to be in control, and the effects diminish somewhat.

Many first-time users may feel very much out of control, but with continued practice, you can stay pretty much stoned around the clock if you want to and still be able to function in the world.

Marijuana is also a natural painkiller that has helped people who have cancer. For that reason alone, it should be legal. The only negative aspect of marijuana that research has shown so far…is that with too much use, some people can become lethargic, or just plain lazy.

So tell me…what's wrong with that?

In the mid-Sixties, possession of marijuana could get you a ten-year prison sentence, but now...marijuana is legal in some states or allowed for medical purposes in others, but across the board, possession is only a misdemeanor offense that only carries a small fine.

Someday...marijuana will be legal in all fifty states.

Hashish is a chemical derivative of the marijuana plant and looks like a dark crumbled resin-type-of-substance, and because of its coarse texture, hashish (or hash) is usually smoked in a pipe.

Hashish is stronger than marijuana and puts you into more of a dream-like state. It's also more likely to put you into an *'out-of-body'* state because the duration of the high is much longer.

Hashish is the drug of choice for the holy men of India who believe that simply by smoking it, they will become united with Lord Shiva. Many of India's *"Sadhus"* stay stoned twenty-four hours a day.

Opium is not as popular now as it used to be, but it's still used a lot in Asia, and it makes you have some really wild dreams.

It comes from the Poppy plant, which is also well-known for its medicinal purposes. Traditionally, dry opium was considered to be an astringent, an analgesic, and a sedative. Poppy has also been used for toothaches and coughs. Opium, and other drugs derived from opium, are addictive and can have toxicological effects with extended use.

The opium that was used by the hippies was usually a black pasty substance, and almost always smoked. Opium is a drug that literally takes you out of your body. A hundred years ago it was used as a means of *'deep dreaming'* in China's once-famous "opium dens."

A war was fought between England and China from 1839 to 1860 because England wanted to continue shipping large quantities of opium to China from India, called, *'The Opium Wars'*...and China lost!

In my opinion, cocaine is the most abused and misunderstood drug in our society and is one of the world's most powerful stimulants of natural origin. South American Indians have used the leaves of the 'Erythroxylon-coca' plant for over five thousand years.

For the Indians, coca-chewing acts as a stimulant, promotes clarity of mind, and creates a positive mood. They also chew the leaves of the plant for social, mystical, medicinal, and religious purposes. In our own country, pain pills like hydrocodone and Lortab come from cocaine.

In its processed form, the white powder can be snorted nasally, smoked, or melted down and injected with a needle. Whichever way, the effects are almost instantaneous, and the drug is highly addictive.

"Crack," on the other hand, is the condensed form of cocaine, and is a more solid substance. It cannot be snorted but must be smoked or melted down. Crack is instantly addictive, because after the first initial high, the user is continually trying to get back to the original feeling that he or she experienced, and it just can't be accomplished.

Cocaine and crack can be very numbing to all parts of your body, including your mind, and sometimes when you're high, you may feel as though you can't move at all, but your body feels good all over.

Because it's a stimulant, cocaine can make you feel very horny but both men and women may find it extremely difficult to have an orgasm.

Too much cocaine can stimulate you enough to cause heart failure, especially for those who have a weakened heart condition, so everyone needs to be very careful about the quantity of cocaine consumed.

Heroin is not only highly addictive, but its use has become a serious problem in the United States. It's processed from morphine, a naturally occurring substance extracted from the seedpod of the Asian poppy.

It appears as a white powder and is often mistaken for cocaine.

Heroin abuse is associated with serious health conditions, including fatal overdoses, spontaneous abortions, and infectious diseases.

If you inject it...you can get HIV, AIDS, and hepatitis.

Another big problem with heroin is that it can take you right to the doorway of death...because death...can be a pleasurable experience.

It's the dying process that causes pain, not the moment of death.

When you reach *the doorway of death*, you experience an extremely pleasant mood and feeling. There's no longer pain when you reach it.

Heroin is an out-of-body experience that takes you right to that very edge of death...and why so many people overdose on the drug.

They find the experience so pleasurable, that in their altered state of consciousness, they won't return to this painful wretched world.

Instead, they choose to step through the doorway and go into the Realm of Death. It's a very dangerous drug so please, don't even try to experiment with it...and just stay away from it entirely.

What's the difference between opium, morphine, and heroin, you might ask? Opium is the pure form. Morphine is refined from opium. Heroin is a synthetic form of morphine. Most pain killers are opiates. The government ranks these drugs' medicinal quality with a schedule number. Opium and morphine are classified as *Schedule II drugs* which means they are very addictive but have pharmaceutical value and viable medical use, but heroin is a *Schedule I drug* which means that it's very addictive and has no pharmaceutical or medical value.

Lastly, there's methamphetamine, also called speed, ice, and crank. Other than potency, they're pretty much the same thing. Chemically, they're made from some pretty nasty stuff that's not good for you.

Speed is not hallucinogenic, but very euphoric and helps to remove physical pain. It gives you a giant boost of energy, dehydrates you, and inhibits your appetite, so you tend to lose a lot of weight.

When you're speeding, your brain is racing. Every problem you have seems to have a viable solution, or else they just don't matter.

Many times, even the most complicated situations have an answer because it simulates your brain to a level where you see the world from various points of view...or at least you think you do.

You believe you're having clarity of thought, but your brain is simply allowing you to think that everything is perfect, when in reality, it is not. On speed, your thought process may become irrational and get you into trouble. Doing something illegal might actually seem to be a good idea at the time, especially if you haven't slept for several days.

Isaac Newton said, "What goes up must come down."

That's what happens with speed, as well as with most drugs.

It might be a nice high while you're doing it, but the next day you're often irritable and the pain is back. Worst of all, you feel depressed and want to get high again...and so the vicious cycle continues.

In today's world, which is now the year 2015, there are a lot more drugs available than what we had in the Sixties. Things like ecstasy, ketamine, GHB, PCP, and bath salts...and the list just keeps growing. But I'm going to stop here because I don't know enough about them.

However, before leaving this subject I want to tell you about one of the mushroom experiences I had, just to try and describe how it felt to have a hallucination. This way, perhaps you won't have to do it too.

Even though I'd taken a lot of LSD in California, I'd never smoked a psychedelic drug before. Larry sold me some mushrooms that were reported to be very visual in nature, so I just had to try them.

He took one-third of an ounce, ground it up to a fine powder, and let it sit for twenty-four hours in one liter of anhydrous methanol.

Then he shook it several times.

Psilocybin extracts better in acidic conditions, so then he added a few drops of concentrated sulfuric acid as well.

The next day, and after a final shaking, Larry poured the solution through two coffee filters and allowed the substance to drip into a glass dish, and then set it out to evaporate over the next three days.

The extracted 'shroom powder' dried very quickly…until finally, there was only some off-white powder left in the dish. When it was scraped out, there it was…a 'pea-size pile' of flaky stuff.

It was a Monday, which was good because on Tuesday I only had night classes. I was alone at the time and had just returned from a class.

I put the powder in an aluminum foil pipe, held it next to a lighter, and started to suck. The smoke was thick, but not too hot, and only lasted a few seconds. Then, I lay back on my bed and held my breath.

Almost immediately I felt the effects. It was as if an immense wave of relaxation was hitting me. At that point, I closed my eyes and felt myself sinking into the incredible depth of my bed, and to me, it felt like being in a womb, warm, and caring. Then I exhaled, realizing that my body was starting to glow with some sort of strange energy.

After several minutes in this womb of life, visuals started to come, and I found myself exploring the evolution of man. Three-dimensional patterns danced on the ceiling from the light in the room, so I tried to figure out what culture they resembled and then related it to all of the things I knew about the people of those times.

Some of the patterns began to look like abstract drawings, as if they were from Africa, or perhaps early petroglyphs from cave drawings. Some even looked like ancient hieroglyphs or the lines found on rune stones discovered in early England. It was truly very fun and surprised me, but the super-fast come-on was almost nauseating.

My body was now buzzing with incredible new energy, and all of this happened within the first ten minutes.

Bringing myself back into the room, I smoked a little more of the powder and then lay back again as I held my breath. When I exhaled and opened my eyes, I was still very much in the living womb, so I tried to focus my attention on where I actually was. My imagination this time took me to a new universe, where my mind was searching out all of the living things that could be living there. It was as if the mushrooms were revealing to me all the life that is around us that cannot be seen.

At that point, I decided to get a grip on where I was before I became lost forever. At first, my room looked normal but then it changed again. I immediately sat up and looked at my watch to find out how long I'd been laying there. It seemed that only about thirty minutes had gone by as deduced from my instantaneous calculation. Looking at the watch again, I found that I had no idea what those numbers meant.

In fact, I didn't have any clue as to what I was doing, or why I was looking at my watch because the time we see on a clock was created four hundred years ago and was not a "true aspect" of anything.

This was followed by the experience of complete vision loss, but in retrospect, I must have blacked out because I sat up again abruptly.

When I opened my eyes this time, my room was totally warped.

The walls were flowing like ocean waves, and I enjoyed some simply awesome visuals of people and things that were repeatedly merging between the haunting shadows created by the slow-moving ceiling fan. And, oh yes…there was also a rather large mountain that seemed to be growing out of my wastebasket.

Then, I had one of those thought-loops which are so common to certain high-frequency experiences. I was thinking about something while lying down, but only a few seconds before I'd been sitting up, but then again…maybe I hadn't been sitting up. I couldn't remember.

It was very much like being in a dream within a dream. That is, you can't really tell if you're in the dream or not or if it was a dream at all.

As I started to watch my room again, I felt that my self-awareness was shrinking. This started to remind me a lot of Alice in Wonderland.

The last thing I recall…was lying back down on the bed with almost no difference in awareness between having my eyes open and having my eyes closed. I decided…my brain wasn't working anymore.

It seemed, that my connection to reality had been altered.

Then, I resurfaced a few minutes later. That was the weirdest part of all, for when I opened my eyes, everything was back to normal.

Obviously, there were still minor visuals going on like beautiful patterns appearing here and there, plus a few extra digits on my watch, but I was finally able to comprehend my surroundings again. However, this went away all too quickly. After an hour, I was left with nothing but a deep feeling of suggestibility. It was as if anything that wanted to enter my deepest subconscious could do it through my wide-open eyes.

Sometime later, I was looking in the mirror at my pupils and found them to be as big as I'd ever seen. It had been a wonderfully incredible day, but I should also add that there are no words to describe the full intensity and personal significance of that experience.

Furthermore, I never had to leave the apartment, which was good, because it could have taken hours to negotiate my way down the stairs.

My best advice to my readers is…*never, to try this alone.*

Time flew by fast, and before I knew it…December arrived.

Donna was going back to Boston to see her parents for Christmas right after exams were over. I decided to see my parents as well, but once Christmas Day had passed, I planned to return to the West Coast to see my friends for the two weeks before classes started again.

Something about California…was always calling me back.

However, before I left, thousands of Berkeley students boycotted their classes in protest of the war just before their school term ended.

I thought…it was a great idea and hoped to encourage the students at NYU to do the same thing next year…after I returned in January.

When I arrived in Oakland, I had almost no trouble finding Diane.

By now, she was well-known in the area and was once again living in some hovel of a house…that they called a commune.

It was obvious…she'd been doing a lot of cocaine, as well.

For the next two weeks, one of my friends at the Psychedelic Shop allowed me to stay in a vacant room he had available

Although Diane officially continued to live with her friends at the commune…we still managed to spend most of our time together.

Our relationship had become one of love, friendship, and mutual respect. I loved her immensely, and she was also one of my best friends, but I respected her space, physically, mentally, and emotionally.

On that New Year's Eve, I experienced something I would have never expected to happen. One of Diane's celebrity friends owned a yacht, and he invited a small group of people to go sailing with him on San Francisco Bay for the countdown. Everyone was going to drop acid about two hours before midnight, celebrate the New Year, and just hang out on the boat until the next morning. It sounded like a great idea.

At eight o'clock we boarded the forty-five-foot yacht with ten other people. It was a little crowded inside, but somehow, we still managed.

I had never met any of these people before. One man was a writer, another was a movie producer, and some of the girls on board said they were up-and-coming actress wanna-bees.

The owner of the yacht was Marco, a successful drug dealer who kept the other guys supplied with plenty of stash. Before he became successful at selling cocaine, Marco had owned an Italian Restaurant that was in the same neighborhood as the commune where Diane was living. I suppose that's how he got to know her and had introduced Diane to the harder drugs. Over time, they had remained friends.

Someone poured champagne into fine crystal glasses and served a plate of chocolate-covered strawberries…and then they began to pass around a couple of joints. The weather was nice, so most of the clothes were already coming off in a various mixture of tops and bottoms.

The people were all very nice and we got to know a little about each other, but I could see that these were well-to-do mainstream people who were not in the same mindset I was. They were not anti-war activists, radicals, hippies, or cultural revolutionaries, but were simply occupied and satisfied in time and space with the life they were living.

It took a while to adjust to that consciousness, but I actually found it to be a refreshing break from my reality, as I was used to being around people who bitched and complained about the establishment, and now here I was about to get all fucked up with the establishment itself.

To me, the boat felt crowded, with ten half-naked people on board, with a lot of uninvited touching, rubbing, and feeling going on.

The other five girls on the boat were all attractive, but Diane, in my opinion, was the best looking of all…and of course, the old guys were always grabbing at her whenever they wanted to cop a feel.

I had to tune into my resistance and try to 'let go' of any feelings about being jealous. After all, these were her friends, and I would be leaving again in two weeks anyway. The truth of the matter was that they had all probably fucked each other before, in one way or another.

Everything went like clockwork. By nine-thirty, we were far out into the Bay and getting close to the ocean. There were other boats around us but we found a secluded area near the far shore. Marco said that as long as we weren't too loud and stayed relatively inconspicuous there would be little chance of being boarded by a patrol boat.

If it did happen, he said…*just throw everything overboard.*

Around ten o'clock, Marco pulled out a black silk purse and dumped a large quantity of powdered cocaine onto the table down in the galley. I had never tried cocaine before, but I was already so high on weed and alcohol that getting even more fucked up really didn't matter, so I just watched how the others were doing it.

Marco took out a razor blade and skillfully chopped up the small lumps in the powder until the entire batch was like confectionary sugar, and then like a surgeon, he spread out twenty or more thin lines.

With the same razor, he cut a plastic straw about four inches long and proceeded to suck up two of the lines with a long and powerful snort. Then he passed the straw to the next person to do the same thing.

Not everyone indulged, but when I saw Diane go for it, I decided to join in as well. When it got to be my turn, I just snorted the first line of cocaine as the others had done. The inside of my nose began to burn almost instantly, and I made a grimacing face.

"Don't worry, that'll go away in just a few seconds," Diane said. "It's just cut with a little speed, that's all."

Within minutes, I could feel my body start to tingle and then found myself shifting to a whole new level. After that, I snorted up the second line as well, and then just lay back on the couch.

Just before eleven o'clock several of us dropped a tab of acid, all at the same time, and then washed it down with our favorite mixed drink.

Within half an hour we were all very fucked up.

In my opinion, we were lucky that no one fell overboard that night.

I seriously doubt that any of us could have saved anybody.

It became obvious that some of the folks were planning some kind of orgy, but it was way too crowded to be having sex inside the cabin.

Diane and I both agreed...*we weren't in the mood at the moment*, so we went up on top of the yacht to wait for midnight to approach.

There was no moon that night, so lying on the deck and facing the sky we could still see tons of stars, and being in the fucked-up condition that I was, they seemed to be dancing all around the sky.

The others came up on top right before the countdown to midnight just to watch the fireworks going off in the distance. There was also some talk about putting on party hats and making some noise as the New Year arrived, but the rest of what happened remains a fog.

And speaking of fogs...that took us all by surprise.

Shortly after the New Year's bash began, one of the biggest and thickest fogs I'd ever seen rolled in...so bad, you couldn't see anything anymore...so all of the partygoers went back inside except for us.

The fog became so thick that Marco had to find a place to anchor and said we would have to stay there until the fog lifted.

Diane and I remained on the top deck for the rest of the night and grooved to the music coming from down below.

I think the rest of the crew was actually having one hell of an orgy down there, but I had no desire to join in, and neither did she.

Apparently, they didn't seem to mind that we had left the party.

By the time morning arrived, Diane and I had made love so many times my body had become a part of hers. Most of the others had come down from the effects of the night before and were either sleeping or simply lying still. Marco, however, managed to come up onto the deck, hoisted the anchor with an electric winch, lifted the sails...and then took us back to the dock where we finally arrived at ten o'clock.

Along the way, I mentioned to Marco some of the things I'd been involved with at NYU. I also explained that I was selling pot to other students and was getting pretty active in the anti-war movement.

He told me that one of his parents was Italian, but the other was from Bolivia, and he had grown up in South America. He said...he'd known many of the great revolutionaries during his life, but that sort of thing no longer interested him. Now, he was just into making money and was flying cocaine in from Mexico every month.

He also told me…that he could get guns and weapons to arm the students…if anyone wanted to buy them.

It only took a moment to consider it before I said, "No thanks."

"But why not? You just said that you were a revolutionary."

"What I said was I wanted to create a revolution of consciousness. Don't you see? It's about creating a revolution of love in this country."

Then I remembered the sign Rosie had on her surfboard, and said, "Going to war to create peace is like fucking in the name of virginity." Marco just laughed and shook his head.

Talk about grooving on a Sunday afternoon, I'll never forget the first-ever '*Human Be-In*' held in Golden Gate Park. I didn't need to be back in New York until the following week, so the timing was perfect.

It was scheduled to be held on January 14, 1967, but The Diggers were suspicious of the event, as they were with anything that involved consumer groups. To them, it was just another calculated way of getting free publicity by the "hip" merchants on Haight Street.

Nonetheless, they still wound up supporting it because most of the 'hip' merchants had agreed to supply free food and other free things. Even the Pranksters agreed to supply ten thousand tabs of acid, which they called 'white lightning,' along with seventy-five turkeys to cook that was pretty close to twenty pounds each.

The *Be-In* was an organized event that first started off with a press conference, posters, and press releases, and then with the support of the Oracle Newspaper, as well as by word of mouth.

In one article, Don wrote, "*The spiritual revolution will be manifest and proven. In unity, we'll shower the country with waves of ecstasy and purification. Fear will be washed away, and ignorance exposed to sunlight. Profits and empire will die on deserted beaches, and violence will be submerged and transmuted in rhythm and dancing."*

He thought it was quite prophetic.

♥ ♥ ♥

As a result of all the successful advertising, over thirty-thousand hippies converged on San Francisco for 'a gathering of the tribes.'

It was an open-air event that was located at the Golden Gate Park polo grounds. What made it so different from other gatherings was that the people were not there to protest anything. They had no demands to make that day, and it was simply a celebration of being together.

Best of all, it was free, but The Diggers were opposed to having a stage full of self-appointed gurus, as well as the fact that there were very few non-white people who had assumed any kind of leadership.

People of notoriety included Allen Ginsberg, who was dressed in a long white garment from India, Gary Snyder blowing his now-famous conch, and an up-and-coming radical yippie named, Jerry Rubin.

Also, and much to my surprise, Timothy Leary was there.

For those who don't know, the press had coined the term *'Yippie'* to describe any hippie who believed in taking violence to the streets.

Ginsberg began the celebration and chanted the *'Hari Om Shiva'* mantra as a gift to the God of the hashish smokers, while Snyder played the background music. Jerry Rubin then tried to explain to the crowd that a yippie was nothing more than a cultural revolutionary hippie and called for a marriage between the Berkeley and Haight-Ashbury tribes.

Leary was tripping so hard that all he could do was to smile really big and say to the crowd, "Hey, dudes! Turn on, tune in, and drop out."

Entertainment was supplied by *The Talking Heads, Moby Grape, Sopwith Camel, The Chosen Few,* and *Jefferson Airplane.*

Because we were already close friends with some of the bands who were there, Diane and I were able to be right up on the main stage and spent a good part of the day passing out turkey sandwiches and tabs of white lightning to anyone who wanted any.

One thing I didn't care for was the fact that the stage's generator truck was being guarded by some of the Hell's Angels because earlier someone had tried to cut the power lines. I had never believed that Hell's Angels represented the hippie culture, and I didn't trust them.

In the field, there were girls in long dresses and miniskirts, people wearing masks, stovepipe hats, leather capes, feathers, body paint, and see-through tops. There were mothers with babies, fathers were with babies, and children with kittens. There were people with tarot cards, kids blowing bubbles, astrologers, Sufi dancers, Hare Krishna chanters, jugglers, and balloons. Some people were high on marijuana, and a lot of people were high on the free acid that was being distributed.

At one point, a single-engine airplane flew overhead and someone in a radiant golden-colored jumpsuit parachuted out and landed in the nearby meadow. The rumor quickly began to spread that everyone had just witnessed *the second coming of Jesus Christ*.

Diane knew I'd be soon leaving to return to school, but sadly asked, "Why do you have to leave again? Why can't you stay forever?"

"I mean, we're good together. When you're here, everything seems to click, but when you're not…I feel like I'm floating in outer space, with nowhere to put my feet, and I feel so totally lost."

As I looked into her sad blue eyes, all I could think of to say was the words from a famous song by Sonny and Cher.

I'm not the one you want, babe. I'm not the one you need.

"But…why aren't you *the one*?" she asked.

"Because I'll only let you down."

Inside, I was feeling as though I was made of stone.

"What do you mean?" she asked again, wanting a better answer.

"You're looking for someone who'll come each time you call and pick you up every time you stumble, but I'm on a mission. You know, I've got this idea in my head...that maybe someday I could become the King of Iceland or some bullshit like that. So let's just keep things the way they are for now and try not to put a definition on it.

"Trust me, it's all good."

"All right," she said with a frown, "but promise you'll come back next summer. I don't know where I'll be, but I know you'll find me."

"I promise," was my reply, not knowing if I would actually keep it.

The new year of 1967 started off with a lot of things for people to talk about. A former actor, Ronald Reagan, became the Governor of California, and a pro-segregationist leader, Lester Maddox, became the Governor of Georgia. *The Beach Boys* band lead guitarist, Carl Wilson, refused to comply with a draft notice to enlist into the military and was charged with draft evasion. Open rebellion against Mao Tse-tung broke out in China, but worst of all, three U.S. astronauts were killed due to a fire in the cockpit. Gus Grissom, Edward White, and Roger Chaffee, all died while still sitting on the *Apollo-1* launch pad.

For the hippies of San Francisco, *the Human-Be-In*...that we'd held at Golden Gate Park, was a grand success...and everyone talked about it for months. The tribes had come together, united in peace, and joined together by love. It seemed...they were finally ready.

It was very possible that the coming year, 1967...for those who had more militant intentions...*would possibly be the perfect time for a new American Revolution to finally begin*...and I wasn't the only one who felt that way...you could actually feel it in the air. Something big was about to happen...but how would it come about, as the energy of love, or the energy of war? The question was...would the energy of love win over the energy of fear? All I could do...was to hope that it would.

Parsley, Sage, Rosemary, and Thyme

Are you going to Scarborough Fair?
Parsley, sage, rosemary, and thyme…
Remember me to the one who lives there…
She once was a true love of mine…
(Artist: Simon and Garfunkel)

♥ ♥ ♥

In California, you could frolic in the parks for most of the year, but not for those who lived on the east coast. Because 1967 turned out to be a very cold New York City winter, the more hardened species of the counterculture were centered near Greenwich Village and Tompkins's Square Park. This winter, like most, the Hotel Chelsea would be filled with writers, poets, filmmakers, and musicians. It was the same hotel where Bob Dylan had lived for a while, as well as Andy Warhol.

It was now January. Frank Zappa, and his *Mothers of Invention*, had just arrived to do a gig at the old Garrick Theater on Bleecker Street. Jim Morrison and Jimi Hendrix also came into town for a while, and everyone stayed at the well-known Hotel Chelsea.

Because I already knew Jim from California and had met Jimi the previous year in the Village, I took a chance and tried calling Morrison.

Fortunately, he was in his room recovering from a hangover.

Jim remembered me from our conversations in the park with Diane and told me how much he had enjoyed it. He also said that since it was a Monday night, most of the musicians were free that evening and that he and Hendrix, and perhaps Zappa, would be going out on the town for a night of boozing and whatever, and invited me to come along.

He also said I could bring someone else if I wanted. I called Drake and asked him if he would like to spend the evening with me, Jim, Jimi, and Frank, and of course…he absolutely crapped in his pants.

♥ ♥ ♥

We met in the lobby of the hotel and almost immediately began to share a joint. Here we were, surrounded by some of the greatest minds, philosophers, poets, and musicians of our time, and we were going out on the town with them to have fun and getting stoned as well.

We wound up going to a new bar called 'Sticky Fingers' where my friend Eddie was playing, so I knew the music would be good and not too loud. Once we arrived, we had a few beers, another joint, and began some heavy conversation about what was going on in America.

There were at least three different levels of awareness going on about the climate in our country among the hippies. The first two were a dichotomy, either to be in favor of love, peace, and passive resistance or to have an armed revolution. However, there was also a third, which was about wanting to escape and to just somehow disappear.

After a while, everyone was pretty high and fucked up...

"What I think we need is to pull the entire underground movement together. You know, have another gathering of the tribes like they did in California, but this time for the whole country," Drake explained.

"And how would you do that?" asked Jimi.

"What you guys need to do is to really make a statement about the new consciousness with a huge outdoor concert where the countryside is beautiful. To hold a magnificent '*Be-In,*' where everyone…hippies, yippies, and even those still uncertain about their politics…could meet together for three or four days of nothing but peace, love, and music.

"There would be no anti-war demonstrations, just a lot of acid, a lot of people getting fucked up, and everyone just spending time moving and grooving on the music while getting high living on the land.

"That would not only change lives but would also scare the hell out of the establishment if they saw such a united force. If they even dared to try and bust up that party, we'd easily have them outnumbered."

Jim replied, "Yeah, that's a pretty far-out thought, man. You know, rock and roll is the new way of communicating for our generation."

"You're saying…if you just believe in rock and roll, then music can save your mortal soul," noted Jimi. "Or…do you believe in magic?"

"I'm saying…that I believe in the magic of a young girl's soul, and I believe in the magic of rock and roll. And therefore, I believe that the magic of the music can set you free," Morrison answered.

Zappa intervened and said, "I've been smiling lately and dreaming about the world as one, and I believe that someday it's going to come. Personally, I think that to have this big concert thing is a good idea, but I don't think it will ultimately change a god-damn thing. Change has to be organic and natural…*you just can't fucking force it to happen.*"

"We all create our own reality," I said back to him, "so three billion people on the planet means three billion realities. I'm just beginning to see that the trees are drawing us near, and now I've got to find out why. I think a huge outdoor concert would be an incredible thing."

Drake then added, "Yeah, just a big gathering with no other agenda. Imagine no possessions…I wonder if you can…no need for greed or hunger, just a brotherhood of man. Imagine…if all the people were sharing all the world. That's what we need more than anything."

Then Jimi replied, "It's almost as though we're stardust, and we are golden, and now we've got to get ourselves back to the garden."

Morrison noted, "That's true, but not all things are known to us. There is *the lake of the known,* and there is *the lake of the unknown.* Most of the time we are in between doorways that lead to the evolution of consciousness. If our music aims to achieve anything, it's to deliver people from their limited ways of how they see and feel the illusion.

"We're going to have to keep the music alive if we're ever going to make this world happen. Let's do it, man, let's do that damn concert."

"I hear you, dude," said Hendrix. "What we have to do, you know, is to continue to carry on, because love is coming. Yes, brothers, love is coming to us all, and baby, *love is all you need.*"

Drake responded, "What you're saying…*is give peace a chance.*"

Frank then interjected, "Just because a man's hair is long and he has that Jesus Christ look, and he's wearing the same costume of clothes that we do, we still have to question if he has a new tolerance, and what his attitude is toward all those who are still struggling in the old political ways. Just look, it's all dying. If you believe there's justice, well, I've got news for you…it's dying, too. If you believe in freedom, it's also dying. If you believe a man should be able to live his own life, it's also dying. Forget rules and regulations, who the fuck needs them? I say open up the door and just leave. For me, that's what I plan to do. I've got to get back to the land and set my soul free."

Jimi quickly responded, "Nah, man, don't you see? There's a time for love, a time for hate, and a time for peace. I swear it's not too late. We really can change the world…we just need to be in unity to do it."

"You know…we all want to change the world," said Morrison.

"I just don't know," Frank noted, "My philosophy is, *live for today*, because chances are…no one will ever give peace a fucking chance. That's just some pipe-dream that some of you still have."

"Well, if the button is pushed…then there'll be no running away. There'll be no one to save with the whole world in a grave," I replied. "That's exactly why we all just have to keep trying."

"You're right," said Zappa. "But tell me…just what does any of this have to do with the price of parsley, sage, rosemary, and thyme?"

"Where do you think we're going anyway, Scarborough Fair?

"People in power will not ever disappear voluntarily.

"Young girls giving flowers to cops and soldiers just doesn't work anymore because their thinking is fostered by the establishment.

"They'd like nothing better…than to squash everyone involved in the peace, love, and nonviolence movements, altogether.

"Besides," Jimi added, "They can't get a handle on our new sexual revolution at all. It scares them. The only way I want to see cops get flowers is with a flowerpot being thrown down from a high window."

Morrison mumbled, "What in the world ever became of sweet baby Jane? She lost her sparkle, and now she ain't the same. She's living on reds, vitamin C, and cocaine. All I can say is, *ain't it a shame?*"

Drake interjected, "Like the Dow Jones Chemical Company says: '*Better living through chemistry.*' Drugs will get you through times of no money better than money will get you through times of no drugs."

Hendrix responded, "It seems to me, that lately, things don't seem the same. Businessmen, they try to drink my wine, and then they want to taste my herb. Everyone is just acting funny, and I don't know why. So, excuse me…while I kiss the sky."

"Are you doing that purple haze shit again?" Zappa retorted.

Then, he looked at all of us like we were crazy and wondered why everyone was now talking about drugs instead of the big concert.

"Remember, my friends," he said. "Yes, a war could create the end of time…but to turn the Earth back to sand would not be a crime!"

Drake then answered, "Forget about war…what we need right now in this country is a revolution of love. Never doubt that it only takes just a small group of thoughtful and committed citizens to change the world, and in fact…it's the only thing that ever has."

Morrison quickly replied, "Yeah, but there can't ever be any kind of large-scale revolution until there's a personal revolution happening on an individual level. That's got to happen first…inside of everyone. It happens one by one by one, then it becomes one with one."

"Then you finally get to the hundredth fucking monkey," I added, "and eventually everyone gets it, dig? Then the revolution succeeds."

And so the night went on, and on, and on. Eddie finally got up onto the stage and played his tunes, then Jim got up and asked to use Eddie's band to introduce his newest release, *Wintertime Love*.

We closed out the revelry that night when everyone joined in with Manfred Mann's *Do-Wah-Diddy*, and Bob Dylan's *The Mighty Quinn*.

Just before sunrise, Frank picked up the tab for all of us, and then like vampires, we headed home to get some sleep. On the way back we ignored the frosty morning air by singing, *A Hazy Shade of Winter*.

It had been an extraordinary evening with some wonderful friends.

My relationship with Donna continued to have its ups and downs, and so did my studies. I was doing well in school but needed something to make me stand out from the other students because I was seriously considering the possibility of graduate school.

Up to now, as far as my involvement with the anti-war movement was concerned, I'd always been in the backdrop of what was going on.

I'd never stepped in, spoke out, or stood up...to become one of the leaders of the underground movement. It was because of the question, *"Did I want to be on the front line...and a part of something...that was starting to become increasingly violent and militant?"*

My objective was to have peace, not to have war...but it almost seemed that in order to become recognized as one of the movement leaders you had to be a strong advocate of some kind of aggressive, activist behavior, which the establishment would always interpret as being violent, or at least being presented with hostile intentions.

Why couldn't the people of the world see peace and war for what they were? It seemed to me that peace, if it were ever going to exist, would not be based on the fear of war, but on the love of peace itself.

It would not be about abstaining, or *not doing* any particular act, but being in a state of consciousness. Until that time came, the human race didn't stand a chance of ever having real peace in the world.

♥ ♥ ♥

Donna once said that coming out of the closet about who you really are is both a courageous and spiritual act, just as she had come out of the closet about her bisexuality. If that were true, and if I was claiming to be an activist for peace...*then the things I do should all be peaceful.*

However, I hadn't been completely honest with Donna about some of my sexual diversions, but then again, she hadn't been completely honest with me either. Donna still didn't know anything about Diane, or about the other women. She didn't know I was selling weed, or about the occasional times I was getting high on LSD and mushrooms.

I never mentioned anything about her and Kathy's lesbian affairs on the side, and for all I knew she could be selling drugs, dropping acid, and bonking all the geeks in the chess club, for that matter.

Maybe we were both hiding some kind of a secret double life.

It was obvious that tension was building up between us. I couldn't put my finger on why but could feel it lurking in the shadows.

♥ ♥ ♥

The news of the Golden Gate Park 'Be-In' was exciting news to the tribes living on the East Coast, but the excitement quickly gave way to a winter of student discontent, and the offensive of even more fully confrontational student politics at NYU.

The most well-known student organizations at that time were the CEWV (Committee to End the War in Vietnam) and the Voice Party, the latter being heavily influenced by the International Socialist Party and the Free Speech Movement, which had begun at Berkeley.

Although Larry was not a student, he was a member of both groups. He told me that these organizations were targeting the University's links with the military, such as various Defense Department contracts, on-campus recruitment by war-related industry, the ROTC program, and the University's cooperation with the Selective Service.

He said…that the coalition groups were seriously considering some kind of possible retaliation that could cause a lot of damage.

I asked myself…*how was it possible for this generation, which is supposed to represent peace and love, to suddenly turn so militant?*

Activities on the NYU campus were beginning to heat up, although it really had nothing to with the war. In February of 1967, the students living on campus held a '*sit-in*' at the NYU Bookstore demanding that they lower prices, improve service, and form a cooperative.

Bookstore workers joined student pickets, bringing students and workers together for the first time. What the strike did was to further politicize the campus, which in turn gave many students the sense they actually held some power. The *sit-in* action was met with criticism by the administration, and some participants received letters of reprimand.

In March 1967, three hundred students turned out for a '*teach-in*' that was held to discuss certain issues about the war in Vietnam, and about university reform. The panelists debated America's involvement in the war, the University's participation in the war effort, and the NYU power structure, which was compared to the royalty of medieval times.

As spring approached, and after everyone saw how the *Be-In* from San Francisco had been such a success, the students of NYU and the hippies of New York City wanted to do one of their own. They decided to hold their own 'Be-In' on Easter Sunday in Central Park.

My job was to help spread the word. Once again, I used the help of Gary's printing press, and it was very successful. Over ten thousand East-Coast hippies celebrated the outdoors. It was fun, but nothing like the one in California, because so many people came to protest the war.

To me…*it didn't feel like a real unified gathering of the tribes.*

During April, plans to hold a huge national protest were already in their final stages at NYU so I began to get involved in the effort.

Students, teachers, and many non-students participated in a variety of activities that were designed to raise the level of campus awareness and participation by having open forums and discussions about the war in Vietnam. The purpose was to initiate as much student action against the war as possible. These included seminars, films, panel discussions, and theatrical performances. Our effort at NYU was a part of similar programs carried out at other campuses all across the country.

These local actions were to be the cornerstones for two massive demonstrations. They were to take place in both New York City and in San Francisco on April 15th. It would be sponsored by a new group I'd joined called the *Student Mobilization Committee.*

It was highly successful. More than two-hundred-thousand people protested in the two cities against the Vietnam War, but to our surprise, seventy thousand 'pro-Vietnam War' supporters countered by holding their own parade in New York City the very next month.

It was obvious that battle lines were being drawn, but for most of them, it wasn't about trying to escape as Zappa had suggested. Instead, it was about choosing between peace and war. *Would it be a revolution born of love…or a revolution based on fear and anger?*

I felt…most people didn't realize that a new American Revolution, was very close to happening…*and it was going to be armed.*

♥ ♥ ♥

The April 15th action had a tremendous impact on public opinion. Americans from all walks of life were beginning to dissent from the war which allowed opposition to the government to become legitimate. The demonstration spurred anti-war sentiment that had been growing over the last several months…including opposition within Congress.

What happened on April 15th was a demonstration by the anti-war movement that would allow people to see the wide breadth of the mass opposition to the war. More than any other single action before, the demonstration convinced a lot of new previously uninvolved groups to participate, and thereby furthered the anti-war movement.

The action was also a demonstration of unity and how consolidated the Student Mobilization Committee (SMC) had become. Our success turned the SMC into an authoritative national committee. It acquired the respect that was necessary to begin organizing the tens of thousands of student activists in a program of actions that were directly aimed at withdrawing the U.S. troops, abolishing the draft, and ending N.Y.U.'s complicity with the genocidal war of U.S. imperialism.

I actually gained some recognition as being one of the movement leaders, and many people were beginning to see me as one who knew what was *really happening*, both on and off campus. However, I was personally being forced into making a decision that I didn't want to make. That is…*was I going to take a stoic Gandhi-type-of-stance that embraced the notion of complete and total non-violence, or was I going to be pushed to the limit by the establishment and begin fighting back to defend my right to life, liberty, and the pursuit of happiness?*

♥ ♥ ♥

It had been a busy winter, and it was time to get back to California. The moment final exams were over…I was on the next flight out.

As for the rest of the world… Australia finally gave its indigenous Aborigine people the right to vote, and the famous revolutionary from Cuba, Ernesto Che Guevara, was killed in Bolivia.

The world's first successful heart transplant patient died thirty days after his operation, and the movie *Bonnie and Clyde* became a top box office hit. Seven thousand Black Power protesters had been arrested in Detroit after thirteen hundred buildings were burned to the ground.

The civil rights movement seemed to remain split over the issue of violence and non-violence. The establishment was still very much the establishment, and the law was as prejudiced and corrupt as ever.

People all over the country were now beginning to talk openly about the possibility of revolution…and *very seriously*, too.

The ugly paradigm of racism was at the forefront of just about every aspect of American life, but white society still seemed numb to it.

World heavyweight boxer, Muhammad Ali, refused induction into the Army after being drafted and said to the press, "Why should they ask me and other so-called negroes to put on a uniform, and then go ten thousand miles around the world to drop bombs on brown people in Vietnam when the so-called negro people in this country are all being treated like dogs…and being denied simple human rights?"

After that, the U.S. Boxing Commission then proceeded to strip him of his World Boxing Championship title….so Ali responded by saying, "I'm not going to miss fighting, you're the ones who will miss me."

President Johnson appointed the first black man in history to serve on the Supreme Court in an effort to ease black and white relations.

Very little changed, and racial tensions remained high. If only we'd changed the paradigm back then…*the world would be different now*.

Chairman Mao Tse-tung's '*Little Red Book*' of quotations about China's cultural revolution became the world's best-selling book but was instantly banned in the USA. So much for *freedom of the press.*

Robert Crumb's *Zap Magazine* became the first underground comic magazine, and the Beatles put out a revolutionary new sound of music with their new album, *Sgt. Pepper's Lonely Hearts Club Band.*

Meanwhile, the rest of America was in love with a new actor named Dustin Hoffman, and everyone flocked in record numbers to see the young college student in the midst of a steamy sexual affair with both Mrs. Robinson and her daughter in a movie called, *The Graduate.*

Sounds of Silence

Beneath the halo of a streetlamp…
I turn my collar to the cold and damp…
When my eyes were stabbed by the flash of a neon light…
That split the night, and touched the sound of silence…
(Artists: Simon and Garfunkel)

It seemed as though the energies were all in place for a revolution. In the summer of 1967, an isolated air strike sparked retaliation by Israel against several of its Arab neighbors in what was to become known as the '*Six-Day War.*' Israel easily won in only six days and captured extensive territory from Egypt, Jordan, and Syria, as well as all of Jerusalem, the West Bank, the Gaza Strip, and the Golan Heights.

China announced the explosion of its first hydrogen bomb, while at the same time…twenty-six countries and four-hundred-million people watched the Beatles perform their new song…*All You Need is Love* being broadcast from the roof of their Abbey Road Studios in London for a special television spectacular. Was '*Love*' really all we needed to survive as a planet? Obviously…there were many who doubted it.

After all, massive race riots had already begun to erupt in Detroit. They spread into Harlem and then into Birmingham…so by the time the summer of 1967 was over, rioting had taken place in one hundred and twenty-seven different U.S. cities…and a lot of people had died.

Black Power was beginning to win over any hope for non-violence within the civil rights movement, and hippies who were calling out for the world to love were struggling with the same indecision.

Would this revolution end with peace, or would it end with war? Many of those who wanted peace…believed they were about to lose, and that another armed American Revolution might be close at hand.

Those of us who believed in love had to remain impeccably vigilant to prevent being won over by those who claimed to be hippies but were advocating violence in the streets. Sometimes…our closest friends.

♥ ♥ ♥

As soon as the spring semester of school was finished it was time to say goodbye to Donna and my friends. I subleased my flat and flew out to San Francisco along with Eddie to spend the summer.

After finding a place to settle in, back in my old neighborhood, we rented a car for a few days and drove down to Monterey where a huge outdoor music festival had been planned for the weekend.

Eddie had actually been invited by Jim to be the backup drummer for *The Doors* because the regular drummer had injured his wrist and couldn't play for several more weeks. Once the concert was over, he and I would go our separate ways. Eddie was hoping that having played for Jim Morrison would open some doors of his own.

♥ ♥ ♥

I hadn't heard from Diane since January and didn't have any idea where she was living, but I figured it wouldn't be much of a problem finding her after the festival was over. I instinctively knew she would be waiting for me to come back, so I guess I was just relying on some kind of psychic telepathic connection to locate her.

People were saying that the '*Monterey International Pop Festival*' idea had been thought up by Alan Pariser, the heir to the 'Sweetheart' paper cup fortune. It sounded to me like Drake's idea…the one we'd discussed during our conversation with Hendrix, Zappa, and Morrison.

Alan had wanted the festival to be more than just a pop music show, so he used music that was popular among the hippies with the hope that it would become a more serious art form, and eventually take its place alongside blues and jazz. The festival itself was tailored like the one a year earlier at the fairgrounds in Monterey, California, which meant it was family-oriented with lots of vendors selling snow cones, popcorn, and cotton candy. It wasn't exactly a real gathering of the tribes.

Funds were raised for the concert, the site was established, and the idea that proceeds would go to charity was also adopted. On June 16th, what was now officially termed "The Summer of Love" was actually given birth. It made me feel good that my friends and I had planted the seeds for the name during the previous summer.

It was a long weekend filled with uniquely amazing sights, sounds, and experiences. Over two hundred thousand people gathered for the three-day-long celebration of music, peace, flower-power, and love. With the huge turnout of young people, there were also a lot of drugs.

Most of the performers agreed to appear for free, with only lodging and travel expenses provided. It was a time of reunion and discovery for both the performers and the audience. Funds raised by the festival went to *The Monterey Pop Foundation* to provide help for worthwhile causes, such as the Haight-Ashbury Free Medical Clinic.

Thirty-two bands appeared that weekend, which included the songs and music of India's Ravi Shankar, Janis Joplin, The Byrds, The Who, Canned Heat, the Mama and the Papas, Moby Grape, Jimi Hendrix, Country Joe and the Fish, Simon and Garfunkel…and Otis Redding.

It was the first time that many of the bands had actually met and were able to see each other perform. For many, it was also the first time they had performed in front of a large audience.

It seemed as though everyone was marveling about the fact that one good group after another appeared on stage. They had a backstage area where food was being cooked and served twenty-four hours a day, as people wandered around having a good time meeting each other.

Jimi Hendrix and Janis Joplin exploded onto the world scene with their intense performances…and the audience was absolutely shocked when Jimi set his guitar on fire after singing *Purple Haze*.

It was amazing to see how people could get together out here in California and have a good time, but on the East Coast, everything had to be so fucking serious. It was almost as though the consciousness of the people in New York just couldn't let go of that god-damn war even for just one weekend of peace, love, and music.

Ed and I wandered around the Fairgrounds area meeting the people, smoking pot, and even took time to roll down one of the grassy hills.

"Holy-moly," Ed yelled after rolling all the way to the bottom.

Then sitting up he said, "I agree with Drake's idea. We need to have an outdoor festival that's even bigger than this and with three times as many people but way out in the countryside in the middle of nowhere. I know it's going to happen, man, I can just feel it. Can you?"

Lying near the bottom of the grassy hill…*I knew she was there.*

Not far away, in a small grove of trees where people were camping next to a psychedelic Volkswagen minibus, I could see the outline of a slender body wearing blue-jean cut-offs. Instantly, I knew it was Diane.

She turned in my direction almost at the exact same time, feeling as though someone was watching her. Then she saw me as well.

"Andy!" she shouted. "*You found me!*"

Haight Street had changed a lot in only six months. It was much more crowded than it was before, with artists, poets, and runaways that looked like high school kids. It seemed as though they were competing to see who could wear the oddest and strangest outfits, not as a form of fashion, but more like beggars. Christian evangelists were on the street right next to the Hare Krishnas and the Moonies...and each of them was trying to convert some new arrival over to their side.

Besides all of the people claiming to be saviors of the world, there were also the usual UFO cults, head shops, and anti-war stuff going on almost everywhere. At times, the atmosphere was much like a medieval street fair, however, there was also more violence and danger.

Rape was becoming a common event...often occurring while a young girl was flat on her back after doing too many drugs. Whoever was with her at the time would simply take advantage of the situation. After all, this was *the free love generation*...so who would care?

Smoking pot and taking LSD was rampant, but the harder drugs were now beginning to take over. Drugs like cocaine, speed, and heroin were rapidly overtaking acid and pot as the drugs of choice.

Those who had become junkies to the harder drugs would do almost anything to get the money for their next hit.

It seemed as if there were more and more wide-eyed young people arriving each day from small-town America, many of whom had come from closely protected middle-class environments.

The Juvenile Justice Commission was returning over two hundred runaways a month to their parents from the Haight-Ashbury district alone, and many of them tried to fight it or just ran away again.

There was a twenty-four-hour switchboard that received hundreds of telephone calls each day from people looking for somewhere to stay or to get help for a bad drug trip – most of whom were naive youngsters who had flocked to San Francisco with flowers in their hair and looking to become one of the beautiful people.

Some of the underground newspapers printed lists with the names of the parents who had left messages for their runaway children.

Fortunately, there was the Haight-Ashbury Free Medical Clinic which was in dire need of the proceeds from the Monterey Pop Festival.

It was open twenty-four hours a day, was located on the corner of Haight and Clayton Street, and was staffed with thirty part-time doctors and nearly one hundred volunteers. Because most of the hippies had no other form of medical services available, and no insurance, the free clinic had become a real lifesaver for the community.

The newspapers said that over seventy-five thousand young people visited Haight-Ashbury that summer. To me, it was like a burned-out battlefield. Many of the old-time residents were now gone, including *The Grateful Dead*. Those still there…were thinking of moving out, either to the countryside or possibly to New Mexico, feeling as though the old hippie days would soon be over.

In August, George Harrison of *the Beatles* visited Haight Street and was booed by the crowd because he refused to sing for them.

George has always supported hippies because he was an acidhead himself, but he said these kids were "just a bunch of hideous, spotty little teenagers who were all terribly dirty and scruffy."

Police busts were beginning to occur regularly. On occasion, they would escalate into violence when someone in the crowd retaliated by throwing a beer bottle at the cops. Then, people would yell something at the cops like "Revolution!" or, perhaps, "Kill the pigs!"

Paranoia was striking deep, and into people's lives it would creep. There would be a man with a gun over there…who was telling them, "You have to beware." Then he'd start and make them afraid…and if they stepped out of line the man would take them away. So you came to know every sound, as everyone looked at what was going down.

One afternoon a band started to play in the middle of Haight Street, and spontaneously, a group of people began to dance…some taking off their clothes…that is, until the police arrived and stopped the music.

The people of the street became very disturbed and started throwing eggs and vegetables at them, but then more cops arrived, and even more violence broke out. As a result, over fifty people were arrested.

As I walked the streets of Haight Ashbury, I was seeing an entire generation being destroyed by the madness. Starving, hysterical, and naked young people were dragging themselves through the streets at the first light of dawn...already looking for another angry fix.

These young-haloed-hipsters yearned for just one more heavenly connection for the night, often just standing there in total poverty with tattered clothes and hollow eyes higher than California Redwoods.

Sitting up until the early hours of the dawn smoking dope within the supernatural darkness of their star-cooled-cold-water flats...while pretending to float across the tops of the city and contemplating the latest music and saying...*look at how cool all this fucking shit is!*

I often thought about ways to describe the situation, but then a song by Simon and Garfunkel came to mind, *Sounds of Silence.*

And in the naked light, I saw
Ten thousand people, maybe more.
People talking without speaking.
People hearing without listening.
People writing songs that voices would never share.
No one dared, to disturb the sounds...of silence

As for Diane, she was simply who she was...a tuned-in, turned-on, dropped-out hippie chick who was being passed around from one guy to another, and from commune to commune, or from band to band.

Out of pure compassion, I decided to enter her world again for a while and even allowed myself to get caught up in her habit of snorting cocaine on a daily basis. Instead of being outdoors in the sunlight, and tripping in the park as we used to, we would lay around the apartment and listen to music...sometimes almost in a comatose state and numb to the world without any quality of life. When it was time for me to return to school in late August, I was more than ready to leave.

♥ ♥ ♥

What I did accomplish during those several quiet weeks of being on such a laid-back cocaine high was a reassessment of my attitudes and values about my role in the anti-war and anti-draft effort.

I finally came to terms with my dilemma, as to whether I would continue to be an advocate for peace and love or give in to the growing militant attitude. What I saw going on all over Haight Street, as well as my own degeneration that summer, led me to make the decision to go ahead and veer away from my previous pacifist stance and to now take the position that if we were going to have a revolution, then it would have to be one of violence...*because it could not be won with flowers*.

Maybe the summer was just too hot, or maybe it was a side-effect of the drugs, but out of sheer frustration, I decided that when I returned to school in the fall...I'd participate more with the protest movement.

And if that meant becoming militant...then so be it.

After all, our country's founding fathers had been nothing but a bunch of pot-smoking junkies from the very beginning. At some point, they decided to put down the pipes and put on the war paint.

♥ ♥ ♥

I was looking forward to getting back to New York.

But when it came time for me to leave, there was nothing more than just a brief goodbye between me and Diane.

She got high that morning, although I'd told her several days in advance that I'd be leaving, she had already forgotten. But there were no tears this time. I'm not sure if she could feel much of anything.

In her usual manner, she chose to sing another song from the same play she'd previously said would soon be a Broadway hit.

She heard it from her celebrity friend who was a screenplay writer. This time she didn't really sing it out loud to me but just mumbled some of the words in her soft and sexy voice while looking right through me with her strung-out anorexic eyes. Diane seemed to be so out of it at times she had no idea what she was talking about. At first, it sounded like a lot of nonsense, but she continued to sing it as best she could:

"We starve, look…at one another short of breath, walking proudly in our winter coats, wearing smells from laboratories, facing a dying nation. A moving paper fantasy, listening for the new told lies, and with supreme visions of lonely tunes. We sing songs…on a spider web sitar, with life all around you, and in you…so let the sunshine in…all across the Atlantic Sea…because I'm a genius-genius, and I believe in God… and I believe that God believes in me. Yes, me! The rest is silence."

"What in hell message are you trying to say?" I asked.

"What I'm saying my love is just this…now that I've dropped out, life just seems so dreary…now please answer my weary query dearie, is it she or is it he…or is it me? Or could it be it or them?"

As far as I was concerned we were finished. I didn't see any reason to continue it. Diane had become just another one of those fucked-up hippie chicks. I grabbed my bag, kissed her on the forehead, and left.

From there, I took a taxi to the airport and returned to school for another semester, knowing I was leaving that midnight cocaine cowboy world behind for good…and never thought twice about going back.

As soon as I arrived on campus, I was ready to go to work but still felt regretful about having allowed myself to get caught up in Diane's world of depression and cocaine addiction. Immediately, I immersed myself more than ever into the energy of the school's anti-war politics.

We planned another massive rally to be held in October. Since the April 15th sentiment against the war had erupted with such explosive passion on campus, we hoped this march would manage to assert itself with even more waves of radical protest and passion. Most of us already knew that it might even result in militant confrontation by the police.

♥ ♥ ♥

As opposition to the Vietnam War deepened across the country, so did public sentiment against having a military draft in the United States. Although they were clearly two separate and distinct issues, it would be rare to find a person who just supported one…without the other.

The recent demonstration in April 1987 had not stressed adequate defiance against the issue of a draft. The new actions, which we began to plan for October, would now totally identify with both the general anti-war sentiment to withdraw the U.S. troops from overseas and our demands to end the military draft as well. Everyone involved with the anti-draft movement saw this as a progressive change for the better.

Although most of these actions revolved around opposition to both the war and the draft, many of the protests and demonstrations were simply against the current norms of society. Protest against the draft, however, had been a much-needed element of the anti-war movement's activities from the beginning, but was now becoming a major focus of both movements. No longer were we just saying, *bring the boys home*, but now we were attacking the military industrial machine itself.

When the anti-draft protests first began as an integral part of the anti-war movement in 1965, Students for a Democratic Society (SDS) and other pacifist leaders had expressly designed it to be an alternative to the development of a mass anti-war movement.

Back then, the isolated protest actions of some individuals were sometimes seen to be a counter-imposition that was in conflict with the anti-war demonstrations. For some organizers, becoming part of the anti-draft movement became an excuse for not wanting to participate in the wider anti-war actions that were taking place.

There was also the issue of money. If one person was raising cash for the anti-draft movement...and another was raising money for the anti-war movement, and someone threw twenty bucks on the table then which organization would get it? Now, it seemed that the two separate movements were finally coming together as one and the same.

Pursuant to the highly coordinated nationwide anti-war effort, there were demonstrations happening in California, Wisconsin, New York, and Washington, D.C., that all took place during October 1967.

This indicated a deep alienation from and active opposition to the evils of war. The demonstrations also expressed a healthy disregard and disrespect for the establishment in general and its institutions.

As anti-draft protests began to reach even larger proportions, they not only reflected the mass sentiment that existed against the war but became more and more in conflict with the state apparatus.

Military conscription has always been a basic tool for America's war-making ability, so they weren't likely to give it up easily.

Faced with all of the new mass opposition to the military draft, the government resorted to even more harsh measures against protesters, such as police brutality, retaliatory draft calls, and long prison terms. However, these repressions only served to intensify the mass protest of the activists even more and won even wider public support for them.

It was apparent...that the establishment was becoming worried.

The direct confrontation that ensued was just another expression of the heightened struggle against the imperialist American war machine. We decided that the job of the new anti-war militants was to organize this confrontation by integrating even more mass protests against the draft in conjunction with the general program of anti-war actions.

The October 1967 demonstrations were an overwhelming success indicating a big advance over the ones that took place in April.

The massive turnout was an embarrassment for the Lyndon Johnson presidential administration. No matter how much Johnson would have liked to prevent the demonstrations, or dampen their impact, he was unable to do so because anti-war sentiment existed at all levels in this country. Despite the urging of his advisers, Johnson did not dare stop the demonstration, but he did retaliate by imposing harsher methods of dealing with smaller and more manageable groups of protesters.

The outstanding characteristic of the marches in October was the militant mood of mass confrontation. When fifty-thousand people stood outside the Pentagon and cheered for a young man who broke through police lines, it indicated a deep defiance of the establishment.

One surprising development was the spontaneous attempt by a large number of activists to speak to the soldiers who were surrounding the Pentagon. They tried to talk with them about the war and the anti-war movement. Very quickly, a new cheer was addressed to these troops, one that was going to be heard a lot more often.

The crowd shouted, "Join us…join us…join us …!"

The authorities would like to have arrested many people that day but were prevented from doing so because of the size and militancy of the demonstrators. It became obvious that most of 'the establishment' was getting worried about the large number of protesters showing up.

Another aspect of the October actions was all of the international ramifications. Coordinated with the various Washington, New York, and San Francisco action committees, demonstrations also occurred in Europe, as well as in Chile, Australia, New Zealand, Japan, Hungary, and elsewhere. In some countries, the demonstrations were the largest and most militant since the end of World War II.

This was the greatest international demonstration in opposition to the Vietnam War held to date. Washington and the establishment were now feeling even more threatened because this new sentiment was now becoming an organized international anti-war movement.

The demonstrations were a preview for the organizers of what the anti-war and anti-draft movements were actually capable of.

In fact, the defiant and militant anti-war sentiment in this country was starting to reach massive proportions, and it seemed to be just a matter of time before the *boiling pot of America...blew up!*

What we also realized, was that actions challenging the war policy of the government...if they were planned correctly...could actually turn out masses of people in every major city in the country.

Some of the more radical political groups summed it up like this:

The evolution of our anti-war movement thus far is the outcome of internal struggles over the political perspectives of all Americans.

Soon, you'll see hundreds of thousands of U.S. citizens coming into the streets saying, 'No! We will not continue with this war any longer!

The myth that American politics rests upon permanent multi-class conformity has begun to crumble. Revolutionaries all over the world have drawn inspiration and encouragement from this new resurgence of radicalism and will continue to fight in their own countries.

Our attempts to find ways of turning this from 'mass action' to that of 'class action' will create even more pressure on the politics within the established order as democratic ideals are continually brought in as a part of the movement. But at each critical point in its development, both the anti-war and anti-draft movements must continue to manifest objectively in such a way that it always appeals to 'class sentiment,' rather than to expose the movement as one that might be perceived by the Wall Street bigots as being 'anti-imperialist' in character.

They also explained...that we must continue to have united mass demonstrations...if we were ever going to win the war here at home.

Once again, those famous words of the American Revolution rang truer than ever…that…*united we stand and divided we fall.*

The anti-war and anti-draft movements were helping to create huge dissonance all over the country, and yet it remained legitimate.

Public confidence in the government was now being shaken.

A precedent for aggressively disagreeing with and challenging the government was being permanently established in America.

The anti-war movement had finally brought into check the previous emergence of wartime hysteria and witch-hunt tactics orchestrated by our country's administration by capitalizing on the deep split which has always prevented the ruling class from uniting behind most war efforts.

We were helping to promote a spirit of domestic struggle during an imperialist war and were fighting a government that was hell-bent on seeking world domination. The fact that people all across the country were speaking out, and beginning to act in a radical manner, was having a profound effect on the political consciousness of those fundamentalist American people who still had a rather large stick up their butt.

We had now become part of an international anti-war movement, and that was forcing a shake up and realignment on a world scale that had the potential of preparing and promoting a mass radicalization of the entire country…*and now, there was no way to stop it.*

♥ ♥ ♥

In November, anti-war protesters in Washington clashed with the police outside the Pentagon and over six hundred people were arrested. In Berkeley, a small group of protesters actually bombed the local draft board office and somehow managed not to get caught after Governor Ronald Reagan called for a further escalation of the Vietnam War.

Also in November, former vice president Richard Nixon announced his plan to run for president in 1968 and was considered to be a Hawk.

In December, a fifty-three-year-old dying man, Louis Washansky, was given a new heart in what was billed as a revolutionary transplant operation in Cape Town, South Africa. Louis died soon afterward as a result of lung complications. However, it wasn't seen as a setback.

On New Year's Eve, Ho Chi Minh sent a New Year's greeting from Hanoi to all of the U.S. anti-war protesters, congratulating them.

By the end of the year, 1967, U.S. casualty reports showed that over seventeen thousand soldiers had died in Vietnam since 1961.

On a lighter note, the Beatles went to India and sat at the feet of a yogi with a long beard. While posing for cameras with *the Maharishi*, the notorious group told reporters...*they were becoming spiritual.*

Their latest film, *Magical Mystery Tour*, aired on the BBC network and got very disappointing reviews. Even the most devoted Beatles fans were turned off and confused by the seemingly pilotless plot.

The controversial musical, "Hair," opened at the end of the year in New York City at the Shakespeare Festival Public Theater. It was just as Diane predicted. Within a few months, it became a Broadway hit. To my surprise, much of the play reminded me of my life with Diane.

I decided to go home at the end of the semester to be with my family for the Christmas holidays, so I took the train back to Pennsylvania.

I was thankful that an actual armed revolution had not yet occurred, but something inside of me just knew the coming year of 1968 would bring even more demonstrations and violence. It was certainly possible *that this year might be the big one*...but hoped we could resist that kind of confrontation. I was already committed to being a part of the new American Revolution one way or another but like so many of the others I was prepared for the worst possible case scenario. All any of us could do was to pray that we wouldn't have to choose between peace or war, but could just experience a revolution of consciousness instead.

Fire and Rain

I've seen fire and I've seen rain...
I've seen sunny days that I thought would never end...
I've seen lonely times when I could not find a friend...
But I always thought that I'd see you again...
(Artist: James Taylor)

I agreed to spend New Year's Eve with Donna in order to try and get our relationship back on track so we both arrived back in New York a few days early. We decided to celebrate it with Tomás and Debbie and took a taxi into China Town for dinner. We were told...1968 would be the *Year of the Monkey*. That being the case, it didn't surprise me at all that the year would start off with a lot of monkey business.

A famous baby doctor, Benjamin Spock, was a national bestselling author, but he was being indicted for his anti-draft activities.

Even though the number of American military men in Vietnam now exceeded five-hundred-thousand troops, the Viet Cong launched the *Tet Offensive*...a big surprise to U.S. forces stationed in South Vietnam because the city of Saigon was directly hit. As a result, U.S. General William Westmoreland was sworn in as U.S. Army Chief of Staff and immediately requested that two-hundred-thousand additional troops be called up as reinforcements. It was a huge setback for the Unites States.

This year should have been named the *Year of the Goddess,* since women's liberation issues had become forefront, and joined in with the other violent political activism that was seen heating up day-by-day.

If you didn't watch out...*Goddess energy could be a real bitch!*

♥ ♥ ♥

Presidential Executive order 11246 prohibited any kind of sexual discrimination by any government contractors and required affirmative action plans for hiring women. For the first time in American history, a female teacher was allowed to teach while being visibly pregnant.

Even though men still referred to women as 'birds' and 'chicks,' or 'my old lady,' dresses were coming off, and women were beginning to wear trousers…as well as suits, which caused quite a sensation.

Mayday Magazine said, *"A whole new generation is finally getting an education about the new look for women…"*

Even the gay community was starting to come out of their closets and into the streets. Homosexuals were becoming more pro-active, in spite of the fact that straight Americans still felt threatened by them.

Sexual issues, as well as drugs, were becoming more prominent in movies. For example, Ringo (from The Beatles), starred as the gardener in the movie, *Candy*, which was about voyeuristic sex and LSD.

Michael Caine starred in the movie, *Alfie*. It not only took on the subject of sex with no strings attached but also the tragedy of abortion.

The Beatles released a full-length animated cartoon that attracted thousands of tripped-out hippies based upon one of their famous songs, *Yellow Submarine*. With a drug-related theme, it made fun of the police with scary-looking characters called, *Screaming Blue Meanies*.

This year was also a time when talking about having a revolution was starting to get serious because very few protest marches had been able to remain peaceful. Fighting in the streets and unruly violence were becoming a normal event…and often predictable, which caused the police to become even more violent and brutal as well.

Many of the people who lived in the city were becoming fed up with all the police violence, or were afraid of it, believing our country was becoming something like a Nazi police state. For that reason, a lot of the more peaceful people retreated into the countryside in order to escape the violence and made efforts to set up communal-type farms.

In some areas of the country, it seemed as if the hippie lifestyle had even spread into the suburbs because just about everyone by now had embraced the hippie counterculture...from Hollywood to dance halls and shopping malls. They wore bell-bottom pants, rose-colored glasses, beads, and chains with peace symbols, or had flowers in their hair.

Even wearing a shirt that resembled an American Flag had become more accepted. It was a style that began with the movie, *Easy Rider,* which starred Peter Fonda and Dennis Hopper.

After our dinner in China Town, I got the feeling that something was up with Donna, but I didn't know what. Whatever passion we used to have was definitely gone. One month later I discovered why.

She was sleeping with a woman by the name of Valerie Solanas, who headed up her own very radical one-woman organization called SCUM that stood for "Society for Cutting up Men." One day I even followed her to the Hotel Chelsea where Valerie was living

Valerie had written a paper called the '*Scum Manifesto,*' which she later self-published in New York City. Part of it read like this:

A true community consists of individuals...not just mere species of members, and not just couples who are simply respecting each other's individuality and privacy...while at the same time, interacting with each other mentally and emotionally as free spirits in a free relationship to each other, cooperating to achieve their common ends.

Traditionalists tell us that the basic unit of society is the family, while hippies say...*it's the tribe*, but no one says the individual.

The hippies babble on about individuality...but they have no more conception of it than anyone else. He desires to get back to nature, back to the wilderness, back to the home of the furry animal...of which he is also one, and away from the city where there is at least a trace of, and only a bare beginning of civilization. This is where he can best live at 'the species level' with his time taken up with simple, non-intellectual activities such as farming, fucking, and bead stringing.

The most important activity of the commune, the one on which it is based, is gangbanging. The hippie is enticed to the commune mainly by the prospect of all the free pussy that's available to him…and the main commodity to be shared, to be had just for the asking. But blinded by greed, he fails to anticipate all the other men he has to share with, or the jealousies, and the possessiveness of the pussies themselves.

Men cannot hope to cooperate or achieve a common end because each man's end is to have all the pussy to himself. The commune is, therefore…doomed to failure, for each hippie will, in panic, grab the first simpleton who digs him…and whisk her off to the suburbs as fast as he can. Thus, the male cannot progress socially but merely swings back and forth from isolation…to that of gangbanging.

After reading Valerie's works, and then discovering that she and Donna had become lovers, I finally understood why Donna had become more cynical about men and less interested in me. I wasn't jealous, but I was feeling a bit angry about the deception, just as when Kathy told me that she and Donna were sleeping together as well.

In February, I confronted her with this new revelation, and to my surprise, she didn't deny it. She was actually angry at me for 'spying' on her and felt betrayed. Donna believed that when a woman had an affair with another woman…it wasn't the same as cheating on her man.

I suppose it's all just a matter of one's perspective, but the bottom line to all of this is…we broke up. Regardless of whether it was the *Year of Monkey,* or the *Year of the Goddess,* Donna had become much more of a women's libber and seemed to prefer women over men when it came to sex. So before things got any worse between us, we decided to part company and to go our separate ways. I cared a lot about Donna, but she had never once shared any of her girlfriends with me.

That fact alone…was one I continued to resent for quite some time.

Now that I no longer had either Diane or Donna, I began to feel a certain sense of emptiness and aloneness that I hadn't felt in a very long time, almost since high school. I began to wonder about relationships in general…perhaps, it was a basic weakness of the human condition, to feel that someone else completes us and makes us feel whole.

*Can't we be whole and complete just by being ourselves, or do we actually need to be connected to another person? What about self-love? Wouldn't that, simply on its own, be enough…*I would ask myself?

I didn't know the answer back then, but I knew that someday I'd have to try and figure it out…shortly after that, I met Lennie.

We met one night at an acid party being held at Larry's apartment.

I was introduced to this short, slender hippie chick with small perky breasts and dark flowing hair that hung down the middle of her back. She reminded me a little of Cher Bono, but was tripping pretty hard, and seemed to be walking around lost in space. I took her hand and told her that everything was going to be all right. It apparently made her feel safe because she clung to my arm for the rest of the evening.

Lennie was raised Jewish, was very smart, and was a freethinker. She enjoyed smoking pot, was against the war as much as I was, loved to have sex, and getting a degree in speech therapy. Her most admirable trait was that she loved to laugh and was always a joy to be with.

She also had an apartment that she shared with her cat named Chip, who was white with a lot of black spots. When Lennie would get really stoned, she would hold him up and say, "Just look at that cookie face."

To me, Lennie was the perfect cross between Diane and Donna.

Right off the bat, I was completely honest with Lennie. I told her all about my adventures in California, and about my past relationships with Donna and Diane. She was appreciative of my honesty.

Lennie shared her past with me as well. She wasn't bisexual at all but was willing to try anything. She had been to a couple of parties where girls had been all over her, including my ex-girlfriend, Donna.

"You know, Andy," she said, "I never did like that sissy bitch."

♥ ♥ ♥

Lennie and I had a lot of our own adventures together, because when you're stoned or tripping, sometimes even the smallest of things can seem pretty major. For example, she liked to get really fucked up and rub 'Ben-Gay Ointment' all over herself just to feel the heat rush. One night, we rubbed it on each other before leaving to see a sold-out movie. The odor of the menthol was so strong that some of the people sitting around us were so annoyed by it…they actually got up and left.

She also liked to make spaghetti, get stoned, and have a food fight at the table. Needless to say, Lennie was a lot of fun to have around.

One evening, she called and said there was a party going on that wasn't planned but just sort of happened…so I went to her apartment and found an odd-looking group in her front room watching television.

They were also smoking pot, drinking beer, and eating popcorn.

A person I didn't know looked at me said, "Hey come on in, we're having a substance abuse party. We've got some shrooms, mescaline, acid, speed, coke, weed, GHB, and whippets…choose your poison."

I wasn't sure if he was serious or not, so I went directly to Lennie's bedroom and tried knocking on her door. After no response, I entered.

Lennie and two of her friends Alice and Nancy were partially nude and sitting on the bed. The room was illuminated by a single black-light psychedelic poster of *Jim Morrison and The Doors*. My white t-shirt glowed with the color of purple haze, and I could smell the strong scent of sandalwood incense mixed with marijuana. Up to now, the two girls had only been mere acquaintances, because April had recently started going out with Drake, and Nancy had been hanging out with Larry.

I wasn't at all bothered about them being there. How could anyone be bothered by two good-looking blonde chicks sitting on the bed with their tops off? Besides, jealousy just wasn't my game anymore.

I sat down next to the three of them. They smiled a lot but said very little until Lennie took my hand in hers. Then, April said, "Welcome to our bad-ass-bitch-boot camp." By now my eyes had adjusted to the dim lighting and I could see that the room had been laced with string from corner to corner and around the bed. Lenny whispered to me that it was 'a spider's lair,' and the bed was a cocoon where they could hide from the spider. If anyone fell off the bed, then the spider would eat them.

Yeah, these girls were pretty fucked-up all right. I suppose whoever the guy in the front room was…*wasn't kidding about the drugs!*

Lennie turned off the black light and then reached up and turned on a strobe light that was directly over the bed. Nancy handed me a freshly lit joint. She said, 'Welcome to our web of sin for naughty little girls."

Apparently, they had all given 'their creation' a different name.

I took a couple of deep drags and tried to feel into whatever it was they were doing. It was nice to be 'getting high' on a bed next to three half-dressed women. It reminded me of my earlier days in Oakland.

"Andy," Lennie started, "I think it's really great that you just let me be who I am…without judgment, and…without anger."

"Well, I think you're really great, too," I replied.

She gave me a push backward causing me to fall on top of April. Then I sat up and pushed her back…we all then proceeded to gently push each other until Nancy finally fell off the bed.

"Ah-ha, you're dead meat now," Lennie yelled.

A moment later I heard a loud knock on the door…it was Larry.

"Anyone in there?" he asked from the other side.

Nancy slowly got up and let him in.

"Looks like you're having a good time," he said looking around. "What's all of this string shit you've got going on?"

"It's our evil spider web. It's going to eat you up," Nancy teased.

"Cool, let's get evil," Larry replied.

Now it was two guys and three dolls and that was enough for me. Besides, the queen-size bed wasn't big enough to hold any more bodies.

I looked at the large mirror on Lennie's dresser and could see all of us sitting there. It looked really funny with the piercing strobe light.

Larry was already stoned, but…we passed around another joint.

He said he had some crystal meth, also known as speed, and wanted to try shooting it up intravenously. He asked if any of us would like to join him. Because Nancy and Larry had been dating for a couple of weeks, I was sure that he and Nancy had already done this before.

I had never done any drugs with needles and was hesitant about doing them that way. Nancy had previously talked to the other two girls and convinced them that it was safe, so they were willing to try it so long as Larry had new insulin syringes for them to use.

Nancy was also a student in the nursing school at NYU and had been trained in how to properly draw blood and give injections.

Larry explained that he would first melt down the meth in a spoon, then fill a syringe half-full of the liquid. Nancy said, she'd have to insert the small needle directly into his bloodstream by going into the biggest available vein in his arm after wiping it clean with alcohol.

Everyone…was wide-eyed with attention.

Lennie turned off the strobe light and turned on the bed light so we could examine each other's arms. When Nancy looked at my arm, she said that my veins were so big they were a junkie's dream.

"Never use someone else's needle because you can catch hepatitis, and all other sorts of disease that way," she warned.

Nancy showed me how to insert the needle so I could do her.

I watched her do it to Larry, then to Lennie, and then to April.

Hesitantly, I slowly inserted a needle into her arm, then she, in turn, did the same to me. Almost immediately I felt different.

From the base of my spine, I could feel a warm tingling sensation coming up my back and throughout my body until it finally reached the top of my head, and I swear my hair started to curl. I was buzzing all over with an incredibly great feeling of euphoria, as was everyone else.

Speed makes you awake and alert, but you also tend to talk a lot.

Sometimes conversations don't make a lot of sense. It's as if your speech is miles behind whatever your mind has already thought.

In only minutes, Alice was trying to explain to us that her idea of a long-term relationship was about two cigarettes after having sex, and then asked the group if there was anything other than an act of Congress that might make her more orgasmic.

"You just have to learn to let go," Nancy replied. "Don't hold back. You have to let go of your stress, your inhibitions, and all of your anger and frustration, and then just have the god-damn orgasm."

Then, April reached over and began to gently rub her fingers across Nancy's breasts and said, "You call these little things boobs?"

"They're fucking perfect and you know it," Nancy snapped.

April didn't have a comeback, because Nancy was right, but then she asked Larry about his opinion on the matter.

"Yeah, I like her boobies...except for the freckles," he joked.

"You bastard," Nancy retorted...with a punch to Larry's side.

"Ouch...bitch!"

"Nancy's freckles make her boobs very erotic," Lennie interjected. "So really, I think you need to apologize to her...and her boobs."

Larry said he was sorry, but the girls were still pissed off and began to get dressed, saying they wanted to go outside to be with the rest of Lennie's guests. After that, we just sat in the living room drinking beer. If there had been a substance abuse party going on, the substances were all gone except for a bag of pot, so we decided to smoke another joint. Larry said the alcohol and the pot would help to take the edge off of the speed because we were all still buzzing like crazy.

Also in the living room was a large, busty blonde named Frieda, a petite brunette named Toni, and a guy with a mustache named Angelo. I had never met any of them before now. There had also been some others, but they had already left with the rest of the stash.

An hour later we were all pretty trashed, but the real party started after Larry wanted to know if we could all fit into the shower together. Not everyone was willing to participate, but five of us did. Very quickly we removed our clothes and then ran into the bathroom.

The tall blonde said she didn't want to be lathered up with Lennie's cheap shampoo, but she did enjoy scrubbing it onto everyone else with the long wooden shower brush. Laughing hysterically throughout the entire get-together, we then wrapped ourselves in towels and headed back into the living room where we got dressed again. Someone said it all happened so quickly it reminded them of a Chinese fire drill.

Then, I noticed that Lennie was missing. I could have sworn she had been in the shower with the rest of us, but apparently, she wasn't.

Several minutes later I found her. She was sitting in the corner of her bedroom with April and Angelo discussing how '*war and peace*' were essentially the same thing as '*fire and rain.*'

"Sometimes the fire is so hot the rain just can't put it out," she said. "Then, you just have to allow the fire to burn until there's nothing left. That's why the peace and love movement isn't able to stop the war."

♥ ♥ ♥

As the night wore on, Toni became paranoid, watching the window. Frieda said it was simply because she wasn't getting enough attention. Then, Toni asked if we could shut off the music because it hurt her ears, and blow out the candles because the apartment might catch on fire.

We all just looked at her kind of strangely.

She started to cry and said, "You all hate me."

"No one hates you," Frieda said, trying to comfort Toni as she ran her fingers through Toni's long brown hair.

"Really?" asked Toni, as her mascara ran down her cheeks.

"I wish I had a body like yours. It's so incredible."

Frieda just laughed and said, "That's touching, thank you."

Then, Frieda held out a tissue and wiped Toni's tears.

Lennie was now out of the bedroom and came over to sit next to Frieda, who began stroking her hair just as she had been doing to Toni.

"She's going to be all right," Lennie assured us. "I'm sure it's just a little too much wild and crazy energy from all these drugs."

Then, Nancy stood up and began to go off on her own soapbox about drugs and sex. She said, "A truly free person is one whose sexual energy has been liberated and is consciously expanding in increasingly more beautiful and complex ways. The sexual revolution we're seeing is not just a part of the atmosphere of freedom that's being generated, but instead, I think it's the very center of it. The reason that drugs, and particularly marijuana, are so popular is because of their innate ability to turn on the physical body. I'll say flatly that the meaning and central issue of the psychedelic experience is the erotic exhilaration one gets from sex and drugs. There's increased freedom in sexual expression in the arts, and the mass media is now symptom number one of our victory in this one arena alone. In my opinion, when you stop exploring with sex and drugs, that's a bad scene. I never want to stop exploring."

"That was some heavy shit," Larry responded clapping his hands.

For the rest of the night, we just relaxed. We smoked more weed, drank more booze, and caressed each other while listening to the music of Janis Joplin. It was like a crazy dream that I'll always remember warmly, although the details have always remained just a bit sketchy.

In the spring of 1968, U.S. troops massacred most of the people living in My Lai, a small village in South Vietnam. As a result, over eighty thousand demonstrators against the War stormed the American Embassy in London. Three hundred protesters were arrested and ninety were hurt. The good news was, that for the first time, the U.S. began to have talks in Paris about bringing peace to the Vietnam offensive.

Violence was also heating up once again within the civil rights movement as Martin Luther King led a march in support of striking Memphis sanitation workers, and then promised to return for another march in April. However, Dr. King had been forewarned that the CIA was plotting his assassination. That night, he told the crowd of listeners that he might not live much longer. The day before his death he said to them, "I don't care if I die, because I've seen the top of the mountain."

The next morning, he was gunned down on his apartment balcony by an unknown assassin. Mobs immediately took to the streets in over one-hundred-and-sixty-seven U.S. cities, and many universities, until they were finally contained by the National Guard. Chicago's mayor, Richard J. Daley, issued a *shoot-to-kill* order to the city's police force for anyone involved in cases of arson, looting, or rioting. The FBI said they were seeking a white man, James Earl Ray, for the murder.

When he was caught…he denied having any involvement.

Many suspected…that our own government was behind the killing.

Even though President Lyndon Johnson had been given credit for passing the Civil Rights Act in 1964, he announced that he would not be seeking re-nomination in 1968. It seemed, our efforts in the anti-war movement had actually caused a popular American president to resign. The slogan with a fist in the air was right, it was...*Power to the People*.

It was becoming increasingly obvious that former Vice-President, Richard Nixon, would be the Republican choice for a new president, but it was uncertain who would be the democratic nominee. Some said it would probably be Senator Robert Kennedy, brother of the former President John Kennedy, but Senator Eugene McCarthy was also close.

The school year came to a close, but this time, I wouldn't be going to California. I hadn't heard from Diane, and the Democratic National Convention was about to take place in Chicago. I really wanted to go, so I talked to my friends and convinced Larry, Nancy, Drake, April, and Lennie that we should all go together. As it turned out, it was the main event that was a turning point in my having to do with my decision as to whether I should remain faithful to the peace and love movement, or do as my friends wanted...and engage in violence with the police

A Whiter Shade of Pale

And so it was that later…
As the miller told his tale…
That her face at first just ghostly…
Turned a whiter shade of pale…
(Artist: Procol Harem)

The summer of 1968 started off wild and crazy, and at times it seemed unbelievable. The movie, *2001: A Space Odyssey*…became the number one hit, not so much because they found proof of alien life on other planets, but to warn us that computers were becoming just a little bit too human. If you tried to disassemble one…*it might try to kill you.*

There was also a standoff going on between the generations that transcended the cold war between the U.S. and Russia, and that of race. Young people in America were not only speaking their minds but many were now being led by a new breed of hippies who no longer preached love and peace. Instead, *the yippies* were planning for an all-out armed revolution and preparing to take over the government.

The famous artist and film producer, Andy Warhol, was shot and seriously injured by Valeria Solanas, who had recently been given an actress role in one of Warhol's films, '*I, A Man,*'…but when Warhol refused to film Valeria's new play, '*Up Your Ass,*' she went absolutely berserk and pointed a gun at him. When Warhol accused her of being a cop who was trying to get him to make an obscene film, she unzipped her pants, exposed herself, and said, "Right, I'm a cop,"…and just to prove she wasn't the law, pulled the trigger and shot him.

His Holiness, Pope Paul VI, issued a decree in the *Humanae Vitae*, his encyclical letter to the Patriarchs, Archbishops, and Bishops, that denounced the use of any form of artificial contraception.

To the disbelief of the entire nation, Senator Robert Kennedy was fatally shot in the head in Los Angeles right after he won the California primary. His killer, a young Palestinian immigrant, Sirhan Sirhan, told police he did it in retaliation for the 'Arab-Israeli Six-Day War.'

James Earl Ray, the accused assassin of Martin Luther King, was finally arrested in London. However, he maintained he was innocent, claiming that he'd been set up *'as a fall guy'* by the CIA.

France exploded its first atomic bomb in the South Pacific.

The musical artists who were finally making it big included such names as Frank Zappa, Tiny Tim, and Janis Joplin. Their music was different in some way from the earlier Sixties, wilder and crazier.

Dr. Benjamin Spock, a successful author and pediatrician was sent to jail for two years for encouraging people to dodge the draft.

Also, the Vietnam War officially became the longest war in U.S. history. The death toll now surpassed thirty-thousand U.S. troops.

♥ ♥ ♥

I'd recently purchased a Volkswagen minibus.

It was yellow and white and wasn't painted with any psychedelic artwork, but Lennie wanted to put a big green marijuana leaf on it.

I told her...*no way in hell.*

We decided to drive the van for its maiden voyage to Chicago to participate in the anti-war movement activities that were being held at the Democratic National Convention which, instead, turned out to be the Democratic national disaster of the year.

Abbie Hoffman was a young, bearded man whom I had briefly met in California at one of the acid tests. He was now a radical hippie leader and a self-proclaimed cultural revolutionary as well.

Hoffman and his co-radical friend, Jerry Rubin, had joined forces with the beat poet, Allen Ginsberg, to sponsor a 'Festival of Life' in Chicago that would coincide with the Democratic Party Convention.

The original intent was to show the nation examples of what hippie alternative lifestyles looked like, however, Abbie, Jerry, and Allen also wanted to launch the *Youth International Party*...a radical political party whose members would be known as the *Yippies*. They planned to run their own candidate for the office of United States President.

It was a pet pig named, *Pigasus*, from the Hog Farm Commune.

"If they can run their pig for president," Abbie stated to the media, "why can't we do the same thing with our pig?"

The idea was to create a combination of a Be-In and Love-Festival, which was to be held as close to the Democratic Party Convention as possible...probably at some of the parks in the inner city.

There would be yogis, poets, musicians, dancers, and speakers.

They even tried to get The Beatles to attend, which turned out to be the inspiration for their song... *You Say You Want a Revolution.*

The biggest problem with having the love festival turned out to be Chicago's Mayor, who didn't like hippies, and was fearful of both their lifestyle and of what they represented. The Mayor refused to give the yippies a permit to hold their festival in any of the parks.

This...proved to be the mayor's ultimate undoing.

Many of the nation's anti-war groups were not hippies or yippies and were in Chicago specifically to protest against L.B.J., but when he withdrew from the presidential race, they had to rethink their position.

There was also a group of coalition leaders such as David Dellinger, Rennie Davis, Tom Hayden, and Black Panther leader, Bobby Seale.

They had taken on the job of organizing the various anti-war groups in an alliance and had planned several marches and demonstrations for the full three days of the convention. Since the yippies had no permit of their own, they tried to coordinate their so-called 'Love Festival' to coincide with the other anti-war coalition activities going on.

In a retaliatory response to the fact that the yippies and hippies were coming anyway, without a permit, and the belief that tens of thousands of young people from the various coalition groups were also about to descend upon the city, Mayor Daley went into a state of panic.

To prepare the city for this impending onslaught of hedonism, he placed eleven thousand police on twelve-hour shifts. He also mobilized five thousand Illinois National Guard troops and had seven thousand U.S. military troops airlifted in from Fort Hood. To top it off, the Mayor even had one thousand agents of the U.S. Secret Service placed at his disposal…all with the blessings of President Lyndon Johnson.

We arrived on Saturday afternoon already knowing that the festival activities and coalition group meetings were scheduled to begin early the next morning. Every hotel and motel in the city was sold out, so we decided to go to Lincoln Park and see what might be happening.

When we got there, we were surprised to find that many people were already dancing, reading poetry, preparing signs, and playing on acoustic guitars. A speaker's platform was being built for the next day. Lennie, Drake, April, and I joined in to help set things up while Larry and Nancy went off to find some drugs.

A short distance away Rennie Davis and Tom Hayden were training a small group of people in karate and other forms of self-defense, whose job would be to protect the speakers on the stage.

One of the famous urban legends that had already arisen from the ensuing confrontation was Jerry Rubin. He sent the Mayor of the city a postcard saying the yippies were planning to spike the water supply of the city with LSD. Immediately, fully armed troops were deployed to guard the city's water treatment facilities…regardless of the truth.

Another story that was circulating said the hippies were planning to use hairspray against the police, and everyone knew the expulsion of hairspray from a can, when set next to a match, was like a homemade flame thrower. Since everyone also knew that hippies were dirty and didn't bathe, they certainly had no other use for hairspray.

As a result, city officials became very worried and banned the sale of any hairspray to anyone who even looked like a hippie.

The media was also in town and were prepared to report about any violence or brutality by the police…not only against the demonstrators but against news crews and bystanders as well.

All of the police, National Guardsmen, and Federal troops that had been deployed were determined to put up a show of force never before seen in this country…even though the number of people at any of the protest sites never exceeded seven thousand people and many of those included hundreds of undercover agents and spectators.

By nightfall, only a thousand young people were in Lincoln Park, and some had come with the intent of spending the night on the lawn, even though the park was to officially close at eleven o'clock at night.

Police officers entered the park at about nine o'clock that night and began hitting and beating people up, even though they had every right to be there and were not disturbing the peace.

The officers seemed to go crazy at times. They would fire tear gas and club protesters almost indiscriminately, regardless of what anyone was doing. Fortunately, none of my friends were harmed, but we were forced to quickly return to our van in order to get away.

We had heard some conversation around the stage that if this should happen, then the organizers planned to retreat to another park that was thirty miles outside of the city and spend the night there.

We drove to a local Handy Market and loaded up with food, beer, and wine. Then, with a map, we proceeded to find the new location.

We arrived about an hour later. Larry, Drake, and I strolled around the park while the three girls stayed in the van to sleep.

In the distance, we could see a small group of people sitting around a fire, which turned out to be many of the same people we had met while building the stage. Everyone was sitting around passing a joint and getting high, so we offered a gallon of wine and a half-lid of grass to the group as an offering. They gladly invited us to be a part of the tribe, so we sat down on one of the logs near the fire.

We passed another joint around the fire and introduced ourselves to everyone. I already knew Abbie Hoffman from an acid test and had met Jerry Rubin from the Be-In at Golden Gate Park.

Abbie explained to those who didn't know him well that he was a native of Worcester, Massachusetts, and had graduated from Brandeis University where he was influenced by the ideas of Herbert Marcuse and Abraham Maslow. Hoffman said it was his desire to become a part of a tradition of great Jewish thinkers like Karl Marx, Sigmund Freud, and Albert Einstein. He began his radical career as a civil rights activist in the South by registering black voters in Mississippi in 1964, but as the Vietnam War heated up, he became more involved in that conflict.

"Freedom of speech is one of the casualties of the existing order," Hoffman said. "The first thing a dying dinosaur empire does is to try to devour its young, and America is a dying empire. Its institutions are crumbling, so the students' role is to teach the established order where the problems lie and create the kinds of dilemmas it just can't deal with. All of us here are living for the revolution, but we're also dying for it."

Abbie then went on to say, in his opinion, that because of the way things were in this country, a college degree was useless.

In his opinion, all of our universities and college campuses should be transformed into training grounds for revolutionaries.

"People have to make up their minds that they are going to destroy the university as it now exists," Hoffman tried to explain to the group.

"If you simply accept that the student's role is just a student, then you're accepting the student's role of being a slave."

Some of the people clapped in support of his words.

Then, Jerry Rubin interjected with some of his own views and said, "It is the duty of every revolutionary to revolt, and I predict that this is going to be a year of violence for many of us, but guess what...I'm all for it, because personally...I find this revolution to be highly sexual.

"The more I revolt, the more I want to make love."

Everyone laughed and cheered, "Right on."

Then, Hoffman mentioned that we should start supporting some of the leaders, such as Timothy Leary, who was personally responsible for hundreds of thousands of people being able to finally break free from established society. He also praised Bobby Seale for being the leader of the Black Panther movement and said that Bobby was one of the great fighters for a renewed political representation in the country.

"The black man has lost too much blood," Abbie explained to us, "and he needs to extract some of it back from the white man."

Then someone yelled, "We're going to take it to the streets, and if they want to fight us, we're going to fight back!"

Abbie said that if he had the opportunity, he would blow his nose on an American flag right in front of a television camera.

In my opinion, Abbie Hoffman was overstepping the line because it was obvious that he wasn't there for a love festival at all but had come to stir up as much trouble as he possibly could.

The truth was...I could never shoot anyone, much less a policeman, and I didn't want to go to prison for the rest of my life, either.

Selling marijuana on campus was one thing, but I just wasn't ready to strap on a machine gun...and become like Che Guevara.

For the rest of the night, we sat up, smoked pot, drank beer, and told our own personal antiwar stories and experiences. Somewhere around three o'clock in the morning, we finally fell asleep.

♥ ♥ ♥

The next day, we returned to the park where a public address system was quickly set up in order to speak to the thousands of people who had gathered there again. A comedian group called 'MC-5' came on first and worked up the crowd yelling, "Up against the wall, motherfucker."

They made fun of the police...even though many of them were watching nearby. Then Allen Ginsberg came on and began to chant the Hindu mantra 'Hare Krishna' for about fifteen minutes to try to calm the crowd. Then, MC-5 came back on and worked them up again.

After that, Jerry Rubin jumped on the stage.

Removing his jacket, he exposed his hairy bare chest to the crowd, and everyone applauded. He was wearing a long red cape, looking like Superman, with a military rifle on a strap hanging over his shoulder.

It wasn't real of course, but it looked real. Then he held up his right hand and gave everyone the peace symbol. The crowd cheered again as Jerry began to make the opening speech.

"Marijuana has become totally rampant in the Army, and now the military is facing both low morale and civil disobedience. Why does marijuana inspire the Viet Cong, and kill the fighting spirit of American troops? Any pot smoker can understand this. It's because marijuana is a truth serum. The Viet Cong are defending their parents, their children, and their homes, and therefore their deaths are noble and heroic.

"The Americans, however, are not fighting for anything you can see, feel, touch, or believe in. Their deaths are futile and wasted, and because they smoke pot, they now see the truth.

"Every soldier must eventually ask himself this serious question: "Why should I die defending...Hamburger Hill?"

"That's why the pot-smoking American soldier points his gun at the officer who ordered him to take that hill in the first place. It's a hill that only the Viet Cong would want. It's their hill, and it belongs to them.

"If the Pentagon tries to stop the use of marijuana in the Army, they'll end up destroying the entire military in the process. However, if the Army Brass will leave the grass smokers alone, then the Army bases will soon be as turned-on, tuned-in, and just as unstoppable as all of our colleges and universities already are…can you dig?"

Loudly, the crowd cheered again.

"What's going to happen when all of those in the American military come home and ask, 'What do you mean we can't smoke pot? We were old enough to fight and old enough to die in Vietnam, but now you're telling us we can't smoke naturally grown plants in our own backyard?' Tell me, what do you think these men and women going to do?"

Everyone laughed, but before Jerry could answer the question a mob of police storm troopers burst from behind the trees in pursuit of anyone who was gathered there. This included news photographers and reporters. The club-swinging militia of law enforcers advanced on the crowd very quickly, and everyone ran in different directions until the park had been completely cleared of demonstrators.

Many people were injured, including seventeen members of the media who had to be taken to the hospital for medical treatment.

Within just a short time, the crowd had been successfully dispersed by the police. The anti-war coalition leaders returned to the previous encampment in order to regroup and figure out what to do next.

Our own little band joined in with them as well.

As we once again, passed around a joint with new-found-friends, it seemed as though we were a part of history in the making…just like the American revolutionary soldiers must have felt…when they were on the run from the British Redcoat soldiers.

If this had been Christmas Eve, I would have suggested we attack the police while they were off guard, just like General Washington did two hundred years earlier against the Hessian troops.

As I was sitting there getting high, I was thinking more and more that maybe I should give up my principles and join in by fighting back. After all, according to history...some of the quotes from our greatest revolutionary statesmen actually supported an armed conflict.

It was Thomas Payne who said...*it's the object of war that makes it honorable, and if there was ever a just war since the world began it's the one in which America is now engaged. It's not a field, or a few acres of ground, but a cause we are defending...and whether we defeat the enemy in one battle, or by degrees, the consequence will be the same.*

To me that sounded like what we were dealing with now.

What if Abbie and Jerry were right? What if it was really true that the members of the Continental Congress were a bunch of pot heads just like us? Wouldn't it be something if history revealed that Benjamin Franklin and Thomas Jefferson stayed stoned a lot back in their day?

That's why they traveled to Europe so often...to mask the truth that they were smuggling in drugs, and why they were such great thinkers!

Little did I know, but while we were staying at the small state park that night...FBI and CIA agents were in the parking lot writing down the license numbers of everyone who had left their vehicles there.

As a result, each vehicle owner eventually became the target of a huge government inquisition on counts of both conspiracy and treason.

♥ ♥ ♥

The main battle began the very next day, on Monday, just outside the Conrad Hilton Hotel. The National Mobilization Committee was headed by David Dellinger, who had organized a pacifist rally that was to start in Grant Park. Most of the park had been sealed off by the police and National Guard troops, but Davis and Hayden had already agreed to have the march anyway, regardless of whether the park was sealed off or not...so the protest began despite the city's attempts to stop it.

Initially, the march was led by Allen Ginsberg, William Burroughs, and others, all with their arms linked together and holding flowers.

I was with my five other friends and located fairly near the front. With only a few blocks underfoot, National Guardsmen blocked our way with machine guns and barbed-wire shields. They would not allow the marchers to go any farther out of the park, or onto the city streets.

After a long standoff, Dellinger announced that the march was over, stating that the government had forced us to abandon our citizen's right to have a peaceable assembly for the redress of grievances.

Reluctantly, the marchers tried to peacefully disassemble, but many couldn't move at all because the police were still blocking the main bridge, which was pretty much the only way to leave.

Without provocation from anyone, the police then fired tear gas at the crowd, which of course caused a panic. The group we were in pushed forward and managed to get across a lightly guarded smaller bridge that took us back to the city across Michigan Avenue. However, we ran straight into the middle of Reverend Ralph David Abernathy's Poor People's Campaign, which was marching up the same avenue and progressing slowly because they had mules and wagons.

Mayor Daley had granted Abernathy a permit to march. Otherwise, he would have been faced with the possibility of a full-scale riot from Chicago's black community. The whole thing was like something out of a comic book...with cops in gas masks amidst the wagons and mules chasing thousands of white and ragged long-haired hippies who were breaking through the group of bewildered black marchers, and at times were trying to join in by pretending to be one of them.

As the Poor People's Campaign neared the Hilton Hotel, the mules and wagons were allowed to cross the intersection, but those of us who were part of the war protest group were herded aside like cattle to be slaughtered, soon finding ourselves separated from the other marchers.

Being surrounded on three sides by rows of hostile and angry cops, I didn't know where Lennie and my other friends were.

Meanwhile, those of us being threatened began to say to each other that we were going to make a stand, and not to be afraid to take on the police even though we had no weapons of our own.

We only had our fists, beer bottles, and rocks to protect us.

Without any warning...the police plunged in at us with their clubs swinging, beating people indiscriminately, and spraying mace.

Instinctively, I fought back as hard as I could and even got in a few good punches...until I was hit across the forehead with a nightstick.

I quickly dropped down on one knee and placed my hands over my head in order to protect myself from another hit as I felt the presence of warm blood streaming down my arms, and my head pounding.

After a while, I felt safe and stood up.

I could hardly see through my swollen eyes...but somehow, I was able to get out of the war zone and find my friends.

Fortunately, all of them had remained unhurt.

Tourists, newsmen, and even people who were just on their way home from work were all attacked and beaten as well. The police were not particularly interested in arresting people but were more into the mode of what resembled some kind of shark-feeding-frenzy.

So many people were injured that the Eugene McCarthy campaign headquarters on the fifteenth floor of the Hilton Hotel was turned into a makeshift hospital for some of the news reporters.

Once we managed to get completely out of harm's way we headed back to the van, which was parked near to where the march had started. We had all seen plenty of violence that day...and were ready to end it.

Because of the blood gushing out of my forehead, I was now like a marked man, and a couple of policemen followed us to where the van was parked. I told Drake to drive, but as he quickly drove away, I could see one of the officers writing down the number of my license plate.

"Let me see your head," Lennie said as she wiped away some of the clotted blood. "I think it's time that we leave for home before someone really gets hurt, or even worse…gets their ass arrested."

"Well, it wasn't our fault. They're the ones who drew first blood," Drake replied, "and by the way…I was really impressed that you were standing toe-to-toe with the cops, even if it was just for a few minutes. We were all watching, and man, you nailed one of those fuckers good."

"Yeah, and it's also a damned good thing you're not behind bars right now," Lennie pointed out with a hint of worry and annoyance.

She was right…I had come very close to getting arrested, and it was time to get out of Dodge. Along the way, we smoked several bowls of weed and sang a popular song by *Country Joe and the Fish.*

It was called the *Vietnam Song,* that went…
And it's 1, 2, 3…what are we fighting for?
Don't ask me, I don't give a damn.
The next stop is Vietnam.
And it's 4, 5, 6…open up the Pearly gates.
Well, there ain't no time to wonder why.
Whoopee, we're all gonna' die.

Over the next two days were allegations against the organizers of the resistance that included all kinds of allegations.

One witness claimed…that Jerry Rubin had urged demonstrators to attack police and incited the rioters in Lincoln Park.

Police officers said they observed Tom Hayden letting the air out of the tires of their police car, and Davis and Dellinger were seen urging demonstrators 'not to let the pigs take the hill'…referring to some high ground near the park. Bobby Seale was also arrested for addressing a crowd in another park, after the police had charged in and beat up the demonstrators, enraging them to smash windows and streetlights.

Two coalition organizers, John Froines and Lee Weiner were also arrested for violent encounters that took place between the police and some of the demonstrators in the streets near Grant Park.

Abbie Hoffman was arrested while having breakfast, just for having the word '*Fuck*' written on his forehead. Allegations by the police also claimed that he'd proposed kidnapping the city's superintendent.

By the fourth day, Hubert Humphrey had emerged as the winner of the presidential nomination for the Democratic Convention and chose Senator Edmund Muskie of Maine to be his running mate.

Also in August, Richard Nixon was nominated for the presidency by the Republicans along with his running mate, Spiro Agnew.

Two weeks after we returned home, I received a letter in the mail from the local FBI office stating that I was being investigated and might have to come to their Brooklyn office at some future date to answer questions. They warned me not to leave town.

Almost everyone who drove to Chicago by car and had parked in one of the lots where the riots took place, now had their name on the FBI's hit list of possible terrorists. Most of the cases were ultimately dropped because there was no way to prove who the drivers were.

The riots led to more than six hundred arrests, but those who were indicted to stand trial in Federal Court were Rennie Davis, Jerry Rubin, Abbie Hoffman, David Dellinger, Tom Hayden, John Froines, Bobby Seale, and Lee Weiner, who became known as the *Chicago Eight*…for *conspiring to cross state lines to incite a riot under the Civil Rights Act*; but Abby claimed…*they crossed state lines 'for peace, to end the war.'*

I returned to school for another semester once the summer was over, but it was still just as wild and crazy as the summer had been.

In September, the Miss America Pageant was upset in Atlantic City after moderator, Burt Parks, rattled off the measurements of all fifty women…including their breast size, waists, and hips.

A finalist…took the microphone out of his hand and announced, "So now, please tell everyone here, Mr. Parks…how big you are?"

He turned a whiter shade of pale, and every color in the rainbow.

Then the contestants, and many in the audience, began to chant, "*Freedom for women! Freedom for women*! …" after a huge banner was dropped from the balcony declaring…*Women's Liberation*.

♥ ♥ ♥

In October, former Alabama Governor, George Wallace, who was thought to be 'obviously racist' by many, announced his candidacy to become the next President of the United States.

When the Olympic Games opened in Mexico City, the American black athletes wore black army berets and black gloves. They made clenched fists as a salute to symbolize *Black Power* in America, which severely embarrassed the U.S. Olympic Association.

Both John Lennon and Yoko Ono were arrested for possession of marijuana in a police raid on Ringo Starr's London apartment.

Jackie Kennedy married a Greek millionaire, Aristotle Onassis.

To everyone's surprise, L.B.J. ordered a temporary cease-fire to the bombings in Vietnam, apparently wanting to leave the White House believing that he finally did something right.

November brought us the big election, but my friends and I were still too young to vote…since twenty-one was the legal voting age.

The Presidential Election was won by Republican, Richard Nixon, who became the 37th U.S. president but only by a very slim margin.

Shirley Chisholm became the first black woman elected to serve in the House of Representatives of Congress.

At the end of November, college campuses all across the country held a national *"Burn Your Draft Card Day."*

In December, America launched its first-ever manned *Apollo* space mission. After *Apollo* 8 was launched into space it finally splashed down in the Pacific. Frank Borman, James Lovell, and William Anders had orbited the Moon ten times in six days. Everyone knew that it was just a matter of time before we actually landed on the moon.

As for me, I was still in outer space, debating the pros and cons of peace and war, but without any idea where I was going to land.

Just about everyone I knew was ready to begin an armed revolution, but after what had happened to me in Chicago, I was beginning to have second thoughts. Fighting with the police, defending a bridge, or trying to bomb a post office, wasn't going to solve a god-damn thing.

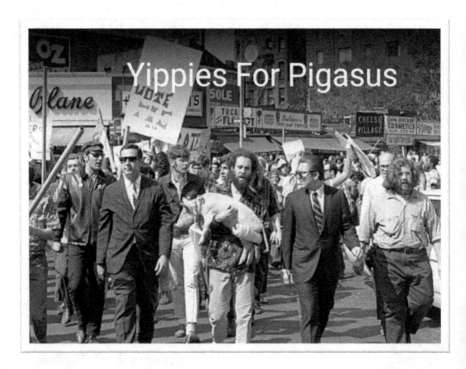

A Bridge Over Troubled Water

When tears are in your eyes, I will dry them all...
I'm on your side...when times get rough...
Like a bridge over troubled water...
I will lay me down...
(Artist: Simon and Garfunkel)

I was about to begin another year at NYU, but quite unknowingly, 1969 would prove to be another year full of extremes...as violence and madness existed alongside achievement, success, and sexuality.

A disenchanted president, Lyndon Johnson, stepped down from the Oval Office while the new and more ambitious, Richard Nixon, had to watch his inaugural parade from behind a bulletproof shield.

Yasser Arafat was elected to become the new leader for what some believed to be a terrorist group, the Palestine Liberation Organization.

Scientists at Cambridge in the United Kingdom announced the first successful *in vitro* fertilization of a human embryo.

The Beatles made their last-ever *live appearance* while playing on the rooftop of their Apple Records Headquarters, at Thirty Seville Row, in London. The police, however, had to be called in to stop the noise when some of the neighbors complained.

Although there'd been many developments in support of Women's Liberation, full-frontal nudity began appearing in '*Playboy Magazine,*' and it didn't take long for its competitor, '*Penthouse,*' to soon follow.

Midnight Cowboy became the only X-rated movie in history to win an Oscar...starring actors Dustin Hoffman and John Voight.

Lastly, the first *Boeing Jumbo Jet* had a successful maiden flight.

As the New Year began, I wasn't sure what to think about the letter I'd received. The last thing I wanted was to be indicted like the others. I was afraid I was being watched, so I stopped selling drugs on campus.

To make things worse, Larry was having a lot of mental problems.

He was becoming more depressed, and angry about life in general.

Larry had despised the government and the military ever since the 'My Lai massacre' occurred in Vietnam, and now he had also witnessed the senseless beatings and stupidity of the police in Chicago.

Sometimes, I would be at his apartment and Larry would turn to me and say, "They're really trying to kill us, now. It's the end of the game."

He was definitely up to something, but I didn't know what it was. Over the course of the semester, I began to sense that he had a plan in mind that he thought would turn the tide in favor of the hippies.

However, Larry just kept it to himself and refused to discuss it.

On several occasions, he'd hinted at wanting to blow up a building on campus that was being used for Army research, and ultimately, that became the focus of his anger. It was called *the Roosevelt Building* and was one-of-a-kind as far as research centers go. It had already been the target of anti-war activists before since it opened in the 1950s.

Over the years, as protests against the war intensified, underground newspapers published stories alleging that university professors and graduate students were conducting secret weapon research that would eventually be used to kill hundreds and thousands of civilians all across Southeast Asia. The possible use of anthrax was also amongst many conversations. The research was being conducted on the top floor of the six-floor brick building. For many of the protesters, the building had become 'public enemy number one' in minds of many.

Ever since I arrived in New York, the number of protests around the university area had grown from simple demonstrations of public discord to riots and fire bombings. This was often countered by police with pepper spray and National Guardsmen using brute force.

Students would abandon classes to protest discriminatory policies, and rally in large numbers to tell the administration how they should run the school. Simply going to class had become difficult for many.

I had expressed to Larry many times that I didn't believe in blowing up buildings, and that it wasn't the answer to winning this war.

He would just argue back, saying that "Vietnam War protesters had raised some fundamental moral questions, many of which, were shared by peaceful and violent activists alike throughout American history," and he cited examples from the abolitionist movement all the way to the creation of the current protest movement.

"The question is," he said, "if you believe your country is engaged in a fundamentally immoral activity…then, just how far are you willing to let it continue before you act?"

At three o'clock in the morning, during the last week of February, someone made an attack on the Roosevelt Building. The explosion was so powerful it damaged several other buildings in the area.

The police found pieces of a homemade bomb atop an eight-story building three blocks from the blast site.

I was almost knocked out of my bed by the blast, and some of the nearby churches lost their windows from the explosion.

When I looked outside, I could see a red glow from the fire, and there was debris flying around in a black cloud of smoke.

Instinctively, I suspected that Larry must have been involved in it, so I quickly got dressed and went to his apartment and knocked on the door several times. When he finally opened it, he pretended that he'd been asleep the whole time…but I knew that he wasn't.

He was flying high on speed.

♥ ♥ ♥

Several days later, investigators said they believed that Larry, along with his cousin Gary, and several other accomplices, had filled several containers with jet fuel, placed it next to the building's loading dock in the wee hours of the morning, and lighted the fuse.

It appeared their intent was not to harm anyone, having assumed the building would be vacant at that particular time. Unfortunately, the blast seriously injured four people who were cleaning one of the floors.

The pain of the event was definitely felt most among the faculty who worked in the physics department inside the Roosevelt Building. They were located on the first floor and basement of the building, and many of their academic projects were totally destroyed, while all of the military research on the upper floors was virtually uninterrupted.

There were a lot of mixed emotions amongst campus protestors. Some of them said the bombing relieved a lot of tension, while others, including the student body president, feared it was just the beginning of worse things to come. Many activists said it discredited the peace movement and gave credence to those who viewed war protesters as dangerous. So it would now be difficult to reclaim the message about how our government was killing soldiers and civilians in Vietnam if the public thought protestors were acting the same way as those they protested against. This group had *almost killed* innocent people in the name of peace, just as our very own government was doing in Vietnam.

"The bombing has definitely had a negative impact on what we are trying to accomplish," said one of the radical student leaders at the time.

As a result, Larry knew he had to get out of town, and Gary decided to go with him. They drove to Canada the very next morning.

"I don't think I can ever come back," Larry told me before he left. "But, what the fuck, I've always wanted to see Canada anyway."

"What were you thinking?" I questioned with harsh disapproval.

"You could be sentenced to *twenty* years in prison…stupid man."

"It just seemed like a good idea at the time," he replied.

After that, I never saw or heard from either of them again.

On a lighter note, my friend, Arnold, always seemed to be hard up for money. Since I was a psychology major, I knew the University was always asking for human guinea pigs for experiments in the clinical laboratory that were being conducted by the graduate students, and they would usually pay ten or twenty dollars for your time.

I recommended that Arnold sign up for one of the tests and he agreed without question. Furthermore, because I was now in my fourth year of studies, one of my graduation requirements was to come up with a psychological experiment that was both a new and original idea.

As it turned out, the experiment Arnold signed up for was just one of your basic 'Rorschach ink blot tests'…where the subject being tested examines a series of ink blots that are about the size of your hand, and then must tell the conductor of the experiment what he sees using his imagination, other than an ink blot. Somehow, the answers you give are supposed to say something about your inner personality.

I already knew Arnold was a 'crazed sex maniac'…so more than likely anything he saw would be sexual in nature. So I told him not to worry about it…if all he saw was a big hairy pussy…just say so.

"They'll probably lock me up…but okay, that's what I'll do."

When he took the test…the questioning went like this:

Examiner: "Okay, Arnold, just allow yourself to breathe and relax. Then tell me what each of these various ink blots reminds you of.

"You're allowed to say whatever it is you think you see…except, you can't say…it looks like an ink blot. So let's begin.

"Which of the following five choices…most closely captures the emotional impact of the ink blot you're seeing in front of you?

"Do you feel happiness, joy, excitement, calmness, or serenity?"

Arnold: "Excitement. It makes me feel…horny."

Examiner: "This is the next one. Does it in any way…make you feel fear, disgust, terror, or feeling trapped?"

Arnold: "Feeling trapped."

Examiner: "Why do you feel trapped?"

Arnold: "Because it reminds me of a big vagina, and man, I would be scared to death of getting trapped inside something like that."

Examiner: "Okay, here's the next ink blot. What does it look like?"

Arnold: "It looks a lot like a vagina, also."

Examiner: "Does it in any way remind you at all of a person, a bug, a flower, an airplane, a ship, a spacecraft, or a jewel?"

Arnold: "I told you, it looks like a pussy. But I guess it could also be a flower that's shaped like a pussy."

Examiner: "Let's try the next one. Do you see anything sexual?"

Arnold: "Yes."

Examiner: "What do you see?"

Arnold: "I see two people having sex."

Examiner: "Does it seem as though it's occurring in the past, the current day, or occurring in the future?"

Arnold: "I don't know. It just looks like two people fucking."

Examiner: "Do you see anything involving aliens, or perhaps any kind of outer space vehicles in this next ink blot?"

Arnold: "Yes."

Examiner: "What do you see?"

Arnold: "Two aliens fucking each other."

Examiner: "Does it make you feel threatened, curious, interested, or does it create a sense of confusion, despair, or gloom?"

Arnold: "Curious, I suppose…I mean, how do aliens have sex?"

Examiner: "All right, here's the next one.

"Do you see a heart, a frog, a flower, a penis, a volcano, or a tree?"

Arnold: "It looks like a penis that's fucking some kind of animal."

Examiner: "What feelings did the ink blot most strongly convey? Humor, passion, calmness, shock, nervousness, cruelty...or nothing?"

Arnold: "Oh, I don't know. I supposed I'm pretty shocked that someone's penis would be fucking an animal."

Examiner: "Do you see any of the following in this next ink blot? A man, woman, and child together...a moose, bear, and tiger together, or a car, bus, and train together? If none of those, what do you see?"

Arnold: "No, I just see a big hairy pussy with wings...like a bat."

Examiner: "What emotions did this ink blot most strongly convey? Did you feel pride, anger, disgust, confusion, fear, happiness, insanity, depression, concern, or was it nothing?"

Arnold: "Well, most definitely I felt some confusion and insanity, because a pussy with wings...well, I mean, I used to get really turned on watching Tinker Bell when I was a child."

Examiner: "All right, which of the following choices most closely resembles what you see in this next ink blot? Do you see a dinosaur, a superhero, an evil creature, a figure that is part-human and part-animal, or do you see a mixture of two different animals?"

Arnold: "I would say that it looks like two big bugs, or perhaps a bee that's having sex with an alien. No, wait a minute. Now I think it looks more like an angel fucking a gargoyle."

Examiner: "An angel wasn't one of the choices."

Arnold: "You said two different animals."

Examiner: "An angel is not an animal."

Arnold: "Then what is an angel?"

Examiner: "Never mind. Are you ready for the next question?"

Arnold: "Of course, I'm ready. This is fun."

Examiner: "What is the strongest image you see in this next one?

"An elf, a mosquito, a wasp, a fly, a dragonfly, a cricket, or an ant?"

Arnold: "I see a fairy fucking an elf."

Examiner: "All right, here's the last one. Which of the following things do you see in this last ink blot? Do you see a blackbird, a flower, two flying creatures, a combination of non-flying creatures, a butterfly, a woman's breast and nipple, a cloud, or none of these?"

Arnold: "Oh, definitely…the breast and nipple."

Examiner: "Was that the only thing you saw?"

Arnold: "Now that you mention it, the whole thing reminds me of a naked woman. Everything I see reminds me of sex…does that mean I'm a sick person? What's wrong with me? Do you have a diagnosis?"

Examiner: "Well…yes, I think so…I mean, on a scale of one to ten, I'd say you're pretty fucked up in the head."

Arnold: "Okay, fine, I'm a ten! Do I still get my twenty dollars?"

That evening, I met Arnold at a local tavern with Scott and Bill, and we shared some pitchers of beer while we talked about the day.

As it turned out, Arnold gave me an incredible idea.

"Instead of ink blots," he explained, "why don't you just show me pictures of women's pussies, then ask me what 'they' look like?"

"Maybe if I looked at a pussy really up close, then I could tell you if it resembled a bat, or a bee, or a fucking elf. I mean, who knows, maybe a hairy vagina would remind me of an ink blot."

As a result of Arnold's over-sexed mind, I went on to invent a new psychological test of my own and wound up getting an excellent grade.

The test was a series of photographs that were shown to a subject, and all the pictures showed a close-up of a woman's twat, which I was able to obtain from the Fine Arts Department. Some of them were old, some were young, some were shaved…and some were not.

In this test, the person would have to tell the examiner what the photograph reminded them of…and of course…the answer could not involve pussy, so the test went something like this:

Examiner: "Do you see any of the following in this photograph of a woman's vagina? Do you see an angel, a heart, a little man in a boat, a salamander, a moose with antlers, a lion, an alien, a scorpion, a spider, a mouse, a skull, a dragon, or none of the above?"

Sigmund Freud must have rolled over in his grave that day because I named it the '*Freudian Psychological Unconscious Sexual Survey*,' called 'Freud's PUSS' for short, which soon became the most popular psychological test on campus. In fact, people were lining up at the door to do it for free…just to see pictures of hairy vaginas.

Because I was scheduled to graduate from NYU in December, very soon I was going to have to be making a choice. I could either face getting drafted and being sent to Vietnam, or I could run off to Canada and become a fugitive…or I could try to get into graduate school which would give me a deferment for at least another two years.

Because of the great success of my *Freud's PUSS test*, I had earned myself a chance of getting an academic scholarship for graduate school. I began filling out all of the necessary paperwork and prepared to take the Graduate Record Examination (the GRE).

Now that Larry and Gary were no longer around, I found myself spending more time with Scott, Bill, and Arnold at the bars, or off with Drake, Lenny, and April…to smoke joints at the Cellar Door.

Lennie was a pretty smart girl and had been an incredible friend. We never argued or fought about anything. I accepted her for who she was, and she felt the same way about me. I loved her natural wisdom, the way she knew things, without having had a formal spiritual teacher.

In some ways, Lennie had always been like a teacher for me, kind of like Jiminy Cricket…who acted as Pinocchio's conscience.

It was like having my own personal guru to get high with, to sleep with, and make love to, all at the same time. If reincarnation were true, then we must have had many previous lifetimes together.

One night I was at her apartment when Drake and April came by and asked if we wanted to share some of their weed. We sat on the floor to share a joint and then began to talk about all kinds of things, which included the little we knew about Tibet and Buddhism in general.

Drake hummed a tune from The Grateful Dead and then alternated it with The Moody Blues, while April was in the kitchen brewing some green tea and honey. When April returned, they sat across from us.

We were sitting in a circle around a big red candle that Lennie had made that very same day from the empty carton of a gallon of vanilla ice cream. It seemed to burn a lot stronger now that most of the smoke in the room had been released from the nearby window.

After quite a long pause, Drake began to speak as if he was just now remembering something about a previous conversation.

"The reason no one will come right out and take a stand on anything is that they don't really know much of anything. You don't know much about me, I don't know much about you, and neither of us knows much about ourselves. No one knows much about love, or much about the revolution, or for that matter, evolution. No one knows how to expand our awareness, or for that matter, even about paying the fucking rent."

"What does anybody know?" April said as she passed another joint. "If you don't know, then maybe you need to ask somebody."

"If anybody knows, Lennie knows," I interjected. "What do you think this whole revolution is about, Lennie? Do you have an opinion?"

Lennie paused for a moment, asked for a toke, and took a big puff.

Then, she slowly said, "Well, in my humble opinion, maybe I do.

"I heard the other day that seventy-one-million people died during World War II. That's almost three percent of the world's population.

"To top it off, with the invention of the atomic bomb, it was the first time in history that mankind could destroy the entire world.

"So what I think…is that God put out a distress call to all of those who had died in World War II and said, '*Sorry, you've got to go back.*'

"The Souls replied, '*But dear God, we all just died horrible deaths, so it's not fair to send us back to that wretched place you call Earth, where there's so much suffering, where all people do is kill each other.*'

"God said, '*That's exactly why you must go back, while the horror of war is still fresh in your minds. I want you all to return and put an end to war forever, and then to create a whole New World for me.*'

"And so it was, that those brave Souls began being born right after World War II ended, but they came in waves. Beginning right around the year 1960, the first wave of those responders started coming of age.

"That's who we all are. Don't you get it? We are the ones God sent to put an end to war forever. We are…*the love generation.* We are here for a reason…to stop this crazy shit and create a whole new world."

"Wow," said Drake. "That's way far fucking out there."

"There's also another thing I'd just love to do," Lennie responded. "I think it would be fantastic to go to India and live in an *ashram*,"

"If we went right now," I replied, "I'm afraid I'd get drafted."

"Why can't we get a student deferment for studying in an ashram," Drake complained. "It's just like being a student! I wonder if anyone's ever gotten a college degree in Enlightenment? Come to think about it, long ago…they used to have Buddhist Universities in India."

Changing the subject, Lennie looked over at me and mentioned, "Last night, I used the *I-Ching*, and the message I got said…I was to prepare myself for the journey of a close friend. Could that be you?"

"Maybe…I suppose. You know I want to see the world."

Drake pointed out, "You know, Andy, if you join the Peace Corps, you can get a deferment from the draft. It's just like being in college. Maybe you could go to India, or Nepal, or maybe even Tibet."

"Yeah," April said. "You could undo some of the damage that U.S. imperialism and the multinational corporations have inflicted on them. Who knows? Maybe you could actually help some of the people."

"That would be a good thing. But first, I would have to get accepted.

"Hell, they're probably looking for really straight people who are from rural America, not someone like me. I've hardly ever been out of the city other than going camping as a Boy Scout."

"I don't think so," Lennie replied, "they just want people who have a college degree. Besides, you don't look like a subversive hippie at all, and you were an Eagle Scout. I'm sure they'd love to have you on their peace team. You said you wanted to travel around the world. This way, you could see the world for free...*and at the government's expense.*"

"It's for two years, why don't you come with me?" I suggested.

"I just can't do that. I want to get my master's degree before I start slacking off too much, otherwise, I'll never go back and get it."

"Well then, are you going to wait for me?" I asked her.

"I'll wait for you to come back," Lennie replied, "but I might not be all that faithful while you're gone."

"You're not all that faithful now," I retorted, "but yeah, I'll guess I'll check it out. I've already put in papers for graduate school, I'm just trying to cover my ass for after graduation in December."

"I hear Nepal is fantastic," Drake commented. "The culture is really intense, and the farmers grow marijuana as a cash crop...but I don't think Americans are allowed to enter Tibet right now."

"Really, why not?" asked April.

"Because communist China took seized it about ten years ago, and the U.S. Government only recognizes Taiwan, not mainland China.

"But Nepal would be a really cool place to go.

"A lot of Tibetans live there, and you can stay stoned all the time."

"I heard *the Buddha* was born there," I commented.

Drake continued, "Yeah, it's really far out, man. It's like…where the hope for enlightenment was born. There are lots of Lamas, mystical gurus, and drugs are *everywhere*. Who could ask for more?"

"Yeah, that's really far fucking out there. I might do the same thing, and try to get a job teaching English," April commented with a puff.

Then, Lennie came up with an off-the-wall-downer when she said, "There are a lot of exotic diseases in Asia. They have malaria, rabies, plague, cholera, smallpox, typhoid, tuberculosis, parasites, and who knows what else. Maybe I don't want you coming home to me."

"There's also cobras, tigers, hyenas, and rhinoceros," I interjected. "Chances are…I won't even make it back!"

"Why can't we just live forever?" asked April.

"Sorry, babe, we all have to die sometime," Drake informed her.

"I don't necessarily believe that," Lennie responded in support of her very stoned, blonde-headed friend. "I don't really think we're even human…we're spirits…who are only temporarily using this body.

"However, I do believe that our physical bodies could last forever if we wanted them to. I mean, what if death is simply nothing more than a belief…that mass consciousness created thousands of years ago?"

"What you're saying doesn't fit the *modus operandi*," Drake noted. "To the best of my knowledge, *no one has ever not died*, so it can't just be a belief. Does anyone else have an opinion about what she just said?"

"I agree with Lennie," April commented. "I think the mind is really the key here. You are what you eat, and as you think, so you are also.

"And a person's health will be…*what they believe their health is*, both on a subconscious and unconscious level."

"Why can't it be on a conscious level?" Lennie asked.

"It could be," said April, "but most of mass consciousness operates in the shadows of the mind. The reason you start an exercise program is to reinforce the belief that your body's becoming thin and healthy.

"If you really believed that you might not have to exercise at all."

I said...I'd recently taken a class in Eastern Philosophy, and the professor discussed a Buddhist term that he referred to as *Dukkha.*

That meant...*everything that comes from our mind is garbage.*"

"According to Buddha, all of the shit we keep inside our brain is the source of human suffering," I explained to my friends.

"Are you saying that everything comes from the mind, including death?" Drake asked to make sure he was understanding correctly.

"It's the fear of death that comes from the mind," replied Lennie. "And I still believe that death is just a belief. I heard that there was once a person called Saint Germaine who lived for over one thousand years, and the only reason he finally died was that he became bored."

"So then, where does God fit into all of this?" Drake proposed. "Does God decide when each of us will die?"

"Don't get me started on that damn subject," Lennie responded.

"I don't know if there is an actual *Supreme Being,* or not, but even if there is one, I don't believe...that 'he or she' is concerned about us.

"Whatever God is...has never cared for humanity, and never will. It's like an absentee landlord, and most of the time...a slum-lord."

"But you just told this beautiful story about God sending all of us back here...to create a whole new world," April interjected.

"It was a story, an allegory, a fable. Truthfully, I'm over all this shit about having to deal with a faceless God. Why can't we ever see God? Why is God so unknowable? It doesn't make sense. Why does God have to be such a mystery? It's time for God to come out of the closet," Lennie ranted. "Maybe, *we sent ourselves* back down here to create a new world. You know, maybe...God had nothing to do with it."

"You've heard the phrase, 'You can't see the forest for all the trees.' We don't see God...for all the people," April tried to explain.

"What if...we're always seeing God, and just don't realize it?"

"Good point," said Drake, taking the initiative.

"That's what meditation is all about.

"After sitting on your butt for years and years trying to find God, it all becomes a big blur, until you can no longer distinguish God from your own butt. Eventually, it all just becomes one and the same.

"You know...like, we're all just part of one big ass hole."

"Hey, speaking of which, are there any more of those Buddhism classes going on? You know, like the one when we first met," I asked.

"Not the same one as before. The old Lama passed away a couple of years ago," Drake answered. "He was a cool dude."

"Actually, there are lots of classes on the subject of Buddhism where I go to meditate," April said. "Next week, our NYU Meditation Center is having a speaker to talk about the *Tibetan Book of the Dead*. It should be really interesting. I don't know much about it, but I think it must have to do with what happens to the soul after you die."

"Cool," I replied. "I think I'll check it out."

We continued to talk and get high late into the night until we all eventually crashed and passed out, but the seeds had been sown about joining the Peace Corps. The next morning, the seeds were already starting to grow, causing the idea to always be in the back of my mind.

Who knows? I thought to myself...*the Peace Corps might very well be an alternative to graduate school. I need to learn more about it.*

The next week, I went to the meditation center on Fifth Avenue and attended the lecture about the *Tibetan Book of the Dead*.

Instead of the lecture being held by a Lama, as I had hoped it would, it was being conducted by a relatively young American.

He was about thirty years old and had lived with Tibetan people for several years in India, at a place called *Dharamsala*. The city had been offered to thousands of Tibetan exiles in 1960 by India, which was sympathetic to the plight of the people because of their connection to the Buddhist teachings. Several other countries had done a similar kind of outreach, like in Nepal, Bhutan, and Sikkim.

As I listened to his words, I was in absolute awe.

"Good evening," he said. "Tonight I would like to share with you some of the information I have learned about the Buddhist view of death. Buddhists and Hindus alike believe the last thought one has at the moment of death determines the character of the next incarnation.

"On this point, Buddha said rebirth arises from two causes: the last thought before one's death, and the last actions of the previous life.

"The stopping of one's last thought is known as 'deceased,' and the appearance of one's first thought is their 'rebirth,' which will simply be the continuation of the last thought.

"Some scriptures in Buddhist traditions are intended to influence the thoughts of the deceased during the transitional period out of body. One of these is the *Bardo Thodol*, called *The Tibetan Book of the Dead*, which is also known as '*The book of natural liberation.*'

"In the Buddhist tradition, the afterlife is known as the '*Bardo,*' which is a gap, or interval of suspension, and is interpreted as an inter-mediate transitional state between death and rebirth. The Bardo refers not only to the interval after death but also to any suspension within the living situation. The text has been used to guide both the living and the deceased because it deals with the principles of 'birth and death' as they occur naturally and constantly in our waking state in this life.

"The Bardo experience is part of our basic psychological makeup. When we breathe in, there's the gap or interval of death, and when we breathe out, the same thing occurs. And so it goes back and forth.

"The Bardo is always present and always with us. Death occurs in every moment of time while we are living in our awareness, and in our intermediate states of consciousness, which we can use in our daily life to practice dying by becoming aware of its existence.

"Death is inevitable. You begin to die as soon as you're born.

"We can choose to ignore this unpleasant fact, busying ourselves with the tasks of present-day life until death inevitably comes to us, or we can face our inescapable fate, and prepare for it in our present life.

"With the decline of conventional religion and of religious values during the last three hundred years in the West and with the triumph of materialistic science and its marvelous technology, people have tended to push the existential fact of death out of their daily consciousness as if they would live forever. Increasingly, old people and the dying are hidden from our view because we are warehousing them in old people's retirement homes, or in sanitized hospital wards.

"Yes, violence and death are relentlessly depicted in films, on TV, and in video games, but these events no longer feel real and we have become desensitized to them. They are more like events depicted in cartoons. They do not touch us at the existential level. We repress the thought of our own mortality, believing that death will not come to us personally until it's too late...when death arrives from an accident or a terminal illness. However, the inevitability of our own death is actually very real and ever-present. Someday, it's going to happen.

"No amount of wishful thinking or distraction with entertainments will make it go away. In denying to ourselves that we will eventually die, we deny the part of ourselves called our *Shadow Self*.

"Death's inevitability is ever a part of our life, here and now, and it will follow us as relentlessly as the shadow follows the body each day; but our modern secular society and scientific rationalistic culture do not prepare us for death, and we've lost touch with the 'art of dying.'

"We could say the Bardo experience is part of the collective psyche of humanity and is located within the atmosphere of psychic energy surrounding our planet earth. This realm of the unconscious psyche is not simply filled with white lights and angels. The shadows are also there. The shadows we deny in ourselves and push out of sight, into our unconscious mind, will most surely meet us face to face in the Bardo, as well as our relatives and spiritual guides.

"You should understand that your physical death does not mean the end of your conscious existence. You have lived before in countless previous lives, and in countless other bodies in this ongoing cycle of existence called Samsara. Whatever actions you have done consciously in these past lives, whether positive or negative, are deposited in the dark unconscious depths of your stream of existence as karmic traces.

"When the appropriate circumstances arise in some future life, these karmic seeds become activated, germinate, and bring their karmic fruits. Thus, the situation you have in your present life…and even your present physical body, is the result of your past karma. But, in the same way, with each choice of your actions you make in this present life, you create new karma whether positive or negative, that will determine the course of your next life…so the situation is far from hopeless.

"In fact, at this very moment, you are actually creating your future lives through your thoughts and actions. All of us carry the seeds of our future karma with us, lifetime after lifetime.

"Each of us is like a mighty river…without any beginning in time, which flows through many different, and varied landscapes.

"Each of these landscapes…is another lifetime.

"When you understand that your present stream of consciousness is like a mighty river, then you know its waters change from moment to moment, so it's never the same, and yet it is still the same river.

"In the past, you have been many people.

"In the future, you will be many more.

"In each lifetime, you have lessons to be learned.

"Know that you are very fortunate because you possess a precious human existence. Such an existence is considered precious because it takes an exceedingly large accumulation of meritorious karma accrued over many lifetimes in order to realize your next human rebirth.

"This is a unique opportunity that should not be wasted. On this earth, it is in human existence that opportunities for spiritual evolution are at their maximum. There are many other possibilities of rebirth, both higher and lower, and there is no guarantee of yet another human existence, except through your actions here and now in this present life.

"Yes, at least for the present you have this precious human body. However, all things are impermanent, all monuments will eventually crumble into dust. Even the great mountains over millions of years will be washed away by the rains, and even the great oceans will eventually dry up in the fires of the sun. Eventually, the sun itself will fade, grow cold, and die. All things are impermanent, and especially this physical human body you now possess. It is certain that you will die eventually.

"The hour of your death is uncertain, but it is both certain and sure it will come unwelcomed and unannounced. For old age, sickness, and death follows all of us relentlessly like the shadow follows the body.

"You cannot flee from your shadow, just as you cannot escape the inevitability of death. You can only face it by discovering what you are.

"Remember…both Light and Dark…come from the same Source.

"This frail body of yours, produced from many past karmic causes and conditions, is unreliable and fragile like the flickering of the flame of a candle left outdoors in a violent windstorm. Certainly, it will not endure long. Nowhere will you find a physical body that is not a vessel for death. No one knows when the Lord of Death will come, for he is almost always unexpected, but it is certain he will come.

"Therefore, you should be mindful of the signs of approaching death, whether these come from an external source or an internal source, and you should always exert yourself on the spiritual path.

"Humans face two kinds of death. The first is a death that is caused by an untimely death, and the second is death that is caused due to the exhaustion of our life force. Before the conclusion of our natural life, untimely death may be turned away by methods of 'long-life practice.' Where the cause of death is due to the exhaustion of our life force, then these methods are of little value. Our situation becomes like that of an oil lamp empty of its fuel, for the flame will soon be extinguished.

"All life involves some kind of suffering, and all that is born...dies. Moment to moment, you die and are then reborn again. Rebirth is an ongoing process because the human soul can be in many bodies at once, just as one candle can light many flames.

"When you see a movie, things seem to be moving, but it's just one frame at a time. Just one moment in time after another moment in time, but it gives the *appearance* that it's moving. That is also like life, which is also moment to moment, from birth to death. Therefore, to have a perfected life is to have one perfect moment after another.

"In fact, each 'now moment' already is perfect.

"People sometimes ask me, 'Is there life after death?'

"The correct question should be, 'How could there not?'

"That takes us right back to Buddha's very first teachings about the 'Four Nobel Truths' where he explained the cause of human suffering, and the liberation of suffering. According to the *Bardo Thodol*, there is also the opportunity for the liberation of suffering after death.

"Buddhists believe...*there is no death*...simply a transformation. There's a transition...from the physical body...to a body of energy.

"So with that said, this is an appropriate 'Bardo' to end this lecture."

Everyone in the class laughed.

I couldn't remember his name, so after it ended, and the speaker sat down, there were some light refreshments for those who were hungry. I took this chance to briefly introduce myself.

"Hi, I'm Andy. I really enjoyed the talk. I was thinking perhaps, about maybe joining the Peace Corps…and going to Nepal."

"Good to meet you. My name is David Humphrey," he said and shook my hand. That's interesting, because so am I.

When spring arrived Simon and Garfunkel played a free concert for two-hundred thousand people in Central Park. By the time they played 'Bridge Over Troubled Water,' it was dark, and people began to hold up matches and lighters. Before you knew it, the whole park was lit up. Ever since that night, people all over the world have been doing the same thing…only now, these days they use cell phones.

Some say that spring represents not only the official end of winter, but it is also the beginning of new life and new beginnings.

That certainly seemed to be the case in many respects.

Spring was no longer just about pretty girls in Easter bonnets, but about pretty boys as well. Ponytails were now being worn by males almost as much as females and both sexes wore hairbands. More and more females were also beginning to wear pants instead of dresses.

This new androgynous look made many of those in the straight community particularly upset as the gay men and women of our country were finally coming out of the closet. As a result, there was now a new *Gay Rights Movement*…that was just beginning.

James Earl Ray was sentenced to prison for ninety-nine years, still claiming to be a pawn in the assassination of Rev. Martin Luther King.

John Lennon married Yoko Ono in Gibraltar and staged a *Bed-In* for world peace at the Amsterdam Hilton Hotel. They unleashed photos of the two of them lying naked in bed together.

In Israel, Golda Meir was elected Prime Minister.

Queen Elizabeth II, a luxury ocean liner, made her maiden voyage.

Sirhan, Robert Kennedy's killer, was sentenced to death.

The Supreme Court ruled, *all school districts must end segregation.*

Singers, George Harrison, and Mick Jagger were both arrested for possession of Marijuana in separate incidents while in London.

In the heaviest bombing raids to date, the U.S. dropped more than three thousand tons of explosives on enemy positions (i.e., villages) near the Cambodian border, but the number of servicemen actually in Vietnam was reduced to five hundred thousand troops.

By now, more than thirty thousand U.S. soldiers were dead.

More than eight million men and women had served in this war, but only five million U.S. troops had served during World War II.

At two o'clock in the morning, I received an emergency telephone call from Diane's sister. She said Diane had tried to kill herself again, but this time it wasn't due to a drug overdose.

It sounded a lot like a case of clinical depression.

Her sister felt that if anyone could help her, it was me.

She asked if I could come to Oakland as soon as possible and see if there was anything that I could do to help the situation.

I felt that I had no choice…and said I'd be there as soon as I could.

My classes for the semester had recently finished, so after telling Lennie what happened, I flew to California the very next morning.

Actually, I was looking somewhat forward to being back in my old neighborhood again and perhaps seeing some of my old friends.

But I had a feeling…my connection to Diane was starting to fade.

Purple Haze All in My Brain

Purple Haze…all in my brain…
Lately, days don't seem the same…
Acting funny, but I don't know why…
Excuse me, while I kiss the sky…
(Artist: Jimi Hendrix)

By the time I arrived in Oakland, in May of 1969, Diane was out of the hospital…and had both of her arms bandaged up to her elbow.

She said she didn't remember a lot about what happened, except for being very depressed for several months and had gone back to using heroin as her escape. She said that I was the only person who had ever shown her any real kindness or concern…but because I didn't return last summer, she had gone deeper and deeper into depression.

Diane's sister said she was sitting in the bathtub and cut both of her forearms with a razor blade. Her roommate was in the other room and heard her crying, opened the door only to see the tub full of blood, and then called 911. When the paramedics arrived, Diane cut the arteries on her wrists, too, right before attempting to run from the paramedics.

The next day, she called her sister from the psych-ward, who still wasn't sure how Diane was able to talk the doctors into letting her out so quickly. They kept her under observation for seventy-two hours and then apparently gave them a nice apology, a bright smile, and promised never to do it again. When I found her at the place, she was living on Telegraph Avenue, she seemed about as normal as ever.

We just picked up…where we'd left off…from the previous time.

♥ ♥ ♥

Diane told me about a new park near the university that had just
been created by the students and people who lived in the community.
They called it '*People's Park.*' She wanted to go there for the afternoon
and have a picnic, smoke some pot, and then go back to the apartment
she shared with Amy, another hippie chick…and her best friend.

Amy was also an artist, and together, the two of them had been able
to set up a t-shirt shop on Haight Street that was actually doing quite
well. Diane said, she hadn't been dating anyone and didn't want to,
admitting that Amy was also her part-time lover.

Right now, she just wanted to get her life back together.

The area just to the south of Berkley was called "hippie high street."
It was actually Telegraph Avenue, which had a lot of old houses that
were usually rented out to students and hippies, so drugs were always
available. The university wasn't happy with the hippie influence being
so close by, so they purchased three acres of land where most of the
buildings were located and then bulldozed them all down.

University officials said they were going to build more dormitories,
however, Governor Reagan had recently cut off funding for any further
student housing, so the land remained vacant for a long time.

There was just no point in allowing good land like that to be wasted.

Some of the Haight Street merchants had the idea to use the site for
a rock concert and brought in a truckload of trees and shrubs to plant.
Within days, hundreds of students and local hippies joined in and were
working at the site. On one weekend, as many as three thousand people
had turned up to build swings, slides, a wading pool, flowerbeds, and
even a sandbox. Within a month, 'People's Park' had been created.

As Diane and I walked through the new communal garden, I was
amazed at how it had all come together so quickly. With all of them
working together in unity…*as One*…they were like little worker bees,

acting from the higher calling of a group soul, with no real leader to tell them what to do. Instinctively, everyone seemed to already know what needed to be done for the highest good of everyone concerned.

It was an action that exemplified one heart, one mind, and one body, and was an act of loving intent. Speaking of which, and after our walk, we went back to her apartment that same afternoon and rekindled the old flame we'd had, which for me, had burned out a long time ago.

The very next morning, shortly before dawn, three hundred police officers sealed off the ten square blocks of the park while city workers bulldozed the gardens and the children's playground. Everyone who saw it, or even heard about it, was totally horrified and very upset.

After the demolition was over, the city erected an eight-foot-high cyclone fence around the property. Everything was completed that very morning, and the entire community was left in shock.

By noon, a protest rally was already in the making.

Diane and I, along with Amy and her two friends Shelly and Sam, attended the rally on the campus quadrangle, where several thousand people showed up to protest the unwanted attack.

The student body president, Dan Siegel, gave an address to the crowd on a quickly made wooden platform. Waving his arms and shouting to the crowd he said, "Come on! Let's go down there and take the park back! This is our park, and it belongs to us! Not them!"

Right from the pages of the American Revolution, instead of a small militia of colonists standing on Lexington Green at Concord facing the 'Red Coats,' a small militia from 'People's Park' marched off across the green grass of the Berkeley campus to face the 'Blue Coats.'

The *'Battle for People's Park'*...then began.

The park itself was only four blocks from where our rather large group of students had assembled, and we stormed off in the direction of the park like a hostile mob in search of the Frankenstein monster.

We were immediately confronted by a large line of police officers. For some reason, someone in our crowd decided to open a fire hydrant, and that act alone was enough to make the police retaliate.

They began by tossing tear gas, but some of the students grabbed the tear gas canisters and threw them back at the police. Then some of the students started throwing rocks and beer bottles. After that, the cops charged into our ranks, beating unarmed students with nightsticks.

There was no doubt that we had them outnumbered, and some of the crowd even managed to turn over a police car and set it on fire, but we didn't have any weapons or any way to protect ourselves.

I wanted to make sure Diane didn't get hurt, so my primary concern was trying to get her to a place of safety, rather than duke it out, or to have my head busted open again by the police as I did in Chicago.

Shouting out to Amy, Sam, and Shelly, I said we should all stick together as police reinforcements began to quickly arrive. That gave the Blue Coats the advantage of the field, and unfortunately, it was the Alameda County Sheriff's Deputies who appeared wearing their bright blue jumpsuits. They looked a lot like…the *Screaming Blue Meanies,* from The Beatles' movie, *Yellow Submarine.*

Instead of nightsticks, they were carrying shotguns loaded with some kind of non-lethal birdshot. It was obvious from the start that these out-of-town guys weren't going to take any crap from anybody.

Almost immediately, the Blue Meanies started firing pellets into the crowd, which stung like crazy. This managed to disburse a lot of the protesters from the open areas to places with more protection.

As we were trying to do the same thing, Diane and I were both hit by the stinging pellets which left small red welts on the unpadded parts of our bodies. Quickly, we found shelter with some other students.

We wound up behind a barricade of trash cans and bicycles near a group of students who were retaliating by throwing rocks and bottles at the deputies and the local police, but then we had to move behind yet another make-shift barrier of tables and chairs when a canister of tear gas sailed over our heads, landing in the street directly behind us.

The dense smoke from the explosion of tear gas caused the driver of a 1953 Plymouth to lose control and led to him crashing into the corner of the newly built Fine Arts Building. He almost hit a group of students who were huddled together behind some bushes.

The driver was Carlos, a young dark-haired lad from Brazil who was friends with Shelly. He managed to climb out the driver's window of his wrecked car, but then just stood there not knowing which way to run until the smell of the tear gas started to overtake him.

Then, he ran in the direction of Shelly who had begun shouting for him to come to us. "Over here, Carlos, you idiot! Get your ass over here before those fucking pigs smash your head in!"

Carlos leaped over the barricade to join our small group, which then caused the police to move in our direction…attacking with large black wooden batons and crowd control shields made of bullet-proof glass.

We decided to fall back, but there were many of those young rebels who resisted and tried their best to fight. Soon, they were either bruised or bleeding from the surging blue marauders' merciless mayhem.

The officers tried to chase us at first, but as rocks, bottles, and beer cans were coming at them from many directions they became distracted and decided to leave us alone. The cops were very brave when pitted against defenseless students but ran when they were under attack.

The five of us were now joined with another small group that was also trying to get away, which brought our total number to twelve.

Knowing we might come under attack at any moment, we followed a gravel road through some trees that led to the athletic field. When we got there, the football team was in the middle of summer tryouts.

We would have to cross the field to get off the campus, but at the moment we were trapped in between the police and the football players. It was like facing an unstoppable force, or an immovable object.

"Hey, man," Sam said, handing me a lit joint. "If we interrupt the football team, we're likely to have a whole new war on our hands."

"Yeah, instead of it being the freaks against the cops, it will be the freaks against the jocks," I replied with a laugh.

Then I took a long toke and passed it to Amy.

"Thanks," she replied. "I say we just do it, and then drop our pants and moon those goons right as we're leaving the field!"

"Maybe if we flashed our tits, they'll feel compelled to protect us from the police," Shelly interjected as she took the joint from Amy.

"Are you suggesting that the male species has an instinctual urge to protect females if they think they might get laid?" Amy noted.

"But, of course," Shelly replied with a laugh after her long exhale, "however, it might make them want to chase us even more."

"I've never had sex with a football player," said Diane, who was next in line for the joint. "Do football players do drugs too?"

"Shit, yeah," said Carlos, "most of them are fucking steroid freaks."

At that moment, an abrupt nearby explosion of tear gas resolved the dilemma, prompting us onto the field. But instead of trying to be quiet, we made as much noise as we could…in the hopes that somehow by acting crazy…it would scare them enough not to chase us.

This was as close as I wanted to be to a near-death experience!

Then, Sam yelled out to the football team at the top of his lungs, "Give peace a chance…you ugly mother-fuckers!" and led the charge of our small brigade across the football field towards the other side.

As we hit the turf, someone else shouted, "*Down with the pigs*!" and "*Jocks suck big ones*!" Of course, this inflaming rhetoric incited the football team to react immediately…but not in a good way.

That's when forty or more blue and gold football jerseys turned in our direction in search of a holocaust, wanting to do nothing more than to kick some peace-freak ass. Being quite stoned, we were somehow able to bolt across the field far in front of the on-coming assault.

Just as she promised, Amy stopped for just a moment to drop her bell-bottom pants and moon the entire team while Shelly lifted up her tie-dye shirt and flashed her small but perky freckled breasts at them.

"Come on, guys!" Diane shouted. "We've got to get out of here!"

With the coach's bullhorn screaming in the background for the team to come back, the sound of the players stampeding in hot pursuit, and the thought of police batons swinging wildly not far behind...we felt like young desperados being chased by a Tombstone Sheriff's Posse.

We crossed the field and safely reached a group of nearby buildings which were part of the campus Sports Administration Complex.

"I think the players have quit chasing us...and I didn't see any cops behind us either," Amy reported, short of breath.

"Let's go around to the back of that red building other there and go inside. I think that's where the players' dressing room is," said Carlos. "I just want to see if there's a water cooler nearby. I'm thirsty as hell."

We all needed a drink, so we did as he suggested.

Not only did we find a water cooler, but the athletic supply room door was open and athletic equipment was everywhere.

"All right, guys," he said, "it's time to level the playing field."

"This is some cool shit," Amy piped in.

Sam handed out the gear as quickly as he could, giving us football and baseball helmets, shin guards, shoulder pads, and chest protectors, and each of us was given our own baseball bat. He kept a catcher's mask for himself, thinking it would help to avoid getting a broken nose.

"We don't want to hurt anyone," Diane said. "We just want them to stop chasing us. That's all...so remember that."

"Ready? All right then, we need to get going," Sam instructed.

Carlos yelled, "And remember…*power to the people!*"

After each of us took a very quick puff from another freshly lit joint, we all yelled at the same time… "*Power to the people!*"

Once again, we stormed outside…feeling rejuvenated and happy, like the true peace and love warriors we were…but luck was with us because as we ran out the door we encountered no one to fight.

We hadn't been seen ducking into the building, so there were no cops to greet us. We decided it was best to get off the campus as quickly as possible and head home. I'm sure we looked funny-as-hell to our friends as we arrived on our street with all of that sports equipment on.

The only thing we were missing…was a football.

By the time we got home most of the skirmish was over for the day. The students had been dispersed, and the cops slacked off, so we hid the gear…to use for another day. Then we went back to Haight Street where there was another rally being held to determine what to do next.

Some of those who had seen us earlier showed up with their own bats and helmets for protection just in case another riot broke out.

At the meeting, they told us that even innocent bystanders had been hit by the shotgun blasts that day. One man was permanently blinded when he was hit in the eye by a pellet, and many had serious injuries. All in all, over a hundred people were hospitalized with minor injuries.

In the minds of the students, there was absolutely no reason why the land could not be used as a park until the dorms were built, but the state officials and university administration would not negotiate.

As a result, unrest continued.

The next day, two thousand National Guardsmen were brought in, armed with bayonets. Seven hundred cops patrolled the area day and night, and public gatherings were banned while curfews were imposed.

The following day, tear gas was thrown at a group of junior high students, who were out for a field trip. It was something totally uncalled for, making most of us feel like we were in Nazi-occupied territory.

On another day, Diane and I were talking with a group of people near the campus and were actually made to lie down on the concrete. Then we were searched for weapons and verbally humiliated.

If any of us tried to move, they threatened to hit us with a riot baton.

When students tried to organize another rally close by, a National Guard helicopter dropped tear gas on the crowd that blanketed most of the campus. The gas wound up getting into a nearby hospital and an elementary school. Troops proceeded to arrest everyone who was not a student…all together over five hundred people were taken to Santa Rita Prison for processing. To everyone's surprise, the troops even built a machine-gun tower inside the park and proudly flew an American flag.

No one could believe that this was really happening.

When hippies and students tried to set up another park on a small piece of public land located on the other side of the campus, the police moved in and destroyed that as well.

Smaller versions of People's Park began popping up everywhere, only to be destroyed by National Guard troops as soon as they were discovered. This whole thing was totally absurd and there was no doubt that it was time to put an end to this utter nonsense.

That evening, I was invited to attend a meeting put together by a coalition of student leaders and Haight Street merchants. It was to be a secret meeting held at the newly built warehouse for 'The Oracle'…run by my friend, Don. He had finally sold the old Psychedelic Shop and was now devoting all his time to running the paper. We all agreed that through *The Oracle*…it would be announced that in just three days we were going to organize another march to protest the shameful behavior of both the police and the National Guard. The announcement would emphasize the peaceful aspects of our protest, and demand that *no more* violence would be tolerated by *anyone* on either side.

In response to our advertising, on May 30th, twenty-five thousand brave and beautiful people, who represented all walks of life, marched peacefully towards the park. Even though it was guarded by police sharpshooters on the rooftops of buildings and ringed with guardsmen holding fixed bayonets, the marchers refused to be stopped again.

'*We, the People*,' gave direct tearful eye contact to the soldiers and proceeded to place flowers in the barrels of the rifles that were being pointed at us. We told them they were still loved by everyone despite what they were being made to do. As the ritual for peace continued, many of the young guardsmen actually had tears in their eyes.

By the time '*the Peoples*' march was over, not one single disruptive act had been committed. It had been the most successful, non-violent protest that had taken place in several months. Seventeen days later, the National Guard troops left the campus. Of course, the fence remained standing in order to prove that they still retained all the power.

However, in our hearts…we knew that we'd won the battle.

'*We, the People*,' had not only stood our ground for something we believed in…but had also changed the lives of many.

Even though the summer of 1969 had just begun, it turned out to be quite the summer to remember. No longer was it about the East Coast and West Coast taking action, but now, students were demonstrating on campuses all across the nation and even in the heartland of America.

At the University of Wisconsin, and also at the University of North Carolina, National Guard troops were using bayonets and tear gas against the students. All the while, the establishment continued to try and blame the conflict on just a small group of white radicals who called themselves Students for a Democratic Society (SDS), claiming that they were responsible for most of the disruptions.

Also that summer, Mary Jo Kopechne drowned after a car accident, and her passenger, Senator Edward Kennedy, fled the scene without reporting it to the police until the next day.

Many believed…he was intoxicated at the time.

Actress Sharon Tate, and four others, were murdered in Hollywood by several followers of a cult leader, Charles Manson, who all lived in a California commune. Charles Manson, a long-haired, crazy hippie, had been in and out of prison for most of his life. Manson and his group of followers became a huge blow to the credibility of the peace and love movement because his actions confirmed to many of those within the establishment that all of us must be dangerous radicals as well.

After the battle in Chicago and the arrest of the 'Chicago Eight,' many people involved in the anti-war movement were convinced that free speech was no longer an American freedom. In fact, a lot of people were fed up with trying to remain peaceful. After all, peace itself hadn't really worked, so maybe now it was time for violence.

As a result, an extremely violent group of students had formed in Greenwich Village. They became known as "Weathermen."

They were a radical faction of the SDS that had recently taken over leadership of the organization at a SDS convention. However, after they took credit for bombing several government buildings that included post offices and draft boards, thirty people in the group were indicted and became fugitives who were mostly hiding in New York City.

The Weathermen issued a political manifesto in several of the local underground papers that summer. The headlines stated very plainly… *You Don't Need a Weatherman to Know Which Way the Wind Blows.*

In the article, they advocated a city-wide, anti-pig movement, and even went so far as to romanticize the Manson family killings. It was decided by the group that the only way to get people's attention about the truth of what's happening in Vietnam was to bring the war home to America, what was interesting was that most of those who belonged to the Weather Underground were not degenerate dropouts but were well educated, upper-middle-class kids from well-to-do white families.

The Weathermen were apparently determined to overthrow the United States Government in the belief that we had criminally waged war in Vietnam and were continuing to persecute minority groups, such as the Black Panthers. Many of the members were articulate, attractive, and charismatic, and spent a lot of time in the news media spotlight.

Figures such as Kathy Boudin, Terry Robbins, Bernadette Dohrn, Mark Rudd, Naomi Jaffe, and Brian Flanagan were said to be sexy, young outlaws by many, much like Bonnie and Clyde, who believed in what they were doing. In addition, they represented youth, exuberance, sex, and drugs. But most of all, they wanted action.

On several occasions, I had the opportunity to talk to some of the members who were staying at April's apartment in what was called a "safe house." April had been a regular member of the SDS for several years and was sympathetic to what the group was doing.

After they went underground, groups of houses were set up all over the city, and around the country, where several people could stay.

Because Larry had been my friend and was now a fugitive for being subversive, they thought I supported the cause and was on their side.

What was interesting to me was that most of them truly believed that by blowing up a building, or vandalizing something, that somehow this would cause the entire United States government to collapse.

As convincing as they were with their political theory…that we had to 'bring the war home' for people to be able to see what was really happening, it just didn't make sense to me. Now, I finally understood what Jimi meant…for I too, had purple haze all in my brain.

In Greenwich Village that summer, a huge riot took place against the police by the gay community that later became known as "the Stonewall riots." The story goes that a group of gay men took to the streets and openly fought with police following a drug raid by the cops on the Stonewall Bar, which was a well-known gay establishment in the Village. Afterward, the group proudly proclaimed, *'Gay Power,'* creating the beginning of gay liberation and the gay rights movement.

In England, Prince Charles officially became the Prince of Wales, and ex-Rolling Stones guitarist, Brian Jones, was found dead in his swimming pool from a drug overdose at his home in Sussex.

After the *Apollo* space program landed a manned lunar module on the moon's surface, Neil Armstrong became the first man in history to actually set foot on the moon. "The Eagle has landed," he said.

"It's a small step for man and a giant leap for mankind."
But he planted an American Flag, instead of one for the World.

The *Equal Rights Amendment* for women fell short by three states and didn't pass continuing the absence of women's right to vote.

To make matters worse, scientists were claiming that two-thirds of the world's forests had been lost to clearance and agriculture.

"If we don't stop deforestation, especially of the rain forests in South America," they said, "then the world could run out of oxygen."

Meanwhile, the Palestine Liberation Organization (PLO) created by Yasser Arafat, quickly became a hostile threat to the security of both Israel and the stability of the entire Middle East.

Despite everything going on in the world, the biggest news of the summer was the event everyone had all been waiting for. It was soon to become known as, *'the Woodstock Music Festival.'*

By the Time We Got to Woodstock

By the time we got to Woodstock...
We were half a million strong...
And I dreamed I saw the bomber death planes...
Turning into butterflies, above our nation...
(Artist: Joni Mitchell)

It turns out...there never was another armed American Revolution that was anywhere close to what we had in 1776...but there's no doubt, the Sixties had undergone a *Revolution in Consciousness.*

Everyone could see that the entire world was now different.

Young people had managed to break out of the molds their parents were stuck in, expanded their awareness, and discovered that music was an effective outlet for expressing their creative ideas.

It was no wonder that the hippies would bring an end to that era in our history with a giant outdoor musical celebration. After all, with the coming together of the tribes at all of the many concerts, and with the *Be-Ins* held in California, everyone who had been in attendance soon realized that this was bound to happen...so those who were part of the new counterculture just decided that they were going to make it happen with their strength in numbers...and nothing could stop them.

True believers still call Woodstock the capstone of an era that had been devoted to human advancements in consciousness and awareness.

Cynics, on the other hand, say it was a fitting and ridiculous end to an era of naivety and irresponsibility. But then, there are also those of us who say...*who cares. it was still one hell of a party!*

The Woodstock Music and Art Fair happened in August of 1969, drawing more than four-hundred-and-fifty thousand people to a large thirty-five-acre pasture in Sullivan County in upstate New York.

For four days, the site became a counter-culture-mini-nation.

Minds were opened, drugs were all but legal, and all of the music and love were free. It began on Friday, August 15th, at 5:07 p.m., with the music of Richie Havens. He sang an awesome and inspiring version of...*Here Comes the Sun.* The festival continued until the mid-morning of Monday, August 18th, when Jimi Hendrix played his own electric guitar adaptation of...*The Star-Spangled Banner.*

The Woodstock festival created one of the nation's worst traffic jams, but it also inspired the creation of a slew of local and state laws to ensure that nothing like this would ever happen again.

"What we have here...*is a 'once-in-a-lifetime' occurrence,*" said the Bethel township local historian, Bert Feldman.

It was a fusion of energy that defined an era, and one that will never be reproduced again. Why it happened, or how it was able to happen, may never really be known. Regardless, it was a truly magical event.

Woodstock was the great gathering of the tribes we had asked for, the quickening, the great calling, or whatever. Somehow, something was *tapped* from the inside – like a nerve of consciousness – and for an unknown reason, everybody felt the inner calling to show up.

The counterculture's biggest bash had ultimately cost more than two million dollars. It was sponsored by four very different young men.

Strangely, the oldest of the four was only twenty-six years old.

John Roberts was heir to a toothpaste manufacturing fortune and a multi-million-dollar trust fund. He'd only been to one rock concert in his entire life, which had been by The Beach Boys.

Joel Rosenman was only twenty-four years old and was also the son of a rich Long Island orthodontist. He was a Yale college graduate, but in 1967, the young and mustached Rosenman was playing guitar for a lounge band in motels from Long Island to Las Vegas.

Artie Kornfield was twenty-five years old and wore a suit, being the vice president of Capitol Records. He smoked hash in the office and was the company's primary connection with the rockers who were starting to sell millions of records to the youth culture.

Michael Lang didn't wear shoes very often, and his friends would describe him as "*a cosmic pixie with a head full of curly black hair that bounced on his shoulders.*" At age twenty-three, he owned what some say was the first headshop to ever exist in the state of Florida.

In 1968, Lang produced one of the biggest rock music shows ever, a two-day pop festival in Miami that attracted forty-thousand people.

To this day, the founders of Woodstock still disagree on who came up with the original idea for the concert. Dulled by time, competition, and countless retelling, no one's recollection is consistent…except that someone decided there really needed to be a huge outdoor rock concert.

Originally, it was scheduled to handle only fifty thousand people, to use a slogan proclaiming, '*Three Days of Peace and Music*'…and to downplay the highly abstract theme of this being the *Age of Aquarius*.

The promoters of the event worried that using the word 'peace' in the slogan might link the anti-war sentiment to the rock concert but they wanted to avoid any violence and thought that perhaps a slogan using the word 'peace' would in some way help to keep order.

Max Yasgur's six-hundred-and-sixty-six-acre dairy farm was about a hundred miles north of New York City. The thirty-five-acre field sloped downward and formed a natural amphitheater, but the stage was so far away…that some people could barely see anything.

However, that didn't matter…*but just to be there*…did.

At the time, it was the largest performing stage that had ever been constructed, and it took an entire month to erect. The audience would be able to hear the music from a huge speaker system mounted on eighty-foot-tall scaffolds located on either side of the stage.

Wavy Gravy and his Hog Farm commune had been asked to come out and help build the site, as well as to provide food and security.

He agreed, saying that if anyone got out of hand, they would stop the fight by throwing a pie in their face. If the crowd became too tense, they planned to throw balloons to the people who would in turn begin tossing them back and forth to each other.

As soon as I heard it was going to happen, I told Diane I had to go.

I even offered to bring her with me, but once again, she refused to return to the East Coast. I asked her to try and not get depressed again, and to quit doing so many hard drugs. I also promised to return as soon as possible. She seemed to be all right with that, so I packed my bags and headed out to attend the festival in upstate New York.

My friends and I drove to upstate New York on the day before the concert and found a room to stay in at an old farmhouse.

We considered ourselves lucky to find a room only five miles away from the festival site. Early the next morning, on '*Woodstock Friday*,' we packed up the van and headed to the festival so we could find a good place to camp. For most people, driving was almost impossible, but we managed to get there before the New York State Freeway was closed. However, the traffic had already come to a total crawl.

When we arrived, we parked the van near the showering area and began to walk around and meet people from all over the country.

Oranges and apples were freely offered to us during our walk.

The feeling of peacefulness seemed to be everywhere.

There was also an acceptance, often by total strangers, who offered us a place on their blankets, to sit down and talk, and share a joint.

We'd purchased our tickets for eighteen dollars each, for the full three days of the festival, which amazingly…lasted four days.

Only a few hours after it opened, the fences were knocked down and it was declared to be a free festival for anyone who showed up.

Throughout the festival, everyone was wearing the latest fashions in hippie-wear. Apparel like bell-bottoms, dashikis, afros, beads, and peace signs were all popular fashion statements. For the next few days, we lived with hardly any food, sleep, or shelter…to speak of.

At one point, I was probably more soaking wet than I ever was in my life, yet, with all these discomforts it was still the most spiritually and emotionally positive experience I'd ever had in my life so far.

The events of Woodstock are not only forever imprinted upon my soul, but upon everyone who was there. Sometimes I wonder how we endured all of the many hardships, and yet could still have such positive feelings about the whole experience when it was over.

It was far more reaching than merely historical significance, and I'd like to think it was no coincidence that Woodstock occurred around the same time that the first human beings landed on the moon.

It was a reflection of something of great…*almost Biblical.*

At ten o'clock that night, we finally made it to within five hundred yards of the stage and stayed close until Joan Baez finished the last set at two o'clock in the morning. I won't describe all the bands that played over the next three days because it would be too lengthy. And after all, a documentary movie is readily available for anyone to watch.

Hippies were everywhere like waves across the ocean and as far as the eye could see. People were dancing, bikers were trying to do some kind of crowd control, and there were little booths set up in the woods selling all kinds of things, like drugs and t-shirts...during these crazy three days of unadulterated freedom and hedonistic experiences.

At one point, I fell asleep under someone's American flag and woke up to the sound of Country Joe and the Fish shouting to the crowd,

"Give me an F! ...Give me a U! ...Give me a C! ...Give me a K!

"What does it spell?"

His voice resounded over the field as everyone yelled out "FUCK!"

And they did it...as loud as they could.

I was so emotionally moved that I started to cry.

Saturday morning opened with Wavy Gravy shouting out to those in the audience with a microphone, "What I have in mind is breakfast in bed for four hundred thousand people." Then, he and others threw out thousands of oranges to the sea of people all around us.

On Saturday afternoon we got closer to the stage and convinced the security guy that we were friends of Wavy Gravy and the Hog Farm, so we got to go backstage...while there, we briefly got to hang out with Jimi Hendrix. Later on, during a rainstorm, we met up with some of my friends from the Hog Farm and helped them distribute food for lunch.

Some of the people who knew me were actually very curious about what we had experienced in Chicago, and about our confrontations with the police in both Berkley and New York City.

I also noticed that even the former presidential candidate, *Pigasus*, was here at Woodstock. I was glad to see he'd made it back safely.

On Sunday, Lennie and I helped to unload the helicopters that had been brought in to deliver cheese sandwiches, apples, and raincoats.

Since the concert had been declared a disaster area by the governor of New York State, people from the surrounding communities prepared many of the needed provisions. Most of the concession stands had sold out of their supplies within only a few hours with no way to replenish their items. However, what the surrounding communities did for us was show the world that even people who were not at the festival were simply working to make this a magical event.

Woodstock was far greater than anyone could've imagined.

Here we were in upstate New York, and instead of thinking about the war, people were loosening up and allowing peace, love, happiness, music, and the experience of *getting back to nature.*

It seemed that east coast consciousness had finally caught up with west coast consciousness. Everyone who came, in some way, shared and contributed to the essence of what became the '*Woodstock story.*'

We were all in communion with each other, to a greater or lesser degree, sharing the experience, the hopes, the hedonism, the desires, and whatever else…as one heart, one mind, and one body.

Words cannot describe Woodstock.

It was incredible, exhilarating, and exciting.

It was even…much more than that.

There were those of us who were trying to be socially responsible for the direction our country was heading and trying to *wake up* fellow citizens, while others were just having fun smoking weed, tripping out, and being irresponsible hippies playing in the mud.

There were Vietnam vets, artists, craftsmen, campers, long-hairs, short-hairs, bikers, babies, young kids, high school kids, college kids, college grads, dropouts, and even conservatives. We saw some people walking around naked. Most certainly…it was all a glorious activity.

Between performers, an announcer would sometimes grab the mic and stop the music until the audience members who climbed up on the speaker scaffolding for a better view came back down. Too much weight up there and the whole thing would come crashing down.

Luckily, there were no catastrophes like that.

Even though the anti-war and anti-draft groups were not included as a part of the Woodstock festival, as the music continued, there were people who were not against the war who had come just to watch and have a good time…and to see a lot of cool bands while observing the peacefulness of those *who were* against the war. It gave them time to pause and think about what we were really trying to accomplish.

For folks who were still undecided on the war effort, chances are, they were asking themselves whether all of these beautiful people had been victims of propaganda instigated by communist organizations.

I wondered…how many converts there'd be…when it was over.

Periodically, we'd get up and move around a bit, and would see lots of happy smiling people just digging the whole thing.

Some of the people were just experiencing the joyful feeling one gets by returning to nature, while others considered dropping out of a culture that was imprisoned by the inertia of its own conservatism.

Idealism was in the air right beside the marijuana smoke. Maybe, what was happening at Woodstock would spread, and perhaps a quiet revolution, or even *evolution*, would take place.

So I also wondered, if Woodstock would be the key that disengaged the U.S.A. from the crazy and unnecessary war in Vietnam.

There was one incident that did take place when Abbie Hoffman ran on-stage while *The Who* was in the middle of performing.

He attempted to make an announcement about the imprisonment of John Sinclair…who was a fellow radical and friend of Abbie's.

The Who's lead guitarist, Pete Townsend, clearly disapproved of the interruption and proceeded to hit Abbie with his guitar, driving him off the stage. The incident was symbolic because it showed how the political counterculture Hoffman symbolized wasn't always supported by the music counterculture, represented by rock groups like *The Who*.

On Sunday, the rains came, and many people didn't have umbrellas, raincoats, plastic tarps, or other protection. People shared whatever makeshift shelters they had, while others simply used cardboard.

Everything...and everybody...got wet.

Places with a lot of foot traffic (like near the stage) had mud that was a foot deep. Whatever was on the ground, got pushed into the mud, and with the rain...came cooling temperatures. The rain put a damper on things, but like anything else, some managed to turn even that into something fun...like mud-sliding down the hill.

Drugs, of course, were pretty rampant. A lot of pot got smoked, and a lot of acid was dropped. Between performances, there were frequent announcements over the public address system to be on the lookout for someone who was passing out tabs of acid in sugar cubes.

"Brown acid...don't take it, people, it's bad," they announced.

The stuff caused a dozen victims to be airlifted out by helicopter medical teams. As a result, some saw Woodstock as being nothing more than a big concert, and the press tried their hardest to defuse our religious experience. They made people think that hippies were just a bunch of drug users, but we all knew that just wasn't true.

No, that's not what it was about.

Not all hippies did drugs.

It was something much greater that pulled us all together for those four days in August of 1969. It was something that went beyond the mere experience of being human, only hinted at in Timothy Leary's psychedelic prayers or Allen Ginsberg's Hindu mantras. It was much more Divine, spiritual, un-nameable, and perhaps even unfathomable.

We were acting in unity, as one celestial being, one Divine Soul, and one consciousness. Together, we were...*as God, also.*

After Woodstock was over, people all over the country began to drop out of mainstream America. They stopped wearing animal furs and eating meat, demanded an end to the war, and began to respect what being a hippie was all about. Hippies were no longer freaks.

They were just...*everyday people.*

♥ ♥ ♥

By Monday morning, most of the masses of people had already left, but Jimi Hendrix wrapped it up on his electric guitar...in a way that it had never been played...*or heard before.*

As I listened, I remembered the signs that pro-war supporters had held in opposition to our protest marches, the ones that said things like, *America, love it or leave it.* But the fact was...we all loved America.

"We were all red-blooded, regardless of what we thought about the war in Vietnam, or whether or not we supported what the President and the government were doing. We loved this land and were all fighting for the same freedoms the early American colonists had fought for.

Admittedly, the thought that we were fighting for the same ideals was confusing, but there just was no way we were going to leave.

Within months, Joni Mitchell and many other artists wrote songs about Woodstock. Even Abbie Hoffman took time to write a book called...*The Woodstock Nation.* Charles Schulz created a character in his 'Peanuts' cartoon strip and named it Woodstock...and the youth of the late 1960s became known as...*the Woodstock Generation.*

Woodstock was a fitting tribute to those who had tried so hard to heal the bleeding soul of our nation...in the name of peace and love, instead of war. It was a symbolic recognition of all the hard work the hippies had voluntarily undertaken...and the transformation that their heroic revolution in consciousness had been able to accomplish.

Jumping Jack Flash

But it's all right now…
In fact, it's a gas…
Yeah, it's all right…
I'm Jumpin' Jack Flash, it's a Gas! Gas! Gas!
(Artist: The Rolling Stones)

The decade of the Sixties had been turbulent, and sometimes our actions seemed to represent a contradiction of philosophies. Some of us had declared war on the establishment *through violent means*, but for those of us who professed that *the principles of non-violence* were the appropriate new consciousness…we were the stronger force.

It was actually…*the peace and love movement*…that prevented an armed revolution from taking place in our country.

♥ ♥ ♥

It had been a truly incredible summer, but the year was hardly over.

In September of 1969, I was back in New York City and was at the student union auditorium signing up for my last semester of classes.

I was very excited because one of the classes could be an elective and I planned to take a philosophy course in Tibetan Buddhism.

While I was there, I happened to see a small desk near the entrance with a sign that posted 'Peace Corps'…reminding me of my promise to check it out as an alternative to going to graduate school.

My chances of getting accepted into graduate school at NYU were almost certain. However, I decided to wander over to the table anyway.

There was a pretty, young, brown-eyed girl with long dark hair who was sitting behind the table. With a rather cheery smile, she asked me, "Have you ever thought about joining the Peace Corps?"

"Yeah, and I'd like to find out if I qualify, or not."

"Great!" she said with excitement. "My name is Kimberly.

"I was in Sierra Leon working for two years as a schoolteacher.

"It was a really incredible experience. Can I give you an application and maybe answer some of your questions?"

"Is it difficult to get in?" I asked.

"All you need is to have a college degree and two years of related experience, but the hardest part is just getting through this application.

"It's twenty pages long and we're going to need a full set of your college transcripts, three sets of fingerprints, a birth certificate, and four letters of recommendation from friends, relatives, or professors.

"On your application, you need to list three countries that you'd be willing to work in, and then list three different job choices."

"What countries are the easiest to get into?" I asked.

"Hardship countries…like Thailand, Pakistan, Nepal, Afghanistan, Bangladesh, and Ceylon. It used to include India, and at one time we had over a thousand volunteers there, but recently, the Peace Corps was asked to leave India because the people thought we were spies for the CIA or something. These days, a lot of people are asking to be sent to South America so they can learn to speak Spanish," she explained.

"Oh, so I don't have to know how to speak the language already?"

"Oh, no…the Peace Corps gives you several months of intensive language training as well as cross-cultural training before you even set foot in a village. You'll learn more in a couple of months than you do with two years of college study…much of it is done in-country."

"I'd really like to live in a Buddhist country, in the mountains, so if I wanted to go to Nepal, what would be the best job to pick?"

"Well, Nepal is the second poorest country in the world right now with Bangladesh being number one. They really have a strong need for people with agricultural experience, so they're looking for people with some farming background. They also need teachers, but these days, everyone wants to be a teacher. So if you want to guarantee yourself a position, then put down agriculture. And…if you don't have any real experience, well…hell, just make something up.

"After all…no one is going to call up some old farmer in Nebraska and ask him if he remembers you shoveling shit for two years."

She was a pretty cool chick, and I wished I could have gotten to know her a little better, but she said she was moving around the country doing this recruiting thing and had to be at Princeton tomorrow.

I thanked her for the information and took the application.

Then it suddenly occurred to me…*there's probably a lot of lonely schoolteachers just like her…living in the Himalayas.*

On the way home, I remembered back to when I was a young kid. My grandmother had lived on a small farm in north Georgia, and my parents and I would visit her every summer. I would help her gather vegetables from the garden, pick eggs from the henhouse, feed the goat, and sometimes even shovel shit from the horse stable.

So the way I figured it, if you were to count up all of those summers, then I really did have about two years of agricultural experience.

*Far out…*I said to myself…*I just might get in after all.*

In September, President Richard Nixon announced the withdrawal of thirty-five thousand troops from Vietnam. It seemed that many of the anti-war groups were now beginning to hold gatherings that were advertised as 'pro-peace rallies,' prayer vigils, or moratoriums, instead of being billed exclusively as an anti-war effort.

Millions of people across the nation observed a one-day Vietnam moratorium on October 16th. It was organized by college students and was called 'Vietnam Moratorium Day.' However, despite the subtle change in climate, there were still a number of massive protests taking place in Washington, D.C., that same month.

In November, President Nixon announced that North Vietnam had rejected his secret U.S. peace proposals. Therefore, the war in Vietnam would continue. The President then said that those who still supported the war effort were the 'great, silent majority.'

On Veterans Day, a small group of citizens and veterans marched down the streets of the nation's capital in a 'pro-war' demonstration.

A few days later, two-hundred-and-fifty-thousand people came to Washington, D.C. to march against the war at the same time that more than one-hundred-thousand marched on the streets of San Francisco.

The news accused a U.S. infantry unit, led by Lt. William Calley, of committing the March 1968 massacre at *My Lai*, a South Vietnamese village where more than four-hundred-and-fifty unarmed and innocent villagers were slaughtered in a U.S. military attack.

The Army announced that Lt. Calley would face a court-martial for the massacre, while on a more positive note, the U.S. military agreed to destroy all of its germ warfare weapons.

I was watching the *Apollo* space crew make a second landing on the moon when I received a telephone call from Lennie. April had called her and said that Mark Rudd (with the Weather Underground) wanted to meet Drake and me at a small café located in the Village. She said that Drake was already on his way. Hesitantly, I accepted the invitation.

When I arrived, Drake was already there…plus, it wasn't just Mark, but a couple of his other friends too. Mark recognized me from our previous meeting at April's apartment and stood up to shake my hand.

"Hey, man. What's up?" I asked.

"All kinds of new things...and I'll tell you about them in a moment. What's going on with you?" he answered.

"I'm graduating next month...but at the moment I don't have any definite plans for the future. I might go to graduate school, or I might even join the Peace Corps," I responded.

"That's what I heard from April. Actually, that's what this is about. You see, Tex...we all want to change the world...and the Peace Corps is pretty far out there all right, but what we really need is to change things here at home. You could help the world much better by staying here, rather than traveling halfway around the world."

"Exactly how is that?" I asked feeling somewhat intrigued.

"You see...we need some new blood in our organization.

"We need smart people, educated people, people who will make us not only look good but who will be able to make things happen. I mean, people like you and Drake, could make a big difference to the group. We need people like you...and I want to offer you both a job."

"You mean...*a real job?*" Drake asked.

"Yeah, man, a real full-time fucking job. You see, we've got money and we can pay you a lot more than you're going to make out there on the streets of New York City even with a bachelor's degree."

"So all I have to do is blow up a few buildings? Is that it?" I asked, feeling like there was some major manipulation in the air.

"You don't have to blow up anything, but we do need people like you who are already part of the revolution to help us with what we're doing. It would include things like helping us recruit new members, organizing more safe houses, doing the planning and the paperwork for setting up covert operations, and implementing intelligence activities. You know, that sort of thing. In other words, to help us run the business without actually getting your hands all that dirty."

"Sounds to me like you need a mob-boss from the Mafia," I noted.

"No, man, they want to bring the war home to the people here in America so that the war will finally come to an end," Drake explained. "When it's all over, they're going to be heroes," he added.

"That's our motto," said Mark. "Yeah, it's *'Bring the War Home.'* That's the only way to end this war, Tex, and there are a lot of people out there who are ready to back us…both financially and with weapons.

"Just look at your friend, Larry…for example.

"Do you remember what he did?"

"Larry was a paranoid schizophrenic who probably should have been on some heavy tranquilizers instead of so much LSD," I snapped.

To avoid any tension, I calmly said, "But, I know what you mean. There are lots of people ready to go to war…when the time is right."

"That's it, man. That's exactly what it's all about…but it's also about getting the right leadership in place. That's what the movement is missing the most right now…*good leadership*. People like Hoffman and Rubin can't pull it off because they're just too much into their own fucking ego, and not level-headed enough, but with some new blood, meaning people like you, I think we can really do it."

"I just don't know if I really want to become an outlaw at this time in my life. I mean, maybe the world does need more outlaws, but I don't know for sure if I want to be one of them."

"Let me tell you something, brother. It may already be too late."

"What do you mean?" I questioned.

"I mean the *Feds*, man. They know everything about you two guys. You know this country has already become a police state. Tex…they know about your experiences in Oakland, and Drake, they know what you were into at Cornell. They also know what you both did in Chicago, and that you were friends with Larry and Gary. They know about your drug contacts, and what you've been doing for the anti-war effort.

"I mean, hey, man, you guys are already outlaws in their books."

"They haven't picked you up yet because there haven't been any warrants issued…but the time is coming, man. It's going to happen.

"You need to either get off the streets or start watching your back, but when you sign on with us, you're going to be completely protected because the Feds won't know where in the hell you are.

"We're going to make it look like you've completely vanished."

I swallowed hard. "Fuck, I never thought about that," I admitted.

When I looked at Drake, I could tell he wasn't bothered at all about what Mark had just said. In fact, he was smiling, almost as if he were thinking…*Man, I'm finally somebody important.*

"You come with us, and we'll teach you how to lay low, and you'll be making some good money, too. After we've won the war and the government has been toppled, you'll be right up there at the top of the organization and maybe even a vice president, or something like that."

"I'll tell you what," I insisted, "I need some time to think about it. I'm going to go ahead and graduate in December and then I'll weigh in on my options. This is new for me. It's very dangerous and I don't want to just rush into anything…you dig?"

"I'll think about it, too," Drake replied.

"Of course. Hey, dudes, we dig it. I didn't expect you to just dive right in…but remember, this is a ground floor opportunity to be right there on top of things when the government falls. When it does, you'll be like the founding fathers of a whole new country. You might be like George Washington or Benjamin Franklin, and believe me, it's just a matter of time before it happens. So let me know something in a couple of weeks. Thanks for coming. See you guys later."

That night, Drake and I met back at April's apartment to talk.

"Hey, man, that was sure a surprise," I said to Drake.

"It sure as fuck was," Drake agreed.

"So what's your take?"

"I could tell you were a little put off by it," he noted, "but it *really* is a ground floor opportunity for both of us."

"I don't know how I feel about being a part of a violent revolution. When I first got into this movement, I thought it was just going to be about peace and love. You know, like what the old Buddhist Lama was trying to teach. But this is a whole new thing...and it's not pretty."

"I know but look at what happened in Chicago. I mean, dude, you tried to be peaceful, but you got your ass kicked by the police anyway and they made you become violent. Peace just isn't working anymore.

"I have to agree with Mark that it's time to bring the war home and take it to the streets. It's the only way American people will understand what the fuck is really going on. It's the only way to open their eyes to the truth. Chairman Mao said, 'Power comes from the barrel of a gun.' So perhaps...peace is not the real answer to solving anything."

"As I said before, when I got into this movement it wasn't about power at all, it was about peace, love, and freedom. Maybe you're just confusing the words, or maybe you're thinking that power can be the same thing. But power is about control, which is about fear. Peace is about freedom, which is also about love. I still have to think about it. At the moment I have to leave, but we'll discuss it again, all right?"

It felt strange to lecture Drake about peace, freedom, and power because up to now, I had always viewed him as being my teacher.

I always thought he was much wiser and more enlightened than me, but over the years something had shifted...as it did for all of us.

There was just something about this god-damn war that had caused many of those in the *peace and love movement* to begin embracing the dark side and turning to violence in the streets. Perhaps it was just a *casualty of war*, but the numbers of those who did will never be known.

I wanted to get the hell out of April's apartment as fast as I could. For all I knew, some donut-eating FBI agent was watching me with a pair of binoculars...or worse, what if there was a sniper on a roof with a rifle pointed at my head. What I did know...*that wasn't who I was.*

Yeah, I was feeling a little scared all right, and also very confused, since I was finally being put to the test about what my beliefs really were on this whole thing. I was being handed the opportunity to become a part of another great American Revolution, which would also mean blowing up buildings...and maybe, even shooting at the cops.

On the other hand, I could easily *'just say no'* to violence altogether and continue to try to change the world through peaceful means, but maybe that would be a waste of time. It was true that most successful revolutions had come from a violent confrontation. Although, in my heart, I was only a consciousness revolutionary...not a violent one.

I'd reached *a threshold moment* in my life and would have to make a choice between peace and war...which also meant love and fear, but I didn't want to be *against* anything, I just wanted *to be for peace.*

However, what can you do when people refuse to wake up to peace?

Do you violently slap them in the face until they do wake up?

I remembered back to my high school geometry class where they'd taught us...that when you multiply two negative numbers, the outcome is a positive number. Could it be that two opposing forces that were hell-bent on destroying each other...would eventually create peace?

Then, I remembered what Jerry Rubin had said in Chicago.

All this talk about revolution is making me horny.

That's what I needed...to get laid. Then, I could make my decision.

April told Lennie what had transpired earlier...so she knew I'd be confused and worried. When I got to her apartment, the first thing we did was smoke a big, fat joint...and got really stoned.

After that, I was able to settle down and relax.

I wasn't sure where the stash had come from, but it was good.

Lennie called it "White Rhino," and said it came from Nepal.

How ironic, since I might be going there, I thought to myself.

"What can I do to help you?" she asked.

"I really need to work off some of this energy. There's so much of it going on inside of me. Do you feel like fooling around?"

"What do you have in mind? Anything in particular?"

"I've been reading a lot of books for my Tibetan Buddhism class, and one of the books was on the subject of tantric sex."

"I've heard about it, myself. It's more of an energy thing, isn't it?"

"Yeah, it's like me being God, and you being Goddess, and together we share the creative energy each one of us holds within us.

"First, we get naked and sit on the floor across from each other with our legs crossed. Then, we become aware of sexual energy as it arises.

"We feel it move up our spine and try to release it from the top of our heads…instead of from…well, you know, the usual way.

"I'll be sending you my energy, and you'll be sending me yours, and together we become One with each other. They say we're supposed to imagine universal cosmic energy…making love to itself."

"Without having an orgasm…is that right?" she noted.

"Well, because it's sexual energy…if you have an orgasm, it stops.

"I think the goal is to get to that stage of pre-orgasm, and then hold on to it for as long as you can. The literature says…you should do your best not to have an orgasm, but if you do…it's all right."

"It probably takes a lot of practice. I like that the best," she said.

"Once the first part is mastered…then together, we try to focus our combined energies. They say…you can make energetic connections in all sorts of ways…even with the stars, and specific constellations."

"I've always loved *the Big Dipper*," she noted.

"Me, too. I also like the star system of the *Pleiades*.

"I've heard…there are some really cool dudes that live there.

"Some say…they're the ones who built the *Sphinx*, in Egypt."

"How do you know where the *Pleiades* star system is?

"Don't you have to have a telescope to see it?"

"No…just imagine it in your mind, and then tell your brain that this is where you're sending your energy. When you make the connection, then the star, or the constellation, will send its energy back to you."

"That's far out let's try it," she said, as she opened her nightstand and took out a white candle and some incense.

For just a moment, we held hands then we kissed each other gently on the lips and allowed our tongues to become intertwined for several minutes as our low vibrating moans of pleasure echoed through the small, one-bedroom apartment blending with the smells of sandalwood and her vanilla flavored candle. The intensity of our sounds, the light of the flame, and the distinctive smell reminded me of something like a far-off memory. I just couldn't put my finger on it. Maybe it had just been a dream I once had. I decided to just let it go.

We released, and then sat cross-legged with our knees still touching and holding each other's hands. Within only a few moments, we were at peace with the world while feeling a sense of both emptiness and fullness, existing together simultaneously. Here we were…just about as close as two people could be with each other, male and female, the masculine and feminine, fused and merged with each other's energy hoping to blend with each other on an even deeper level.

I could feel an entrenched feeling of heat beginning to rise from the base of my spine, as it slowly tried to find its way up my spinal column.

Then, the heat began to spread even further across my lower back, as though it was expanding and glowing. The feeling continued rising into my head, causing me to feel like I had a halo surrounding me.

Then I realized…what I was feeling…was most likely from the effects of the White Rhino, rather than from anything mystical.

After many minutes passed, my mind was swirling and spinning as the feelings continued to engulf me, but I was determined to continue and allow this to be real whether it was drug-induced or not.

Still sitting cross-legged, I became embraced by the spirit of my own soul. Inwardly, I knew this was no more than my imagination, but I also knew I'd made a connection with an aspect of my Higher Self.

It did not exist in the material plane, but was part of me, somewhere in the cosmos of what we call *the mind*. It was the part of me that was speaking out, demanding to be heard, echoing over and over in my head…*go to the monastery, so you may learn what you need to know.*

Moments later, the vision faded, but the awareness of it remained.

I continued to feel a deep warm glow throughout my body.

It was as though…I'd just come out of the oven…ready to eat.

Then, I opened my eyes and saw Lennie was smiling at me.

She looked very peaceful as she stared back before she laid her head on my shoulder and said, "That was so goddamn intense."

"It was for me, too…baby."

"Oh…I just fucking love you, Andy."

"And I love fucking you, Lennie."

"I was up inside of a golden pyramid, and you and I were one and the same…just pure golden light…and together, we spread our love all over the world. It was so incredible watching us do that."

"I think I went to Tibet," I told her.

"That's really far out, dude," she replied. "I think everyone should get stoned and have sex in the afternoon, don't you think?"

"Well, we didn't actually have sex…you know, in a biblical way."

"To me, it was both sexual and biblical. Besides, you don't have to have your dick inside someone to have a sexual experience," she said.

"But you do have to…for a biblical experience," I noted.

"Shut up, that's stupid. I'm just saying that perhaps the world would be a better place if people would treat sex more like a sacred ritual, rather than being an act of personal self-gratification."

"Yeah, I agree with you," I replied. "In fact, what if everyone got naked at the same time each day, got with their partner, and for just ten minutes…sent loving energy to the whole world. Then, there would be no war, or any crime, because everyone would be having sex instead.

"That's some heavy shit," Lennie surmised, "but I'd take it another step further and say…*screw for peace, or don't screw at all.*"

"Unfortunately, the world's not ready for that yet," I pointed out, but what you just said would make a great new button."

"So what's up with you wanting to go to Tibet? Is that where you really want to go? What are you going to do…leave this wonderful land of the holy dollar bill…for the land of the blessed Buddha?"

"It means, that I'm seriously considering joining the Peace Corps if they'll take me. I could go to Nepal and teach farming."

"How could you? You don't even know what a cow looks like.

"I don't care if people call you Tex. You're a city boy."

"Hey there, Miss Know-It-All, what they want is people with a few years of farm experience, and every summer while I was growing up, my family would spend two months at my grandmother's farm in north Georgia, and I'd help her do stuff. You know, farmer-type of stuff."

"The way I see it…all those summers add up to several years."

"What did you really do…at your grandmother's farm?"

"I would pick tomatoes, corn, and other vegetables, and I'd gather eggs from the hen house. Plus, she had a goat, and we used to go into the woods to find wild blackberries. I've even picked a few apples."

"Sounds like you did a lot of picking and pulling. Is that what they need over there in Nepal…pickers, and pullers?"

"Now you're making fun of me."

"Sorry, baby. I know you've been thinking about it a lot, and I'm sure you have all kinds of talents that have yet to be discovered."

"I've been having dreams about it, too, and with all the violence we see going on in the world, I feel like I've lost my way. Maybe I need to take a break and find out what's missing in my life. It's like…there's a big piece of the puzzle out there waiting for me. Do you understand?"

"Andy…you're free, white, and single. You can do whatever the fuck you want. I don't want to hold you back…but want you to know that I really love you. And…I suppose I could handle it…if our sexually casual, chemically tolerant, emotionally comfortable, and generally fun-loving relationship should suddenly come to an abrupt halt."

I just gave Lennie a big hug and quit talking about it.

I knew she could handle me leaving if I decided to go, so there was really no reason to continue discussing it.

By now, it was time to prepare for final exams and to write a final paper as well. This year, winter came unexpectedly early, and I began to feel a slight wave of depression setting in.

I was feeling down about having to deal with way too many things. With the Weathermen, the Peace Corps, the FBI, the CIA, graduate school, and you name it, I was feeling just a bit overwhelmed about all of it. Then, I received a telephone call from a friend who said the guy who had given the talk about the Buddhist view of death was going to do some kind of mystical séance, and that anyone who attended would have the opportunity to make contact with the spirit world.

It sounded kind of spooky, but I really wanted to go.

David Humphrey's séance turned out to be more than just a regular, old-fashioned, run-of-the-mill séance. Instead, it was based upon the teachings from the *Tibetan Book of the Dead*. The group was limited to only thirty people, and I was fortunate enough to be included for, as it turned out, this experience actually changed my life.

He started, "The *Tibetan Book of the Dead* is not only for the dead but for the living. It is not only to read to offer liberation to those souls who are recently departed, but it also teaches those of us who are alive how to die to the old self and to be reborn as a spiritual being.

"This evening, I am going to allow you to die. I want you to see yourself actually dying to your physical body and to experience death. When you return, you will be in a new body, and that new body will be the new you, that is…a new being embodied with a new spirit.

"In this guided meditation you will be taken through three phases of your inevitable future, known as the *Bardo*…there are three Bardos in the intermediate state between your death and your rebirth.

"First, you will contract a terminal illness of your choice and then the various signs of impending death will appear for you. Then, you will enter into the process of dying, characterized by experiencing the progressive dissolution of the five elements of your body.

"The five elements of earth, water, fire, air, and open space…also correspond to your physical body's five psychic energies.

"Earth relates to the psychic energies found in *flesh and bones*.

"Water relates to the psychic energies of *blood and bodily fluids*.

"Fire relates to the psychic energies of *inner heat and digestion*.

"Air relates to the psychic energies of *breath and nervous system.*

"Open space relates to the psychic energies of *consciousness*.

"Thus, earth dissolves into water, water into fire, fire into air, and air into space. As your energies dissolve, you'll have many experiences and visions, as well as external physical signs observable to others in your presence…and internal experiences which only you are aware of.

"Finally, your respiration, *or outer breathing*, will cease…and all those around you will think you are dead. *But you are not yet dead*, and can even be revived and resuscitated, because the circulation of your psychic energy, *or inner breathing*…will continue for a while.

"During this time, you will have further interior experiences, such as the inner dissolution of your psyche or emotions, and your mind or thought process. Although to outsiders you may appear cold, inert, and surely dead, your consciousness remains in your body dwelling secretly in your heart center where slight warmth may be detected.

"Even your inner breathing will cease as the last of your remaining psychic energies gather in your heart center and are absorbed there.

Then, he paused for a moment and took a drink of water.

"If everyone is ready, let's begin, as I allow the lights in the room to become dark. Just relax, take a deep breath and close your eyes."

The room became quiet and still as the lights were dimmed so that we could barely see. I got comfortable in my chair, crossed my legs, and took a deep breath. I thought I was prepared for just about anything.

Then, he began again… "The time for the death of your physical body has come upon you, as it must come to all mortal beings.

"What you are about to experience…is the *Bardo of Dying*…which began with your present terminal illness.

"You are now lying on your death bed, at your final resting place, and although the time of your death has come, this is not the end.

"As you draw in your last few breaths, you will notice that you still have a stream of 'conscious experience' that continues. What is most important is to keep your mind peaceful and calm, but fully alert. There is nothing more to be done in this life, so it's time to let everything go."

"The time has now come for you to seek the path of light to the other shore…beyond this present life and outside the portals of death. This begins your journey through the gateway into a new existence.

"There is nothing to fear. You've made this same journey countless times before, so you will not become lost because 'the guide' will point the way. Yes, you must leave this present life behind, with all its joys and sorrows, and you must also leave behind your possessions, all your friends and family…and all your lovers and enemies.

"You must leave behind your present physical body, to which you are so inordinately attached. However, the death of your physical body is not the end, it is only a transition, a new beginning, a resurrection.

"The continuum of your consciousness does not cease even with the death of your physical body and your material brain.

"Even without a physical body, your consciousness continues in space because it is the nature of space and light.

"Your stream of consciousness continues to flow onward toward an unknown destiny, even after your physical death. It is like a current of warm tropical water flowing through the great ocean of consciousness and is ever-changing, yet it is ever the same current.

'Your karma cannot be fully exhausted in this present lifetime alone, and so karma is what propels your stream of consciousness into new lives and new existences. Always remember, *death is not the end*, there is only the transformation from one dimension to another."

As he spoke, I found myself getting older and older, until I was a very old man, close to a hundred. I found myself high in the mountains among some very large rocks…but trees and bushes were also there.

In the foreground was a wolf, and it seemed to beckon me toward the edge of a cliff. Then, I saw myself sitting on a rock at twilight, overlooking a big city that was lit up as night began to fall.

Then, I realized that this was the place where I would die someday. *But how will I be buried?* I thought.

I looked at the wolf…and then heard him speak.

"When you are dead," the wolf said, "I will take care of your body.

"There will be no need for a funeral…or any burial."

Then David continued, "Yes, that which is called death has finally come upon you. Therefore, you should consider matters carefully.

"You have arrived at the time of your death, and so now you should adopt the attitude of the enlightened state of mind, thinking of all other living beings, whose numbers are as vast as the sky itself. You are now surrounded with boundless thoughts of friendliness and compassion."

I looked at the wolf and realized that we were of the same spirit.

In fact, all that I was now in my current physical body, would soon become the body of the wolf after he partook of my flesh.

"For the sake of all living beings, at the moment of death, you will come to recognize the *'Clear Light of Reality'* as the very nature of your own mind. Come to the realization of that which you really are, and act only for the good of others. If you do not attain this realization, then recognize the *Bardo* for what it is, the intermediate state between death and rebirth, and recognize all the visions seen in the lights of the *Bardo* to be the visible manifestations of the energy arising from the nature of your own mind. *This*, you must remember above all else.

"At this time, when both your outer and your inner breathing have ceased, although your consciousness has not yet exited your former physical body, you will find yourself in a vast dark space, like the sky at midnight, void of stars. You're not unconscious but just suspended in the darkness of space as if someone has turned out the light.

"Now…you'll find yourself in a totally dark room.

"How long this experience of total darkness remains depends on individual karma. But then the dawn of the *'Clear Light of Awareness'* will come inevitably upon you, because now your body and your mind have all been stripped from you…as if you're completely naked.

"However, you do not cease to exist."

He was right…*there was a part of me that still existed.*

Gently, I felt myself stepping out of my physical body, discarding it like an old suit of clothes. I was now just a glowing shimmering light.

Under me, I could see my former body lying there, dead.

The wolf walked over to my body and looked up at me.

Then, I gave him my approval to do what he was there to do.

"The space all about you will appear to become like the vast open cloudless sky in the east at dawn. This light grows brighter and brighter, as when the sun, still invisible, approaches the horizon from below.

"If, at this time, you can recognize this 'Clear Light of Awareness' to be a self-manifestation arising out of the 'Nature of your own Mind,' you will then merge into this light. Becoming One with it, you are being delivered from the delusions of cyclical existence and the necessity for future rebirths in the suffering realm of Samsara. Instead, you are now ascending beyond the stars and returning home with no further need for you to enter the experience of this *Bardo state*, for you have now passed beyond the beginning-less cycle of life, death, and rebirth.

"Unfortunately, you have failed to recognize this 'Clear Light' as your own mind reflected in the mirror of empty space, so you fall away from it in confusion, and in fear of losing yourself in its radiance.

"You seek to avoid it and flee from its clear brilliance. You fade away into unconsciousness and fall back into the outer darkness.

"Having fled from the dawn of the 'Clear Light of Awareness,' which was nothing more than your own mind, you descend again into the darkness of night and experience a brief period of unconsciousness.

"Next, you enter into the 'after-life, after-death' experience known as the intermediate state between death and rebirth. However, during this time of unconsciousness, which lasts for an uncertain period of time, your memories and your past karma begin to reawaken, like the dreams that come upon you in the night when you fall asleep.

There was a short pause...

"Your mind and your psyche begin to function and operate again with thoughts and emotions," he said. "Then, as you awaken from your state of unconsciousness, you find yourself again in the *Bardo*.

"You discover yourself inhabiting a subtle light-body composed of psychic energy, with your mind and your sense faculties functioning intact. This is a mind-made body you have created, a subtle energy structure that embodies and encompasses your consciousness, created by your memories and your past karma. This is not something physical, but only an immaterial 'Spirit-Body of Energy and Light.'

"Now, you are truly dead and departed from the world, and yet your spirit-body resembles the previous physical body you possessed before you died in almost every way, including your clothes. However, it is free of all diseases, feels no pain, and suffers no infirmities or absence of limbs. At first, finding yourself in this body, you feel pulled to visit your old haunts and familiar scenes. You try to speak to your old friends and relatives, but they cannot see or hear you anymore.

"Gradually, familiar scenes begin to fade away and you find your mind increasingly distracted. You wander through many strange and alien landscapes, always searching for something, but never quite knowing what that might be. Eventually, the sky opens up before you, becoming a deep blue color. During successive cycles, you may come to experience five lesser clear lights showing up in five extraordinary primary colors, all in succession: white, blue, yellow, red, and green.

"Then, these bright clear lights may become as big as mountains and even come to fill the entire sky before you. In these lights, you may see visions of the celestial hierarchies that span the heavens. You also see whatever gods you worship, sitting on their thrones, surrounded by choirs of angels, coming to you from the heights of heaven.

"Still, you fail to recognize these secondary Clear Lights, and these peaceful serene images as being self-manifestations of your own mind.

"So you attempt to flee from them in fear of being overwhelmed, but these images are nothing more than manifestations coming from your own purified consciousness. They come from deep within you but are projected into space. Still, you fail to recognize them, and fear them out of ignorance, so in terror…you flee from them and therefore fall once more from the fullness of Reality…into deprivation.

"Once again, you will faint and find yourself in yet another state of unconsciousness. Next, however, you then awaken in the *Third Bardo*, the *Bardo* of the *Process of Rebirth*. Here, you find yourself once more inhabiting a subtle body composed of psychic energy, but with your mind and sense faculties totally intact. Nevertheless, this is still just an immaterial spirit body that also resembles the body you possessed in your previous life. There is much more confusion here. It is like you find yourself in a dream, where the scenes change all around you with increasing rapidity and instability. Failing to find your old body, you enter into the process of rebirth and now set out once again seeking a new birthplace, but with a greater feeling of desperation.

"Along the way you encounter many different spirit beings who are like yourself, who are also searching, but these encounters are only fleeting and give little comfort. You see many visions of colored lights and hear strange and frightening sounds like thunder and experience many varied landscapes like you are in a dream.

"You're experiencing your personal karma in a very visible form.

"But again, you fail to recognize these as karmic visions created by your own mind, so the winds of your own karma drive you relentlessly onward, like a frail leaf blown about, to-and-fro, by the autumn winds.

"At last, you come to stand before the gates of Hell itself, in the 'Hall of Judgment' within the great 'Court of Justice.'

"Entering within this awesome structure, which is also your own creation, you find yourself in the presence of the Judge of the Dead.

"He is stern and terrifying in his appearance and holds the mirror of your own karma in front of you. In it, you see the face of your own Soul reflected back at you…as it really is…but you do not recognize it.

"All of the good and the evil that you believe to have done during your life are weighed before you in the full view of this court. If you can recognize that the dark and solemn form of the judge is actually your own conscience manifesting itself in a visible form before you, then even here, in the court of karma, you can obtain full liberation.

"If not, lights that are the pathways to future rebirth in *Samsara* will begin to manifest right before you. You must take one of these roads. You are irresistibly drawn to one of them, and you make a choice."

I had only briefly seen myself in the mirror, at the entranceway to the Hall of Judgment. I saw who I was, and what I'd become.

He was right…I had to make a choice.

Would I become a criminal, a terrorist, or some kind of outlaw?

Would I become a fugitive from justice, simply because my ways of pacifism would give way to my hatred for the establishment?

Would I join the ranks of the Weather Underground or some other league that worshiped the violent dark side?

Was I going to become just like those whom I was trying to stop?

My God, I thought. *What am I doing to myself?*

Then David said, "Suddenly, the winds of your karma become like a hurricane…and the mirror of your karma is blown out of your hand."

Then, the winds blew…and I found myself in a dark, empty space.

It was intensely quiet…and I was confused.

Would I give in to violence, just as so many had done in the past, or would I retain the spiritual values I had found in this decade?

The only way I could ever become the spiritually enlightened being who I wanted to be…was to choose peace and love, not war and fear. So there, it was done. I'd made a clear choice and had chosen wisely.

"By now, you have made your choice," David stated in an almost uncanny way. "In this dull light, the form of your old body from your previous life begins to fade away, but more and more, your physical form begins to resemble the body you will have in your future rebirth. Impulsively, you will search for a place of rebirth in accordance with the unconscious propensities of your karma. Then you see it.

"You see a place where your future parents are seen making love, and you feel attracted to them. At the moment of conception, when the white element...*the sperm of your father*...unites with the red element ...*the egg of your mother*...you are irresistibly drawn near to her womb.

"Once you know the fetus is safe, you will enter it, and now...you know...that you are about to embark on a new life...in a new body.

"In only a matter of time, you will be reborn."

There was another short pause...

"Slowly, you come back into this room. Soon, you will open your eyes, but they will be new eyes, and you will be in a brand-new body.

"You are now a new spiritual being made of light, love, and peace.

"And with that, I bid you all, goodnight. Thank you for coming."

Perhaps Lennie and April had been right about death simply being an illusion, for I had just been allowed to witness how I would die...and it would be a death that I would create when I became much older.

I also saw what I could easily become as well if I continued on my present path...and I didn't like what I had seen.

No, I wasn't going to start the 1970s with the violent overthrow of the United States, and no, I wasn't going to become a member of the notorious Weather Underground. Instead...somehow, I was going to stick it out and retain my non-violent nature.

For me, the decision was now made. From this day forward, my life would only be about peace...not about war.

It would have been nice if Woodstock had been the final big event of the Sixties, and for the decade to have ended on such an incredibly positive note. But…life is often full of unresolved paradoxes, foibles, confusions, perplexities, and entanglements. In this case, it seemed as though the hand of the devil himself…moved in quickly.

In only three short months, all that we had worked so very hard to create from the success of Woodstock was about to come suddenly crashing down with an earth-shaking and shattering end.

♥ ♥ ♥

Just as the month of December began, I received a telephone call from Diane, which was very unusual. She wanted me to meet her for a one-day Rolling Stones concert being held near San Francisco which was to take place on December 6th. Since she had missed Woodstock, this would be her big chance to experience the same phenomena.

All of my classes and term papers were pretty much finished and now it was just a matter of waiting for graduation, so I agreed to meet her and attend the concert. In fact, I was looking forward to it.

With all the violence and rioting going on in America during this time, what happened at Altamont isn't at all surprising, and perhaps what is even more surprising is the fact that it didn't happen sooner.

The concert itself degenerated into chaotic mass mayhem when the booze-bellied-acid-headed Hell's Angels were hired to keep order in front of the stage to protect the Rolling Stones.

Instead, they proceeded to discharge their task by violently beating the concertgoers at every opportunity. Altamont's violence was capped by the murder of a young black man, Meredith Hunter.

In fact, it was even captured on film.

For many, Hunter's murder cemented the festival's reputation as a fitting end to a decade…that had not lived up to its own expectations.

First planned for Candlestick Park, and then Golden Gate Park, the free concert was moved again to Sears Point Raceway after its permit was withdrawn. The stage was already completed at Sears Point when that venue fell through there, as well. The deal to perform the concert at Altamont Raceway was struck at the last minute.

In the aftermath of Woodstock, there was a general euphoria that 'the peace and love community' had finally triumphed, and could, even in the midst of anarchy, overcome anyone who might have any interest in violence. Some people did raise concerns about the public's safety, but those voices were overwhelmed with the usual pacifist confidence.

However, Altamont, or something that was very much like it, would have been inevitable in any case. After all...*it was the crazy Sixties*.

It was a time that was steeped in violence and there was nothing that could stop that violence from eventually encroaching upon the counterculture, even if was just another rock festival.

Given the large crowds of people, the lack of sanitary facilities, the bad drugs, and the shortages of food and water, most rock festivals were catastrophes just waiting to happen. People would get angry when they were uncomfortable, or if they were being felt ripped off.

The Hell's Angels were hired by the Rolling Stones as security for several reasons. The Grateful Dead had a long-standing relationship with the Angels and had used them for security on several occasions without incident, and the Stones had used the Hell's Angels for security in London over the summer for one of their free concerts in Hyde Park.

At Altamont, the Angels acted just like they always did...drinking alcohol, smoking marijuana, and dropping acid. The Angels probably abused more drugs in varying combinations than anyone else.

There were no other security forces except the Hell's Angels.

If one of them got out of line...there'd be no one to stop them.

The Angels most popular choice of weapon for the day was to use a pool cue, which they used to beat people over the head. The other popular weapon was the beer can. They assumed that the best way to calm an angry crowd would be to throw full cans of beer at them.

The Rolling Stones might not have put on a free concert if they didn't think their fans expected it of them after Woodstock. They might not have hired the Hell's Angels if the gang hadn't been held in such high esteem by Hollywood, and the Haight-Ashbury rock and roll elite.

The fact that the Altamont festival was held in the San Francisco Bay Area just four months after Woodstock was absolutely horrific, in part because several more people died during the one-day event.

Bay Area filmmakers captured it all on film in the landmark movie, *Gimme' Shelter*, vividly illustrating a major turning point in American pop culture. Starting with a set by *The Flying Burrito Brothers*, the event seemed to begin well even if some tempers were short.

By the time *Jefferson Airplane* took the stage, there had already been some clashes between audience members and the Angels.

Things started to get out of hand after the bikers were instructed not to let anybody on the stage. They were only too happy to comply with their orders by using the end of a lead-weighted cue stick.

The scuffles became so bad that Jefferson Airplane began to have difficulty finishing songs. After one of the band members was knocked unconscious, members of the group began having verbal confrontations with the biker gang using microphones to argue back and forth.

Grace Slick even tried to calm the crowd down a couple of times by declaring, "You shouldn't be putting your body on other people's bodies unless your intent is for loving them."

However, her pleas went unheeded.

With night falling, The Rolling Stones were the marquee act on the bill, and launched their set called '*Sympathy for the Devil*,' but barely got into it before more scuffles brought the song to a halt.

Like Slick, Jagger began pleading with his "brothers and sisters" to cool out, but even Keith Richards was getting so pissed off that he threatened to leave the stage. Jagger eventually managed to get some of the audience in front of the stage to sit down but even this tactic failed. More fights broke out and more songs were abandoned before they could be finished. Bad vibes clearly hung over the winter evening as the incendiary flares and flames blew up around the stage.

Because it was a free festival, no admission was charged to get in, which meant that anybody off the street could show up, and more than three-hundred thousand did. Furthermore, drugs had been taken by many in attendance, and in dangerously large quantities.

Meredith Hunter, an eighteen-year-old black man, was near the stage with a knife and a gun. As the Hell's Angels attacked him with their pool cues, Mick sang his song about how groovy it is to be Satan.

It was being sung in a perfect setting as Hunter was beaten to death by the Angels while the Stones are playing their asses off.

The incident was so swift that nobody knew what happened.

Then, Hunter was taken outside and zipped up in a body bag.

The Rolling Stones finished their set with Mick Jagger bouncing around and singing, *Jumping Jack Flash*. Only then…did the crowd begin to disperse, but it marked a foreboding return of mob violence to the normally placid outdoor rock festivals of the past. After that, the Stones would only perform stadium gigs behind tall chain-link fences.

Tragically, three other people also died at the Altamont concert.

Two people died in sleeping bags after being run over by cars, and one unidentified person drowned. Even the most incomplete reports show that this was a festival dominated by violence.

The fact that this free concert resulted in both destruction and death shocked the entire Woodstock Nation. After all, over four hundred and fifty thousand people coexisted peacefully for four days in a muddy field in New York just to listen to music. But at Altamont, instead of the widespread notion of joy, and an outpouring of goodness, there was fear and pain. When it was over, the establishment claimed that it simply went to prove that the hippie counterculture's advocacy of 'peace and love' had not succeeded. In fact, they claimed, nothing had really changed, and especially…the human impulse for violence.

Years later, *American Pie* became one of the most mysterious songs of all time, as Don McLean told the story of this tragic event.

The words would go something like this:

Jack be nimble, Jack be quick, Jack Flash sat on a candlestick,
Because fire is the devil's only friend.

And as I watched him on the stage, my hands were clenched in fists of rage, no angel born in hell could break that Satan's spell.

And as the flames climbed high into the night, to light the sacrificial rite, I saw Satan laughing with delight...

The day the music died.

Just as the death of Buddy Holly and the others had marked the end of the previous decade, so the sacrificial death of Meredith Hunter at Altamont had marked the end of the Sixties-style of rock and roll, with its Love-Ins, Be-Ins, and the days of peaceful outdoor concerts.

Once again, it became '*the day the music died,*' but this time, it was the death of a kind of music that once held so much meaning.

"*Hey, it's just life. Wake up and smell the thorns,*" someone said.

The 'peace and love movement' had gained some ground over the last six years, but now it was time to wake up from that dream as well and to face a whole new music, a new mood, and a new consciousness.

It was time to face…the coming decade of the Seventies.

However, one last question still begged to be answered.

Had we learned anything from this great movement, or would the lessons of the Sixties have to be repeated in the not-so-distant future?

Diane and I ended the weekend on a somber note feeling bad that the concert wasn't even close to what we had expected or hoped for.

I flew back to New York the following day. To make matters even more surprising, Diane wrote to me soon after and said that she was moving out of Amy's apartment and was hooking up with one of the Hells Angels she had met at the concert. In her letter, she said she was very happy and enjoyed riding on the back of a big Harley.

As far as I was concerned, this time it really was over between us. Hells Angels were not hippies, they didn't believe in love and peace, and if that was the direction Diane was going…so be it.

Besides the tragedy of Altamont, later that month the elite injected even more bad raps into the blood of the 'peace and love movement.'

Charles Manson's acid-head hippie family commune was convicted for the brutal slaying of pregnant actress Sharon Tate.

At the conspiracy trial of the Chicago Eight, Black Panther leader Bobby Seal was forced to sit in front of a jury…shackled in chains.

Both trials tarnished everything the hippies had tried to do.

December of 1969 was a hell-of-a-way to end the decade that was supposed to be about freedom and the expansion of consciousness.

It had been a decade troubled with an unjust war that caused more than forty-thousand U.S. deaths and had brought violence into the streets all the way to the heartland of America.

It had been a decade when the leaders who represented all the new countercultures were torn between peace and war.

The voice of many had raised their fists in defiance of authority and declared…*we shall overcome*, while the voice of others had only raised two fingers in hope and declared…*give peace a chance.*

Yes, it had been a decade of paradoxes all right, and now there were even more widespread protests going on against renewed bombings in Vietnam, and the illegal invasion of Cambodia by the U.S.

I graduated from NYU with a bachelor's degree in psychology and a minor in political science. My head professor had already invited me to begin a two-year master's degree program in clinical psychology.

That way, I didn't have to worry about that damned draft anymore.

Although I'd mailed in my application for the Peace Corps, I was told that the training sessions for agriculture took place in the summer, and if I were to be accepted, I would hear from them in the spring.

I told Mark I wasn't interested in his executive position with the Weather Underground, but Drake had other things in mind. That being the case, I settled back and enjoyed New Year's Eve in Times Square while tripping on mushrooms with Lennie, Tomás, and Debbie.

As we stood there awaiting the countdown for the big red ball to fall at midnight, we could only speculate about what the new decade of the Seventies would bring. Then, a single ghostly voice from behind me began to softly sing the song from the Broadway musical, *Hair.*

It was the same song that Diane had once sung to me.

We stop, look, at one another short of breath, standing proudly in our winter coats, wearing smells from laboratories, and facing a dying nation, like a moving paper fantasy, we listen for the new told lies…

So…let the sunshine…let the 'sun' shine in…

Moments later, everyone around us began to sing the same song in unison until the big red ball came down and the fifty-thousand people who were in Times Square began to cheer and hug each other.

It was now the year, 1970, and *'the Sixties'* was officially over.

As I gave Lennie a kiss and a hug, I asked her, "Do you ever wonder why everyone is cheering so loud? Is it because a new decade is here, or because the previous decade has ended?"

"It's because…they're just happy to still be alive," she answered.

"Personally," I interjected, "I feel sad that it's over…but looking back…we sure had a *hell-of-a-good time*, didn't we?"

Lennie looked at me with tears running down her cheeks and said, "I'm feeling sad too…but I doubt that any of us will ever know for sure just what this crazy-ass decade was really about.

"However, I do know one thing…I'm sure going to miss it."

You Say You Want a Revolution

You say you want a revolution…
We all want to change the world…
But if you want money for people with minds that hate…
All I can tell you is brother you'll have to wait…
It's going to be, all right…it's going to be, all right…
(Artist: The Beatles)

I doubt that even God knew what the 1970s would bring.

Sure, there was still that horrible war going on in Vietnam, and it would continue for several more years, but as Neil Diamond said in one of his songs…*good times, never seemed so good.*

The Nixon administration kept promising peace with the right hand and then escalating the war with the left. Thus, Richard Nixon became known as '*Tricky Dick*.' The term '*hippie*' would become a common household name that would be used for years to come, as would LSD.

However, cocaine became the drug of choice for the Hollywood set, while heroin and speed were becoming increasingly popular.

Another bookmark that signified the beginning of the new decade was the breakup of the Beatles in 1970. When they split up it seemed like a terrible death to many of their fans, leaving a big hole in popular music because the sounds and lyrics that had inspired a new generation began to fragment and splinter off…as if they had lost their leader.

Many of the newer bands that were being formed were advocating violence instead of love. Alice Cooper would later make jokes that his group was the one that drove a stake directly into the heart of the peace and love generation. He not only rejected the message of the hippie movement but then reversed it to advocate hate and war by performing stage antics that included simulated rape and murder. Ironically, it was Cooper's depravity of consciousness that made him such a big star.

There would be more of the same talk about revolution, and many more anti-war protests. There was also lots of work to be done in the battle against racism…for both women's rights and gay rights.

No doubt, there was still a lot of love left over from the Sixties, but for many, the Seventies was the beginning of an even groovier decade. It was okay for men to cry and for wives to swap. No one cared if you wore bellbottoms, knits, polyester, platforms, skirts, or suits.

The new music had fewer messages about war and peace. Instead, it was now about sensitivity and feelings. People were caught up in the new "I and Me" generation, letting go of all the martyrdom and the need to save the world. Now, it was about saving yourself, or how to get a little action on the side that would get your rocks off.

Instead of focusing so much on drugs, sex, rock and roll, there was now a different focus. What developed was a greater awareness of a new spirituality. The eastern and western philosophies were starting to come together, not so much to create a new religion, but rather to form a kind of fusion that connected religions and spiritual groups from all around the world. It was no longer about breaking free from the molds of the past, but rather…the Seventies was a time of re-defining yourself and discovering just who and what you were really all about.

By the time 1970 came to America, East Coast consciousness and West Coast consciousness had pretty much come together, but many of the former hippies began to 'sell out' to the old American capitalism.

It seemed…that everybody was competing to be on the same page.

Corporate greed became rampant, as companies like *McDonald's* and *Coca-Cola* could now be found in most third-world countries.

People in poor countries were imitating those in more developed countries, while people in the so-called civilized Western world were trying to go back to a more laid-back lifestyle that could only be found in poorer countries. Everyone wanted to be like somebody else.

It reminded me of a book by Dr. Seuss called, *The Sneetches*.

Allen Ginsberg had gone to India to study eastern philosophy in the early Sixties, and Dr. Richard Alpert, the former LSD guru, went there to do the same in the late Sixties. Both came back as self-proclaimed spiritual gurus. Alpert adopted the Hindu name, *Ram Dass*, and then became one of the new pioneers of American Buddhism.

Even *the Beatles* had gone to India to sit at the foot of a holy man, *the Maharishi*, and then chanted some mantras in front of television cameras pretending to be somehow magically enlightened.

So by the end of the Sixties...the stage had already been set for a whole new drama in spiritual awareness to begin.

Even the teachings from the Eastern religions had been arriving in the U.S. since the early Sixties, but with the dawning of the Seventies, the spiritual traffic increased exponentially...and was everywhere.

Tibetan Lamas, Zen Masters from Japan, Hindu Priests, yogis, and tantric practitioners were flocking to the West by the thousands, as well as masses of Chinese herbalists and acupuncturists. Not only did they build empowerment centers for spiritual learning...but many of their North American students became the new lineage holders of that same sacred knowledge and wisdom that had never before left their native countries. Americans could now become enlightened masters as well,

If you didn't have the money to go to India...you could still sit at the foot of a real guru just by finding one in the 'yellow pages.'

In response to easterners coming west...hundreds of thousands of young people from the U.S., Canada, England, and Europe flocked to South Asia, to places like India, Nepal, Burma, Ceylon, and Indonesia, not only to see the world…but many still wanted to find a teacher to show them the path to enlightenment. It seemed; *the East* was heading west at the same time *the West* was heading east. It's a wonder they didn't bump into each other at the airport, or at bus stops along the way.

That's actually how many of them traveled. A European charter bus that began in Germany would travel non-stop through the famous cities of Istanbul, Tehran, Kabul, and Lahore. After crossing the Khyber Pass, it would then unload its cargo of young men and women somewhere in downtown New Delhi…and the five-day trip didn't cost a whole lot.

The route from Turkey to India soon became known to many as the '*hippie highway.*' From New Delhi, the young seekers of knowledge could catch one of India's many trains or buses to other cities, such as Bombay, Madras, Benares, Calcutta, Darjeeling, Kashmir…or even Kathmandu. Some would go to Burma or Bhutan, but the roads that lead into Tibet still remained closed to all western foreigners after the horrible Chinese invasion that had taken place in the year, 1952.

A large number of the Lamas, monks, and citizens from Tibet had managed to flee from their own country and were now living in either Nepal, Northern India, or Burma. The Tibetan culture and its ancient teachings had been saved and could now be accessed and experienced in these places by the youthful westerners who sought them out.

It wasn't surprising that there were a lot of single young women traveling along the hippie highway to India by themselves. After all, the Sixties was about '*free love*'…for many of them, it was often quite easy to hook up with a group, or some young dude going in the same direction…that is, for a while at least, until their paths separated.

Then, another young man could easily be found.

South Asia was especially attractive to former hippies…because there were almost no laws against the use of drugs…India and Nepal were already famous for their powerful ganja (*marijuana*) and hashish.

Interestingly, ganja was commonly smoked by all of the holy men in India, known as *Sadhus*, and many of the older men and women who lived in India and Nepal were regular pot smokers. Because of the high currency exchange in India, you could purchase an entire kilo of pot for about two American dollars, and no one would try to arrest you.

However, with the massive arrival of the western youth culture to the home of Hinduism and Buddhism, they also brought their LSD with them, and just about any other drug you could think of.

Soon, head shops and ganja restaurants began springing up all over India and Nepal. You could go out to dinner, or shopping in the bazaar, and to get totally stoned and fucked up anytime that you wanted, never feeling any paranoia about getting arrested. For many young travelers, that experience alone was often worth the cost of the trip.

Not only that, but both the Indian and Nepalese people were very friendly and courteous to the young westerners, and even to the ones with long hair. Young people didn't have to worry about being mugged or robbed, which was not always the case in the more violent Muslim countries like Turkey, Iraq, Iran, Afghanistan, and Pakistan.

India and Nepal became the new '*hippie heaven,*' second only to Amsterdam, so New Delhi and Kathmandu were definitely among the most popular places to visit. By the early Seventies, South Asia had become a spiritual drug paradise where you could get high and also find God at the same time. However, living conditions were often harsh since most of the cheap hotels and youth hostels were very primitive by western standards. After all, these were very poor countries, so most of them had no air conditioning, ice, hot water, or bathtubs.

But these hardships didn't bother most world travelers...because hippies didn't stay in posh hotels, and were used to sleeping on floors, camping out, being dirty...and not taking a shower every day.

Most of them said...*they felt right at home.*

♥ ♥ ♥

In January 1970, I was still living in New York City and would have loved to have done what thousands of other young people were doing that year. It was so much easier for the Europeans to travel to India than it was for young Americans like me. Not only because of the distance but also because of the war. Anyone my age who dropped out of school was likely to get drafted within just a few months.

I already had an *A-1 draft status* and could easily get pulled into the military at a moment's notice if I didn't keep my student deferment in effect. Therefore, I had to become a full-time graduate student.

Life for me hadn't really changed much. I still believed in the words of Bob Dylan…*that everybody must get stoned*…but my resolution for the new decade had been to stop smoking cigarettes. Therefore, I had to replace the habit by smoking as much marijuana as possible.

"Here you go, Andy," Lennie said as she passed me a joint with one hand, and a freshly opened beer can with the other.

"How are things going with the new students you're teaching?"

What she was referring to was that I had been assigned to teach an *Introductory to Psychology* class for incoming freshmen and found the whole thing appalling. My interests had shifted to eastern philosophy.

I firmly believed that the founding fathers of our modern western psychology (including Freud, Jung, and Pavlov) didn't know what the fuck they were talking about at the time.

Sigmund Freud had written his theories about the Id, the ego, and the mind…*while high on cocaine*…more than a hundred years ago.

So the entire period that had given birth to western psychology and psychoanalysis…came from men who were high on drugs. However, Buddhist psychology was more than twenty-five hundred years old and based upon the personal experiences of meditation practitioners who had spent their entire lives studying the human mind.

Think about it...*who would you rather believe?*

To answer Lennie's query...I honestly replied, "At times, I have trouble answering their questions because I don't believe in the answers that the Psychology Department wants me to give. I mean, these kids are looking for some profound human truths that Freud and Pavlov just didn't have back in their day. For example, they said...that *who we are* is more a function of the unconscious mind, which lies hidden within the psyche. I believe that in just the last one hundred years, our human consciousness has actually evolved. In other words, a lot of what used to be 'unconscious programming' for most people...has now become much more conscious...but you won't find that in the textbooks."

"It must be frustrating," she said as she took another big hit.

"Even the word 'consciousness' means something entirely different in the Buddhist teachings. It's everywhere...and is all-pervasive."

"Is there anyone you can talk to?"

"Not really, my department head is Professor Perkins."

"Is he that short, stubby bald guy with a beard whose stomach looks like he swallowed a beer keg?" she asked.

"Yeah, and he's always wearing the same brown jacket, blue shirt, and red tie. He also has his big ass crammed into a pair of wrinkled khaki Levi's and wears *John Lennon* glasses. With that short goatee, he reminds me of a *Bolshevik* revolutionary, like a *Trotsky wanna-be*. What's worse...he drives me crazy," I complained.

April was with us as well and asked if I knew what the difference was between Buddhism and Christianity.

"Christians believe in *sin and salvation*, which can only be attained by accepting Jesus Christ as one's savior, who's also the Son of God," I clarified. "Buddhists believe that only ignorance and enlightenment exist, that both sin and salvation come from the mind. Buddhists also believe Buddha was a human who attained enlightenment, not a god."

"So tell me, are Buddhists atheists?" Lennie asked.

"No," I replied, "they're non-theistic. It means…even if God exists, one's enlightenment doesn't depend on God…it's a state of wholeness and balance that comes from within. One continues the cycle of birth, death, and rebirth until he or she attains that enlightened state of mind, and after they die because there's no more karmic need to have rebirth, so the cycle ends. Then, they're said to have reached *Nirvana*."

"I'm a bit confused about what an 'enlightened mind' actually is," admitted Lennie. "What do you think it means?"

"Well, you can't really define enlightenment because the moment you try to describe it, or put a label on it, it becomes limited, and true enlightenment has no limitations…it has no boxes, walls, borders, or boundaries, like a wide-open sky. For example, Christianity puts God into a box by telling you what to believe…but in Buddhism, the box never existed. Just yesterday, I was thinking about that same question. This is the definition I came up with. I've still got it here somewhere."

I dug into my pockets and pulled out a wrinkled-up paper.

Then I opened up the page and began to read:

"Enlightenment is not only about higher consciousness and one's expanded awareness, but it is also about being truly authentic. It's about being you and about being real. However, there's also a paradox there, because according to Buddhist doctrine…the '*Self*' does not exist.

"Belief in a *real Self* is just part of the illusion we experience in the physical plane. *Impermanence* is all that's real. A belief in an immortal ever-lasting Soul, *or even in God*…cannot exist separate and apart from this principle of impermanence. Therefore, it's about seeing through the illusion that we're faced with every day and being authentic.

"However, *I do believe in an afterlife*, but it doesn't require a God who sits at the top of a pyramid scheme. I believe, there's no difference, or separation, between life and death, or between time and space.

"Death is nothing more than a continuation of life, and vice-versa.

"It's all, transformation…

"In life, we prepare for death. In death, we prepare for a new life. One cannot fear death or life if they want to experience enlightenment. That's what words like '*freedom, illumination,* and *liberation*' mean. It's to be free from the fear of death…*and the fear of life.*"

"I like that definition," she said. "And when I become enlightened, I'll let you know if it's actually true."

Just then the telephone rang. It was Drake talking in a panic.

"Dude, you really need to get over here quick. Something's coming down heavy and you don't want to miss it!"

When I arrived at Drake's apartment, I couldn't believe my eyes. Timothy Leary was sitting in his living room. He had recently escaped from the San Luis Obispo Prison with the assistance of the Weather Underground and was planning to join Eldredge Cleaver in Algiers.

For now, he was in Drake's apartment, which was operating as a safe house for the Weathermen. The previous year, he had planned to run for the Governor of California, but he was set up by the authorities and was arrested for possession of marijuana. After going to trial, he was found guilty and was sentenced to ten years behind bars.

Dr. Leary vaguely remembered me when we shook hands.

He was sitting in sweatpants at a table in the living room and we chatted for several hours. Occasionally, he would inhale a balloon full of nitrous oxide, which he called "pure brain food."

He hadn't changed too much since the time we met, except now it seemed as if his mind was more expanded than before. In his opinion, because of all his LSD experiences, his DNA structure had now taken on a god-like intelligence that was rapidly propelling him toward the next phase in the evolutionary script for humanity.

This included being able to escape from the planet and experience even more exponential growth in cognitive intelligence.

Eventually, he hoped to experience immortality.

He had built this vision around a rather unique model for all human consciousness. He divided them into eight circuits, four terrestrials, and four post-terrestrials. Then, he linked those to other traditional human psychological systems such as the *Tarot*, the *I-Ching*, and *astrology*.

I never did quite understand what the hell he was talking about.

Leary also talked a lot about his eventual death and said that he was prepared for his brain to be frozen but wanted to make it clear that he might change his mind and decide not to do it.

"If I could be brought back to life," he said, "the condition of my brain might be of some interest to science. Somehow, I'm going to plan my own death. After all, you plan for college. Therefore, you should plan for dying. In my case and for many years, I've been planning this."

I told him about my experience at the séance and he became elated.

"I was a student of the *Tibetan Book of the Dead* for many years," he explained. "*Ram Dass* and I wrote a book about it in 1964, and it's just now becoming accepted among mainstreamists."

"Really?" I replied.

"And more importantly, did you know the LSD experience is very much like the experience of death, and that one can actually become enlightened while they are tripping their ass out on LSD?"

"Sure, I think that may be possible," I remarked while noticing that Leary himself had not yet claimed to be fully enlightened.

"I'm going to attempt one final experiment in mental exploration before I die. You see, there's a period of time after the heart stops, but before the brain actually dies. Obviously, this offers an opportunity to explore just how long that interval might be.

"It could be…several minutes.

"In my dying room, when I'm wired up and close to inarticulate, I'll still be able to type with my fingers, or maybe by blinking my eyes. The key thing…is that on my front wall will be a large screen, so I can word-process and communicate. I'm hoping that Richard and I can come up with something that a spirit can communicate with."

I enjoyed talking with Dr. Leary that day and wished him well in his future life as a fugitive. Even though he had been in prison for a year, he never lost his charm or his upbeat positive personality.

To me, his mind was more expanded than anyone I had ever met.

Although my admiration for him dramatically increased after our meeting, I was convinced that he might just be a little whacked out but meeting him again made me want to finish graduate school, get my Ph.D., and then perhaps, take off where he had left.

On April 30, 1970, the first 'National Earth Day' took place, and was observed all across America. Because it happened, a number of important safeguards were later set in place that protected the earth's ecology by monitoring pollution activity. Within only a short time, the Environmental Protection Agency was established by the government.

For me, it became a day that I'd remember for other reasons.

Drake, April, Tomás, Debbie, Lennie, and I were in Central Park to celebrate the event. However, one of Drake's 'new' friends was also hanging out with us. What I didn't know, was that he was connected to the Weather Underground's system of safe houses.

By then, Dr. Leary was long gone and was already safe in Algiers.

Law enforcement officials found out that he had been staying in New York City, and were watching people like Drake and his friends very closely. They already had orders to pick up anyone connected with the Weather Underground, and anyone else who might be part of it.

I felt pretty certain that Federal officers didn't know who I was.

However, because Drake and I hung out together, I was sure my face had appeared in some of their intelligence-gathering photographs.

For all they knew…Drake and I were working together.

We had just smoked a joint, as we usually did, when Drake leaned over to me and said, "Don't piss in your pants but I think there are some cops over there in the trees that have us staked out."

I looked to my left and saw three men in dark jackets and sunglasses who appeared to be staring in our direction.

"I see what you mean," I replied.

We gathered our group together and told them we needed to leave right away. Otherwise, there was a chance we could all get busted.

April and Lennie became a little upset because they had just dropped a tab of acid each and didn't understand what was going on, but they followed us anyway. We packed up our blankets and Frisbees, and headed in the opposite direction, from those surveying us.

Then, Drake saw another agent to our left and one more to our right. It appeared as though we were being surrounded.

"But we haven't done anything wrong," April whined.

We managed to get close to the announcer's platform to mingle into the crowd as much as we could, but the federal agents pushed through the sea of people and even knocked a few of them over as they tried to reach us. Drake and his friend were both pulled down at the same time by two men, and the struggle caused hundreds of people to scramble, creating commotion and chaos in all directions.

Drake was able to get away, but his friend remained on the ground.

As we watched the commotion, it was clear that one of the agents had placed a small plastic bag in the boy's back pocket just as the other one was throwing on a pair of handcuffs. Our small group was able to run out of the meadow and into the trees, and then quickly left the park, but we all knew…it had been a really close call for everyone.

"What the fuck is happening?" Lennie yelled at the two of us.

"Why in the hell are they after us?"

"I'm not sure," Drake responded, "but I think we better split up and go in different directions. Everyone needs to pair up and take off.

"We'll get together later tonight and figure out how to handle this."

"It better be with a pipe and some freshly imported Turkish hash," April joked in an effort to break up the anxiety.

"Yeah," Tomás interjected, "the pigs were starting to get a bit ugly, and I don't know why. Anyone got a cigarette?"

Lennie handed Tomás her pack of Camels and added, "I thought you recently quit smoking these things?"

"That was yesterday, but yesterday's gone. You know, it's like the way that song goes…*sha na, na na na, just live for today.*"

"Did you see the way they tackled that guy?" April said, butting in. "Those pigs even put some drugs in his back pocket, just so they would have grounds to arrest him. They sure don't fight fair at all…by the way, who was he and why were they after him?"

"His name is Brian, and he works with me," Drake interjected.

"I guess that explains it," I noted. "It's about the Weathermen."

"I'll try to give you a better explanation later. Look, we really need to get out of here. Tex, is your van around here somewhere?"

"It's not anywhere close."

"We need to get out of this area for a couple of hours…all right?"

Drake was bleeding from the nose and had a cut on his lip, so April used her yellow and blue tie-dyed shirt to wipe it off. She gave him a big kiss and said, "Look what those fucking pigs did to you, baby."

"Come on, guys," interjected Lennie. "Cut the shit. Those jerks could be here any minute. I don't want to spend the night in jail."

"What do you mean…*spend the night?*" I rudely commented.

"They just busted that guy out there by planting some drugs on him.

"Something like that could put you away for a couple of years."

"They don't have to plant anything on us," Tomás reminded us.

"The shit we've got ain't exactly chewing tobacco. By the way, does anyone know where Debbie went? I haven't seen her in a while."

"Maybe she hooked up with those cops," April replied with a laugh.

"That's not funny," replied Tomás, "I'm really worried."

"Having a girlfriend is just too much responsibility for me."

"There she is!" Lennie yelled as Debbie came barreling around the corner with a fearful look on her face.

"Where were you?" Tomás demanded. "I thought you were lost."

"Sorry, I had to pee really badly. Don't be mad. That whole incident just scared the piss right out of me. I'm really high right now from that joint we smoked, and I didn't know how to ask you guys to slow up and wait for me, or to tell me what's going on. I'm a little scared right now, so try and keep an eye on me from now on, all right?"

"We've got you covered," Drake stated confidently. "Maybe we shouldn't split up after all. Instead, let's try to sneak out in one of those service vans over there behind that restaurant. I think I know how to hot-wire the ignition with my pocketknife. Andy, why don't you go and check if one of the doors is unlocked?"

Quickly, Tomás and I checked the several vans parked in the area Drake had pointed to and in only minutes we found one.

"Over here, guys!" Tomás shouted. "There are no seats in the back, so just find a place to sit on the floor."

Drake climbed into the driver's seat and fumbled with the wires, while I sat in the front. April and Lennie opened the side door and found a comfortable position leaning against the side panel of the van.

Tomás led Debbie by the hand and cautiously led her to the back.

Having found a moment of apparent relaxation, April instinctively reached into her blouse and pulled out a fully rolled joint.

Then she lit it, took a long toke, and began to pass it around to the others who were now sprawled out on the floor, laughing loudly.

"Everybody needs to stop making so much noise," Drake told them as he watched the collective smoke going around.

"We've got to get out of here first, and then we can party."

Drake found a white painter's hat on the floorboard and put it on, and then slowly drove out onto one of the main streets. I could see from where I was sitting that there was still pandemonium going on in the park as several more police cars had recently pulled up.

The chaos of the riot had given way to the incarceration of others, and because thousands of *Earth Day* gatherers were now trying to leave the park, it looked as though some kind of *mob scene* was going on.

Fooled by the van's appearance as a service vehicle, we were able to leave the area unchallenged by the local authority.

"Hey, you guys, see if you can crank up some music while you're sitting there. Would you like a hit off of this joint?" April asked.

I began to search the radio for a decent underground FM station as April passed the joint to the front seat. After taking a good long drag, Drake reached out his hand and said, "Hey, don't *Bogart* that joint."

Just then, the voice of Tom Petty was blaring on the radio loud and clear, as he sang his latest underground hit tune.

Call out the instigator because there's something in the air.
We have got to get it together...because the revolution's here.
And you know that it's right...

"Yeah, you motherfuckers!" April shouted. "We know it's right! And we are free-fucking-falling right now...aren't we baby?"

Later that evening, we went to one of the local pubs to have a beer, and Drake explained to everyone that he and some of his friends were working closely with the Weather Underground. It seemed as though the Feds were on to them about the Timothy Leary matter, but so far as he knew, they didn't know where he lived. He said that agents might be looking for some connection to the rest of us as well.

He suggested, that after tonight we shouldn't have any more contact with him, at least for a while, or until things had cooled down a bit.

April was obviously very upset but left with Drake anyway. A few minutes later, Tomás and Debbie left too, leaving Lennie and me alone.

While we were still in the pub, we were sitting next to an older guy and overheard him say to his friend that he knew all about tantric sex, claiming he had done the whole sexual circuit during his lifetime.

Because Lennie and I had an interest in that subject, we decided to ask him to tell us some of what he knew. However, like most guys at a bar, he had too much to drink and one hell of a story to tell.

"Is it my age?" Bruce asked, looking at us. "Or because I'm unable to form relationships? What I'm noticing, is that I'm getting less and less pussy in my life. I still find sexual energy to be nice and exciting, but I find the pure act itself to be rather boring and uninspiring.

"For me, a good orgasm is more quickly achieved without someone else's support, but still, one can always be on the lookout for new kicks, you know, something a little wild on the side… like getting really high, role-playing, exploring fetishes, or pretending to fuck in outer space."

Lennie looked at me as if to say…*why didn't I think of that one?*

"While growing up, I always knew there was more," he continued. "I've spent quite some time in my life studying things like personal sex and sensual cultures, doing tantra, tantric massage, and yoga, which is all very good. After all, one needs to know the heart chakra from the one in your ass, as well as to know for yourself if you're feeling horny, or if it's just the cocaine kicking in. During my first years of practicing tantra, I had a hard time finding women who understood those things, you know, like being with a man who was in touch with his emotions.

"Since then, I've overcome my rather arrogant and esoteric desire to heal women with my *the Shiva lingam*, which means, *holy penis*."

Lennie poked me in the side…indicating she wanted to leave.

"With tantra, there's much more time to experience the loving flow of sexual energy between a lovely Shakti, and myself, Shiva. But you know, I'm not asking for a cosmic orgy every night or even just a hot *yoni priestess* in my life. All that I want is just a bit of understanding and tenderness beyond the old 'in and out' mechanism."

"What is your definition of tantric sex?" I asked Bruce.

"Tantra starts like everything else. This is not just tantric snobbery. It's that I'm just a firm believer that proper love-making must include a set of skills that goes way beyond a simple erection or wetness."

"First, one must know their own anatomy, their partner's anatomy, the erogenous zones, the effects of hormones, and the excitement that plays out across the human body. Also included is the knowledge about how to operate your genitals and all the different sexual positions.

"In later stages, you can add all sorts of games, external pleasure tools, and of course…the use of drugs as well.

"The next big area of skill is your sexual psyche, and how the mind and emotions interact with sexual energies. You must know both the side effects to the mind and the emotional side effects as well. This can actually be quite a task, but a very fulfilling one, for this is where we can learn to be more open, to heal our wounds of love, and to learn to show some true affection. Since our sex life lives next door to our ego, there's lots of potential for conflicts, such as fear, hunger, and madness, so to master your sexual psyche means to confront your ego.

"For some people, the last skill to master in the area of tantric sex is that of sexual magic, or what some call *sacred spirituality*.

"They find this to be the most exciting because they expect there to be some form of magical enlightenment just from simple penetration.

"Maybe they've watched too much advertising, but some kind of spiritual-energetic exchange will always happen when making love.

"So…in a lot of ways…the tantric experience is all made up.

"Just because you call it tantra, chant some mantras, meditate, or breathe a little harder, isn't going to change anything about an orgasm.

"I don't care if you've read all the tantric literature in the world, nothing *fantastic* is going to happen until you learn to use the energies consciously, instead of remaining unaware at the animalistic level.

"Tantra is about consciously exchanging energy with your partner by moving and weaving the love and putting out an energy that goes way beyond the satisfaction of an actual physical orgasm.

"It's a deep experience that has a lasting effect on your psyche, and leaves your body humming with all kinds of new energy."

The stuff this guy was talking about wasn't making a lot of sense to either of us, so Lennie and I finally said goodnight and went home. After all, this was just a guy we had met in a bar. However, I became even more determined to find out the truth and to discover what tantra was really all about. If I got into the Peace Corps and went to Nepal, then I'd find out for certain what the big deal was about tantric sex.

That May, U.S. and South Vietnamese troops attacked communist areas in Cambodia…which directly contradicted the repeated pledges Nixon had made to pull U.S. forces out of Southeast Asia.

On May 4th, at Kent State University, unarmed students began to protest about our country going into Cambodia, and four of the student protesters were shot dead by a group of nervous National Guardsmen.

That same day, eleven other students were seriously wounded.

The next day, two students were killed at Jackson State University in Mississippi. None of us could understand why this was happening.

It was absolutely…the worst possible thing that could take place.

What happened at Kent State was a terrible blow to the peace and love movement. Although the incident at Altamont symbolized the end of the music from the Sixties, after the Kent State massacre, just about everybody in the movement was ready to take up arms and fight back.

It took a lot of restraint to keep on singing...*Give Peace a Chance.* Anti-war protests and outrage began to erupt across the entire country, including a protest demonstration that was over one hundred thousand strong in Washington, D.C., right in front of the Capital.

I drove down in my van with a small group of friends who I knew were devout pacifists. It became the first time I was ever arrested.

We had gathered in Lafayette Park across from the White House and briefly paused to take a deep breath. Once we crossed the police barricade, we knew our arrests would begin, almost immediately.

We had talked about this possibility on the way to the Capital and everyone agreed that if it came to this, we would not back down.

By the same token, we would not resort to violence either.

We agreed...it was all we could do since we were coming in peace.

To my surprise, the arrests went smoothly because the police acted more humanely and considerate than in Chicago. Of course, it helped a lot that most of us helped them do their job by not fighting back, and by sticking our arms out in front of us for the handcuffs.

The police were not only scared of being accused of overreacting but most of them were disappointed and saddened about the incident at Kent State, wishing it had never occurred at all.

We sang songs in the paddy wagon, and then later when we go to the jail, in the holding cells as well. We recited poetry to each other and told stories about our lives to some we didn't know...but the concrete floor of the cell was cold, and as the crowd grew, at times there was no place to sit, but throughout it all...we remained loving and peaceful.

The miracle was…that after six hours of holding us at the station, and after the protest march ended, we were given a stern warning not to return to Washington again…and then let go.

They hadn't photographed us, fingerprinted us…or even fed us.

We were elated about being let go, not having to post a bond or go before a judge, but I'm sure it was also our peaceful, loving intent that allowed the miracle to happen. After that…we tripped out in D.C.

♥ ♥ ♥

Two more really big things happened that week.

First, I received an official letter stating that I'd been accepted into the Peace Corps program in Nepal. Agricultural training would begin in July at a former migrant labor camp near Davis, California.

However, I had to undergo a psychological examination in Dallas, Texas, just two weeks from now. Inside the letter was an airplane ticket to get me there and back…and an overnight hotel voucher.

The second big event was that the guy who had gotten arrested that afternoon in Central Park spilled his guts out to the Federal agents and told them about his involvement with the Weather Underground, about Timothy Leary, what he knew about the rest of us…and worst of all, he told them where Drake was living. Two days later, an early morning raid took place…Drake and April were both arrested.

Instead of being charged with subversive activities…it was for drug possession. When I heard about it, I became quite concerned because so far as I knew I could easily be next on their hit list.

That was the catalyst that helped me finally make my decision.

The world was just too crazy right now, and I couldn't take it.

I didn't want to think about peace or war anymore. I didn't want to decide whether or not to fight with the police. All I wanted was to get the hell out of Dodge before I got shot by Wyatt Earp, or beaten up by the Screaming Blue Meanies…*I had the right to disappear.*

The Eve of Destruction

And you tell me…
Over and over again, my friend…
You don't believe…
We're on the eve of destruction…
(Artist: Barry McGuire)

By the middle of May 1970…there was a lot of very positive news circulating throughout the New York University Campus.

Abbie Hoffman, Jerry Rubin, and all of the other members of the 'Chicago 8' were acquitted of the conspiracy charges.

President Richard Nixon requested that Congress support a bill that would allow eighteen-year-old men and women to vote.

The State of New York passed an abortion law that was the most liberal that ever existed in the United States.

The World Trade Center had finally been completed.

To top it off…the first New York City Marathon was held.

Despite all the good news, after the tragic arrest of Drake and April, the Kent State massacre, and my arrest in Washington DC, I was pretty bummed out. There were not only times when I was feeling angry but also disturbed, totally dismayed, and completely disappointed with the human race. A part of me still wanted to pick up a gun and fight back, and yet the stronger part of my intellect still said to give peace a chance. The real saving grace was that I had been accepted into the Peace Corps to go to Nepal and could perhaps recuperate in *the land of Buddha.*

There was no doubt about it…I'd made my decision.

I'd be living on the other side of the world for the next two years.

To hell with fighting for a cause, or some stupid revolution.

Perhaps by going there, I could find some sense of the peace and freedom I desperately longed for. However, if I stayed in New York, chances are I'd eventually end up like Drake by getting arrested.

Although he and April were quickly released on bond, they had to stand trial and face the possibility of going to prison for a long time.

I'd been given this window of opportunity and needed to take it. Besides, I remembered sitting in the student cafeteria at Berkeley four years ago and thinking what it would be like to go to India, travel around the world, and then to come back, experienced in the ways of eastern wisdom and perhaps a little enlightened. Hey, this was a dream that was about to come true, so how could I possibly say no?

The Weathermen were never going to overthrow the government, but now, here I was getting ready to become an ambassador of goodwill for the very government they wanted to destroy.

*Imagine that…*I thought to myself…*working for the United States*!

The right arm of Uncle Sam wanted to arrest me for terrorism and conspiracy, while the left arm wanted to send me around the world as their representative for peace.

That's quite the paradox!

♥ ♥ ♥

In order to start preparing for my trip to Nepal, I decided to take a meditation course at the Buddhist Center, so I went there one evening.

The short two-hour course was on *Vipassana* meditation. It was a form of awareness training where you just sit on a meditation cushion with your eyes open and try to be aware of what's going on around you.

First, you focus on your breath, and then continue breathing in and then out. As your thoughts begin to rise, you just relax and see what's going on inside your head, and then you let the thoughts go.

As you will find, many of the same things continue to keep coming up, and you begin to see what kind of garbage you tend to hang on to.

Whatever happens, you just sit there, not reacting to the thoughts. For example, let's say the thought of eating a banana comes into your head. Normally, you'd get up, find a banana, and then eat it…but with awareness practice, you just remain sitting on your meditation cushion.

Eventually, any thoughts you have about eating the banana seem to go away…and then an entirely new thought arises. For instance, you might begin to worry…that you forget to pay your Visa bill.

They told us not to expect anything unusual to happen, or to have any great insight, for that matter. Since I smoked a joint before I went, my experience turned out to be 'quite different' anyway.

As I sat there observing my thoughts, with my legs crossed and my hands upon my knees…I found that I immediately had trouble staying comfortable. My muscles ached and my back began to hurt.

I just couldn't seem to keep my thoughts together.

Finally, I just gave in to the pain until my legs became numb.

Sitting there, I was feeling a little light-headed, and then my focus shifted as I saw myself in front of a large, dark quiet cave.

In my mind, I stood up and entered the darkness, first observing bats that were flying in all directions. I realized that I was no longer in my body, and no longer felt any connection to it, but I didn't panic, and just decided to allow the experience to unfold.

The bats disappeared, and as the darkness cleared away, I could see that I was now overlooking a plateau of some desolate hills, and in the foreground, I could see a city made of bricks and mud.

Then, I saw monasteries similar to the ones I'd seen in pictures of Nepal, and there were people wearing robes while walking the streets.

I was seated in a half-lotus position in front of a small fire.

Across from me, was an old man in a long saffron robe.

He resembled a Tibetan lama perhaps, who was also seated.

His face seemed strangely familiar.

As he silently turned a prayer wheel in his right hand and held a long white crystal wand in his left, the old man chanted softly.

Then, he gently looked up to gaze at me with loving eyes.

He handed me the wand and said, *"Here's your destiny…take it."*

Staring at the old crystal wand, I saw it was scraped and scarred.

"Why is it made from crystal?" I asked.

"It holds the magic of the world within it. It is why water is wet, why the sky is blue, and why fire burns. It is a wand that can turn lead into gold, shit into nectar, and chaos into enlightenment. But it is more than a mere wand…*it is a Sword of Light*, one whose vibration holds the world in balance, and keeps mankind from destroying each other."

"Is it a sword, or is it a wand?" I again asked.

"It is both. Most people believe that their individual reality is like a box, and do not ever attempt to change the shape of their box.

"But reality is more like a bubble, and the shape of the bubble can be changed anytime you want to change it. And so it is with individual realities, with national realities, and with the world's reality.

"A time will come when the shape of the bubble must be changed, for humans, for countries, and for the Earth. So take hold of this wand, this sword, and place it into your heart and keep it there safe.

"You will know when the time has come to use it."

Then, the vision began to give way as the meditation instructor chimed the bell, signaling the meditation was over, and time to leave.

I felt as though I had been in a deep sleep.

I didn't understand anything I had seen or heard, and sure as hell didn't know what the wand was all about.

Before getting up I created another vision of the magical wand.

Then, I placed it into my heart, just as the old lama had instructed.

As I left the building, it began to sink in that I'd be leaving in less than a month. I needed to tell people about my decision to leave and to say goodbye, especially to my close friends…and of course, to Lennie.

♥ ♥ ♥

The next day, I caught up with Drake and April.

"So tell me, don't you think it's quite ironic that we both wound up in jail just a couple of days apart?" I asked.

"Yeah, you were lucky. They didn't book you. The pigs found some weed in our apartment, so if they do find some connection with me and the Weathermen, they'll add even more charges. If the heat gets too hot around here, I may have to disappear for a while," said Drake.

"I've already made my decision. I'm joining the Peace Corps."

"What in the hell do you want to do that for?" Drake asked, raising his voice angrily. "We've worked hard for this. Hey, I know hundreds of guys who are ready to go to war with this country right now. They've got guns, water, food…they have places to hide, like in the mountains, in the canyons, and in the desert. *The revolution is here, man.*"

"He's right, you know," April interjected. "But still, I can't believe that *The Beatles* won't help us out with a couple of million dollars!"

"Drake," I replied, "when we first met, you were the one who was talking about peace and love…but look at you now!

"Instead of love, all you're doing is talking about war."

"Back then," he retorted, "it was about changing the consciousness of this country. We gave peace a chance, but it just didn't work.

"Don't you see…we're the true patriots of this country!" he noted. "It isn't those fucking red necks called 'the silent majority.'

"If I have to kill one of them in the name of peace, I will, because the establishment is dividing us…they're making us go to war against each other because of their fucking imperialistic policies.

"Here, give me a hit off of that joint."

He took the joint and toked it hard.

"I wish you would listen to what he's telling you," April interjected, obviously trying to draw me back into their fold. "Everybody's talking revolution these days, especially after what just happened at Kent State.

"Why do you still want to be a pacifist?

"The pigs almost knocked your teeth out in Chicago.

"Not to mention...that last week you got arrested."

"I still think peace is the only answer," I replied, "*just give it time*."

"Wait until they start shooting at you," April retorted.

"If they shoot at me, maybe I won't shoot back...or maybe I will.

"Look, guys, I don't really know for sure what I would do...maybe it depends upon the situation...and you just deal with it at the moment; but I'm not going to be a doormat for anyone, and I would never allow some stupid cop to run over me, or take my life, and hopefully it won't ever come to that. But if this world is ever going to live in peace, it has to start sometime, somewhere, so why can't it start right now, with me, or with you, or with the guy sitting at that table over there?

"Remember the saying: '*The journey of a thousand miles begins with a single step*'...well perhaps, the first step just needs to be taken."

"Why do you think you'll be safe anywhere you go?" asked April.

"I plan to create a bubble of protection around me that will prevent that from ever happening," I replied. "That will be my own reality."

"That sounds like a bullshit bubble to me," she pointed out.

"No, what I'm saying is, it's not running away or about being safe. It's about learning to find inner peace. When I come back, the stupid war will be over, but a lot of people will still be at war with themselves. I just can't belong to a group that blows up government buildings, any more than I can join an Army that drops napalm bombs on villagers.

"I'd never allow some bullshit sergeant, who's never smoked pot, tripped on acid, or walked in a peace march make me kill someone.

"So think about it...why would I do the same for the Weathermen? It's like what Grace Slick said in, *White Rabbit...when the men on the chessboard stand up and tell you where to go...*the whole thing has just become so absurd...I'm getting the fuck off the chessboard."

"But what about the revolution, man?" Drake demanded.

"If people like you are running off to the Peace Corps, the pigs will wind up winning everything. You're worth more to us over here than you are to them over there. It seems as though we're losing everyone.

"What the hell is going on? What are we doing wrong?"

"When I first went to California," I answered, "I thought that being in the 'peace and love movement' would be just *for peace*, but then it seemed to change. I soon realized; it was also...*against war!*

"I don't understand," April replied.

"Our generation was born from parents who had just experienced the World War, so I think that some of that ancestral karma must have been passed on to us, which is why the movement failed."

"What are you talking about?" she asked again.

"We're not always just for peace. We were also against things, too. We're so busy fighting the establishment, that many times, I can't tell the fucking difference between them and us. There's too much hate in our generation, too much anger, and too much energy being exhausted about protesting the war and being 'against' so many things.

"Perhaps the secret...*is not to be against anything.*"

"Huh?" April said.

"Hopefully, we can pass along our peaceful karma to our own kids, and maybe they will be the ones who will eventually figure it all out."

"So you're saying, we should teach our children about what we did, and just hope they don't make the same mistakes?" Drake pointed out.

"Yeah...everything should just be for *peace* and nothing else.

"The reason you should want peace is because you love peace.

"Don't be for peace just because you're against war…to be against anything creates limitation…don't even be against Richard Nixon.

"To be free, we must *be for peace* in all aspects of life. That's what enlightenment is about…*it's having no walls, borders, or boundaries.*

"If peace is ever going to be achieved in this world it will have to come from all of us wanting to *be peace*, not from being against war.

"Until that shift in consciousness occurs, none of us stand a chance of achieving anything, because our hate will eventually turn against us, and then we become the very enemy we were fighting against."

"Isn't that just talk? You know, spiritual rhetoric?" April noted.

"No," I replied. "The energy of peace and love that our generation expressed was very strong. It has acted as a balancing point to keep the potential for violence down to a minimum, but now we're in the streets *fighting against* the war and the draft, so the atmosphere has changed.

"Without the energy of 'peace and love' to balance people's anger, it's possible that the violence we've already seen in the streets could become a hell of a lot worse…*if we don't teach our children well.*

"Otherwise, a new armed American Revolution could happen."

"You said before…that you might shoot back if you were shot at," Drake reminded me. "Is that still your truth?"

"Only if I were to lose sight of my values and my inner conscious.

"Otherwise, there's just no way would I ever do that. I suppose that if I ever got so terribly caught up in a moment of hate, then something like that could happen, but for the most part…it's not who I am."

"The farm boy from Texas has come a long way since we first met five years ago. You've become quite the heavenly saint, haven't you?"

"The truth is, Drake, choosing love over fear isn't that hard to do, *because love always wins.* For the last four years, I've been fighting a war against something *out there*…now it's time to fight the war inside. The war without and the war within…*they need to come into balance.*"

The next afternoon, I caught a plane out of LaGuardia and flew into the Dallas airport. From there I caught a cab that took me downtown.

The letter had included vouchers for the airplane and the hotel, but it said…if I kept receipts for the taxi and meals, I could submit those by mail and get reimbursed. But, by the time I arrived at the moderately priced hotel, it was already late in the evening, so I went to bed knowing that the interview, *scheduled for tomorrow*, was only six blocks away.

I wanted to be at my very best and to show the psychologist only my absolute, peak performance potential. *That meant, staying sober…*

The next morning, I put on a suit and tie that hadn't been worn since my high school graduation. Then, I checked out of the hotel and walked to the government office building for the psychological interview.

It was scheduled for ten o'clock, and I didn't know what to expect. Would it be another inkblot test, or a clinical assessment for attention deficit disorder, or perhaps even a battery of tests for a neurological evaluation? The letter didn't say how long the interview would actually take but my flight to return home wasn't until three o'clock.

I don't know why, but I was just a little nervous. Even though I was a graduate student in psychology, I didn't want to be psychoanalyzed or probed about my lack of farming experience. When I put down on the application that I had two years of agricultural background, I didn't say that I'd only been ten years old at the time.

♥ ♥ ♥

The office was on the fifth floor, so I took the elevator to suite 504. The door simply had 'Testing' written on a piece of paper in big letters taped to it. I quietly went into the waiting room and sat down.

The secretary took my name and said it would be a few minutes.

There was a person ahead of me who had a nine-thirty appointment.

That's good, I thought…*it will only take thirty minutes.*

When the first interviewee came out, I was a little taken back.

This guy was obviously…not a farmer either.

He looked more like a long-haired hippie from Haight Street.

He also…seemed to be very happy.

"Hey, man, are you next?" the guy asked me.

"Yeah, so…how was it. Did he get inside your head?"

The guy just laughed and said, "Naw…Rick's a cool dude.

Then he said, "Hi, my name is Sal."

"You must be Italian," I took note.

"Yeah, it's Salvatore. I'm actually, from Pittsburgh."

"I'm Andy…my friends in New York call me Tex because I used to live here in Texas, but no one here in Dallas would call me that.

"Tell me about your interview."

"That shrink in there…don't worry about anything, man.

"You're already in," Sal assured me. "See you in Nepal."

Loving his attitude…I said goodbye and went into the office.

Rick was sitting behind a big desk. He was a tall slender white guy, about thirty-five years old, and very clean-cut, but he had a big grin on his face…almost as if he'd just smoked a joint.

"Hi, Andy, good to meet you," he said. "I'm Rick."

"Hi, Rick. It's good to meet you, too," I replied as I shook his hand and then sat down in a comfortable leather chair across from him.

"Did you have any problem getting here?"

"No, not at all. Tell me, are you a psychiatrist, or a psychologist?"

"I have a Ph.D. in Psychology. Why?"

"Just interested. I'm a graduate student in psychology."

"That's great…do you have any questions about anything?"

"No," I replied. "I've already read most of the materials they sent."

"Good…well then, I guess that about does it.

"If there's nothing else you want to say…then you're free to go."

I couldn't believe it was over that fast.

"That wasn't much of a psychological evaluation," I commented.

"Well, it's obvious to me that you're not a nut case. I can tell by the way you present yourself and how you talk," he explained.

"After all, you have to be a little bit crazy if you want to become a Peace Corps Volunteer in the first place. With that being said, all we really care about is to make sure that you're not totally psychotic.

"I think you'll be just fine."

"Well, I suppose it's nice to know that being a little bit crazy is one of the requirements for the job," I joked.

Rick just laughed.

I just stood up, shook his hand again, and left.

The whole thing had taken less than ten minutes, so I spent the rest of the day in a bar near the airport and waited for my plane to take me back home. The experience left me in total awe about the efficiency of our government, and the way that taxpayer's money was being used.

Two weeks after the interview in Dallas, I received confirmation of my acceptance, along with a large packet of even more materials and information about Nepali culture and politics.

They also sent me a book that described some of the common words and phrases used in the Nepali language, and a copy of the Sanskrit alphabet, so that I could practice writing the language at home.

The language of Nepal was relatively new…having been created from several other languages and dialects. The country had more than eighty different cultural tribes of people, often separated by mountain ranges, who all had their own separate language. In an effort that would allow all of the people to communicate, the "Nepali" language had been created. For the most part, it was half Hindi and half Tibetan.

The alphabet itself was in *Sanskrit*, like Hindi.

I spent day after day trying to figure out the pronunciations.

It was going to be a lot of work…but I knew I could do it.

As the time to leave drew near, I began to wonder about Diane, and what she might be doing these days. After all, our training was to be at a former migrant labor camp located near The University of California at Davis…and that was only a two-hour drive from Berkeley.

Shortly before I returned to my parents' house in Pennsylvania, Lennie held a very stoned farewell party for me in her apartment, and most of my old friends were there to see me off, including Scott, Bill, Arnold, Tomás, Debbie, Drake, and April.

They had been my comrades in arms and in hugs over the last few years and I was going to miss them…some, I would never see again.

We discussed some of the events of the last four-and-a-half years, and about the politics of the day…while indulging in bottles of beer, wine, and whiskey, and of course, we smoked lots of pot.

After midnight, the party started to break up and I began saying my final goodbyes among many tearful eyes. The most moving experience before everyone left was when April and Lennie said they had a going away surprise for me. I had never heard either one of them sing before, and I just couldn't believe how beautiful their voices were as they sang.

April and Lennie began to sing a well-known song by the group, *Peter, Paul, and Mary* called, 'Where Have All the Flowers Gone?'

When they did…tears ran down my cheeks because I realized that I might never see any of my dearest and closest friends again.

Where have all the soldiers gone, a long time passing?
Where have all the soldiers gone, a long, long time ago?
Where have all the soldiers gone? To the graveyards every one.
When will they ever learn? When will they ever learn?

♥ ♥ ♥

During the last week, Lennie and I had practiced many different sexual tantra techniques, but on this particular night, it was different.

After everyone left the party we got undressed and then sat together facing each other for several minutes passing a joint back and forth, touching each other lightly across the arms, chest, and legs.

When we were finished, she gently scooted her body onto me and wrapped her legs around me…squeezing back and forth, until my erect penis was fully inside of her. Then, we hugged each other tightly.

At the beginning of the experience was the usual dance of energy throughout our bodies as our deep breathing began. My experience of this was far deeper and much more prolonged than ever before.

I felt a small vibration in my solar plexus, and then the heat began coming up my back until I became extremely hot all over. It felt as if my flesh was melting away, leaving only a sequence of bright colors.

Then I could feel Lennie's small body trembling, and I knew she was experiencing the same thing that I was. Perhaps this time we would actually merge our energies with each other.

I was both *nothing and everything* all at the same time, and I felt united with *God, Goddess, and All-That-Is*. The feeling seemed to be the melting away of old thoughts, ideas, and beliefs within our bodies. After a few moments, I felt free and released from any expectations.

I was actually dissolving into a huge vortex moving into itself, like a wave breaking on the beach, and covered my whole visual space.

It was made of pastel colors, pale blue, coral pink, and lavender, and it seemed to have a texture within it. At the same time, I felt that we were both parts of the same vortex. I was neither in the vortex, nor was I out of it, but instead I was simply at the center of it.

It became a sensuous experience as our two energies seemed to completely merge. The creation of a cosmic orgasm was in the making.

We recited the lines that we'd already practiced several times.

"I am God," I said quietly to her.

"I am Goddess," she said back to me.

Then, we took several deep breaths together, at the same time.

Lennie said, "I am fire and earth. My spirit is fire. My body is earth. The two are like a volcano, explosive and powerful.

"At my heart is where they meet.

"My heart is where my love resides.

"Its energy attracts the love of others, and it cannot be stopped.

"It reshapes the earth because it holds a power that transforms."

I said, "I am wind and water. My spirit is wind. My body is water. The two are like a hurricane, volatile and unpredictable.

"At my heart is where they meet.

"My heart is where my love resides.

"Its energy attracts the love of others, and it cannot be stopped.

"It reshapes the earth because it holds a power that transforms."

All I remember is pulsating rushes of energy moving up and down my spine, as sexual energy flowed through me…until I exploded, and then listening to her moan with sensual delight.

We continued to kiss each other for a very long time.

Afterward, there was no more talking.

We just laid back and tried to sleep.

Throughout the entire night, I thought about a lot of things but still continued having the experience of being a totally clear observer.

It seemed…that we'd experienced an enduring unconditional love.

It was a moment in time I'd remember forever…

After that, all I remember is sitting up in bed, and being back at my parents' house in Pennsylvania. I took a very deep breath, reached into my jeans lying on the floor, and pulled out a cigarette. After lighting it and taking a long drag, I gently leaned against the headboard to think.

Had the last five years of my life been nothing more than a dream? It almost seemed like it…but no, *it had all been very real.*

A part of me was in awe that I was still alive and was very grateful that I wasn't sitting in a prison cell for the crimes of treason, obstruction of justice, selling drugs, or perhaps…for assaulting a police officer.

It seemed as it was only a short while ago that I had graduated from high school. Now, I had just graduated from college, and the world had turned upside down. I felt as though many lifetimes had passed, but then I thought back to that early spring evening back in 1965, when this journey had first started, and I tried to remember how it all began.

In a dream, I was trying to catch a football, but it seems even back then I realized, *nothing really mattered.* It didn't make any difference if we won the game or lost. However, these last four years had brought about a change of consciousness within me…but would it have turned out the same without my awareness? Still, no one would ever know if I'd been part of it or not. Like most…*I would never be remembered.*

No one would ever know that I'd lived in New York or California, I could have just as easily lived in Canada…or worse, going to prison.

Could it be…that nothing really matters? Then, instantly the song, *Bohemian Rhapsody,* by the rock group Queen, came to my mind.

Just got to get out of here…because nothing really matters, anyone can see, nothing really matters…nothing really matters, to me.

Eventually, I went back asleep…but when I awoke, I knew exactly where I was…feeling that I now had a new sense of purpose, going to Nepal, as a Peace Corps Volunteer. The past still felt like a dream, but as before, it wasn't about winning or losing, it was only about one thing.

I was just going to try my very best to catch that fucking football.

If Allen Ginsberg, Richard Alpert, and The Beatles could go off to India in search of enlightenment…then by God, I could too!

It was June 1971, and I was ready…to leave this 'old world' behind.

I was ready to travel to another universe in some other galaxy very far, far away…to let everything go, and not even think about the past.

All I wanted was to get the garbage from the last four years out of my head…the world would have to *just fix itself*…without me.

I also decided to quit doing drugs, other than perhaps some hashish now and then. After all, Nepal was famous for that.

Who knows…I might even become a vegetarian!

I was waiting to board my plane when my parents decided to give me their parting words. My father said, "Son, I hope that while you're there you'll have good medical treatment available and life insurance."

My mother gave her advice, "Just make sure you don't get married, or think about bringing *one of those people* back home with you."

Neither one said…*I'm proud of you*, or…*have a good time*.

I just looked at them both very strangely, as if they were from some distant planet, and hugged them goodbye. After all, they were from that other generation, the one that time was slowly leaving behind.

As I was sitting in my seat, waiting for the *Boeing 747* to leave the runway, a copy of *U.S.A. Today* was lying next to me…so I decided to catch up with some of the news before I left the country.

The U.S. Senate was trying to curb school segregation by creating 'a mandatory busing program' in some of the southern states.

Soviet cosmonauts set a record of being in space for seventeen days.

The first nuclear non-proliferation treaty had just gone into effect.

The FDA had approved the use of childproof safety caps and had also approved the use of lithium to treat manic-depressive disorders.

The first female jockey in history raced in the Kentucky Derby.

A new national railway service had been formed, called *Amtrak*.

A 'floppy disc' had just been invented for use in home computers.

A Jumbo Jet, like the one I was on, had just been hijacked to Cuba.

And…an earthquake in Peru had just killed thousands of people, leaving over a hundred thousand villagers homeless.

I thought to myself…*what was I thinking? There are still enough nuclear bombs in the world to blow all of us up by tomorrow morning.*

Then I realized…*the world may seem just a little crazy at times, but it's nowhere close to becoming the Eve of Destruction.*

It seemed to me that there were a lot of really good things going on out there but the truth was…I didn't know for sure what kind of shape the world was in right now, but whatever it was…*it was what it was.*

"Is that it?" I asked myself. "Yes, it is," I answered.

Then, a song by *Peter, Paul, and Mary* began singing in my head.

I'm leaving on a jet plane,
I don't know when I'll be back again.
Oh, babe, I hate to go…

As the plane gently lifted off from the runway, and into the future, a number of odd and interesting thoughts began to cross my mind.

Was this journey going to really be about finding freedom?

Would it be the kind we'd talked about on so many occasions?

Would I be able to discover what enlightenment was all about, and would I find the kind of peace I'd been searching for all this time?

Was joining the Peace Corps really going to be about peace, or was it just another form of war, like a wolf hidden beneath a sheepskin?

I didn't have any idea what I was about to get into, but I did know one thing…I was sure as hell going to give it my best shot.

All I could do…was settle into my seat and close my eyes.

An inner knowingness told me…*your future is looking fantastic.*

This was going to be…*the kick-ass adventure of a lifetime*…as a Peace Corps Volunteer in Nepal…in search of enlightenment.

Commentary: When Will They Ever Learn?

And they shall beat their swords into plow shears...
And turn their spears into pruning hooks...
Nations shall not lift swords against Nations...
Nor shall they train for war anymore...
(Artist: God...Isaiah 2:4)

In January 1973, the United States fostered a peace treaty between North Vietnam, South Vietnam...the war was now officially over.

In March 1975, an offensive by the North Vietnamese began.

The South Vietnamese Government was defeated in fifty-five days.

The war against communism in Vietnam had lasted nineteen years, from 1956 to 1975, and at the time was the longest war in U.S. history, but there were many who said...*it had all been for nothing.*

As of January 2015, forty years from when the Vietnam War ended, the war in Afghanistan...*against terrorism*...became the longest war in United States history. Once again, some say...*it's all for naught.*

How many more times will we have to repeat this atrocity?

How many new *longest wars* will we have...*all for no reason?*

When will they ever learn?

In the introduction of this book, I talked about the meaning of '*American Pie.*' It was a piece of the pie people wanted...during a time before the American way of life became so dysfunctional.

But some people say...the reason for the dysfunction...is because it was a side-effect of the long and drawn-out Vietnam War.

It had a devastating effect on all of us.

Just think about…how the war impacted us.

Statistics show that as a result of the Vietnam War, there were more than forty-eight thousand U.S. soldiers *killed in action*, and more than three-hundred-thousand soldiers *wounded in action*. There were also more than twenty-five hundred soldiers who went *missing in action*.

Those casualties do not include more than three-hundred-thousand soldiers who returned from the war with severe cases of post-traumatic stress disorder or the millions of families whose lives were torn apart.

It does not include those who were injured or even died protesting the war…or the tens of thousands who were arrested while conducting peaceful demonstrations against the war and the military draft.

Many of the aspects of the Sixties are now being repeated, now that a New Age is upon us…and violence may again return to the streets of America, especially if the military draft should be reinstated.

If such violence erupts, there may not be a *peace & love movement* in place…to keep bloodshed off the streets.

The era of the Sixties had been one of the most violent decades in our country's history, but the next time, it could become much worse. It's time or us to stop identifying as Americans, Europeans, Russians, or Chinese, or have a nationalized ego, and become world citizens.

It's time for the people upon this planet to bring an end to war.

We can never truly address the complexities of our world problems, so long as we remain under the threat of world war.

We are about to begin the third decade of a whole new millennium, and it's bringing us many challenges. However, if war is not eliminated from the planet in the very near future…so that other problems facing humanity can be addressed…the effect could be devastating.

So what will it be? Are you on the bus…*or off the bus?*

And by the way…where have all the hippies gone?

Did they sell their Souls to corporate America…every one?

The only kind of revolution that can ever bring peace to the world will not be a political revolution or a cultural revolution. Neither one has ever worked in the past because the world is still at war. In order to have lasting peace, there must be a 'revolution of consciousness.'

Conflict resolution is best achieved with consciousness revolution.

That begins…by learning to get out of your mind…to get unstuck, and to let go of all the limitations that you hold 'with your beliefs.'

Eventually, this new awareness will begin to manifest within the physical reality. Conscious love and wisdom will transform themselves into *active intelligence*…which then becomes *intelligent activity.*

The world can only change organically from the inside out.

One-by-One-by-One eventually becomes *One-with-One-with-One.*

That's what it means to have a real *consciousness revolution.*

The lesson from the Sixties was…*not to be against anything.*

Instead, it was to be for peace…and allow peace to be real.

This way, things like global warming, overpopulation, starvation, polluted rivers and oceans, contaminated soil, dirty air, deforestation, the disappearance of wildlife and natural resources…can all finally be addressed…without the looming threat of war holding it back.

The remaining years of this current decade do not belong to any one person, to any one religion, or any one country, but they belong to all of those who are here upon the planet at this time of great transition.

We are all here…*to help create a better world.*

We can bring an end to war…by living life at the highest vibrational frequency possible, which means…*to live love every day*…and do the best we can with what we have available to us at the time.

It will not the meek who shall inherit the Earth…

It will be…*the peacemakers.*

As a side note...most people agree that it's only a matter of time before every state in America legalizes marijuana for medical use.

Plus, in 2017, doctors did several studies on patients who suffered from depression, personality, and mood disorders. They discovered that micro-doses of LSD and psychedelic mushrooms helped significantly.

They expect that soon...these will replace the drug, Prozac.

Wouldn't it be something...if the last fifty-five years being 'at war' with drugs was not only a huge waste of time...but of lives as well?

♥ ♥ ♥

If you enjoyed reading this book and delving into the mind of the author, Anderson Andrews, I'm sure you'll like the next book in this series of novels about his extraordinary life. Although they're fiction, all of his books are based on true events. In *Peace Corps Nepal*...Andy goes off to live for 2-years in the Himalayan Kingdom as a volunteer. There, he discovers the true meaning of freedom and the potential for his own enlightenment...by becoming a student of an old tantric lama and reading the sacred and mystical teachings of Tibetan Buddhism.

In that book, you'll discover new revelations that are guaranteed to unlock new potentials, expand awareness, and awaken consciousness.

THE DARK SIDE OF LIGHT
Amorous Memoirs of a Former Trial Lawyer
A collection of true stories, some funny, some tragic.
www.TheDarkSideofLight.com

A SENSUAL SEDUCTION
Transformation of the Shadow Self
Jut a bit raunchy, but written for Sexual Healing
www.ASensualSeduction.com

THE CRYSTAL TRILOGY
A Story of Conscious Transformation
www.TheCrystalTrilogy.com

THE CRYSTAL PRISON
Part One
www.TheCrystalPrison.com

THE CRYSTAL CHRYSALIS
Part Two
www.TheCrystalChrysalis.com

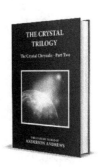

THE CRYSTAL CASTLE
Part Three
www.TheCrystalCastle.net

**If this is going to be your last lifetime on Earth,
these are the last books on Earth you'll ever need to read.**

THE ACTIVATION
What if God Were One of Us?
The Best Spiritual Fiction Novel Ever Written
www.TheActivation.net

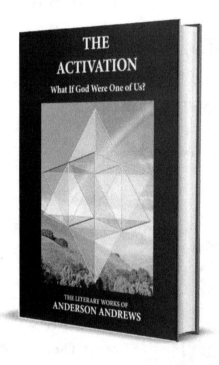

'NEW' BOOK OF THE DEAD
Transformation for the Afterlife
A Book about Life, Death, and Rebirth
www.NewBookoftheDead.com

Anderson Andrews is the author of nine transformational novels on sale at Amazon.com and hundreds of other internet bookstores.

Transformational Books & Novels, Inc. began publishing in 2004, with Anderson Andrews...who set out to write transformational books *for those who knew there was 'something more'*...books that offered a cross between fiction and inspirational non-fiction. The first book that was published was, *The Activation, What if God Were One of Us.*

As of this date...seven of his nine books are fictional novels based on actual events he experienced during his life that he felt would inspire future generations...including his non-fiction book about the Afterlife, *'New' Book of the Dead.* Soon, *Transformational Books* will offer other stimulating novels from authors of transformational fiction as well.

His goal is to create new paradigms for a New World based on love and compassion. Humanity must learn to work in unity to create world peace by establishing a solid foundation of love in all aspects of life, that up to now have been fear-based in third-density awareness.

As humanity comes into fourth-density awareness, they will need to have foundations for living that are based on *the Plan for Ascension.*

The arena that needs the most work is about healing ourselves.

Our wounded masculine and wounded feminine are why the world is in chaos, and why we have racism, which is infused into nearly every aspect of our current reality. Racism in our world must come to an end, and people must realize that the ego is just a fabricated illusion.

Please support us in our cause by purchasing our books.

You will learn so many things that you never knew before and will awaken to new realizations...such as, why we must raise the vibration of the criminal justice system from one that is fear-based and hell-bent on punishment, to one that realizes, *the incarceration of most offenders does nothing good*...it only creates even more problems for society.

Instead, we should help offenders recover from their mistakes.

Please read all three books of the epic novel, *The Crystal Trilogy*. It's a fictional novel that combines the true story of a lawyer who makes a grave error in judgment when he borrows money from his own client trust account, combined with true stories about his thirty-five years of spiritual teachings and his personal relationship with the Universe.

Part One is called, *The Crystal Prison*, about breaking free from the toxic fear-based hypnotic matrix of mass consciousness.

Part Two is called, *The Crystal Chrysalis*, a place of quiet and safety where real spiritual transformation can begin taking place.

Part Three is called, *The Crystal Castle*, about the Higher Realms of human consciousness that are part of our spiritual evolution.

Find out what happens when you shine some light into the darkness.

These three books are an exciting reading experience, filled with spiritual wisdom and advice for what we need to create new paradigms.

After you've read, *The Crystal Trilogy*...you will be the judge of this important question, one that needs to be discussed on social media. *Should first-time non-violent offenders always get a second chance, or are we a nation that only cares about punishment and payback?*

It's my hope, that together we'll be able to create a bridge over these very troubled waters...because like climate change, prison sentencing is a problem that in one way or another affects all of us. It not only ruins the lives of those incarcerated but for their families as well.

One out of every twelve Americans winds up in prison.

You could find yourself in a very similar predicament someday.

Time is of the essence, and your support is greatly appreciated.

This is my 25-point prison reform platform for the times we live in. For a detailed explanation of what these all mean...visit my website at, *www.4Peace.org*, where we also accept donations that allow us to send free books to prison libraries all over the country.

Twenty-Five-Point Plan for a New Prison Paradigm

1. No incarceration for first-time non-violent offenders...
2. Eliminate the current non-refundable bail bond system...
3. We must eliminate 'for profit' prison-run corporations ...
4. Offer better pay and training for prison guards ...
5. Judges must consider prior good deeds at sentencing ...
6. More relaxed standards for parole or early release ...
7. Meaningful rehabilitation available for all inmates ...
8. Humane living conditions provided for all inmates ...
9. No more mandatory hard labor for those incarcerated ...
10. Minimum wages paid to inmates performing labor services ...
11. No mandatory work-release for restitution or fines owed ...
12. Forgiveness training given to victims of the incarcerated ...
13. Support services available for families of those incarcerated ...
14. Support services available for all recently released inmates ...
15. No discrimination allowed against recently released inmates ...
16. The maximum age for nonviolent offenders is 70-years old ...
17. No suspension of Social Security benefits for incarceration ...
18. We must restore full voting rights to all convicted felons...
19. Elimination of the death penalty as a means of punishment ...
20. Elimination of seg and solitary confinement as punishment ...
21. We must stop prosecuting minors as adult offenders ...
22. We must stop incarcerating the mentally ill ...
23. Mandatory mental health services to all violent offenders ...
24. We must encourage judges to give shorter sentences ...
25. Begin replacing judges and juries with artificial intelligence ...

Transformational Novels' Newest Book
MY LAST SPRING BREAK
Dawn of a New Earth
The Twelve have gathered …
what they do this week will change the world.
www.MyLastSpringBreak.com

TRANSFORMATIONAL BOOKS & NOVELS

**If you are an aspiring writer and have a
transformational novel you'd like to write,
visit www.TranformationalBooksAndNovels.com**

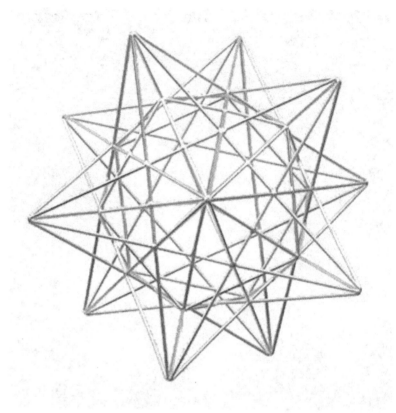

Raise your vibrational frequency to its highest level
Transformational Crystals
www.TransformationalCrystals.com

CPSIA information can be obtained
at www.ICGtesting.com
Printed in the USA
JSHW041101220522
25995JS00007B/51